Dedication

*As ever, my work is dedicated to my wonderful,
ever-extending family and friends without
whom there would be no purpose in life.*

Flimsy .... but good
flimsy. Big oil.
You'll enjoy.

A Confusion of Mandarins

R u.

by

Ron Culley

**Grosvenor House
Publishing Limited**

This book is published by
Grosvenor House Publishing Ltd
28-30 High Street, Guildford, Surrey, GU1 3EL.
www.grosvenorhousepublishing.co.uk

A CIP record for this book
is available from the British Library

ISBN 978-1-908596-57-4

Preface

This book took a lot of primary research. In previous books, my imagination, the reading rooms in The Mitchell Library and the internet provided a sufficient lode to mine. The narrative of 'A Confusion of Mandarins' came to me over time and permitted me to scope a plan of work which involved me travelling to places such as Icelandic glaciers in the middle of winter, Spanish yachting marinas in the height of summer and dingy Glasgow bars in various weathers in order to establish the nuances that help give credibility to a story line.

I am indebted to the many people who gave some of their valuable time to assist my understanding. It really was appreciated. To my family and friends who gave their encouragement, I am indebted. Individually, each was a strength. Collectively, they have been indispensible. To those who read my earlier books and who have favoured me with their comments and feedback; many thanks. In important ways, you are the people who matter most and you have sustained me when I wondered what the hell I was doing when I stood alone at the side of a gigantic glacier in a freezing Iceland miles from anywhere with no signal on my cell phone and a punctured tyre on my car.

I confess I enjoyed writing this book. Inevitably there were times when I stared blankly at the screen willing the next sentence to appear. Often this tested me but in the end I got there and what you have in your hands or on your screen is the result. I have written the book as an entertainment and hope that readers not attuned to the Glasgow *patois* make it past the second chapter. For those who do, relax, it gets easier.

I hope you enjoy it.

Ron Culley

Preamble

The construction of *Novonikolayevsk,* Russia's third largest city began in 1921 as a direct consequence of the new economic policies of Vladimir Ilyich Lenin. Given the general absence of romance and subtlety during those revolutionary years, in 1926 the town was renamed *Novosibirsk*, which translated means New Siberian City. Over the years, *Novosibirsk* became the dynamic hub of the Russian oil industry as the nation powered its way to the top of the world oil production league.

Following the free market reforms of Presidents Mikhail Gorbachev and Boris Yeltsin, Russia's petroleum output fell sharply, but rebounded in the mid-1990s after the privatisation of the industry, higher world oil prices, the use of foreign technology and the re-exploitation of old oil fields previously believed to be spent.

Earlier, in 1988, as *perestroika* opened up opportunities for entrepreneurs in the Soviet Union, a young street criminal from the 'New Siberian City' took a chance to legitimize his underworld business, buying shares in local oil companies following gang wars that saw him last man standing. Dmitriy Ivanov was now a very wealthy man. Friendly with senior politicians, he further bought his way into their affections as well as into more and more oil fields. Over only five years, he took control of the Verhne-Chonskoye Field, the Talakan Field and the North-Caucasus Basin giving him huge influence within the emerging Russia. The following five years saw him take a controlling interest in oil and gas from Kazakhstan and consolidate his grip on power as well as creating a business model that served not only to grow his profits substantially but also did this within an increasingly fortified headquarters in Novosibirsk which contained a compound that would have been the envy of NATO had they but been able to penetrate its walls.

Now, in the year of our Lord 1997, Ivanov's company produced more oil than Libya. In consequence, he was also as rich as Croesus…but he wanted more.

CHAPTER ONE

Sir Alistair Barrington's prostate gland was busily trying to kill him although he was unaware of this. In consequence of his condition, regular visits to the private lavatory in his office irked him as they were always frustratingly brief but yet had the advantage of returning him expeditiously to his busy desk.

Sir Alistair had been a very senior civil servant; a Mandarin, as members of the fourth estate earlier referred to him. The office provided for the job with which he was now entrusted was located deep within marble-faceted premises on London's Embankment. Faded but deep-piled carpets on the sixth floor gave his room a certain still silence, the only intrusion being the monotonous and languid ticking of an antique William Clement long-case striking clock which sounded the time on each hour.

Most of his time on that sunny London morning had been taken up by reading various communications. Three short phone calls and one visit to his office by Miss Hetherington, whose timid knock on his door reminded him that it was ten o'clock and time for a cup of tea, proved to be the only time he'd spoken since his arrival at his desk at six-thirty that morning. As she placed the Josiah Spode bone china teacup before him on his desk, the clock struck as it always did upon the arrival of his morning cup of tea.

"Thank you, Miss Hetherington," said Barrington without raising his gaze from the file he was reading. "That will be all at present." He began to note some neat, handwritten comments in the margins of the front sheet of a file and said, "Oh, before you leave. I received a phone call to say that Brigadier Garrick has asked to meet with me at eleven o'clock this morning."

"Yes, Sir Alistair. He's actually on his way over right now. I didn't want to disrupt your schedule, but from his phone call, I suspect he'll be here any minute."

Sir Alistair looked up at his secretary, trying to understand why an important member of Her Majesty's Intelligence Services would be so anxious to arrive early in the hope of seeing him before the appointed hour.

"Must be important. Please show him in when he arrives. Can you bring another cup?"

Sir Alistair Bartholomew Barrington had been a very senior civil servant within the United Kingdom's security services and had had a long and distinguished career. Educated at Cambridge University where he read politics and economics, he was a young recruit to the service in the late nineteen-sixties and was recruited only after a most thorough sifting process as a consequence of a number of embarrassing setbacks within MI5 when a number of senior officers were found to be Soviet agents. Matters within the security services had deteriorated so much prior to Barrington's employ that in June 1963, the then Prime Minister Harold Macmillan tasked the Master of the Rolls, Lord Denning, with examining the operation of the security service.

Demonstrating a particular talent for his job in counter-espionage, Barrington found himself promoted frequently within the service but soon saw his primary area of expertise in Warsaw Pact countries overtaken by new challenges which emanated from Northern Ireland. Still he progressed and found himself sent to Israel, Baghdad and to Zagreb as the interests of the United Kingdom ebbed and flowed.

In the mid-nineteen nineties, the Privy Council of her majesty's government decided to establish a new, secret organisation that would operate at some distance from senior political control and to one side of the civil service and armed forces in order that a measure of discretion and flexibility denied the formal services could serve the narrow interests of the country. Someone was needed to head it and the powers that be turned to Barrington as someone who had proved his mettle but who was also steeped in the traditions of British security. Barrington had been a field officer but what set him apart from many of his peers and what gained him his relentless promotions through the ranks was his capacity for listening, his understanding of the human condition and its frailties. His interrogation techniques; softly spoken, gentlemanly and cerebral had consistently produced remarkable results. As he approached what would have been an opportunity for early retirement from the service, he stepped down from his role in the security services with some small internal fanfare just sufficiently subtle to signal his departure and capture the quiet attention of the wider intelligence community. Then, after a six week holiday during which he cruised his beloved Caribbean, he was given a sinecure role in a *faux* international trade organisation as a cover for his new duties. He was also given a not insubstantial budget and asked to use operatives who were talented but who could not be connected to MI5 or MI6.

Barrington quite understood the significance of his new role given the new ethical freedom he would possess. He was about to become the 'go-to' person for awkward security problems within the UK that required solutions denied the formal forces of law and order. Over the years, he anonymously and successfully took care of a substantial amount of dirty washing for the security services from behind a plate on the door of his suite of offices which declared him as Worldwide Trade's *'Director of International Trade and Business Relations'*. Only a handful of very senior people knew of the existence and remit of 'The Unit'.

Miss Hetherington's trademark timid tap on the door alerted Barrington to the arrival of his visitor. The door opened and his secretary entered accompanied by the besuited, ramrod-straight figure of Brigadier Charles Garrick. The two men shook hands warmly and sat in a couple of brown, distressed leather armchairs in an area of Barrington's office that had been set aside for more informal meetings.

"You'll join me in a cup of tea," said Barrington.

"Thanks for seeing me. Tea would be lovely. No milk," he replied, redirecting his comments to Miss Hetherington.

"Well now Brigadier, I haven't seen you since you wanted some business taken care of in Tripoli. Must be three years ago now."

"Yes, Sir Alistair. Thanks for that. It went very well."

"So I gather. And now you have further problems?"

"Hmmm."

Miss Hetherington poured a cup of tea for the Brigadier who thanked her and waited until she'd left the room as silently as she'd arrived.

"As ever, Sir Alistair, this comes from the top; the very top. Our friends in the Foreign and Commonwealth Office have leaned on the Director General of MI5 to have us speak with you privately. It has been made clear to me that our conversation must not be made known to anyone and that no notes of our chat may be taken. My request for a meeting was made verbally this morning to avoid leaving any audit trail that links our two selves."

"Of course. I understand," acknowledged Sir Alistair.

"Your ability to deal with matters informally has been determined as crucial in a matter of some sensitivity. The FCO needs deniability."

"Exactly why we were set up," said Barrington.

Garrick leaned forward in his seat, elbows on thighs and prepared to tell his story.

"I'm sure you have scores of operations underway at any one time but we have urgent need of a covert mission. Sources within Russia have indicated to us that they have one or more rogue agents. Our Russian desk has confirmed that the Ruskies are at sixes and sevens over Chechnya. As you know, they've just signed a pretty humiliating peace deal with the Chechens. They've just spent two years and God knows how much money providing overwhelming manpower, much better weapons and complete air superiority to deal with a small piece of geography within their own country but they've not been able to bring about effective control due to lots of damaging Chechen guerrilla raids. It's been a real shock to their system and when the Chechen guerrillas took hostages in Budyonnovsk hospital in 1995, it sent one or two of the old stagers off the page."

"So some have gone native?"

"Yes. And just as they're furious about the direction of travel taken by President Yeltsin, they're equally opposed to those they see as their traditional enemies...we in the west! Chechnya is a nation at the moment ruled by warlords. Kidnapping, hostage-taking, robberies and murder are committed routinely and the Russians are fast losing patience...but not fast enough for the fundamentalists within their ranks. We think the Russians are preparing for round two but at the moment there are a lot of angry, disconsolate Russian agents involved in that theatre."

He sipped from his cup of tea and continued.

"Up to a point, Chechnya is none of our business. But our information is that there are those who want to carry the fight to our shores…to bring back the good old days. We understand that they've lost one or two agents who have disappeared into the ether and we believe them to be undercover, on the loose and targeting their motherland as well as its new European allies so as to encourage familiar enmities."

"And why might you wish this matter dealt with below the radar?"

"These rogue agents are serious people…resourceful people. They've re-routed some of the considerable monies that were to be deployed within Chechnya and have purchasing ability that would permit very serious attacks on our interests. We don't want diplomatic incidents. The Soviets would be embarrassed if Russians were linked to mainland atrocities here and we do not want to test their abilities to commit those atrocities on our shores or against our interests abroad. So, somewhat surprisingly, they're very keen to work in partnership with HMG on this one."

Sir Alistair pondered the information he'd just been given.

"So we face the prospect of trained but disaffected agents operating on our soil…"

Garrick interrupted. "Not necessarily, Sir Alistair. We understand they want to move against our interests.

That might be overseas and might also involve an attack on our allies."

"Quite," responded Barrington, accepting the logic of Garrick's analysis. "Then you don't give me much to work on."

Garrick reached into a briefcase he'd brought with him, removed a buff folder and handed it to Sir Alistair.

"This might help. The Russians have been more than helpful. They list among their concerns, agents they have in Iceland, Berlin, Algiers, Spain and Paris. They're obviously keen to avoid any spill-over and have assured us of every cooperation. As you'd imagine, they've their own agents working on this but want us kept up to speed. They've provided us with the names of missing, presumed defecting Russian personnel along with some fellow-travelers who are listed along with such personal information we have to hand within but remember that with the money they've got they could easily hire mercenaries to supplement their effort."

"Hmmm. They're actually asking us to scrutinize some of their field agents and report to them on our success in eliminating them and you want this dealt with so we have deniability?"

"Yes. It would be embarrassing for both us and the Russians if they were fingered as having agents who could crow about striking against British interests. They'd have to be macho, we'd have to be indignant. There would have to be expulsions… counter-expulsions. It could set us back years. Not to mention the political, economic and human costs if there was some sort of major incident."

"So if it ends up in court or in the press you'd want the ability to point the finger elsewhere?"

"Indeed so. But we'd also be relieved if they were neutralised without a lot of fuss and didn't get anywhere near either the courts or the media."

"Then we'll work on that basis. As ever, this conversation didn't take place. We'll move on the matter directly."

After Brigadier Garrick left, Barrington asked Miss Hetherington for another cup of tea. He always did his best thinking sipping a cup of tea. Dressed immaculately in his navy pin-stripe suit, crisp white shirt, club tie and highly polished black shoes, he stood, looking out onto the River Thames, cup in hand, mulling over the import of what Garrick had told him.

He decided a phone call was needed but first his bladder protested that evacuation was necessary. Barrington paid another visit to his private bathroom to relieve himself and, as ever, was depressed at the few milliliters he expressed. Scrupulous as ever, he washed his hands thoroughly and returned to his desk where, on his secure line, he placed a call to a man called Brand, ostensibly a flower-shop owner in Oxford but who was, in fact, a most effective comrade-in-arms. A man who had killed many times for his country.

CHAPTER TWO

Outside the Thistle Bar in Glasgow's docklands, dogs barked distantly in the murk. A fine, still Scottish mist of rain soaked anyone walking the dark, forbidding streets.

Inside the bar, Andy McCutcheon slowly lifted his glass and contemplated its amber contents before raising it to his lips and emptying it. Placing the now empty glass on the bar-top with his right hand, his left ponderously deepened his jacket pocket and carefully removed the substantial amounts of small change he'd assembled over the evening. A boozer's pocket. Clumsily placing the coins on the bar, he spread them flat in order to calculate his ability to buy one more drink. Satisfied, he slowly slid his empty whisky glass towards the elderly lady who stood behind the bar, shaking her head at his appetite.

"Get me another wee Grouse, Elsie. Ah'm just wantin' wan fur the road." He began to isolate the higher denominations from the spread with his nicotine stained forefinger.

"Jus' goin' home presen'ly. See ma wife 'f she's up."

"Andy, you've had enough whisky. You're pished. Away home now before…"

"Ah says a *Grouse*."

"Keep yer hair oan. Ah'll get ye yer bloody whisky." She lifted his squat glass to a position beneath a whisky bottle on the gantry. "Jeeesus, Andy. When you're drunk you're a right crabbit pain in the arse. Away up the road an' see Jessie like a good boy."

"Elsie, do ah huv tae c'mplain to wee Tam 'bout the way you talk to long servin' cus'mers 'n this place? Coz ah can see it comin' if you don't buck yer ideas up here, by the way. Now give us that Grouse. Is ma money...?"

The sharp crash of the door splintering and smashing against the interior wall of the pub startled Elsie and the six remaining regulars other than Andy whose befuddled brain registered the event only an instant before a baseball bat knocked him from his already precarious position on the bar stool, breaking his right clavicle in the process.

The larger of the two besuited men handed the now redundant bat to his colleague and rolled the wailing drunk over onto his back on the bar-room floor. He spoke directly to his contorted face.

"Ah've tae make sure ye know that this wee message is comin' direct frae Arthur Hanlon, pal. Just in case ye think this is you just bein' unlucky like, an' gettin' beat up by a couple of bad men just for the hell of it."

While the spectators stood gawping at the attack, silently being dared to move by the other suit who blocked the doorway, Andy was lifted screaming onto a wooden chair.

"Ah want ye tae know this gives me nae pleasure at a' ma man. It's just a wee bit o' business. Frankly, ah'd rather be hame daein' the inside of the windaes."

On one knee now, the assailant reached behind him and drew a heavy, round-head hammer from the waistband underneath his jacket. Swinging it upwards in a powerful arc, he brought the flattened head upwards against Andy's chin, fracturing his jaw and sending him reeling backwards in the chair.

"Ah never really liked this next bit, but it's kinda becomin' ma trade mark," said Benjy Reid, Arthur Hanlon's number one enforcer, to a now only semi-conscious Andy.

"It's ma signature tune if ye like. So's people know it wis me that popped in tae say hello."

He looked over his shoulder at the onlookers. "Sorry tae bother ye's a'. Ah'll no' be long an' then we'll get away so ye's can a' get on wi' yer drinkin'."

With no resistance forthcoming from his victim, Reid had little difficulty unbuckling Andy's belt, unzipping his trousers and pulling them down below his knees. He addressed his victim directly while clearly aware of the others in the vicinity. "See, yer mammy was right, pal. Ye should always wear clean underwear in case ye get hit wi' a bus or a big man gies ye a kickin' and shows them aff tae the entire pub." He shook his head at the grubby pants, which still covered Andy's genitals and, hamming it up for his audience, held his nose in mock disgust before returning to the job in hand.

"Down we go," said Reid, tugging the undergarments lower. "See, this is the tricky bit so if ye'll just sit still a minute ah'll try tae dae this so's ye don't get hurt, coz this kinda' thing could get ye a right sore yin." So saying, Reid produced a six-inch nail and with another hammy look to Elsie, who was now frozen in silent tears, positioned it over Kyle's scrotum.

"Now then, pal. Mister Hanlon would like me to remind ye that ye owe him three hundred an' forty quid and he's gettin' a bit pissed aff that you've no been in touch. So anyway, here we go."

He smiled a wide grin at Elsie. "Ah need the aid of ma beautiful assistant for this bit."

He signaled to his partner by gesturing with his chin. "Jimmy, would ye haud this gentleman nice an' safe here?"

Jimmy Foy held Andy back in the chair while Reid re-positioned the nail and began to hammer.

Rhythmic blows drove the large nail in to the seat of the chair via his victim's scrotum, each blow accompanied by a scream, particularly when Reid laid in to the final blows with significantly more vigour.

"Well, ah think that's a job well done," said Reid getting to his feet and brushing the dust from his knees. He turned to Elsie. "Wan guy jist widn'y keep still wance. He made me miss an ah went an' hit him right on his ba's. It jist ruined his whole evenin', so it did."

Reid grimaced a smile in the direction of the others. "Now listen everybody, ah don't imagine that Mister Kyle here'll want tae make a song an' dance about oor wee discussion. But jist in case, let me help us a' by explainin' where we staun'. You willn'y say anythin' aboot his tae nobody...no' even yer best pals. No' even yer wifes. Nobody!" He looked at them all evenly. "Or ah'll be back." He gestured with his hammer. "An' ah'll bring ma carpentry set. So let's no' get silly nur nuthin'. Eh no'?" He smiled a repeat of his stage grin at the nearest drinker and brought his face to within inches of the slack-jawed innocent in front of him inviting acknowledgment of his proposition. "Eh?"

His accomplice gathered up the baseball bat and took the hammer from Reid who caught his glance and, eyebrows raised in silent quiz, asked himself the question he presumed was resting, unasked, in Foy's mind. *Huv we time for a quick wan 'fore we go?*

A tremulous voice spoke behind him, hesitating between each syllable. "His... name's... McCutcheon."

Reid's brows furrowed in a light, unconcerned frown at the audacity of an interruption.

"Whit?"

"His name's...Andy McCutcheon."

His look darkened as the posed question registered.

"Whitd'ye mean, his name's Andy McCutcheon?"

"That's his name so it is. Eh, Elsie?"

Elsie let out the wail she'd been suppressing since Reid and Foy had entered the bar.

"Whit huv ye's done tae tha' poor aul' man?"

"How? Is he no' Angus Kyle?"

Bravado overtook Elsie.

"Naw, ya choob. He's Andy McCutcheon." She pointed to a figure sitting alone at a table near a blanked out window. "That's Angus Kyle!"

Reid and Foy turned, slow and curious...as if choreographed, to focus upon a figure, arms folded across his chest, sitting in a gloomy alcove staring fixedly into his half-empty pint tumbler. They mirrored a synchronised look at each other. Reid spoke to Foy slowly, between gritted teeth.

"You told me he wid be wearin' a black jaikit an' a bunnet."

"Ah know. But that's whit he *was* wearin'!"

"But he's no' the right guy!"

"Maybe no'. But he wis wearin' the right stuff."

Reid nodded his acceptance of Foy's logic and scanned the bar-room, slowly registering the attitudes of its occupants before fixing on the muffled agonies of McCutcheon.

"Christ, ah'm helly a sorry there pal. Seems ah've made a wee mistake."

If Andy McCutcheon acknowledged the apology, he wasn't able to communicate it to his tormentor. A thought occurred to Foy.

"Here Benji, ah only brought the one nail."

Reid's irritation with himself found expression in his heightening contempt of Foy.

"Naw, right enough. Ah suppose ye'd imagine we'd manage tae hammer the right set of ba's intae a chair withoot the need fur another nail. Wouldn't ye?"

"So whit we gonny dae Benji? Yer hammer husn'y got wan of they heads that gets nails oot."

Reid pursed his lips as he considered his next move. He slowly levered himself off the bar and stepped over to the seated, slumped, moaning pain of McCutcheon. Scanning the bar-room again for any sign of trouble or derision, he lifted McCutcheon gently upright and inspected his handiwork. He looked at Elsie, apologetically and felt a need to explain his discomfiture.

"Ah'm no usually aroon tae dae anythin' aboot this bit. Ah suppose ah've never really wunnered how they got the nails oot," he mused. He addressed Foy thoughtfully. "Maybe ye wid need a claw hammer."

"Don't be daft Benji. Ye wid hurt him even more and he's no' even the guy ye were meant tae hurt." They fell silent for a second until Foy spoke again. "Maybe ye could hit it oot from underneath."

"Ah canny really....it's a' wee spars of wood beneath the chair. Ah couldn'y get a right swing at it."

"Maybe no'....but ye could mibes hit at it a wee bit at a time."

"Ah've no' got the time. An' ah've goat ma reputation tae think of as well."

"Some reputation. Ye've jist went an' gave the wrang guy a doin'."

"Jist shut it, Foy or you'll be the next wan that gets the doin'."

"Don't I know you?"

Reid and Foy broke off from their deliberations and turned to face their questioner.

"Are you no' that guy Kyle?" asked Reid.

"Aye. And if ah'm no' mistaken, you're Plooky Reid."

Reid's gaze narrowed, focusing upon this stranger who called him by a name now almost forgotten.

"How're ye callin' me that?" quizzed Reid, still confused.

"Coz that was yer name when we were pals."

"Who the fu...Christ, Gus....Gus Kyle." Reid stepped back slightly and looked Kyle up and down. "Jesus, so it is..." His face lit up. "Christ, Jimmy, it's Gus Kyle. Man, ah've no' seen ye since we left school."

"Aye, since *you* left more like. Ah got to stay. They put you in the Kibble Approved School for all those break-ins and settin' fire tae the gymnasium."

"Christ, you did more than me as ah recall. Ah jist got caught."

"True enough. I worked out early that if you got caught and went to court, you were just putting yourself in the hands of fifteen people who weren't even smart enough get out of jury duty. It was easier just not gettin' caught."

He laughed in recollection. Kyle and Reid smiled at one another, warm in their memories of an uproarious adolescence. Kyle broke the silence.

"So this is you now, then."

"Aye, this is me."

"An' they said ye'd never make anythin' of yourself," said Kyle, comfortable in his mocking.

"It's a livin'."

Kyle smiled, nodding at McCutcheon. "Well, I was most impressed. Very professional. Except it was the wrong guy. Ah'm almost inclined tae pay Hanlon his money."

"Well, it would save me nailin' yer ba's tae the floor," said Reid with the slightest edge to his smiled retort.

Kyle laughed out loud. "Aye, but ah could aye kick yer heid in when we were boys."

"That wis more than thirty year ago. An' anyway, ah've got a pal an' a baseball bat."

"Even so, even so."

Kyle paused. "Your boss Hanlon's an arse. Ah borrowed fifty quid off him when I was drunk a couple of months back an' he jacks it up tae more than three hundred notes. That's no' right Plooky. Ah've already given him a hundred an' that seems no' a bad return on his investment."

"Business is business, Gus."

"Aye, right enough." They eyed one another. "Tell ye what, Plooky. How'd ye no' go back tae Hanlon an' tell him you've nailed me to the cross an' we'll have a pint an' a blether an' both of us'll walk away from this. For auld time's sake."

"Canny dae that, Gus."

"How no'?"

Reid repeated the words he'd used in many a bar-room, knowing that they would not be received by his old school pal in quite the same way. He shifted self-consciously.

"Cos ah'm a professional."

Kyle's laugh exploded into Reid's consciousness.

"Gie's peace. A professional?" he ridiculed. "Let me guess. You're on the dole. You get backhanders from Hanlon an' maybe one or two others. You live in a council house somewhere when you're no' in the pub. Maybe even stayin' wi yer mammy still....?"

"That's a' shite. Ah'm married an' ah happen tae have stayed in Edinburgh for a year."

"Well done. No' bad Plooky. But ah'll bet the rest's true."

"Aye, well ah happen tae have chose tae stay in a council estate, by the way. It's a' gettin' modernised an' everythin'. An ah'm only stayin' wi' the mother in the meantime cause ma marriage is goin' through a wee bad patch."

"Sorry tae hear tha' Plooky...."

Reid shifted uncomfortably. "Gaunny call me Benji. That's the name ah go under noo. Plooky wis ma name jist when ah wis wee."

Kyle laughed again. "Is this your stage name then? Your *professional* name?"

"Look Gus. Stoap windin' me up or ah'll forget we was friends wanst."

"An' dae what Benji? Beat me up like that auld guy over there?"

Reid decided that it might be wise to remind Kyle of the proximity of his assistant. "Jimmy, haud me back. This guy's gettin' right oan ma tits."

Kyle understood bar-room Glasgow as did Reid. There was no way back now other than benevolent or overpowering intervention. Both knew they'd trade insults. Rituals would be observed. But shortly, one of them would be rendered senseless – urgently, bloodily and violently.

"So ah'm gettin' on your tits? Mind you, it widny be difficult. You've got a fine pair there, Plooky. Ah bet they're bigger than yer wife's."

"Heh, jist you leave ma Senga oot o' this." Reid's sense of honour was offended, however artificially, as part of the choreography of the bar-room rammy.

"Senga? snorted Kyle. "No' wee Senga Snotters? Ye married *her*?"

Reid affected injury. "She grew up beautiful, by the way. Wance she'd goat her adenoids oot she turned intae a right princess. An' noo she's Senga Reid. An' naebudy slags aff ma wife."

"Oh, ah'll grant ye she'll have turned into a looker, Plooky. She wis bonny right enough. Ah well remember her looks a' right. An' ah take it a' back. Ye huvn'y got bigger tits than her."

"How? Whit are you insinuatin', eh? Are you sayin' sumthin' Kyle? If you're sayin' ma wife's a slag, ya basturd…"

Reid launched a swing at Kyle, clutching an empty beer glass in his right hand. It met with no resistance, Kyle having leaned back to avoid the blow he'd provoked and had therefore anticipated. A survivor of too many brawls, Kyle went directly to Reid's knee with his boot, crunching bone and cartilage, causing the immediate immobilisation of his opponent. Reid's defeat became inevitable when his thinning hair was grasped firmly, tugging his face upward to meet Kyle's forehead descending at speed. With vicious ferocity, both collided and Reid fell back, his nose burst like a ripe tomato. Blood splattered out, covering his shirt like a red bib.

Kyle turned to Foy who stood, catatonic; frozen in fright. He gestured at his own baseball bat as if he'd just realised he was holding it. "No problems here big man… will ah just put this bat down on the floor, like?"

"Not unless you cover the shaft in grease!"

"Grease? Why would ah...?"

"That way it won't be as painful when I shove it up your arse if you make one stupid move!"

"No need, Mister." Carefully, Foy placed both the bat and hammer on the floor and stepped back.

Kyle evaluated the situation and decided that Foy was no threat. He turned again to the fallen Reid and, having assessed that his injuries had disabled him quite completely, stamped sharply on his right hand, breaking two fingers and thereby ensuring that he wouldn't be able to contemplate retaliation for quite some time.

"For auld times. Eh, Plooky?"

Smoothing back his hair, he turned to Elsie and nodded in the direction of the quiet moaning of McCutcheon.

"You'd better get somebody to look at that old guy over there. Probably better phone an ambulance. He looks in a bad way."

Reid was still conscious and was attempting painfully to wipe some of the blood from his face with the back of his hand. Kyle knelt beside him and spoke quietly into a newly crimsoned ear.

"You know Benji, you're in wi' a right twisted lot, so ye are. Your pal Hanlon's a real bad man. But ah'm goin' to give ye a bit of advice for auld time's sake, eh? Ah dare say you'll earn a livin' beatin' up auld men when you've got the element of surprise, a pal and a baseball bat. But the first time you come up against anybody decent, they're goin' to kill you, so maybe you want to chuck it now."

Kyle stood up and surveyed the carnage. He nodded to Elsie. "Ah'll be off then. Sorry about the mess, Misses."

Reid lay back on the bloody bar-room floor helplessly eyeing his assailant as he bid his farewells. Gus Kyle caught his glance. He shook his head ruefully as he grimaced a farewell to Reid and Foy.

"Don't you guys come back here. Tell Hanlon we're square and if he stays away from me no one'll get hurt." He lifted the remainder of his unfinished pint and swallowed it in one gulp. Placing the glass gently on the bar and collecting his cap, he left the premises.

CHAPTER THREE

"Ladies and Gentlemen, the President of the United States of America".

A grim looking Bill Clinton stepped up onto a portico and placed his hands on a lectern on which some notes had earlier been placed.

"Thank you, General Hess. Let me begin by thanking everyone who is a part of the Grand Forks Air Force Base for what you do for our national security and especially for what you have done to support the people of the Grand Forks communities in these last few days following the floods caused by the Red River. I'm very proud of you. Thank you."

As he spoke, the crosshairs of the telescopic lens of a powerful Barrett M82 Sniper Rifle fell across his chest.

"As I think all of you know, I have just come from touring the devastation of the floods as well as a very moving community meeting, presided over by Mayor Owens, attended by Mayor Stauss and other mayors, the entire congressional delegation from North Dakota and from South Dakota, Senator Grams and Senator Wellstone from Minnesota, Congressman Collin Peterson from Minnesota, and the Governors from North Dakota and Minnesota...."

The crosshairs moved up slowly to rest on his forehead.

"We know that this rebuilding is going to be a long-term prospect, and we also know that there are some very immediate and pressing human needs that many people have. Before I left this morning......."

"Baaaang..." a whispered voice mimicked the shooting of a rifle.

A commentator's voice on the ageing television set was saying something about how more would be heard from the President after the break following which an advertisement appeared in which a talking head was smiling and reassuring viewers of the merits of a new hair colourant for males.

The crosshairs centred on the bridge of the hirsute actor's nose...

"Baaaang...you're dead!" whispered a drunken Jack Bryson before he gently placed the rifle at his side taking care to protect the telescopic sights located above the trigger. He lifted a whisky glass to his lips.

"Baaaang," he murmured to no one in particular as he swallowed the contents of the glass of Macallan 18 year old malt whisky. Impoverished he might have been, but compromising on his whisky wasn't in prospect.

"Another round please. No pun intended," he slurred to no one, pleased at his wit and smiling at his companion whisky glass.

Footsteps on the tenement stairs outside preceded a key being turned in the lock in Bryson's front door admitting a drenched Angus Kyle who entered the rather shabby living room in which sat the armchair rifleman. He looked at the rifle beside the armchair.

"Jesus, Jack! I thought we agreed that you'd keep that hidden beneath the floorboards. I might have brought home a woman friend or someone!" Kyle removed his wet overcoat and threw it over a chair by the window.

"Aye, fat chance Gus," smiled Bryson. "I was just playing soldiers. No harm done."

"Gimme a drop of that whisky. My quiet pint in the Thistle Bar was interrupted," said Kyle.

Bryson placed his glass on a nearby table on which stood his half empty bottle of Macallan and six dead bottles of beer. He looked up slowly.

"What happened? Were you being pestered by all your women friends?"

"Nah. I was being tapped for the money that that loan shark Hanlon figures he's owed but the two eejits he sent beat up the wrong guy. An auld fellah. They nailed his fuckin' balls to a chair. I sent them packin' but I dare say that Hanlon won't let it rest. I suppose I'll need to see him face to face and invite him to stand back. He's had his money back with interest."

"They nailed his ba's tae a *what*? Christ, is that what passes for gangsterism in Glasgow these days?" He paused to pour two glasses of whisky three fingers deep and handed one over to the now seated Kyle. "Anyway, who cares about Hanlon?" Bryson asked rhetorically. "Say the word and the two of us'll wander over to his HQ and sort him out. His type would take us about four minutes of our sinful lives to deal with."

"Ach, we're due to leave Glasgow soon enough. He can keep."

Kyle sipped at his glass and nodded at the rifle.

"Can we not put that back under the floor? Just in case someone gets lost and wanders in looking for the cocktail bar."

"Aye, sure," said Bryson resignedly as he lifted the powerful, twenty-eight pound armament as if it were a small plastic toy and walked into the bedroom where floorboards had been removed to provide for a place of concealment. It would be found immediately by any professional search but would remain out of harm's way should anyone be sufficiently unwise or unlucky to breach the front door of the flat Bryson and Kyle were using as a temporary home base.

"No phone call yet from the Colonel?"

Kyle shook his head. "Nothing yet but I wish he'd get in touch. We could be doing with the money and much as I enjoy little more than sitting here in this dump watching you drink both of us to death, I can't wait to have Brand's small commission explained to us. The one he gave us in Palestine was fun...although for the life of me, I can't see what use he has for our talents here in Glasgow."

"Drinkin' ourselves to death has its attractions, said Bryson morosely.

"I mean, who'd miss us except your daughter Rachael and you've already given her all of your hard earned money so she's now well set up."

"Aye. But better she benefited than your bookies did," responded Kyle, repeating a rebuke he'd made on many occasions to his friend. "The day you pass, the bookmaking fraternity will line the streets in solemn sadness at your inability to share your ill-gotten gains with them anymore."

And so the evening passed, mostly in quiet contemplation. Initially the TV would present a moment which inspired an inebriated comment. Disinterestedly, Kyle would glance occasionally at a self improvement book on English grammar he was reading but gradually their eyes closed and tiredness brought on by a gross surfeit of alcohol saw each of them fall asleep in the chairs in which they'd sat for six days now whilst awaiting further contact from a man they knew only as Colonel Brand.

Gus Kyle and Jack Bryson had been boyhood friends in Glasgow – Bryson a year younger than Kyle's forty years and in consequence reduced to the subordinate in the relationship unless they were on active duty when their lives depended equally upon the other. Career soldiers, they had each excelled and both were accepted into the SAS in their late twenties. Tours of duty in Northern Ireland and Bosnia had seen their reputations soar: real hard men who could be expected to deliver the results asked of them – even when these seemed to be outrageously unrealistic. Both had mastered all of the arts of warfare but Kyle was accepted by Bryson as the brains of the operation who specialised in surveillance and he himself basked in the glory of his armed forces' nickname of OSOK Bryson…One Shot, One Kill Bryson…due to his unparalleled mastery of the sniper's Barrett M82 .50-caliber long-range rifle.

Many times he had engaged targets over one mile away with precision. Bryson's gun fired one of the most powerful rounds in the world, the .50 Browning machine gun cartridge and he was known as being routinely capable of hitting a five inch target at a distance of two kilometers. But the most impressive characteristic of this monster of a rifle was its fear factor. The bullet, traveling faster than the speed of sound provided for a silent and effective kill. Typically, the target would drop dead a few moments before the actual sound of the shot was heard. The bullet, which was the size of a decent Havana cigar, could also puncture a foot thick block of concrete, or over one inch of armour plating without causing much rifle recoil. Bryson had also mastered the ability of firing off all ten rounds in the magazine in less than ten seconds without losing accuracy, thereby rendering small groups of combatants dead almost before they heard the shots.

He left the SAS because he had been found drunk just once too often, in which condition, he couldn't hit a barn door with a banjo. Kyle left along with him out of his sense of loyalty… as well as being found culpable of punching out the four Military Policemen who had arrested Bryson.

Amongst Kyle's many abilities was his capacity as a natural born thief. In his younger days in Glasgow, his agility and bravery had seen him access windows and rooftops that defeated other men. In the army, he became known as the Quartermaster, so adept was he at acquiring anything his men sought – either as a supplement to their field weaponry or as a supplement to their leisure hours. Booze, videos, cigarettes, even once a billiard table, would be supplied on request.

It took a little more ingenuity and planning but Bryson's Barrett rifle and one hundred rounds of ammunition were not only stolen but transported back home to Glasgow by Kyle without too much difficulty…although the discovery of its loss back in a nearby American base in Tuzla in Bosnia and Herzegovina caused merry hell.

Both men had a fearsome reputation, even within the SAS, as the most brutally effective street fighters in the company. No one was particularly keen to engage them in training due to their athleticism and their comprehensive mastery of most martial arts. They were fighting machines par excellence.

Kyle's phone rang, awaking him from the intoxicated sleep into which he'd fallen. Still clad in yesterday's clothing, he glowered at the time on the face of his phone while trying to determine who was phoning him at 3.30 in the morning. Bryson was also awake now and seated bolt upright.

"Yes?"

"Mr. Kyle? I do hope that I haven't awakened you?"

"Colonel Brand? It's yourself. No, I was just finishing the Times' crossword puzzle."

"What a disciplined life you must lead. Are you in the company of Mr. Bryson?"

"Aye. He's reading the Beano".

Brand ignored Kyle's banter.

"Let me cut to the chase, Kyle. I have need of your services again. Can you and your colleague meet me tomorrow, or rather today at nine o'clock, six hours from now?"

"We can if you're in Scotland, Colonel. Just say where and we'll be there. Should we bring anything?"

"You will need the same equipment you used in Palestine. You'll be travelling and will require your passport. Clothes necessary for a two week holiday in the sun. One kit bag each should suffice."

Kyle laughed and directed his response to Bryson, singing the first line of Cliff Richard's hit song. "Hey Jack, *We're all goin' on our summer holidaaayzzz. No more workin' for a week or two'....*"

Brand grimaced at the other end of the phone. "As you might imagine Mr. Kyle, there may be some activity required of each of you. I'll explain when we meet. Be ready to travel immediately our meeting concludes. The Copthorne Hotel, George Square. Suite 104. Name of McLeod if asked. Don't go to reception. Come straight up."

"Yes sir."

Kyle ended the call and placed the phone on the arm of his chair. "Sounds interesting. Two weeks' work, bring our weaponry, sunshine all the way and it looks like we get to meet the Colonel."

"Hate to point this out Gus but the sun shone bright in Bosnia and you were never finished bitchin' about the heat."

"True enough," he replied, accepting the point. "Maybe we should get started. Bring the weapons out and we'll dismantle and oil them."

Bryson made his way through to a bedroom and removed five floorboards beneath which were placed his beloved Barrett rifle, two Heckler and Koch HK P7 rifles, three hunting knives, two IMI Uzi semi automatic machine pistols, a box of M84 stun grenades as well as boxes of the appropriate rounds needed to ensure their lethality. Grunting, he removed everything to the settee in the living room where only minutes before he'd been slumbering and patted his pockets for the oil cloth he'd stuffed there earlier.

Unfortunately for Joe Hanlon and the three thugs he'd brought with him to avenge the injury done to Benji Reid, it took him three kicks to unhinge the rather flimsy wooden door of Kyle's flat. More than sufficient warning.

The four men bundled into the flat, each carrying a baseball bat. Two each also held a knife.

As they barged their way through the door, they faced both Kyle and Bryson standing together, each holding an Uzi machine pistol in one hand and a rifle in the other. Each pointed menacingly at the four visitors.

Arthur Hanlon's attack roar stuck in his throat as he spread his arms to hold back the initial rush of his three assistants, his face contorted. His surprised eyebrows fled somewhere near his receding hairline.

"Holy Mother of God," he exclaimed, immediately recognising the weakness of his position. He took a breath. "Jesus Christ….Gus…..this is all one big misunderstanding."

Bryson took the lead. "You want me to shoot them all in the head, Gus?"

"Let's wait to hear what they want, Jack. Maybe they come in peace."

"We do, Gus, we do," pleaded Hanlon now with his hands clasped together as if in prayer, his baseball bat cast urgently on the carpet. "We just wanted to let you know that the loan is now paid in full as far as I'm concerned. Everything's squared away. We're fine you and me." He threw his arms wide. "I just came to tell you."

Kyle pursed his lips. "You ok, Benji?" he asked of his adolescent friend, now sporting a series of bandages and plasters which held his nose together.

"Fide add daddy, Guz," said Reid, enunciating his words as well as his broken and bloody nose would permit.

Kyle raised his pistol and pointed it at Hanlon's head. "And we won't hear from you again regarding the money?"

"A big misunderstanding, just like ah say, Gus." He straightened his tie and attempted to regain some composure. "It would probably be wise if we just went on our way if you're okay with that."

"I still think I should shoot them all in the head, Gus." Bryson nodded towards a bag on the settee. "I've a silencer in there. Nobody would hear anything and nobody would miss this bunch of clowns."

"Please Gus. Let bygones be bygones," pleaded Hanlon.

Kyle lowered his pistol. "Put a hundred pounds behind the bar in the Stag's Head for the regulars, another hundred to fix the door and put a grand in the pocket of that old man you beat up tonight. Leave these bats and knives on the floor and don't speak of this again."

Hanlon nodded several times as if this was a wise solution to a delicate problem and one to which he'd been giving positive consideration all evening.

"Okay, beat it...and I'll be checking that money is paid over today. If it's not, we'll pay you a visit."

The four men stumbled down the stairs, their weapons lying where they dropped them in the apartment.

"We should have nailed that eejit's balls to a chair just to teach him a lesson," grouched Bryson. "An eye for an eye, a testicle for a testicle."

Kyle shrugged. "Trust me. I know Arthur Hanlon and he'll be much more upset at losing money. Anyway we want to get away from Glasgow with the least possible background noise."

The anonymous flatted dwelling house used temporarily by Bryson and Kyle was located down near the docks in Glasgow; in the Govan area to be precise. It wasn't the most salubrious area of a Glasgow which had experienced a remarkable renaissance in the previous decade but which had still left some small pockets as sumps inhabited largely by junkies, drunks and thieves. Kyle knew the area well and knew also that no one would be reporting a noisy altercation to the police. Still, their door was smashed beyond economical repair and they were due to leave for ever in a few hours. No sense in taking chances. Kyle thought quickly.

"Let's get packed quickly and move off, Jack. We can sleep when we're on our holidays."

They packed two kit bags for their trip....but were aware that, given the arsenal they had just secreted within them, they would be in rather more trouble than having an unannounced extra bottle of malt whisky in their briefcase were they to be taken aside by Border Control. Colonel Brand had better be making some pretty impressive arrangements if they were not to be spending the next few years in a prison cell somewhere.

CHAPTER FOUR

In his compound on the banks of the River Ob, Dmitriy Ivanov waited impatiently for his visitor to be admitted to his luxurious personal apartment. The double doors opened simultaneously and his butler, before retiring gracefully from the room, announced the arrival of Anatoly Borovsky, the head of Russia's new Federal Security Services.

"Comrade Borovsky! You are most welcome. I hope your journey from Moscow was not too tiresome."

"Any travel outside Moscow is tiresome. I come here because I *have* to not because I want to." He accepted the glass of vodka offered him by Ivanov. "I am most interested in why you felt it necessary to call me down here for a confidential chat. You must know that complete confidentiality in Russia means you can tell only one other person...and he is then free to share or sell that secret over vodka!"

"If your journey to Novosibirsk was as much of a trial as you present it, let me get straight to the point." Both men sipped at their glass and sat down facing each other on Ivanov's comfortable sofas.

"Very well, Comrade Borovsky, I have need of your services...or rather, the Motherland would benefit were you to feel it possible to assist my proposition."

"I am sure that each is indistinguishable, one from the other," Borovsky said sarcastically. "So just tell me... what might that be that proposition, Comrade Ivanov?"

"Mother Russia now produces more oil than any other nation on earth. I personally produce more oil that some members of OPEC."

"This much is known to me."

"Despite our dominance of the world in terms of market share, Comrade Borovsky, oil prices are still set by OPEC and western oil...essentially America and Saudi Arabia. Hardly our friends. Our economy is not as developed as Europe or the USA and so we depend more on our raw materials...like oil. Presently our oil is sufficient to meet the needs of the motherland and we export the rest in order to afford the military adventures we so enjoy in places like Chechnya...even if these are not exactly what we would seek in terms of success."

"Do not toy with me comrade. Please do me the favour of coming to the proposition you want to make. I am impatient to return to Moscow."

"Very well. Some weeks ago, I made arrangements to strike at the heart of OPEC and western oil interests. I want to see their infrastructure damaged, I want to see oil prices rise substantially at a point when the only market that can respond to demand is Russia. I would like to do this in such a way that would instill mistrust between the west and OPEC...and I would like to see results soon."

"You are aware, of course, that we are on a new path...one of *glasnost*, of openness with our friends in the west?"

"Of course, comrade...but business is business. The Russian economy would benefit dramatically if we were able to deliver these results. As would I, I concede."

"Perhaps you underestimate the ability of the west to see beyond the initial act and to establish blame. It could set us back years."

"I understand the risks, Comrade Borovsky. But, if you'll forgive me, I have already thought of this and have arranged matters so that any blame will fall on Muslim extremists...not us!"

Borovsky took a final sip of his vodka and placed his glass softly upon the table.

"Comrade Ivanov. If you have already put your plans into action, you must tell me everything. My sole objective is to advance the interests of the Motherland and to minimise any harm that might befall her. You must understand my concern if you have acted without the approval of the state."

"Let me be clear, comrade. The only reason I am telling you *anything* is to guard against your people in the FSS descending upon my organisation at some point in order to have me answer some trumped up charge of income tax evasion or whatever you would invent to see me brought down. I have the resources to take care of the implementation of this operation…what I need from you is to misdirect the west to ensure that they believe my invention that my actions are, in fact, the work of Muslim extremists. This is in the interests of both of us and will cost you nothing."

"And how exactly would you have me do that, comrade?"

Ivanov paused before proceeding.

"The west knows we are in some disarray in Chechnya. If they believed that we have members of the security forces who would wish a return to the old days and that they threaten both Russian and western interests, we could make common cause with them and persuade them that a new culture of cooperation now exists between us…that Islamic extremism is much more of a threat to us both and that we should coordinate our efforts to defeat this new enemy."

"And you can have them believe that their enemy in this is Islam?"

Ivanov nodded. "I have already taken steps to persuade MI5 of a need for them to collaborate with us in order to see off a potential attack by your operatives…or one or two disaffected among them…to damage western interests. However, I've also taken steps to employ the well known Muslim terrorist, the Scorpion. He thinks he is being paid via Iran to advance the Muslim *jihad* against the west but unknown to him, he works for me and his involvement will inevitably persuade the USA because

Islamic extremism acts against what they see as Muslim betrayers in Riyadh as much as western interests. The west will believe it is they who are responsible if OPEC is damaged along with the west."

Borovsky lifted his empty glass.

"Indeed, comrade. Perhaps my journey from Moscow wasn't such a trial after all. If you refill my glass, we could discuss this plan of yours further?"

Ivanov reached for the bottle of vodka.

"Delighted, Comrade Borovsky."

* * *

Loud, repeated *beeeeps* heralded the imminent arrival of baggage on the now revolving carrousel at Malaga Airport in Spain. Liam Brannigan and his new wife Susan waited patiently for their suitcases so that they might continue their journey to Puerto Banus and the luxury 77 meter super-yacht they'd hired for this latest leg in their six week long honeymoon, 'doing Europe'.

Liam hugged Susan close and kissed her forehead affectionately.

"Tired, darling?"

"Exhausted. But we'll soon be out of here. It's not much of a drive to the yacht according to Dad." She nuzzled into his chest. "I can't wait to get on board. It sounds just fabulous.

A seven star hotel afloat with a crew whose only task is looking after you and me. I'll feel seriously pampered."

Dr. Liam Brannigan, a thirty year old economist from Dublin, had wed twenty-five year old Miss Susan Lattanzi of Las Vegas, Nevada only three weeks before. After a fortnight with his extended family in Dublin and a tour of the Emerald Isle, they'd spent a week in Glasgow where Liam had studied for his PhD and where also he still had a lot of old acquaintances. Now the honeymoon continued aboard the luxury, twelve berth, tri-decked motor cruiser 'Ventura' courtesy of Susan's father, ex-Senator Joe Lattanzi for whom Liam worked as Chief Executive. As a sop to Liam who initially resisted the generosity of the honeymoon gift of a fortnight's lease of the cruiser, Joe asked him to assess the area around the rich Spanish playground of Puerto Banus for his next hotel development now that his latest in Las Vegas was approaching completion. Liam accepted his request knowing that it was only Joe's way of making the offer easier for him to agree. But he was interested in having a look round in any case. As Joe's chief executive and project manager on his new hotel on the Strip, he had begun to come by a genuine interest in large scale developments. Anyway, Joe didn't want a report, just his gut feeling for the port's developmental potential.

Susan was one of nature's natural beauties. Now aged twenty-five, she had previously devoted herself to caring for her mother and father on their stud farm outside Vegas. Her friendship with Liam, her father's right-hand man, had developed slowly over some years and Joe and Liz had been overjoyed at the union, so highly had they come to view Liam's personal qualities. Slim and tall, Susan had always preferred to dress in blue jeans with a straw Stetson and a denim shirt tied at the midriff. Her mother was always attempting to have her dress more elegantly and less as if she was 'going to a rodeo' but both she and Liam were more comfortable in casual wear, disguising the fact that they were already very wealthy young people. Upon their return to America, Joe had informed them that he would retire properly and that they would head up the family business with all the substantial millions of dollars that would be conveyed to them in the process.

But tonight she was dressed for travel in sweatpants and comfortable top. She's still the most beautiful woman I've seen on this trip. *America, Ireland, Scotland and now Spain*, thought Liam, as they snuggled together awaiting their cases.

Shortly, their belongings having been collected, they found themselves ensconced in the rear of a large black Mercedes being driven the short, forty minute journey along the coast to Puerto Banus, the 'millionaires' playground' so beloved of film stars, entrepreneurs and the wealthy.

It was dusk now. The car approached the harbour and slowed to a safe pace as the driver manoeuvred along the narrow concrete moorings at which were docked various sizes of motor yachts. Gently resting immediately opposite elegant restaurants, cocktail bars and expensive shops, sleek craft glimmered and purred in the moonlight, accommodating those who could afford to berth in this most exclusive bolt-hole.

The driver continued to drive gingerly until he came to the berth hosting the 'Ventura'. The throaty growl of the luxury car was quieted. Quickly he stepped out, opened the door for Susan and invited her to step on board while he took responsibility for the on-board transportation of luggage.

Standing on the deck next to the gangplank awaiting her new guests was Captain Kimberly Williams. Dressed in a crisp white shirt with epaulettes and creased, black tailored trousers she smiled widely as Susan and Liam stepped on board. Shaking their hands warmly, she introduced herself and gestured towards the main cabin on that deck where a bottle of freshly opened Krug Champagne was being poured into two glasses by a steward. Comfortable yellow leather armchairs accommodated each of the three of them once the honeymooning couple had been relieved of their jackets.

The tri-decked 'Ventura' had been bought direct from the boatbuilders in France only four years earlier and was a 77 meter motor cruiser capable of accommodating some twelve guests in complete luxury. Berthed at the exclusive port of Puerto Banus, it rubbed shoulders with craft which were equally sumptuous. Sleek and powerful, it had the capacity to cruise slowly around the beautiful ports of the Costa del Sol or make longer trips across substantial bodies of water. It reeked of luxury and fine living and its fixtures and fitments were all top of the range. 'A floating palace' was the trite but equally accurate description Joe Lattanzi had offered when announcing his contribution to his daughter's honeymoon with Liam.

Introductions over, the conversation turned to the luxurious quality of the fixtures and fittings of the cruiser.

"I mean, Jeeesus…, it's just amazing", said Liam, looking round at Italian marble and Spanish leather, stone artifacts and the finest carpeting. "I can't believe how spacious and beautiful it is!"

"Thanks, I'll show you around once you've finished your Champagne," Kim said proudly. "I'm very pleased with how things have turned out. It's the finest ship of the line in my humble opinion", she smiled. "The Ventura can carry twelve guests in eight cabins and also has scope for nine staff. I've kept it down to three staff plus me to permit a more homely, unobtrusive feel to your time on board. That said, we all turn our hands to a multitude of tasks. As well as being the owner and captain of this vessel, I can turn my hand to engineering duties, I can pass muster in the kitchen and look after cooking duties if needs be and I'm also a qualified masseuse should either of you have aching muscles or just want to relax on board."

"Wowee", exclaimed Susan. "Where did you find time to become so accomplished?"

Kim shrugged, "I started young but I try to do something new every year. I'm lucky. My mother set me up with the Ventura. I could never have bought it on my own. My new adventure this year has been to become a member of the local beach volleyball team and we're doing quite well."

Susan and Kim fell into easy conversation and despite himself, Liam found himself outside the interaction, assessing Kim, taking in her even, dimpled smile which showed off her perfect white teeth, her slim but muscular frame and her short blond hair that framed an impossibly pretty face. He calculated she must be in her mid-thirties and was obviously lithe and athletic. *Jeez… she's the real deal. She's completely gorgeous and obviously very competent. Hmmm, sharp and charming…….I'm going to enjoy being around these two women over the next two weeks. They'd turn the head of a man whose neck was in traction!*

CHAPTER FIVE

Kyle and Bryson waited until sunrise and the reawakening of the city of Glasgow before hailing a taxi on Govan Road and setting off for the city centre, leaving their dank, urine stained close-mouth behind them. Although there would be guaranteed to be a few Transport Police officers in and around the railway station at Queen Street, they figured that two guys sitting with luggage and having a quiet coffee in a crowded transit point would blend in easily and unobtrusively while they awaited their appointment with the Colonel. The station also had the benefit of being located right next door to the Copthorne Hotel.

"So what do you figure to this guy Colonel Brand?" asked Bryson over a coffee in the station concourse. "I mean we know hee-haw about him. We don't even know who he reports to or who pays him to pay us!"

Kyle pursed his lips. "The Palestinian mission made me think he was British Intelligence." He thought again and shrugged his shoulders. "Perhaps Israeli or American. Taking out five Hamas boys in Khan Yunis and rescuing a man whose name we didn't know didn't seem to me to be something that would be paid for by *al Qaeda* or the Syrians. Whoever it was needed deniability and was prepared to pay for it. And he paid us well."

Bryson nodded. "Aye, so well that you ended up borrowing money from a loan shark!" He smiled, "Mind you, I'll grant you it was well organised. Good Intel. Everything in the place it was meant to be and at the time it was meant to be there. Couldn't complain. I suppose he's *Kosher*, even if he's not Israeli."

At three minutes to nine precisely, Kyle and Bryson lifted their kit bags and walked down the exit stairs from the station entering the Copthorne, going straight to the lifts unchallenged and making their way to Suite 104.

Kyle smiled at the hotel housekeeping assistant who ventured "Good morning!" at him in the corridor and waited until she entered the room she was cleaning before knocking on the Colonel's door.

Almost immediately the door was opened by a tall, pale man with a deep, red scar which cleaved his left eye from above his eyebrow to his cheek. Aged around fifty, his hair was black, combed into a neat shed, silvered at the temples.

"Gentlemen, your punctuality does you credit. Most professional." He stepped back to reveal another occupant in the room, a small man, who lifted each of the kit bags brought by Kyle and Bryson and upon being gestured to by Brand, took them one at a time across the corridor into suite 105 and closed the door.

Bryson narrowed his eyes at being separated from his Barrett rifle.

"Please do not be concerned," said Brand. "I just want to be in a separate room from the contents of your luggage lest we're visited by the authorities while we talk. You will have them back untouched as soon as we are finished."

The three men settled into armchairs and the Colonel moved to pour coffee for them.

"I trust your injuries have healed since you returned from the Gaza Strip?" asked Brand.

"A few cuts and bruises. Our arrival wasn't expected and it was a textbook operation. I hope that every job we do for you goes as well."

"Let's hope so. I must say I was very impressed by you both which is why I'd like you to undertake a task which is rather more complex and rather less action-orientated this time. It involves you working undercover although you'll both be using your real names and background."

"How much?" interrupted Bryson.

Brand paused, mildly irritated at Bryson's interjection. He smiled nevertheless, although his eyes betrayed his annoyance.

"I have Euros to the value of ten thousand pounds here which you will each take away with you today to defray any expenses incurred in your mission. A further fifty thousand pounds sterling will be deposited in your bank accounts upon your return. If only one of you returns or if, God forbid, both of you perish, the money will find its way to whomsoever you nominate.

"Tell you what," said Bryson, why don't you tell us what's involved and we'll tell you if it's worth risking life and limb for sixty grand."

"Alas, Mr. Bryson, every operation has its budget. Money doesn't grow on trees."

"Neither does a new leg if I leave one behind."

"Well, let me explain and we can discuss whether this is a fair price." He accepted a coffee from his newly returned assistant and continued. "The *al Qaeda* effort operating out of Sudan is funded by the illicit sale of opium from the poppy fields of Pakistan and Afghanistan. It's moved through Peshawar or Islamabad to Karachi and on to Europe. A large shipment is being tracked and our intelligence suggests that its destination is Spain where it will be processed and circulated across the European mainland, but will be targeted ultimately on Britain and Russia. The gang who are handling this are headed by a London mobster who's been hiding out in Spain for some years. I know him. A thoroughly bad man. Marcus Perry."

Brand sipped at his coffee and continued. "He's surrounded by a small army of around twenty thugs, most of whom lead a life of luxury out on the Costa del Sol. He can afford to look after his men. One of them, we know, is a plant put there by the Russians but we don't know who he is. You must use your initiative to uncover this man and report to me. Indeed, you might find this person to be of assistance as the mission here is to befriend and infiltrate the gang as far as is possible and stop these drugs finding their way onto the market. Should you inflict casualties on either the couriers or the Perry people, no one will cry into their beer as long as we have complete deniability. One very important consideration is that the drugs haul must be obtained intact, the boxes must remain completely undisturbed and they should be protected until I can make arrangements for their uplift."

Kyle spoke. "How do we find this mob?"

"They're based in Marbella. Hotel rooms have been booked there for you for two weeks from tomorrow. We think that if we don't succeed within this timeframe, we'll be too late. Perry owns the Red Lion pub in Marbella and can be found there most nights eating and drinking with some of his men. He always has his people around him but his right hand man is a Glaswegian just like you two and you might find it possible to befriend him. His name's Cammy Spence.

"Yeah, I've heard his name," said Kyle. "Didn't I read that he was arrested some years ago in Spain when someone who owed him money was found dead with all ten toes amputated?

Brand shook his head. "That was his boss, Perry. He was released when a witness mysteriously disappeared. But it's a crime that's characteristic of the gang. They're not to be trifled with. Our information was that the man they killed told them everything they wanted to know after the second of his toes was amputated by a set of pliers...but they cut the rest off anyway, one at a time. Like I say, I know this man. He's an evil bastard."

He put his hand in his jacket pocket and took out a room key which he threw to Kyle. "In the room across the hallway with your kit bags I've laid out files and photographs which you'll spend the rest of the day reading and memorising. I've booked a private flight from Prestwick tonight. It'll land in Murcia Airport, a small facility where we've paid to ensure that you can land without the usual protocols being observed. You'll be driven to your hotel and given the keys of a four by four which will be at your disposal for two weeks. Your cover story reflects reality. You are two friends recently decommissioned from the SAS who are now soldiers of fortune, looking for ways to use your talents to earn money. This is just a holiday for you on the Costa del Sol. You're no friends of Her Majesty's Government. They can check you out and you'll pass scrutiny."

"Who are we working for? asked Kyle.

"Why, you're working for me, Mr. Kyle."

"Aye, very good... and who do *you* work for?"

"I work for myself, Mr. Kyle. And you don't need to know with whom I'm contracted. It would not be in anyone's interest for that to be known. The fact of the matter is that you'll be working without any official recognition. If you so much as drop litter or are apprehended for violent activity, possessing drugs or large amounts of money, you're on your own. We need deniability. I'll get you in and out safely just like I did in Khan Yunis unless you're in police custody. I'll supply you with everything you'll need by way of materials and information and I'll pay you a substantial fee but you're on your own otherwise. If anything goes wrong, no one's ever heard of you."

Kyle shook his head. "And if it's only sixty grand you're offering, *they* won't ever hear of us either. Putting the hems on a drugs haul like you describe merits a larger fee. If this Perry fellah is as violent as you say, this'll cost more." Kyle stroked his chin and pondered. "Here's the deal. You got us cheap the last time...too cheap. We take your Euros today. You pay us each one hundred thousand pounds and put it in our accounts today using a retention money guarantee with the *Raiffeisenbank* in Hamburg. They'll draw up something quickly for your signature."

Brand's pallid face lost what colour it had. Bryson's face portrayed astonishment. His friend and comrade was a fighting machine, not an accountant. *Where the hell did that come from?* he asked himself.

Brand blanched. "One hundred and ten thousand pounds each? When I add my ancillary costs, the total sum would amount to something approaching the guts of a quarter of a million pounds, Kyle. A lot of money I'd prefer to use on other operations."

"It's no skin off our nose, Colonel. If you can get cheaper operatives who can deliver the results you want, you go right ahead. Jack and I might just go on holiday anyway," shrugged Kyle, knowing well they didn't have enough money between them to purchase the cheapest high street package holiday on offer.

Brand gripped his coffee cup tightly and grimaced angrily. "You well know that I can't come up with other people quickly enough."

"Well that just seems like bad planning, Colonel. It doesn't auger well for other aspects of the operation."

Brand slowly placed his cup down gently on a saucer that sat on a nearby table trying to control his anger.

"You have me over a barrel, Kyle so I must accept". He wrestled with his next utterance which came through gritted teeth.

"But I want success. I want to know the name of the Russians' inside man. I want these oafs dealt with severely and the consignment must not fall into the hands of Perry and his men under any circumstances. There will be thirteen boxes. They must not be opened. They must be protected at all costs for evidential purposes and I should be informed immediately. I'll let you know what to do once you have the boxes under your control. In no circumstances should the boxes be tampered with. You'll phone me every day without fail and advise me of progress. You'll work round the clock if need be, but you'll deliver success. I cannot be out that kind of money and end up with anything that is less than optimal," grimaced Brand.

Kyle rose from his chair and approached the still seated Colonel. He offered his hand.

"Let's shake on it, Colonel. Then you get to work on the finances and we'll make a start on your files next door."

With obvious irritation, Brand shook his hand and his assistant led them out to the hotel room across the hallway.

Closing the room door behind them, Bryson pushed Kyle playfully.

"A retention money guarantee with the *Raiffeisenbank* in Hamburg? …where the fuck did that come from?"

Kyle smiled. "I don't just get into pub fights when I'm off duty. I've been working out how we can improve our fee earning potential with a greater guarantee of actually being paid at the end of it."

"Well done, wee man. I just about pissed myself when you upped the ante."

A running joke between the two friends was Bryson's description of Kyle as 'wee man'. Standing almost six feet in his stocking soles, Kyle was anything but small but when compared with Bryson's six feet five inch athletic frame, his broad, muscular shoulders and narrow hips, any man might reasonably be described as 'wee'.

After three hours reading, discussing and memorising files and photographs, the room door opened admitting Brand and his assistant who carried a tray of sandwiches and a pot of coffee.

"Lunch, gentlemen," said Brand. "All making sense? Any questions?"

Bryson took a cluster of three sandwiches and began to inspect their contents.

"All seems straightforward. What makes you think that Perry and his mob are the type who can be befriended? Won't they be suspicious of new people around them so close to a big drugs deal like this one? Your file says here that it's a three million pound consignment."

"And a street value of thirty million plus.... But Perry and Spence may have a capacity for overconfidence. They've been above the law for years. We have to hope that your considerable personal charm and your reputations as two rogue soldiers who bear a grudge against the British State for curtailing your military service will have them lower their guard."

Brand opened a large manila envelope he was carrying and threw two mobile phone kits underhand at the seated men. The only number on these is mine. One of you must contact me every day. He fished inside the envelope a second time and withdrew two key rings.

"The metal badge on this key ring should be recognised by the sleeper planted by the Russians. Only he will understand it to be a secret symbol used by the Federal Security Service of the Russian Federation and it may make it more likely that he would make himself known to you and assist you. I also need to know who he is...for professional reasons...or at least, reasons that needn't concern you."

He handed a further envelope each to Jack and Gus. "Your Euros. I don't need receipts or change and I expect to have all of the financial arrangements and money transfers we agreed completed before you leave this hotel which I expect to be at four o'clock. You fly from Prestwick at five-thirty in a private Lear jet 45. You'll use your passports and go through normal procedures. Your luggage will be taken care of by me. I've already made arrangements here and at Murcia Airport so that it will pass through uninspected. You'll be met at the airport and taken by car to your Marbella hotel. Then you're on your own. Memorise these files and photographs, gentlemen. Nothing leaves this room with you except your kitbags, your Euros and passports, your key rings and phones."

Brand turned and placed his hand on the door handle. He paused before leaving.

"I wish you good fortune. Keep in touch.....daily!"

Both men signaled their agreement. Brand closed the door leaving Bryson and Kyle with grins on their faces.

"Might make a few bob on this one, Gus!"

"Here's hoping."

Lifting his new phone from his lap, he powered it, dialed Directory Enquiries and asked for the number for the Thistle Bar in Govan.

"Figure I'd better check that Hanlon's paid up," he said to no one in particular.

Minutes later, satisfied that his instructions had been carried out and having left his mobile number with Elsie to ensure that old man McCutcheon had been looked after, despite Brand's specific instructions to use the phone for operational reasons only, he ended the call and looked at his watch, anticipating Bryson's inevitable proposition.

"Sun's over the yard-arm. Mini-bar or downstairs bar?"

CHAPTER SIX

Arbab Khan sliced his razor sharp *nushtar* diagonally across the head of the golf ball-sized head of the poppy plant and watched the white latex ooze gather and flow. Now aged twenty-seven, he had tended his family's poppy plot in Pukhtunkhwa since he was old enough to walk. The Khan family was fortunate. In a desolate part of a mountainous terrain in North West Pakistan, their one acre farm would normally have been considered worthless but its westerly orientation optimised sun exposure and was on a mountain slope whose thirty degree gradient and elevation of 3,800 feet above sea level ensured absolutely perfect conditions for the growth of the opium poppy plant.

As he moved along the row, Arbab also tended his crop of beans, cabbages and squash which the family grew among the poppy flowers for personal consumption or, in a good year, as a cash crop. His poppy cuts were shallow to avoid lancing the hollow inner chambers, creating the 'poppy tears' which dried to a sticky brown resin and which Arbab would collect the following morning. His harvest each year produced four or five kilograms of raw opium, enough to keep his family alive for the following year.

Previously, Arbab's family merely bagged and transported the strongly scented, jelly-like base opium to the market in Peshawar but the younger man was more entrepreneurial than his father. In the hills close to the family farm he had built a concealed if crude laboratory in a small cave which was capable of refining the opium he'd harvested into a sticky, brown morphine base he then pressed into bricks and dried in the sun. Mules took the more refined product to market where it was added to the quantities traded by others until a quantity had been amassed that permitted a cache of 356 kgs. of high-grade heroin to be assembled with a potential street value of £33 million. Arbab saw very little of this money. As the first link in the chain, he would be satisfied with his exchange, unaware in any precise terms that the percentage growth in value would see it multiply many thousands of times as it passed through the hands of traffickers…but it would keep his family alive for another year. Wrapped in bricks of brown paper and parcel tape and packed in thirteen large cartons provided by the local drugs overlord, the drugs were secreted inside a packing case marked 'Hempseed' and would travel by train from Peshawar to Karachi then along the Persian Gulf to the port of Abadan, a coastal town in Iran, by means of a *baghlah dhow*.

The consignment arrived at Abadan. In the port, a swarthy Iranian called Farrokh Hassan watched at a distance as the dhow unloaded its contraband to a dockside pallet prior to it being loaded onto a waiting truck. He put a phone to his right cheek and gave instructions in *Farsi* to a man on the other end of the call who nodded in turn to a dockhand standing with some others near the *dhow*.

A blow to the chin sent the smallest of the group spinning and in a blink, all four were engaged in a fist-fight which moved inexorably towards the *dhow*. One of the group in an apparent attempt to escape the violence jumped on to the *dhow* and was pursued by the other three who continued the fight. On board, the two Indians responsible for the carriage of the drugs from Karachi started to protest and were immediately caught up in the melee which resulted in each of them being thrown into the waters of the harbour along with two of the assailants.

Hassan again lifted his phone to his ear having dialed another number and moments later a police car rounded a corner, only employing its siren as it screeched to a halt on the dockside. Two tough-looking police officers emerged and, grabbing the two spectating dockhands, spoke urgently to the combatants in the water insisting they present themselves passively before them on the wharf. A drawn pistol and a pair of threatening night-sticks did the trick and all six were gathered and prodded towards the police car where chaotic explanations and counter-explanations resolved eventually that all six were free to go. Handshakes and smiles of regret ended the fifteen minute incident. It also served to veil the smooth substitution on the dock of the pallet by a fork-lift truck which clinically removed the thirteen cartons of drugs from the packing case and substituted them with others. Once the side had been reattached the case looked untouched.

Three rows away, watched over by the tall Iranian and a nervous looking fork-lift driver, the dockhands who minutes earlier were fighting, were now placing the case on the back of a truck.

Walking watchfully behind the storage sheds, Hassan took a wad of bills from his pocket and peeled some off which he handed to the driver of the fork-lift. Saying some words of thanks in *Farsi*, he then approached the waiting police car and handed the balance of the money through its window, inviting the two police officers inside to settle with the other four dockside actors who had helped implement his ruse. Returning to the dock where he could see the packing case being loaded, he moved back into the shade of the storage sheds and removed a small transponder from his pocket. Switching it on, he shielded the device from light with his cupped left hand and noted with satisfaction a blinking green light telling him what he already knew; that his consignment could be tracked for as long as he was within a couple of miles of the receivers he'd placed in and around the case and its contents.

Unaware of the exchange that had taken place, the two Indians regained their *dhow* and after much head-shaking about the violent nature of Iranians, sat in wait for the arrival of two Iranian couriers who would take the consignment on the next leg of the journey. Half an hour later they arrived and following much shaking of hands, the two Indians innocently bid farewell to the truck which slowly moved off the wharf.

A difficult and dangerous journey through Iran by truck into Syria was followed by onward progress into Beirut where the new consignment was transferred to a paint-flaked fishing boat in the harbour. The Iranian part of the journey troubled the couriers most as in the year previously, three of their comrades had been caught in Abadan and now were confined in leg irons in a broiling hot, corrugated-iron roofed prison, essentially a collection of wooden cages, and forbidden to move from their cell where they were to contemplate the error of their ways for the next 23 years. The couriers saw themselves as entrepreneurs. They understood risk and reward but the risk of incarceration in an Iranian jail in sub-human conditions was not one that appealed. They must be cautious. They must be observant. Too late they were observant.

At every stage in a drugs journey the product becomes more expensive and heightened security makes discovery more likely but this time they'd made it through, transferred the sealed boxes, and had successfully hidden the contents on the creaky old boat. New couriers, five fresh men, travelled on board, three who owned the vessel and who would steer it to the sleepy, mediaeval Spanish port of Altea; and two brothers, Egyptians Husani and Tarik Aswad who now owned the shipment and who intended collecting £3 million when they transferred the packages they still thought contained drugs to Perry's men in Spain.

After three weeks travelling, the shipment arrived in Altea and Tarik Aswad nervously scoped the harbour area on the look-out for trouble as the fishing boat slowly made its way towards a docking place.

Anxiously, he shouted for his brother.

"Husani, I see no red pick-up truck. There are no vehicles waiting. That was the arrangement but there is no one here to meet us. This is very bad. We will be arrested by the infidels if we can't move things quickly."

Tarik was joined on deck by Husani.

"We will be successful, my brother. Be patient. They will be here soon.

No sooner had the dilapidated fishing boat tied up at the quay than a red Dodge pick-up appeared at the end of the dock. Two Egyptian cousins could be seen in the front seats.

"Allah is merciful," cried Tarik.

Despite the late hour, the two brothers, Husani and Tarik Aswad with the help of their two Egyptian cousins, anxiously transferred the packing case to the pick-up, covering it with a tarpaulin before joining them in the rear seats.

From a darkened car window not one hundred steps away, Hassan sat impassively in the rear of his car watching the boxes he'd substituted being transferred to the Dodge. As it pulled out of the harbour he spoke to his driver without looking at him.

"Follow them. If you lose them, you die."

Anxiously the brothers drove out of the port towards the gloom of a less populated, dark land mass. After ten minutes they turned off the road, extinguished their headlights and the five men embraced.

"It has been such a long time since we saw you," laughed Tarik happily. "We have been so worried for the past weeks. At any moment we might have been found by the authorities."

The eldest cousin Masud responded.

"Allah has looked kindly on you both and has brought you safely to us. Now we face even greater dangers as we sell this powder to the infidels. We must expect them to try to deceive us so we must be careful, but first we must sleep. We have a house not far from here and we will arrive shortly. We will be safe there and can plan how we will exchange our goods for the infidels' money. Allah be praised!"

* * *

Liam and Susan awoke to a shaft of sunlight highlighting a framed photograph on the wall of their motor cruiser, the Ventura, promising a blue sky and a relaxing day.

"Breakfast or shower?" asked Liam.

Susan leaned over and kissed her husband, throwing back the duvet. "Breakfast. I'm starving, and I can't wait to try those beautiful dressing gowns. They're so fluffy. Let's go and see what our shipmates are up to."

Wrapping themselves in their blindingly white dressing gowns, they walked tentatively along the deep carpeted, ivory coloured hallway towards what Kim had the previous evening presented as the dining room. It was deserted, but noises off suggested activity above deck. Susan clutched excitedly at Liam's arm, smiling her astonished approval as they passed an unlit gymnasium and a library. Stepping out onto the sunlit deck area they found Kim and one of her staff arranging a table groaning with food.

"Morning," said Kim, smiling a welcome. "Champagne to start or would you prefer a fruit drink?"

"Kim, you're terrible. You'll have us bewildered before lunchtime," said Susan.

"Well, I'm on holiday so I'll have a go at the champers," said Liam.

Breakfast was a languid affair. They barely dented the food available, although Liam had three glasses of Champagne, eventually deferring to Susan's rebuke that he should slow down before falling down.

"What are your plans for the day?" asked Kim. "Have you made any or are you just going to lie around on the Ventura? If you wished we could take her out and show you something of the coast around here. It's beautiful."

"We've not discussed it," said Susan, but I'd love to see you put the boat through its paces."

"Sounds great," said Liam. "How about we get unpacked, showered and dressed and after lunch you take us on a coastal tour of the area? Perhaps you could dock at Marbella and we could have a look round later on and take in the sights?"

"Sure, that would be no trouble at all. Put some sun oil on. You'll find some in the en suite. If you're spending time on deck at all you might burn with the sun as high in the sky as it is today. I'll start making preparations."

* * *

Marbella is known for its wealthy celebrity, its cosmopolitan atmosphere, its trendy wine bars, restaurants and its marina. Certain of its narrow walkways, however, host less salubrious bars. In one close to the harbour was situated the Red Lion Pub. Decked out in Union Flag bunting and advertising 'Great British Breakfasts' and beers indigenous to the UK, it catered for a cadre of shaven-headed, Bulldog Brits who spouted right-wing slogans and vile vitriol at the foreigners in whose country they resided. A bar where the criminal classes met, where most things, including human lives, could be bought and sold and where for a price, young men and women could be directed to a hotel room for company with no questions asked once a fee had been paid.

In a gloomy back room of the Red Lion, its owner, Marcus Perry gestured to his second-in-command, Cammy Spence, bringing him to his side. Standing at a small corner bar which could accommodate only perhaps a dozen customers, Perry surveyed the room which was furnished in spartan fashion. Its stained and sticky carpets hadn't been cleaned since laid some ten years previously. Few patrons saw the tiny rear bar unless they had cause to deal with the management of the establishment in order to settle a dispute of some sort - and then always at the management's invitation. On occasion, certain of those invited to the rear bar never saw daylight again. With no natural light and a nearby exit into a normally deserted back alleyway, it was a convenient location in which to conduct the kind of violent and illicit business for which Perry's people had developed a reputation.

"I thought you were meant to be the brains of this fackin' operation," growled Perry.

"What's buggin' you Boss?"

"That's three days and we've not heard a whisper from these fackin' Arabs. We've got three million pounds sterling sitting in bags just waiting for the law to stumble across them because we can't complete the deal you told me would be all tied up be last weekend. Fackin' Arabs!"

He turned round and leaned his back against the bar, looking for something on which to vent his wrath. "Look at the fackin' mess in 'ere."

"'Appy!... 'Appy!" he shouted.

A man appeared almost instantly, running and holding a wash cloth.

"Yes, Mr. Perry. Sorry Mr. Perry."

"Never mind 'sorry', 'Appy. This place is like a fackin' shithouse. Clean it up!"

"Yes, Mr. Perry. Sorry, Mr. Perry."

Quietness descended on the small room as Happy gathered up the detritus from a previous evening's drinking, collected the glasses and wiped the tables. As he went about his work he softly murmured a mantra.....

"Sorry, Mr. Perry. Really sorry, Mr. Perry. Won't happen again, Mr. Perry."

"Fackin' shut up, 'Appy. You're beginin' to annoy me."

"Sorry, Mr. Perry. Really sorry, Mr. Perry. Won't happen again, Mr. Perry."

Spence pulled up a barstool so he could speak quietly into Perry's left ear.

"Look, Boss, keep your nerve. This mob needs us as much as we need them. They're careful. I'm glad they're careful. We're ready to do business as soon as we hear from them. The money's ready, our men are available, the boys are ready to dilute the heroin, we have outlets all set up. We're well placed to make millions....millions. Just relax!"

Perry resisted his blandishments. "I can't believe that these fackin' Arabs wouldn't deal in money transfers. It's all guaranteed but no... they give us a product, they want a product in return. Hard cash. It's fackin' medieval and it leaves us at the mercy of the law while we sit here on our arses with bags of cash just waiting to be discovered."

Spence nodded. "Remember Boss. This deal suits us. They only get it if we can't find a way to relieve them of their stuff without having to pay for it. Right now, it's still only insurance money and we might not need to pay it. If it was an electronic money transfer, it would be a straight business deal."

Spence was more than *consiglieri* to Perry, he was also his director of operations...his right hand man, his conscience, his director of finance....his everything. He could speak to Perry as no other mortal could. He was a mature, sixty year old hard man but he was measured, intelligent and was shoulder to shoulder with Perry who rightly understood the qualities that Spence brought to his operations.

Three of Perry's gang members entered the small bar. The tallest and heaviest, a six and a half foot ex-bouncer, a Londoner called Terry Cole, spoke on their behalf.

"Boss, me and the boys was hoping we could have a few beers tonight. That's three days we've been on alert waiting for you to give us the nod for the meet with the Arabs. Three days without a drink."

Perry's rheumy-eyed look would have melted glass but before he could unleash his temper on the men making the request, Spence intervened.

"It'll be ok, boss. Nothing's going to happen today. Allow the boys to let off a little steam. We've eight of them in the bar and ten on the end of a phone. We can afford to stand them down. We wouldn't respond to any Arab request anyway without looking at all sides of the meet carefully. We'd need to build in some time for planning."

Perry looked at Spence with the resigned look of a man who knew the advice he was receiving, while unwelcome, was probably sound. He shrugged and grimaced at Cole.

"Well, you'd all better fackin' behave yourselves. I don't want to have to bail you out of a Spanish jail because you've been arrested having a few beers." He thought further. "And stay close."

"I'll go along to make sure they're ok," said Spence.

Smiling, Cole asked, "Can we take Happy?"

"Sure," said Spence, speaking for his boss.

Happy stood on the sidelines of the conversation smiling widely, "Thank you Mr. Spence. Thank you Mr. Perry." He wiped the table nearest the group. "Thank you Mr. Cole," and in a lower register, "Can I get pancakes, Mr. Cole? I love pancakes."

"As long as you look after us Happy. You going to look after us, Happy?"

Happy nodded his head excitedly. For the past four years he had been adopted by Perry's gang as a general factotum. Now in his mid-thirties, Happy had waited their tables, cleaned the bar, run errands and been the butt of their jokes when drink had made them incautious. Happy was not one of nature's intellectuals but his reward was their avuncular affection, occasional abuse, minor financial support and benevolent social interaction. He slept in an airless one room apartment on the outskirts of Marbella. On nights out, Happy was useful. He couldn't drive a car but was constantly on alert, looking for someone who needed a new pack of cigarettes, a drink from the bar, glasses cleaned away or a taxi hailed. He didn't interrupt. He didn't intrude. He helped them relax. He helped them be lazy.

Happy had a Spanish girlfriend called Maria although no one in the gang had met her. Happy was reticent when speaking of her. She lived in Barcelona and the gang had managed to elicit from him that she had had occasion to be seen by a doctor on account of a depressive illness. Thenceforward the couple was known by the gang midst much amusement as 'Happy and Sad'. Every so often Happy would be dropped at the local rail station and waved goodbye as he set off excitedly to see the love of his live in the big city. Despite being something of a social inadequate, he somehow managed to maintain his relationship with Maria even to the extent of going on holiday with her a few times each year. When all things were considered, he may have been poor, unemployed and unintelligent but Happy was happy!

CHAPTER SEVEN

The Lear jet carrying Bryson and Kyle from Prestwick Airport had transported the twosome to Murcia in no little comfort and both men had taken considerable advantage of the well-stocked bar, especially Bryson whose gigantic appetite for booze dwarfed that of Kyle who put his arm around him, steadying him and escorting him from the plane.

"C'mon Jack, I know we usually play good cop, bad cop, but we're not going to get this job done if it's good cop, drunk cop!"

True to his word, Brand had arranged for the two kit bags to be placed in the rear of their black Landrover on arrival and without inspection. They'd been taken to their hotel in Marbella where the driver parked and left them at the front door, handing them the keys and walking off anonymously into the busy streets without so much as a goodbye.

The following morning had been spent sleeping and sobering up, and the afternoon walking round Marbella avoiding areas where they might run up against their targets. After a late shower, they each checked that the weapons they carried were intact and having been satisfied that everything was in place, put everything back in their kit bags. Occasionally in the past they'd had to leave their accommodation in a hurry and so always lived out of their luggage so as to minimise any delay in departing the premises.

"So what d'ye think Gus, will we go see what this Red Lion pub's like now?"

"Well, we don't need to rush our fences, Jack. Why don't we get a couple of pints of Guinness in and stroll past the place later?"

"Sounds like a plan, Gus. You're on the bell. This job'll probably mean that we get to spend fewer time in the pub than we usually would…"

"Less, Jack…less. Less time. You use *less* when you're referring to something that can't be counted or doesn't have a plural like time or money, air, or music or rain."

Bryson smiled despite himself. "See you and that fuckin' self improvement book."

"Always handy to be able to communicate in the Queen's English."

Kyle patted his denim pockets to check he had his wallet, phone and Brand's special key ring then picked up the hotel room keycard from the desk in front of him.

"Let's head off."

* * *

Liam and Susan had enjoyed a wonderfully relaxing day sailing on the Mediterranean. The Ventura had sailed westwards towards Gibraltar keeping close to the coast so her guests could see views of an arid Spanish landscape dotted with occasional ports. Kim had remained in the wheelhouse for the majority of the time but had relinquished her post to Miguel, one of her staff, and had accepted Susan's invitation to join them for lunch. Heading back towards port that afternoon, both Susan and Liam dozed on the sun deck before taking a Jacuzzi together and accepting yet more Krug Champagne from Kim.

"I could get used to this, Kim. I'm so relaxed," grinned Susan.

She stood and looked towards the coast sipping at her glass. "Where are we? Close to Puerto Banus?"

"Yes. But I thought we might dock in Marbella this evening and you could look around the town. It's beautiful and you could decide whether you want to dine ashore at one of their lovely bistros or whether you'd like us to rustle something up here. Alternatively, if you're after something more vigorous, I could organise the jet-ski and we could moor off the harbour while you zip around for a while."

Susan turned to her husband who had joined them, her raised eyebrows inviting his opinion.

"To be honest, I'd quite like to continue this day of rest, darling," said Liam. "Why don't we ask Kim to find a temporary berth in Marbella? We could do some shopping and find somewhere to eat." He covered the top of his glass with his hand, refusing the Champagne top-up he was being offered by an attentive steward.

"I'm starving," he teased. "Kim hasn't been giving us enough to eat and drink while we've been on board."

Kim smiled and swung a friendly hand at him that languished in mid-air and said, "Well, that would be no trouble at all. Marbella's lovely and we'll just wait in the marina until you're ready to come back aboard."

Ninety minutes later, the Ventura nosed its way into the harbour at Marbella and after docking, Liam and Susan stepped off into the dusk to wander around the bars and bistros.

* * *

Several blocks away, Spence, man-mountain Cole and eight of their associates sat together at a table outside an Irish bar close to The Red Lion lest their services were needed quickly - a compromise earlier brokered by Spence. Cole gave a handwritten list of drinks to Happy for the fourth time.

"On you go, Happy. Another round for the boys. Get that Guinness flowing."

Happy took the list and entered the bar proffering it to one of the bar staff.

"More drink please. Tray please." He finished eating a pancake he'd been given by Cole. "To carry it outside please."

Outside, Cole was speaking to Spence.

"What's the deal with these Arabs, Cammy? We've been sitting around for the best part of a week doing bugger all. Some of the guys think they've reneged on the deal."

Spence shrugged and sipped a mouthful of stout.

Cole continued. "You can't trust Arabs, Cammy. Don't know if enough people know that. Them and the Hebrews. Untrustworthy bastards the lot of them. We should just take the chance to blow them away if they actually *do* show up. Mop-top bastards!"

Spence looked at Cole and began to remind him that Mop-top was usually an affectionate reference to the hairstyles of the Beatles, but desisted on the basis that the more common insult, Rag-head, was more likely to get Cole into trouble if repeated elsewhere so he merely patted him on his shoulder.

"Well you're having the drink you asked for so enjoy yourself. You never know the minute when we'll be asked to jump to it."

"Mop-top bastards!"

Two hours passed. Spence, Cole and their team became more drunk and raucous. In a bistro nearby, Susan and Liam dined on an excellent seafood meal and together consumed an expensive bottle of chilled *Sauvignon Blanc*. Not far away in a sports bar, Kyle and Bryson finished watching Manchester United overtake a one-nil half-time lead and beat Liverpool at football in the evening's big match.

Just another quiet night in Marbella.

CHAPTER EIGHT

"Good game," ventured Kyle.

"Aye, and if it hadn't been for a buggered knee when you were sixteen you'd have been out there tonight scoring the winner," said Bryson.

"Too true, big man. I was a wonder in the box. A better player than you any day. You have the build of a centre half and the footballing intelligence of one as well. Stop everything that comes your way. Take out your own team players if needs be but don't let anyone score. Don't let anyone pass!" He laughed and put his arm awkwardly around the shoulder of his friend Bryson who towered above him. "Mind you, I'm glad we were on the same team or I'd have *two* buggered knees by now."

The two men paid their bar bill and stepped outside into the heavy Mediterranean air.

"Jesus, it's warm tonight. I'm a northern European, Jack. I prefer the cold air...or mild air and cold Guinness," said Kyle.

"To be honest, I prefer warm air and warm beer. Like I'm on holiday but the beer's from Scotland," responded Bryson.

They surveyed the streetscape before them.

"Okay, wee man, will we head off and see what London gangsters look like in Spain?"

"Jack, have you never come across that wonderful philosophy of the Country and Western fraternity? asked Kyle. "'*One day at a time, sweet Jesus*'," he sang. "You're a hell of a man for going straight for the goal, Jack. You should have been the centre-forward, not me." He shook his head. "Remember the plan. We make these guys our best friends. We're two pissed off soldiers. Ex-SAS. Dishonourably discharged. Down on our luck and lookin' to make a few bob. And we're handy."

"That's the plan, Gus. Let's go find the Red Lion."

* * *

Susan had spent some time in a shoe shop and was considering the purchase of a pair of trainers, ignoring the rows of expensive, strapless *Manolo Blahniks* banked in front of her.

"Just coming, darling," she exclaimed, anticipating Liam's mounting frustration at her ambivalence over the red or green soled sailing shoes.

After a few minutes further deliberation, she decided to purchase neither pair and exited to see her husband seated on a bench, pointedly looking at the watch-face of the *Audemars Piguet* he'd received as a wedding present from a friend of his father-in-law.

"Twenty minutes?" said Liam with raised eyebrows, offset by his smile, "I've bought and sold hotel chains in less time".

Taking hands, they walked slowly along the narrow lanes that housed yet more shoe shops, boutiques, bars and restaurants.

Innocently, in one of the boutiques and oblivious to the passing couple, stood Cammy Spence, separated from his charges and looking to purchase some jewellery for his youthful blond partner of five years now.

Up ahead, Susan pointed out the clutch of Union Flags that denoted the location of the Red Lion. "Look, darling. A British pub. Perhaps they'll sell your lager"...a recognition of Liam's preference for Tennent's Lager ever since his years spent in Glasgow studying for his PhD.

"I doubt it, Susan. It'll be warm English beer in there, I'd guess."

The alleyway was becoming more crowded as they approached. More revelers were in evidence. A group of them were larking about up ahead. Intuitively, Liam drew Susan closer to his side.

"Hello, darlin' whatcha doin' with that loser? Come over here to a real man and I'll give you somefin' you've never 'ad before!" shouted one of Cole's men, laughing.

Liam spoke into her ear. "Careful, darling. That one's got leprosy," he said jocularly.

Susan nudged him playfully in the ribs and they continued walking.

"Hey, good-lookin'. Come and join the boys. Ditch lover-boy and get it on wiv some real men."

"Just keep walking, Susan. These guys look like they've had a few. We don't want trouble."

One of Cole's thugs separated himself from the throng and approached Susan from behind. He grabbed her arm and wheeled her round.

"Whassup with you, bitch. You too good for the likes of us?"

Susan squealed and wrestled with her attacker. "Let me go!"

Liam's hand took the drunk's wrist firmly and twisted it so he stumbled off-balance.

"We want no trouble here. Just go back to your friends and enjoy your evening."

The drunk swung lazily at Liam who leaned back easily, avoiding the blow and punched him squarely on the jaw, knocking him backwards. As one man, Cole's team rose and made for Liam who went down in a flurry of blows, the first of which burst his nose and covered his chest with blood. Two of his assailants grabbed beer bottles and made for him as he lay on the ground being kicked by the others.

Susan cried as she attempted to force the men from their attack with no effect whatsoever.

"Leave him, you pigs. Liam! Liam!"

Just as the drunk closest to the fray drew his arm back to break a bottle over Liam's head, Kyle stepped forward and chopped fiercely at his throat. The drunk fell in a crumpled heap, instantly immobilised; his weapon useless. Bryson jabbed another in both eyes with two stiff fingers, temporarily blinding him then slammed the heel of his palm into his attacker's eye-socket, fracturing it, before turning his attention to another attacker with a bottle. A short, single punch to the chin left him concussed and incapacitated. Wheeling round, Kyle kicked the gargantuan Cole in the groin and followed the blow with a scissors kick to his involuntarily lowered face. With a strangled cry, Cole stood suddenly erect before his knees gave way and he collapsed to the ground like a great bear shot through the heart. Two men came simultaneously at Bryson who held up a convenient bench stopping them in their tracks before stepping over it and downing both men with two short, simple but deadly effective punches; one left, one right. Both surrendered immediately to unconsciousness. Kyle kicked one of the remaining assailants on his ankle, causing what the doctor would later tell him was a bimalleolar fracture and right ankle dislocation then turned to see Bryson deflecting a blow aimed at him and slapping the remaining drunk back-handed across the face, fracturing his lower angular mandible and sending him unconscious, crashing through a flimsy barrier erected to isolate one outdoor bar area from another.

The fight had lasted less than ten seconds. Each of the eight assailants lay spread-eagled on the ground. Kyle contemplated the clutter of groaning or unconscious men. He pursed his lips signifying his satisfaction with a job well done. Catching Bryson's gaze he gestured at their fallen adversaries and nodded his approval...

"Efficient!"

All the while, Happy had danced anxiously on the outskirts of the affray.

"No hitting! No hitting!"

Bryson and Kyle recognised a non-combatant immediately and turned their attention to Liam and Susan, having again checked to ensure that there was no remaining threat from any of the gang members.

Kyle turned his attention to Susan and Liam.

"You all right folks?"

Susan was in tears and knelt beside Liam, cradling his head in her lap.

"Liam, talk to me. Are you ok?"

Bryson joined Susan beside Liam who was conscious but in pain.

"Anything broken?"

"Jesus. What was all that about? We were just out for an evening stroll," said Liam, wiping blood from his mouth and chin. As he regained his poise, his thoughts were of Susan. "Susan, are you all right? Did these bastards hurt you?"

"I'm fine Liam but look at you. There's blood everywhere."

Liam acknowledged Bryson who helped him to his feet. "Thank God you guys came along. You saved our bacon."

Kyle and Bryson hovered over Liam as he recovered his composure. "I've burst my feckin' nose again. Every time I get involved in the smallest scrap, my nose lets me down immediately!"

"You'll be fine," said Bryson, satisfied that Liam was damaged only superficially. He gestured to Kyle. "Let's drag these idiots out of the middle of this alley so the good people of Marbella can walk past without tripping."

Kyle nodded and they both took an arm each of the nearest fallen drunk and pulled him to the side of the alleyway just outside the Red Lion.

"Don't either of you move a muscle or I'll shoot you both in the fuckin' head."

Kyle and Bryson turned to see Cammy Spence standing in the middle of the lane with a gun held close to his body at waist level.

"You did a fair amount of damage to my men, there boys. I ought to shoot you right now." He moved sideways, stepping awkwardly over the groaning body of Cole so he faced them both directly. He gestured with his gun towards the Red Lion. "Now, very carefully, I want you to step through that pub door there. One stupid move and you might not come out again."

Bryson and Kyle exchanged glances. A Glasgow accent. Balding. Aged about sixty and looking exactly like the photograph they'd studied back in the Copthorne Hotel. Standing outside the Red Lion? They both realised they were speaking to Cammy Spence.... *Shit!..so much for befriending the gang members,* thought Kyle.

Suddenly, Spence felt the cold barrel of a gun push behind his right ear. "You're not the only gun in town, Mister. Place yours slowly on the table beside you and stand to your left or you can kiss goodbye to your good looks. Don't think about anything clever. I'll drop you before you can move."

Spence froze. *What's the odds someone else has a gun in this street?* he thought.

"Even if you had one, you wouldn't shoot me in cold blood. Not with all these witnesses."

"I wouldn't shoot you dead, for sure. Just so you'd wish that I had."

Spence held his position while he considered his options. After what seemed like an eternity to Liam, he laid his gun on the table where Kyle immediately snatched it up.

"Thank the good Lord," said a relieved Liam setting down an empty bottle of beer whose cold neck had masqueraded as the barrel of a handgun.

Spence looked at the bottle philosophically, confirming to himself that he'd been conned. He shrugged his shoulders.

"Them's the odds, I suppose. I figured it wasn't a gun…but I couldn't take the chance I might be wrong."

Kyle holstered the gun in his belt having decided to effect a rapprochement as far as might be possible given their task.

"No offence Mister. We weren't looking for trouble but your boys were well out of order. We'll be going on our way now. Next time we meet, we'll buy you a pint. From your accent, it seems like we hail from the same corner of the world. Now, no funny stuff. We're going to walk away. I'm going to keep your weapon and both of us'll hope it isn't tied to another crime. We won't involve the law if you don't but don't try to follow us. Just look after these idiots on the floor"

Putting his left arm around Susan and holding his bruised ribs with his other arm, Liam limped painfully towards the end of the lane and pushed his way through the small crowd that had gathered spontaneously to watch the efficient demolition of Spence's gang.

Bryson helped them move through the crowd. He spoke urgently to Liam.

"Listen! These are bad people and you don't want mixed up with them. Do you live close by? Are you holidaying in town?"

"We're lucky. We're actually staying on a motor cruiser. In ten minutes time we'll be out in the middle of the Med and away from all this. What about you two? Are you in danger from them?"

"Perhaps...and maybe the police'll want a chat if they find us given that the locals witnessed the threat of gunplay. But these fallen heroes will think twice about coming after us given the licking they've received."

Liam stopped walking and turned painfully to face Bryson.

"Look, why don't you come on board with us? There's loads of room on the boat and it would help me sleep tonight knowing you were both safe. I pretty much owe you my life."

Bryson considered the offer and eyed Kyle.

"What d'ye think Gus. A motor cruiser in the Med or taking shifts in our hotel to ensure there's no sneak attack?"

Kyle was busy removing the rounds from Spence's gun and placing them in his pocket.

"Makes sense.... but we'll need to get our stuff from the hotel first." He looked at Liam. "That okay with you?

It's not far from the harbour if that's where you're berthed."

Liam nodded and began to move toward the harbour but Bryson sought one more piece of information from him before agreeing the offer.

"Is there strong drink on board this luxury cruiser?"

"Jesus, you fairly like your whisky and wine…," said Kyle.

"Jesus and me are as one on this…I mean, he didn't turn the water into Lucozade, did he?"

Liam smiled and nodded his affirmation. "The place is feckin' swimmin' in the stuff."

* * *

Ten minutes later Kyle had helped a still distressed Susan and Liam back to the harbour where they were joined shortly thereafter by Bryson who turned the corner having returned from the hotel, carrying two heavy kit bags as if they were filled with papier mâché.

Kyle supported a still limping Liam and Susan led the way along the dock until they arrived at the berth which temporarily accommodated the Ventura.

"I suppose it'll have to do, eh Gus? Beggars can't be choosers," said Bryson as he took in the splendour of the super-yacht which Susan was boarding.

Kim had noticed her guests approach the vessel and was on hand to meet them.

"Good God Susan, what happened?"

"Liam was attacked by a mob and these men saved us. We're all still in danger. Can we take them on board and head for the open sea? One man had a gun so we should go right now in case we were followed."

"Of course…but we're short of fuel….just enough to get out of harm's way. Your friends can use any of the guest rooms you want to. They're all made up and ready for occupancy." Kim left them to take the cruiser out of the harbour.

* * *

Bryson dumped the kit bags on the deck. They clinked as they met the ground. Kyle looked at Bryson reproachfully.

"Hotel mini-bar?"

"Emergency rations, Gus. Left the Toblerone." He stepped back on to the dock to release the ropes holding the Ventura in place.

"Off you go!" He waved at Kim who was looking down at him from the wheelhouse. Kim nudged the quietly gurgling cruiser gently from the berth while Bryson stood aft and kept his eyes on the harbour to establish that they were not being pursued by anyone. Satisfied eventually, he turned and went inside where Kyle and Susan were attending to Liam. Susan had cleaned up the blood from Liam's face and left to get fresh clothes. Kyle was gently prodding Liam's ribs.

"Painful?"

"Only when I breathe", said Liam helpfully.

Bryson smiled. "Some days you're a pigeon...some days you're the statue."

Kyle looked disapprovingly at Bryson.

"With ribs there's not a lot we can do without an X-Ray. We've got some anti-inflamatories and some powerful analgesics in the kit bags. We'll get them down you and have you checked out in a hospital tomorrow. With any luck it's just bruising. By the way, before I forget, that was a pretty impressive move when you held that bottle to that fellah's head. You saved our bacon, too you know, sailor."

* * *

Face pressed against a wall, a still pained, still cursing Terry Cole eyed the boat as it pulled out of the harbour noting its distinctive red upper deck colouring glinting in the harbour floodlights. Too far away to catch its name he nevertheless was able later to describe its deck configuration, colouring and the fact that it 'kind of turned right' upon leaving the harbour.

* * *

Half an hour later the Ventura was well out to sea, the lights of Marbella twinkling on the horizon behind them. Kim had had one of her crew rustle up some snacks and coffee although both Kyle and Bryson, delighted at their good fortune, had accepted instead the offer of Champagne with disbelieving looks at each other. Introductions had taken place with the two ex-soldiers presenting the same story to their new hosts as would have been told to Marcus Perry.

Liam had been cleaned up and had benefitted from the drugs administered by Kyle as well as an illicit glass of Champagne against Susan's express wishes.

"What about you two?" asked Susan. "Are you ok?"

"I'm okay but I may have pulled a muscle in my back," said Kyle conversationally. "I wasn't balanced when I dropped that last man."

Before Bryson could say that he was fine, thank you very much, Kim interjected.

"Is it painful?" she asked Kyle and without waiting for a reply said, "Hold on. Give me a minute and I'll fix it. I'll be back in a second." So saying, she walked briskly to her treatment room and prepared her sturdy massage table, heating some oil and spreading some fresh towels on the table.

She returned to the lounge where Kyle, Bryson and Brannigan were each having their glass topped up by an attentive steward. "Ok, Gus. I'm ready. Do you want to come through?"

"Come through?" asked Kyle.

"Yeah. Let's see if we can't fix that back of yours."
Kim smiled. "Don't worry. I know what I'm doing."
She pointed at a nearby table. "You can leave your glass
there."

Kyle stood, uncertain of what was expected of him.
Kim led him through to the treatment room. "I'll give
you a couple of minutes. Take off your clothes down to
your pants and lie face down under that towel on the
massage bed."

"And you're going to do exactly what?" asked Kyle.

"I'm going to make that muscle in your back feel a lot
better. Listening to what went on tonight, we all might
need you in tip-top condition." She hesitated. "Also,
what you both did tonight. Wow! Impressive. I'm glad
you're the good guys." Kim walked to the door. "Two
minutes...now get under that towel. I'm the Captain.
That's an order."

"Yes Ma'am."

Back in the lounge, Susan was making an effort to help
Liam through to their stateroom.

"Let's get you to bed and you can rest up. We'll see how
you feel in the morning."

Kim arrived in the lounge in order to allow Kyle privacy
for a moment.

"Kim, we're going to lie down," said Susan. It's been an eventful night but I feel safe now out here with all you guys looking after us." She held up a hand to the room in a farewell gesture. "Night all."

"Night...and thanks again, Jack." said Liam, as they moved slowly towards their stateroom.

Bryson acknowledged their departure while pouring two miniature bottles of whisky he'd rescued from the hotel into a crystal glass. He looked at Kim. "Can any craft get out here and close to us without you knowing about it?"

"Nope. We have the latest technology. Miguel will be in the wheelhouse all night. He'll be able to see anything that moves along this coast. Don't worry. We're safe as long as we're afloat. If needs be we're the fastest ship in the fleet." She lifted the two empty whisky miniatures Jack had deposited on the table. "And you don't need to bring alcohol on board this vessel, Jack. Just let Miguel know your pleasure any time of the day or night and it will be given to you."

Bryson toasted her generosity.

"Couldn't be sure. Need a regular supply." He burped..."Medical condition. What you doin' with Gus?"

"I'm a qualified masseuse. Thought I'd have a go at fixing his back."

"No shit? Did I mention that I think I've a groin strain?"

"Hmmm. Cold shower'll fix that for sure," grinned Kim. "I'll go fix your pal."

Kyle was lying face down as had been directed by Kim who entered and took a moment to warm her hands with the oil she'd been heating. Carefully she carried some over to the table and dripped it liberally over Kyle's back. "Now where does it hurt? Lower back?"

"Left shoulder."

"Okay. Just relax."

For a few minutes Kim worked on the area silently and then moved her deep thumb strokes in a wider arc to balance the therapeutic effects across both shoulder areas. "Your muscles are like steel. You must work out."

"It's second nature now. Soldiering does that."

Silence descended again and Kim found herself lost in the act of ministering to the physical structure of a person. She'd not been able to utilise her talents much in the past year since she completed the course and found it as therapeutic as did the patient but more because she found herself transported in thought during the process. It relaxed her.

"I'm sorry. I needn't have asked you to strip to your briefs," said Kim. "Force of habit. I forgot it was just your back I was dealing with."

"No sweat." Kyle surrendered to the massage. A further silence.

"It's been a while since someone touched my back tenderly. Usually they're breaking a chair over it."

"No woman in your life to tend to your various wounds?" asked Kim impishly.

Kyle didn't answer immediately. A silence hung in the air. Then he spoke.

"The only woman in my life is my daughter Rachael. I'm divorced ten years now. A youthful marriage. We grew apart... well, to be more accurate, she grew apart from me. It can be difficult being a soldier's wife when I was always away from home and she's worrying if I'm okay or lying dead in a ditch."

"I'm sorry. I didn't mean to pry."

"It's okay. I'm over it now but it was hard at the time. I came back from a tour of duty in Northern Ireland and discovered some pretty raunchy letters in a drawer that made it clear that she was more than close to someone else while I was away."

"She didn't try to fix things with you?"

"She did, but I wouldn't play ball and then it all went south. You know the old saying, 'Hell hath no fury like the lawyer of a woman scorned'. When *they* get involved it's all over bar the shouting."

They fell into another silence, broken after some moments by Kyle who hadn't spoken of these things to anyone other than Bryson. He would later wonder what possessed him to unburden himself to a woman he hardly knew but continued despite himself.

"Maths teacher. Some guy called Samuels. Turns out he was a childhood sweetheart. I didn't quarrel. Just packed my bags and left, swearing that the only people I'd trust in the future would be me and my comrade in arms, Jack Bryson."

"That's a shame. You must have been terribly hurt."

"It's funny…I'm a professional soldier. I've been trained to avoid injury and I think I'm pretty much as good as they come. I've been trained to inflict pain but also to avoid pain. It never occurred to me that a woman could pierce my armour more effectively than any knife."

Another silence. Kim continued to knead Kyle's muscular shoulders thinking, *Ten years ago? These wounds seem fairly fresh.*

"So you've kept women at a distance?"

"It's easier this way. I know my capabilities and they don't include dealing with the fairer sex. I take the view that 99% of them give the rest a bad name. Give me a mountain and I'll climb it… a river and I'll cross it…carrying Jack on my back if needs be. But women are more fearsome than any terrorist I've had to deal with."

A silence resumed, this time until Kim broke it some thirty minutes later by gently stilling her hand between Kyle's shoulder blades indicating the end of the session.

"How's that, Gus? Feel better?"

"That was amazing. Thanks Kim. I appreciate your help."

"Just rest for a moment and I'll get you a glass of water. You need some liquid intake after a massage to cleanse the toxins from your body...and I mean water, not alcohol."

As Kyle lay face down, Kim wiped the oil from her hands and gazed at his resting form. *This guy's in good shape, she thought. Physically... but he's a tortured soul. And no tattoos? That's a first. A soldier with some sense of decorum and good taste!* Her gaze fell on the narrow folded towel covering Kyle's buttocks and she reflected further. *Bet he's got a tattoo on his backside. The Scottish Saltire...or 'Love and Hate' ...one word on either cheek!*

After dressing, Kyle returned to a now empty dining area. Kim appeared and directed him towards a room that had been set aside for him.

"Thanks again, Kim. Where have you stashed Jack? I need to speak with him before I sleep."

She pointed at a door. "He's next to your room. Just knock."

Kyle nodded and moved towards his friend's stateroom. He knocked once and entered almost simultaneously, closing the door behind him. Bryson was seated on the bed looking inside his kit bag for the remaining contents of the hotel mini-bar which he'd piled on the bed.

"Well we've really messed things up now, eh?" said Kyle.

"Never mind the job. That's quite a looker you've managed to pull! I tried to interest her in my groin but she wasn't playing."

"Aye, very good," smiled Kyle. "So what do we do now?"

"Frankly, my friend, I'm in no rush to leave this gin palace! Luxury, safety and the best bevy a man can drink….not to mention a couple of extremely attractive young ladies? This beats having a gun pointed at you by some considerable distance. Yesterday morning we were living the dream… sitting in a pissy hovel in Glasgow. I prefer this place."

"Tell you what," countered Kyle. "That bit of quick thinking by Liam got us out of a tricky situation. We owe him as much as he figures he owes us." He sat beside Bryson on the bed and returned to his friend's earlier comments. "This place is exceptional," he said, looking round the stateroom. "But we need to put our thinking caps on."

"Well, at least when we phone the Colonel we can tell him that we've met Spence and his men and that we made quite an impact!"

Kyle laughed. "Well, we'll need to go ashore tomorrow and have Liam's ribs looked at and anyway, by all accounts the boat's almost out of fuel. Suppose we take tomorrow to get things back in order and then, I guess, we have to face up to Spence again and buy him that pint I offered."

"Sounds like that would be an interesting chat. Okay, one more day afloat...but my groin needs attention. I think I'll ask Kim one more time."

"Trust me big man, you're not in her class." Kyle picked up his phone. "I'll go phone the Colonel if I can get a signal and spin him a line. I'll tell him we made contact with Spence in the Red Lion and that we're going to phone Perry tomorrow night and suggest a pint. I'll miss out the bit about us maiming eight of his best men."

Kyle left Bryson's stateroom and noticed Kim sitting in a yellow armchair with a glass of Champagne in her hand. She stood when he entered, placing her drink on the table in front of her.

"Sorry...I'm afraid the only time I get to relax is when my guests go to bed."

"Don't let me stop you. In fact why don't I pour myself a glass and join you...that is if you can relax in the company of a guest."

"I'd be delighted. After your heroics today, we can refuse you nothing."

"Please don't mistake heroics for us just doing what we've been trained for over too many years. These poor drunks didn't stand a chance against me and Jack. I'm not proud that my one skill in life is an ability to commit violence very effectively."

"But I see a tenderness as well," said Kim. There's a lot more to you than just being a tough guy."

"Well, if there is, it's well hidden...even from me. I care for Jack, I care for my skills and I care for my daughter. That's about it."

"Maybe I'm more like you than I care to confess," pondered Kim. I care for the Ventura and that's about it too."

"No family?" asked Kyle.

"No brothers or sisters and my mother and father are both gone. My mum set me up with this boat. Not really invested in friends, just the staff on board. I'm envious of the friendship you have with Jack. He seems a character but it's obvious that you're both very close."

"Well, I wouldn't take him to tea with the Archbishop but he and I have saved each other's life so often we're in debt to each other a hundred times over. It's a wonderful feeling just knowing that whatever happens, there's a guy out there who'll travel to the ends of the earth to help you out of a fix."

"He certainly seems to like his whisky."

"He does, but like many others with his affliction, his favourite drink is his *next* one...*whatever* it is. He'd drink the contents of his thermometer if that was all that was available but he's my brother from another mother so I look after him and he looks after me. Good arrangement."

Kim nodded and a silence ensued, broken by Gus who suddenly had a thought.

"You must meet a lot of nice people here on board. Perhaps you could make friends with one of your guests if you came across someone special."

"Pardon?" said Kim, rather nonplussed.

Kyle realised his comment was open to interpretation.

"Eh...Sorry I wasn't meaning me...there's no way I'm special...I meant someone like Susan... she seems lovely and just the kind of person you'd get on with."

Kim smiled at Gus's discomfiture. "Well, I think you're special, Gus. Susan's lovely too. Maybe I'll try to reprioritise once this season's over. You should do the same. You can't spend the rest of your days doing this stuff...or can you?"

"Well Kim, it really is all I know. I'm rubbish with money, rubbish with women, rubbish with everything. I'm trying to do a bit of self-improvement and I'm reading up on English Grammar at the moment but apart from telling Jack that he's just finished a sentence in a preposition, I don't get much chance to use my newly acquired knowledge. Sometimes I get a bit despondent but then I have a drink with Jack and we go off on an adventure, I get to practice my skills and I don't think about it until I relax again…like tonight."

"Glad I've cheered you up," smiled Kim.

"You have actually. I don't remember the last time I spoke to a civilised woman…or at least the last time a civilised woman spoke to me."

"Well, this civilised woman thinks you're okay, Gus Kyle so don't you go defining yourself as nothing but muscle. There's a lovely man within that tough guy. I look forward to seeing more of him…but"…She finished the contents of her glass…"I'm off to bed, I'm up sharp to cater for you lot in the morning."

"'Night," said Gus as Kim collected her glass and left.

She's nice, he thought.

CHAPTER NINE

On board the Ventura, everyone rose for breakfast when a passing cruise ship decided to sound its horn a mile astern, its long blast acting as an alarm clock.

Kim's staff had been busy setting a table loaded with healthy food, a day earlier having asked Susan her preferences. Kyle and Bryson would have been more comfortable with bacon rolls and coffee but salmon, scrambled eggs and Champagne - Kim's signature beverage when on board - were more than welcome although Bryson's vast appetite drew light-hearted comments from Liam and Kyle as he picked away at everything on the table.

"How are the ribs this morning?" asked Kyle.

"Still sore, but I'm breathing easier."

"A visit to a hospital will tell us what's what." He looked at Bryson as he began addressing the company with the proposition they had worked on the previous evening before they'd gone to bed. "With Kim's permission, Jack and I think it would be wise to head for another port where we can access X-Ray facilities and Kim can fuel up. Is there somewhere close so we can avoid Marbella?" he asked Kim.

"Home port, I suppose. Puerto Banus. There's a hospital and refueling facilities there."

Bryson interjected. "Gus and I are pretty sure we weren't followed but we shouldn't take chances, not with violent men who have handguns. If Gus takes Liam to hospital today, I'll stay on board to make sure there's no funny business. Now you can't keep the Ventura out at sea for ever so we may as well bite the bullet. Gus and I propose that we take a day to get the analysis on Liam's injury done and tomorrow we'll try to make peace with the boss of the men who attacked us."

Kim's hand flew to her mouth. "Jack, do you really think that's a good idea?"

"You can't spend the rest of your time in Marbella hoping that these men don't connect you to me and Jack", said Kyle. "And you two want to enjoy your honeymoon without looking over your shoulder. Anyway, we can be quite persuasive when we want to be."

Susan supported Kim. "Well I agree with Kim. It's far too dangerous. Shouldn't we just inform the police?"

Kyle shook his head. "No police, I'm afraid. And not just rogue's honour because I told their boss we wouldn't involve the cops. We'd all have a lot of explaining to do concerning weapons; Jack and I have our own police issues and in any event, these guys live and operate here in Marbella and they'll be connected with the city's underworld. Kim's cruiser would have to be well insured if there was a trial and she was implicated. You get to go home to America and me and Jack can leave but Kim lives and works here. Her boat would be found at the bottom of the Mediterranean within a week of a verdict being handed down."

"I'm with the guys on this," said Liam. "No police." He directed his comment to Bryson who was busily engaged in putting the remaining salmon cuts on to his plate. "But are you sure that getting in touch with those people is a bright idea. Might they not just exact revenge for their beating last night?"

"They might try," said Bryson shaping his mouth to accommodate an impromptu salmon sandwich he'd just fashioned. "Gus and I will try just as hard to persuade their top man that they started it and that it was a fair fight. There's still honour amongst thieves, you know. There's a code and they'll know that they breached it, not us."

The morning passed easily with the boys chatting in the Jacuzzi, the powerful jets of water easing their aching muscles. Susan and Kim chatted in the wheelhouse as Kim steered the Ventura back to Puerto Banus.

"Liam seems an absolutely wonderful man, Susan. Had you known him long before you married?"

"For years he was my best friend but our feelings for one another didn't surface until he witnessed a shooting in Las Vegas and my father took him out to live on our ranch for a while to ensure his safety." She inspected her wedding ring fondly. "He means everything to me. Before I was involved with him, my world centred on my mother and father but he's such a wonderful man. I love him deeply and when he was assaulted last night I was beside myself with worry. Thank God that Gus and Jack happened along."

Kim pulled back on the throttle and reduced speed as they closed on the port.

"The way Liam described their performance last night, it's clear they're accomplished soldiers. SAS-trained troops seem quite able at seeing off your average ruffian!"

"What about you, Kim. Is there a man in your life?"

"Nope. To be honest, my life has focused on the Ventura for the past few years. Seeing it commissioned and then staffing it and sailing it has occupied me completely."

"And before that?"

"A couple of guys. Couple of years each. Didn't go anywhere. I'm thirty-four so I'm in no rush to find my special man. But when I do, I hope I'm in love with him as much as you are with Liam." Kim slowed further to allow another yacht to cross her path comfortably.

"Nearly there and then we'll get Liam to the hospital."

* * *

Twenty minutes later the Ventura was tied up at the berth and Kim was organising the refueling. Kyle and Liam set off to walk the few paces towards a waiting taxi while Bryson set himself up at the rear of the boat so he could have a clear view of the harbour although he would walk around the boat now and again to check all aspects. Armed only with a chilled bottle of beer and a large whisky chaser, he put on his sunglasses and settled down for what he hoped would be a quiet afternoon. He was unsettled only by Kim taking out a mobile massage table, setting it up on the foredeck and massaging Susan's back. As she lay in the sunshine being ministered to by Kim, her bikini top was unfastened at the back so as to permit Kim unfettered access to her shoulder blades. 'Astonishing girl-on-girl action...' as he would report, almost drooling, to Kyle later on.

* * *

After Liam had had X-Rays taken of his rib-cage, he sat with Kyle in a waiting room while the images were inspected. Gus anticipated the Doctor's comments.

"The Doctor will probably just want to check that you've not punctured a lung, which you haven't or we'd know about it by now because you wouldn't be breathing properly. A bust rib will heal on its own but the bad news is that it hurts a lot and there's really not much you can do about it. Just rest."

"How come you know so much about this?"

"In my business, you have to be able to deal with pretty much anything that's thrown at you and that includes dealing with most medical emergencies. You'll be okay."

After a few minutes, a nurse appeared and invited Liam into the Doctor's consulting room. As Liam entered, the Doctor was examining the images that had just been taken. "Have a seat, Mr. Brannigan." He pondered the X-Rays. "From what I can see here, you've escaped with bruising. No matter, the treatment's going to be the same as if you had damaged a rib. Simple pain medication. I'm going to prescribe some non-steroidal anti-inflammatory drugs. I'll also give you some pain killers as you'll feel a bit uncomfortable for a while but you're okay. Breathing will be painful but it's important to keep your lungs healthy. Practice taking deep breaths. If you start coughing up any blood or find it hard to breathe, come back and see me but all being well you'll just experience some discomfort."

"So my marathon run tomorrow is in question?" asked Liam jocularly.

"For the next few days, sitting up in bed will test you!"

* * *

A taxi took both men back to the harbour where they rejoined the Ventura.

"The Doctor says I'm fine," said Liam as a concerned Susan came to meet him as he boarded. "But he also says if I don't get some tender lovin' from my wife, dawn 'till dusk, I might regress."

"Then you're good as doomed," said Susan smiling, putting her arm around his neck and kissing him.

Dinner that night was punctuated by a lot of laughter as Gus, Jack and Liam joked and teased much to the entertainment of everyone at the table. After some early Champagne, the three men had elected to drink the Guinness that Susan had suggested Kim bring on board for their guests.

Kim and Susan took their Champagne glasses out to the deck and each leaned on the rail. Looking into the dark water that lapped at the side of the boat, Kim took a sip of her drink.

"You know, I'm really uncomfortable about Gus and Jack trying to sue for peace with these hooligans tomorrow. They shouldn't trust this code that Jack talks about. They might just shoot first and ask questions later."

"I'm with you on that one," Susan said. "Having said that, these guys are ex-SAS. They really knocked these people around yesterday. I watched them. It was pretty impressive in a horrible kind of way. I hate violence. It really shakes me up...all that testosterone. But fair play to Gus and Jack, they dealt with these thugs in jig-time."

Inside, Liam, Jack and Gus had removed themselves and their Guinness and were seated in the comfortable, yellow leather armchairs.

"So are you kind of soldiers of fortune?" asked Liam. "Mercenaries?"

"Kind of," repeated Kyle. But we only take commissions from the good guys. We kind of have to believe that we're doing a bit of good. There's no way we'd be caught up working against the interests of the UK. We hardly spent all these years in the Army to work against our old buddies."

"Enough work out there?" asked Liam.

"There's about thirty-odd armed national conflicts out there worldwide right now," responded Bryson.

"Yeah. Involving populations totaling more than two billion people," said Kyle. And that's only wars where the powers that be have defined them as such. It doesn't take account of situations where they need people like us to deal with awkward things. Increasingly we have to deal with what we call non-state actors...rebels, dissidents, guerrillas...armies don't have a lot of success with them. It's people like us they call on. Lots of these conflicts are fuelled by drugs...some estimates figure that the world spends the same on illegal drugs as it does on legal drugs, so yeah, there's enough work out there.

"And I've to believe you guys are here on holiday?"

"Even people like us need some rest and recuperation from time to time and last I checked, Spain was still in NATO," said Bryson.

"Yeah...sorry we got you involved last night. That must have been the last thing you were looking for if you're trying to get away from your usual excitement."

"No problem. And it let us meet you good people and spend a couple of nights on the Ventura. We'd never have experienced this kind of luxury if we hadn't met up with you," said Kyle. "It's been brilliant!"

"Well, we're here for two weeks. You can stay on board as long as you like while we're here."

"It's your honeymoon, man. Spend time with your bride."

"We don't need to live in one another's pockets. Think about it. We enjoy your company."

Bryson and Kyle passed a look which said *'perhaps'*.

"We'll see," said Kyle.

CHAPTER TEN

The Lear Jet had been called again into service but this time transported Colonel Brand to a grey, drizzled Reykjavik in Iceland. After a couple of hours flying time from Prestwick, the plane banked over the black, rocky landscape that surrounded the trim and tidy township of Grindavik and began to lower its undercarriage for a landing at the Reykjavik air base; Brand having eschewed the more usual landing at the American-built Keflavik airport some forty-seven kilometers outside the city. The Colonel was a man in a hurry and Reykjavik Airport was situated almost in the city centre itself.

A car stood ready on the apron awaiting Brand's descent from the jet. Holding the passenger's door open was one of Brand's contractors, Sam Strachan. Chubby and out of shape, he stood, agitated at his boss's arrival. Reykjavik didn't usually see much action beyond delivering occasional signals that so-and-so had just passed through.

While the engine whine was still high in its descendency, the Lear door opened and Brand stepped from the plane into a summer rain-storm. Shrugging his neck into his coat and turning its collar up as he did so, he nodded to the casually dressed driver of the vehicle as they walked towards the car, simultaneously asking him the questions he'd wanted answered throughout the duration of the flight.

"Are you absolutely certain they're meeting today? You're convinced it's them? We still have time?"

"We've been bugging their phone calls all week," said Strachan. "Although its heavily coded messages they pass between them, we're pretty certain that they intend to meet around one hour from now in a coffee shop near the harbour on Laugavegur."

Brand swore. "I don't like dealing with these things on the hoof. Planning is crucial and we're going in blind here. We don't have accurate descriptions of them, we don't know if this meeting will throw up anything useful and we can't be entirely sure we're not about to ruin the day of two perfectly innocent people!"

"Well, we've been on the heels of one of them now for two years. There's been times I've thought she was a figment of my imagination but the intelligence we've received suggests that she's only too real and that she's here and intent upon mischief."

Brand closed the rear door of the car having thrown a case in the back of the vehicle.

"Let's get the Customs formalities over with. I want to have a look at the files on these two on the way there."

Two Manila folders, one green, one red, were taken from a locked briefcase and handed to Brand.

"These are summarised versions. The complete files would have taken the entire back seat."

Brand harrumphed and read. The first file told of the activities of Svetlana Petrova who had taken up the cause of revolution...any revolution...during her time at university in St Petersburg. Her grades were superb...straight 'A's. Her ability as a track athlete excited various Russian sports federations but a quiet word from more important people let it be known that her precocious talents had also been spotted by the successor organisation to the Russian KGB now named the Federal Security Service of the Russian Federation. After a period of training, she had been used most effectively on tasks associated with grooming men important to the FSS who were swept away by her beauty and charm complimented by her expensive tastes in clothes and cars. Although no absolute evidence was presented in the file, western case officers had her pinned circumstantially as the assassin in four political murders in Dubai, Karachi, Bonn and irritatingly, Cambridge in England.

Petrova had eluded all western attempts to apprehend or neutralise her despite an all-out attempt to secure her arrest during a police hunt only a year earlier. Members of the British security services had been hot on her shapely heels after the shooting on campus of Cambridge Professor Iain Macleod, who had been busily engaged in developing new radar technology designed to counter expensive Russian investments in this area. Sam Strachan, now in Reykjavik, came closest, chasing her through a market square before losing her...an inevitability given her athletic ability and Strachan's rotund and out of condition body.

Her public apprehension and conviction would have been a wounding blow to Anglo/Russian relationships but her violation of usually observed protocols had been so acute, so blatant, that HMG had taken the view that her malfeasance must be dealt with - and dealt with severely. But now she was being fingered as a Russian dissident, working against the interests of the Motherland.

Brand turned the page and began to read of the latest assignment to which British sources placed deep within the Kremlin had alerted them. Details were thin but it was evident that Ms Petrova's beauty was to be placed in the service of someone who might deal a blow to the rise and rise of western influence.

The Russians had much on their mind that year. They were worried about Chechnya. They'd just seen off an insurrection by dint of ignoring the fact that they'd been thwarted by the Chechen people while yet declaring a victory to their own people. The new Premier appointed by the President, wasn't satisfied that the matter had been resolved appropriately and had determined to exact revenge. The west stood by helplessly even while they bolstered their arsenals against yesterday's war threats.

Brand was concerned. A top asset like Svetlana Petrova working in collaboration with any one of a number of talented operators against the west could present formidable problems to be resolved. It certainly hinted at a mission of some significance if she had determined to get involved.

He closed the file so as to scan the details relating to the second individual prior to arriving at the meeting point.

In doing so he quizzed Strachan, now an established operative in Iceland and Nordic countries, completely unused to activity such as was being visited upon him by Brand.

"I take it you brought the items I asked for?"

"Everything. I've two Walther PPK pistols in a diplomatic bag. Silencers as well. Got the needles and sedative as well. I left the automatic pistols back in the office. If we had to use them in the busiest street in Reykjavik it's quite likely we'd make the evening news…something I'm sure we'd rather want to avoid. I brought a rifle microphone as well, just in case we get a chance at distance to listen in to their chat." Strachan looked intently at the two phials of Flunitrazepam. "I haven't used this stuff before," he said. "Does it work instantly?"

Brand took one of the phials. "Intravenous injection of some anesthetics can knock someone out in less than 30 seconds, but two milliliters of this stuff taken as an intramuscular injection will take a few minutes. Think of all the safari shows where the hunters trail after the tracked wildlife waiting for the drug to finally take effect. We use pretty much the same stuff but once we inject they have no option but to submit to its effects."

He nodded his satisfaction at the rest of the equipment and turned to the red file, which was as truncated as the first. It spoke of a man called Krzysztof Kalinowski who was a strategist in Russia's Federal Security Service. A big brain, tactically astute, but non- operational. An able adversary for one so young. Not one for carrying guns or engaging in field matters, he was a fast-tracked, serially promoted, Polish-born, Russian-raised member of the security services, increasingly trusted with important responsibilities.

Brand had heard of him but had never met him. By all accounts, Kalinowski was a creative tactician as well as a strategist. *What on earth was he mixed up with Petrova for?* thought Brand.

The advice he had received from Barrington was that that the Russians were gearing up for a second, more brutal approach to a final resolution of the Chechen issue but that certain of their agents had gone native. Further dispatches included Petrova's name on a list of alleged rogue agents. But Kalinowski's name wasn't on it.

Brand closed the red file and laid it on top of Petrova's green file. Neither file contained photographs of their subject.

"I gather that you're the only one who can potentially identify Petrova," he said to Strachan. Can you identify Kalinowski?"

"Perhaps," said Strachan. "I mostly saw Petrova from the rear as I chased her and I've a ten year old image of Kalinowski locked somewhere in my brain. I met him years ago in Stockholm at a dinner. With luck, if it is him, I'll ID him as well as Petrova."

"Well, let's hope so. This could be a very important snatch if it is them. If we can pull this off without alerting anyone, they could just disappear and everyone would be saved a great deal of heartache."

Drawing the car into an otherwise unoccupied entry just off Laugavegur, Strachan switched off the engine and turned in his seat so as to face Brand.

"Okay, we're here. We think they're going to meet in the coffee house behind us just across the road. How do you want to play it?"

Brand opened his door and eased himself out of the car so he could better see the anticipated location of the rendezvous. Strachan followed suit.

"We have a clear view from this entry," said Brand. "Set up the microphone and we'll see if we can pick anything up that confirms their identity. If it's them, I'm going in with the Walther. I'll approach Petrova. You stand behind Kalinowski. Our job is to get them out and into this car without anyone being aware of any fuss. Once in the car, I'll cover them and you use a syringe. One sharp stab to the neck. It'll be easier dealing with them if they're both unconscious for a bit."

Ten, then fifteen minutes passed. Twenty. Strachan carefully observed all who approached the coffee house but showed no interest in any of the shoppers who ambled by. One or two people entered and left the shop without his comment. Simultaneously, he scanned the conversations inside the shop but only picked up social chit-chat in *Islenska*; no one spoke English even though most Icelanders could flick a switch in their head and converse seamlessly in either language.

Frustrated, he whispered at Brand. "They're late. We may have been rumbled."

"Give them time. Give them time."

More minutes passed. Brand was getting edgy.

"Jesus, it's the bloody' nun!"

"What? said Brand.

"Look! There's a nun and a priest at the table near the door. They're speaking to each other in English. I can't see her face because she's wearing a cowl on her head but the build's right."

"The *build's* right? What are they saying? I'm not threatening a nun with a gun just because you see someone who's built like a fucking woman you chased a year ago."

Strachan listened intently. "It's small talk...small talk...a meeting in Rome...Brother Farrokh...she's saying she needs more money...she's..."

Brand interrupted. "Brother *Farrokh*? An *Arab* Catholic? Figure the odds on that, eh?" His hand pulled at his chin as he contemplated his next move. "Okay, let's do it. If we make a mistake we get out of here fast and all that happens is a story in tomorrow's papers that no one can explain. No one gets hurt. But if it is them, you cover Kalinowski from behind him. Don't show your weapon. I'll deal with Petrova."

As casually as their nerve allowed, the men removed Brand's case from the rear seat, replaced the microphone in the boot of the car and hidden by the raised boot lid which concealed their actions, checked their guns were armed and affixed their silencer. Each held their gun beneath their coat, readied a syringe which they each placed inverted in their inside coat pockets and at a nod from Brand, they moved along the alley towards the front door of the coffee shop.

"Try to make sure you don't inject yourself, Strachan".

Entering, Brand preceded Strachan. Casually they moved towards the table occupied by the two clerics dressed in black.

Brand smiled widely as if greeting an old friend.

"*Prevyet! Kakimi sudbami,*" he said to the nun, indicating in Russian that fate had brought them together that day.

The nun looked at him surprised. Trying to place him.

Brand continued his bonhomie while drawing back his coat, showing his concealed right hand pointing the Walther directly at her groin.

"My friend also has a silenced gun pointed at your neck," he said, now serious, to the priest.

His smile returned lest another customer glanced in their direction.

"We leave together quietly or we shoot you both here and now and leave without you."

Exchanging glances, both rose slowly. The nun wordlessly gesturing to Brand that they acceded to his request. Strachan threw a few *Kronur* on the table, opened the door and backed out into the street, followed by the nun and the priest...Brand immediately behind murmuring imprecations that they should maintain their present decorum or he'd shoot them.

Crossing the road and approaching the car, Strachan opened it and gestured to them both to sit in the rear. Once they were seated, Brand opened the rear door at his side and pointed the gun inwards.

"Look at me! Both of you!"

Each of them complied with his command, awaiting his next order. While they were looking to their right, Strachan plunged a syringe into the blindsided neck of the priest whose left hand moved to the sting. Reacting to his cry, the nun turned her face to the left leaving Brand a simple task of rendering her imminently as senseless as her colleague, using a hypodermic just as had done Strachan.

"You'll both be asleep in a moment but you'll come to no further harm. We move as soon as you're unconscious."

Moments later, each had succumbed. Throwing his spent syringe on the floor of the car, Brand looked at Strachan. "Now all we need to do is establish that we've not assaulted and kidnapped God's representatives on earth for no good reason."

He followed Strachan's example with the priest and fastened a seat belt around the nun to maintain a semi-erect posture while they were driving.

"Take us to the safe house."

CHAPTER ELEVEN

The white van pulled up just outside Puerto Banus Harbour. It was three o'clock in the morning. "Looks quiet," said Cole to Spence who sat behind the wheel observing the dock. "Looks like that cruiser over there. It fits the description perfectly," he said, nodding in the general direction of the Ventura which had been spotted earlier by one of Spence's contacts after Marcus Perry had put out an all points bulletin, threatening everyone within earshot with mayhem if the boat wasn't sighted by morning.

Cafes and restaurants had closed and those who were resident on the motor yachts and cruisers berthed there were all asleep. On the Ventura, everyone had gone to bed around midnight after a night's eating, drinking and laughing although Bryson had spent a further hour alone with an excellent bottle of Old Pulteney.

Satisfied that there was no activity in the harbour, Spence half-turned in his seat to address the men crouched in the rear of the vehicle. "Now, you know how dangerous these men are but we must take them clean. No gun play, no violence unless you're in danger. Cole, you know your job. Don't mess up...and do not under any circumstances try to get your own back for the other night. Understand?" Reaching for the keys, he turned the engine off and spoke again. "I'll stay here. You all know what you've to do. So go...and go quietly."

The dock along which was berthed the Ventura was protected by a sturdy gate with a solid looking lock. It may as well not have existed once one of the gang made at it with his lock-shim, opening the device as if he had used a key. Silently with Cole in the lead, the group of seven men made their way directly to the Ventura. As they closed, they drew their weapons, and made their way aboard unobstructed. Again, the lock of the door of the main deck surrendered immediately and quietly to the attentions of the lock-picker using a wafer-pick and they entered, pistols pointing in front of them, safety catch off. No matter Spence's imprecations, they intended to shoot first. Better a blazing row from the boss than a bullet in the chest or a killer blow to the throat from two men who now had a special place in the gang's folklore so searing had been the experience of many of them only two nights earlier.

Bryson slumbered peacefully in his Queen-size bed as outside, Cole leaned gently against the unlocked door of the stateroom. Opening it slightly, he could see the substantial frame of Bryson, almost filling the Queen-sized bed. He nodded at one of his men who approached the door next to his and placed his hand upon the handle. Gingerly, he too looked inside and identified a large male shape lying in the bed. Two of the men went downstairs stealthily to the staff quarters leaving three others who took the same approach as Cole in tentatively testing the occupancy of a room.

Satisfied that all was in place, Cole took a beat then gestured to his subordinate to act. As one man, they each moved quickly towards the sleeping forms in their respective rooms. Almost simultaneously they woke the slumbering occupants with a menacing gun under the chin and a growled instruction not to move. Once realisation had dawned upon Bryson and Kyle that they were in no position to react effectively, Cole shouted to his men, "Now!" signaling the entry of the others to the rest of the cabins. They easily gained advantage over the sleeping staff and guests. Now standing back and gesturing with his gun, Cole directed Bryson outside into the hallway where Kyle was already positioned against a wall, arms aloft.

They awaited the appearance of the rest of the crew and guests. Fortunately no one assembled in a state of *deshabille* although Bryson, being Bryson, couldn't but help notice how alluring both Kim and Susan looked in their diaphanous, flimsy night attire despite him being held at pistol point and in danger of his life.

Cole spoke. "You two!" He faced Kyle and Bryson. "Just remember if you make a wrong move, you won't be the only ones to die tonight. These lovely ladies could easy catch a bullet."

Content that his message had been received, he turned to Susan and Kim. "Both of you...into that room." One of the gunmen, an older man, stepped forward and opened the door wide so they could enter the stateroom just vacated by Kim.

"You three the staff?" he asked the two elderly women and a man who had emerged from the stairwell. They nodded and were promptly escorted into another room, separating them from Susan and Kim.

"Now you!" He pointed at Brannigan. "You and your friends... in there, and no nonsense." Liam moved stiffly into a vacant room with Kyle and Bryson.

One man with his gun still held ready for action followed the three crew members into their room and one entered after Susan and Kim. "The rest of you stay here," instructed Cole to the remainder of his men while keeping his gun trained on Bryson all the while. He entered the room.

"Well, gentlemen, this is a real pleasure. You didn't say goodbye when you left us the other night."

Kyle sat easily in a chair with his arms at his side. He spoke confidently. "Look, we're no danger to you now. Certainly, the ladies aren't any part of this. Why not leave them out of it?"

"Because, they're going to be our insurance policy, sonny boy. They won't be harmed as long as you three behave and do as you're told!"

Liam still held one arm across his ribcage. "Mister! If you touch my wife in the slightest you'd better kill me dead here and now as I'll make it my business to hunt you down for the rest of my life until I find you."

"Somehow, I don't think you're in a position to be making threats, Mr.?....yeah, first let's get acquainted. Tell me your names."

Kyle took responsibility. "Gus Kyle. Holidaymaker. These two are my friends, Jack Bryson and Liam

Brannigan, also holidaymakers. We meant no harm the other night but your men were bang out of order. You'd have done the same thing. You really don't need those guns. You'll be frightening the women."

"They *should* be frightened, Kyle. They're in deep trouble if you make a wrong move. Now you boys just sit still while I make a call." Cole moved outside the cabin door and spoke quietly into his mobile phone, still holding a pistol pointed in the general direction of the three men.

While he was distracted, Bryson whispered to Kyle. "How the fuck did these people find us? There was no way we were followed."

Before Kyle could respond that he had no idea either, Cole ended his call.

"Ok, you're coming with me to meet my boss. The ladies and the staff will stay here on board. They'll be kept in the rooms they're in just now. They'll be looked after, fed and will have their television to keep them entertained. If all goes well with you guys, you'll be returned to them and can continue your holiday."

He shouted for one of his men. "Harry!" A man entered the room carrying a small rucksack. Cole indicated the three men by waving his gun. "Watch them get dressed then cuff 'em."

Next door, Susan was in full flow.

"You absolutely don't know who you're dealing with, Buddy. I can have muscle here in ten minutes. I know people. You wouldn't believe the people I know. I know the top people. People you've never heard of Buster."

Her captor, old Eddie Crompton wasn't the most gifted of Cole's men.

"Listen darlin', I just do what I'm told... and I'm told to sit here wiv you two and not let you do anyfin' stupid while my boss has a chat wiv your men. My old girl lets off steam same as you and I just sit wiv my ears shut...same as here. So why don't you quieten up and give us all a break 'till I know what's 'appenin' next?"

Cole left a man in each of the two rooms holding the prisoners and an additional man up on deck for surveillance purposes as well as to permit a shift system supervising the prisoners. The rest shuffled quietly off the boat as they had arrived and, with the three men in tow, shortly arrived at Spence's van where they all boarded for the short trip back into Marbella.

* * *

After some twenty minutes, the van slowed and made its way along the rear lane abutting the Red Lion. Stopping and pulling on the handbrake, Spence instructed one of his men to move the van whilst himself alighting and accompanying the rest of the vehicle's occupants into the pub through the back door. Cole opened the door to a darkened room and signaled to Kyle, Bryson and Brannigan that they should enter. As they did, he closed the door behind them and locked it leaving them on their own. Bryson turned on a light.

"Jesus, would you look at this," exclaimed Liam. "I think we're in the Wolf's Lair!"

The three men looked around at walls covered in Nazi memorabilia. Large scale photographs of Hitler speaking at Nuremberg rallies, stormtroopers, Nazi insignia and scarlet and black flags covered the walls. Less obvious but present were slogans in German atop photographs of shaven-headed, angry men. Other than that the room was obviously set out as a meeting room with some basic chairs surrounding a table in the centre. Their hands cuffed in front of them made manoeuvring more straightforward so each of them found it easy to sit down and await the attentions of their captors.

Kyle spoke first.

"Jack, put your key ring out on show," he said, simultaneously digging into the pocket of his jeans and taking out the key ring left him by Colonel Brand and affixing it to the denim belt loop on his waist-band. Bryson followed suit.

"What are these? asked Liam.

Kyle thought quickly. "SAS insignia. If any of these guys did a bit of soldiering, they might be more inclined to give us a break if they recognised them. Now, I think we listen to these guys. If they'd wanted to take revenge, they would just have shot us or beaten us on board the Ventura. We have the lives of five people other than ourselves to think of."

He looked at Brannigan. "So don't let's get emotional here, Liam. We deal with this rationally and see whether we can't keep ourselves alive and look after the people on the boat. We don't have room for democracy in situations like this so you follow my line unquestioningly. Jack and I understand conflict. We're a team and you need to stay on your toes and try not to freelance. Do you understand?"

Liam nodded his assent. "Every man jack of them had a gun when they took the boat. These are serious people all right. And they don't appear to have much of a liberal philosophy if you look at these pictures on the walls. Trust me, guys. I'm with you. You say jump… I jump!"

Bryson repeated the question he'd asked earlier. "Gus, how did these people know where we were? I swear to God that I checked on the retreat from the fight and stood guard the following day and there was no way that we were followed. Absolutely no way!"

"A lucky observation?" suggested Liam.

"I don't believe in luck in situations like this," said Bryson.

The door opened to admit Marcus Perry and Cammy Spence. Both carried pistols.

"You fackin' bastards. You put my men in hospital, you fackahs," said Perry, his spittle spraying delinquently as he raged. "I'm going to shoot you all in the balls, you fackahs. I've got a business to run and my men are all fackin' facked, you fackahs!"

Spence, who holstered his gun in his waistband, intervened.

"We're not exactly pleased at your antics." He looked at Perry, trying to calm him as he'd done a thousand times before. "But we want you to know that we understand the action you took was to protect your woman and that our people were drunk and out of line!"

"You three are fackin' lucky that we've got someone here who gives a shit whether you live or fackin' die, you fackin' fackahs!"

Perry and Spence sat at the rectangular table at the point furthest from their captives.

Spence spoke first. "We have a problem. We're engaged in some business that the Spanish police would prefer we weren't involved in. Everything was set up perfectly, but you guys have knocked the stuffing out of our plan because of the beating you gave our people the other night. Two of you at least are street fighters, probably army or police. You!" He pointed at Brannigan. "Are you uniform?"

Again Kyle took the lead to avoid Brannigan responding.

"Look...let's put our cards on the table...we hardly know this guy. Me and the big fellah here are ex-SAS. We stumbled across your men beating up a woman. We stopped them. He's got bugger all to do with what happened next. Your people might be good enough when there's ten of them beating up a honeymooning couple but frankly, we would have put twice that number to sleep! Your men were amateurs. We have no interest in you or your business interests. Just let us go and no one will be any the wiser. We've not informed the police and have no inclination…"

"Shat…The…Fack…App…!" interrupted Perry. I'm out a lot of money because of you and you're going to make it up to me. Tell 'em how, Cammy!"

Spence allowed a moment to pass before continuing. "I figured you both for soldier types and now we need you to play a part in our operation. If you do, and everything goes ok, you'll be returned to your ship without being damaged. If you mess us about, we have your women and staff on board and a phone call from us will see them shot. That seems straightforward enough to me. Are you guys in or will I make a phone call?"

"Depends what you want us to do," said Bryson. "We have some talents but they might not be what you need."

"Presumably you can shoot a fackin' gun?" asked Perry, rhetorically. "And presumably you don't want the fackin' women shot?"

"We don't care one way or the other," interrupted Bryson. "These people mean nothing to Gus and me. Shoot them if you want to. We don't give two shits….." He paused. "Of course, if we were in on the deal…"

He allowed the significance of his comment to float in mid-air.

Perry laughed despite his anger. "You cheeky bastard. We've got you handcuffed in a fackin' room. We could shoot you and no one would fackin' know and you try to talk a deal wiv us?"

Bryson had the good grace to smile in response.

"Look, me and Kyle here are pros. We're down on our luck. We could do with some work and we're no friends of the police. This fellah here's a tourist. He'd get in our way. If we'd be of use to you, let's talk a deal. If not, why didn't you just shoot us on the boat? We just need an incentive. We've no relationship with the people on the boat. Shoot the fuckers if you want but it won't motivate us one way or the other."

Perry sucked deeply on a cigarette and placed a glass recently emptied of whisky gently on the table. Looking directly at Bryson, he growled an instruction to his lieutenant through his ochre teeth.

"Okay Cammy," he said slowly, "take the fackin' civilian in the van. Drive somewhere quiet and shoot the fackah. Shoot the fackah in the fackin' head. Once he's dead, cut his fackin' head off and bring it back here and we'll see whether Mister SAS here still doesn't give a shit."

Spence rose and beckoned to Liam, who sat still, his eyes like saucers, his mouth agape.

"Take him...and shoot the women while you're at it," said Bryson unmoved. Liam looked at Bryson as if he'd just grown another head.

With a sigh that transmogrified into a groan, Kyle raised both of his handcuffed hands, fingertips pointed at the ceiling, palms outward in surrender. "Leave him alone. We don't want bloodshed. We just want looked after. We're better bets than any of the men you're hiring right now and we'd rather drink with you than fight with you."

Silence...then Spence caught Perry's gaze. "A chat outside, boss?"

"Yeah, we'll chat... but I still want to shoot that fackin' civilian," he snarled in the direction of Liam. They left.

Liam was first to break the silence as the door closed. "Jesus, Jack...thanks for nothing. Now these guys want to shoot me."

Kyle disagreed. "No they don't, Liam. They want us to act as strong-arms for them and they're not too sophisticated at persuasion. Threats are what they know best. But at the end of the day, they're businessmen. In a moment they're going to come back in here and tell us that they've given thought to our offer and they want to let bygones be bygones. They might even send you back to the Ventura."

"Here's hoping," responded Liam.

Five minutes elapsed and the three men sat in the gloomy room looking at the fascist wall-hangings, commenting occasionally and awaiting the verdict of Perry and Spence. Kyle repeated his earlier guidance to Liam to follow their line of direction without demur.

"We need to stay focused, Liam if we all want to get out of this alive."

"Yeah…. but I'd feel more comfortable about that if Jack stopped encouraging them to shoot me and cut my feckin' head off."

Bryson smiled as another silence descended on the small room.

"What do those German words mean… *'Nationalsozialistische Deutsche Arbeiterpartei'?* asked Bryson," scanning the walls again; struggling with the German pronunciation.

"It's German for Nazi," responded Liam. It comes from conjoining the first two letters, NA with the first two in the 'socialist' part of the word, ZI. National Socialist. It stands for the National Socialist German Workers Party, although it wasn't quite as socialist as people like Fidel Castro would have wished."

Bryson looked at him as if to ask, *how the fuck do you know all this stuff?*

"I studied German history for a while at university," said Brannigan reading Bryson's unspoken enquiry.

"I think you're right about this being the Wolf's Lair," said Bryson. "It's a bloody shrine to Hitler and his pals."

Kyle agreed. "Well, the probability is that the bunch of boys who hang around Perry are fellow travelers so we'd better be prepared to adopt their belief system while we're doing business with them. It'll do no harm for them to think we're not that keen on foreigners or Commies... Gypsies, Jews and Blacks are also fair game in their eyes." He shifted in his uncomfortable wooden seat. "We don't need to go over the top, just enough for them to figure we're not Guardian readers."

Still they waited.

CHAPTER TWELVE

Susan slumbered on the stateroom's queen-sized bed. Kim held intermittent exchanges with old Eddie as he sat in the chair observing them.

"It's probably safer for you to holster your gun, you know. We aren't going anywhere... especially with you holding the three men. Why not just put it away and we can all feel a bit more relaxed. We could be in here some time."

"Nah, you'd take advantage of me somehow. I get paid well to do my job and over the years I learned to do exactly like I'm told and I don't make too many mistakes. The day I start thinking for m'self is the day people stop paying me wages."

Kim changed tack.

"Been out in Spain long?"

Eddie didn't answer, trying to figure out what advantage would be conceded if he did. Eventually he decided it was just social chit-chat.

"Must be twelve years now. Me and the misses. London's too cold for me in the winter. It makes me wheeze. And people here are nice. I don't get involved in too many situations like this, you know, because I'm too old but your boys really took care of my boss's main men there and there's no one left to help out so I'm called out of my retirement."

"You seem like a nice man. How did you end up holding two women captive with a gun in your hand?"

Eddie shuffled uncomfortably in his chair. He wrestled with his next sentence.

"I...Nah...I wouldn't shoot you, dahlin'. I don't have it in me. When I was younger I was a bit of a lad. I was a thief...a good thief. But I wouldn't shoot no one. 'Specially a woman. But you need to stay in here, love. Not everyone in this mob's as old and soft as me. I wouldn't hurt you, dahlin' but I'd need to make a phone call and other people would get involved and they wouldn't fink twice."

Kim smiled. "I didn't imagine you were a gangster. Are your friends on board a cuddly as you are?"

Eddie smiled, despite himself.

"Nah!...we're all clapped out. Ernie next door is a pensioner who only cares about getting back on shore to put a bet on the first race at Chepstow tomorrow. The guy on deck is a bit 'andy but he's deaf as a fackin' bat...sorry 'bout the language there dahlin'. Bad 'abits die 'ard."

Susan decided not to correct Eddie's poor grasp of simile.

"You know, you're quite charming. Not at all what I thought at first." Kim stood up from the edge of the bed on which Susan continued to sleep. She smiled at Eddie. "Mind if I help myself to a drink from the mini-bar? It might help me sleep."

"You go right ahead, dahlin'. I might join you if you don't mind. All this excitement ain't good for me."

"Well, what's your poison?" She opened the door of the small refrigerator. "We've got everything in here."

"Any malt whisky, dahlin'? I love a nice malt."

Kim inspected the interior of the mini-bar. "How about a twelve year old Glenmorangie? There's a miniature here, and some still water."

"My favourite. Really nice, love! No ice. Just a little water."

"I'm a wine buff myself," said Kim removing a bottle of *Chablis* from the inside door compartment. Calculating the distance between the mini-fridge and her captor, she removed the full-sized bottle by its neck and swung it swiftly in an arc, sweeping the gun from Eddie's hand and onto the floor where she picked it up, leveling it at his chest.

"You're a lovely man and I don't want to hurt you but I'm not the lovely woman you think I am and I wouldn't hesitate to make your wife a widow and take my chances with the two has-beens you brought on board with you."

Andy held his pained hand and shook his head ruefully.

"My misses'll fackin' kill me...and I don't suppose Mr. Perry will be too chuffed!" He sat back in his armchair and his brow furrowed as he considered further consequences. "And wait 'till the boys down the pub hear about this."

Kim froze then slowly retreated, keeping the gun pointed at Eddie until she reached the sleeping form of Susan. She made a face. "Perry? Marcus Perry? You people are here on his instructions?"

"P'raps...what's it to you?"

Kim looked at the ceiling in exasperation. "Shit...no matter."

With her left hand she shook her guest awake. "Susan...Susan...."

Susan awoke and almost instantly appreciated their change of fortune. "My God. Oh, Kim, sorry I fell asleep...my Lord."

"No matter. Take the draw cord from the two dressing gowns. Tie his hands tightly behind his back....better yet, you hold this gun...and shoot him in the leg if he moves... I'm more comfortable with ropes and knots. I'll tie him up."

A few moments later, Eddie had been immobilised in his chair. Kim turned to Susan. "Right, this is no time for modesty." She moved to her wardrobe and hurriedly took out some clothes. "No underwear, I'm afraid. Just these. We look about the same size."

Susan looked at Kim, taking her lead.

"You can close your eyes like a gentlemen or tell the boys down the pub this as well," said Kim steadily holding Eddie's gaze as she pulled her silk chemise over her head, momentarily revealing her perfectly toned, naked body for his inspection as she gathered up a couple of pairs of jeans and two black T-shirts from the bed where she'd thrown them. She threw a set to Susan who shrugged and removed her nightshirt, presenting a sight only Liam had viewed in recent years, almost giving Eddie a heart attack. The girls dressed quickly.

"Sorry about this Mister but we need you to keep quiet." Kim took a pair of long socks and placed a small round bar of soap inside one forcing it into Eddie's mouth and tying the sock tightly round his neck, doubling the second sock round as well for good measure. "This'll remind you to watch your language in front of young ladies…"

She held her hand out to Susan, silently asking her for the gun.

"I think first of all we look after the man on the deck," she whispered. Susan nodded her agreement and gently opened the door leading into the hallway. Moving towards the stairs they could see the outline of their captor seated in the comfortable leather seating on deck...fast asleep. On her tip-toes now, she moved behind him to a curl of rope used for general docking purposes and handed it to Susan before stepping behind the sleeping man. He held a gun loosely in his hands. Stopping for a second to ensure her balance, Kim leaned over and snatched the gun, awakening the man. Two guns pointed at his forehead encouraged his statue-like immobility.

Kim spoke quietly. "Do not move. Do not speak." The man scowled his concurrence. Again, Kim handed a gun to Susan and took responsibility for tying his hands but this time the extra rope available permitted a more thorough job.

"So far, so good," said Kim. "Now for the one next door to us."

They returned to the deck from which they'd emerged minutes before and approached the door next to theirs. Susan listened, ear to the door. She spoke quietly. "Can't hear anything."

Kim took the handle of the door and turned it slowly, opening the door slightly. As it opened she could increasingly see more of the room. Each of the three members of her staff were seated upon the bed and beneath them was positioned their guard face down on the mattress. Kim took a moment to ensure that she understood what she witnessed before opening the door fully. "How long have you had him like this?" she asked with a broad grin on her face.

Miguel answered. "The man he fell asleep after half an hour. We took his gun and sat on him like *theece*. For all we know he could be dead by now. I don' know how he could breathe with Graciana on top of him. We have his gun as well. We didn't know about the other men."

Graciana slapped Miguel on the back of his head for his cheek.

Susan spoke. "Why don't we bring the three men together in this room? They'll be easier to guard that way."

"Agreed," said Kim. "I'll get them. I need them all tied properly. Graciana, will you stay in here with them along with Juanita? I'll leave one of the guns with you but if we restrain them properly, you won't need it. Miguel, once Susan and I leave the Ventura, can you take her out about half a mile or so from Puerto Banus and await my call? I don't want the boat seen easily from the port....There's one tied up next door and you can take the gag out of his mouth now, but watch him, he's charming!"

So saying, Kim stuffed her phone and purse into her tight jeans and stuck a revolver in the waistband underneath her T shirt. She turned to Susan and proffered the second gun. "Take this and we'll gather our prisoners. Then we'll get off the Ventura. Let's go."

* * *

The door opened and Spence entered. There was no sign of Perry.

"Boss wants me to handle this." He sat down at the table. "You!" He gestured at Liam. "You a honeymoon couple?"

"You're half right," responded Liam accurately.

"Want to stay married, alive, in one piece?"

"I do that…most certainly want that."

"Then you go back to your wife on the boat and wait there 'till our men tell you to get on with your holiday. No funny business…and if your pals here mess up, you get it in the neck too!"

Liam caught Kyle's wink, intending to convey, 'I told you so', and clasped his cuffed hands together as if thanking the Lord.

Cole took Liam to the front door of the Red Lion and shoved him roughly into the pedestrianised walkway where the earlier fracas had taken place. "I see you again when my boss isn't looking, you get another beating. Understand, Irish?"

Liam nodded and Cole re-entered the pub.

Spence sat with Kyle and Bryson. Taking a key from his pocket, he uncuffed first Gus then Jack. "Let's be friends, boys. No hard feelings."

Bryson rubbed his wrists. "Depends whether there's money in it for us. When we say we're soldiers of fortune, we're trying to put across the fact that we don't work for charity."

"Me and the Boss were talking about that. We reckon we could put ten grand each your way if you take care of a bit of business that our people were going to deal with before you put them down."

Kyle engaged. "Ten grand's a lot of money for doing legal things. What's the score? Are you asking us to break the law? he asked rhetorically. What's the chances we'd be caught?"

"I need to get serious here boys. If I tell you what the job is, you're in up to your neck. If you back out, you get shot. My boss was quite specific about that. He can't have people on the street knowing his business without them being part of the job."

"Seems fair," said Kyle. "We're up for that. Nothing happens to our friends on the boat, you pay us ten grand and maybe we could do more work with you in the future if everything goes well?"

"Perfect," said Spence offering his hand to both men in turn. "Now… that's a Glasgow accent isn't it?"

For the next ten minutes, they exchanged information about themselves and stories about their home city before Bryson interrupted, impatiently insisting that Spence tell them about the task in hand.

"Okay, guys, let's get right to it. We're expecting a shipment any time now. Don't need to say what it is but you wouldn't be far wrong if you figured it was something to do with the drugs business. The people we're dealing with are pretty new to us. They're Arabs from Egypt and we worry that what they're trying to do is to relieve us of the money we've put together without giving us the drugs in exchange. We don't trust them and we've got to figure that they don't trust us so we'd prefer to organise things so that we keep the drugs and they don't get the money if we possibly can. They get *shot*...they get shot."

"Where's the meet to take place?" asked Kyle.

"We haven't worked that out yet."

"Then if you get us a map we'll look for somewhere where we've got the advantage. We control the drop and we want somewhere isolated if there are boxes or bags to transfer from one vehicle to another. Better yet if you just take control of their vehicle once you've checked the cargo. Have you someone who can check the consignment's purity?"

Spence leaned back in his chair and shouted. "Happy...Happy!"

External footsteps signaled Happy's arrival and he entered the room.

"Happy, there's a map under the bar. It's a map of Andalucía. Can you bring it in here and rustle us up a cup of coffee while you're at it? Map first."

"Right, Mr. Spence."

Happy left and Kyle thumbed at the posters behind him. "What's all this then, Cammy?"

Tired now, Spence rubbed his eyes. "Good customer care, Gus. A few of the people we get in here are pretty right wing. They hate every fucker. Me?...it doesn't bother me one way or the other but if our drinkers want to come in here and salute Adolph, I don't give a flyin' fuck so long as they pay good money for our drink and mind their own business."

Bryson spoke business. "Gus here's a trained negotiator. You could do worse than letting him square away the details of the arrangements if and when these guys phone."

"I'll check with the Boss. He might not be so keen on that idea. He's more likely to want to go with people he knows. We'll see."

"Sure...but remember, we're pros and we want to make sure that everything's in order before we put our heads above the parapet," said Bryson. "It's our necks on the block so if we don't like the arrangements we don't go in."

"Then you get shot," said Spence. "Simple!"

"Doubt it Cammy. You need us now and we just want to make sure that everything goes off alright."

"Then you get fuckin' *shot*," repeated Spence and left the room impatiently to find the map he'd asked Happy to fetch only moments before.

Kyle looked at Bryson. "Everyone wants to shoot everyone else today."

Spence walked along the narrow, dank corridor and into the small rear bar where Perry stood alone, a glass of whisky and a cigarette in the same hand.

"Well?

"They'll do it. Ten grand each."

"Good. Just remember... use them... and when they've delivered for us, shoot them both. Disappear them. I want no one around other than our people who know anything about this. Trust no one. That's how we've managed to survive this far."

CHAPTER THIRTEEN

Spence had just nodded off on a couch in a room in a back room of the Red Lion he'd commandeered years before as an office and a sometime bedroom when an operation required his close attentions. His boss, Marcus Perry had driven home drunkenly to his walled villa where he lived alone following the suicide of his wife some five years earlier.

Still in the small back room of the Red Lion, Bryson and Kyle had accepted Spence's invitation to try to get some shut-eye. With only a chair and a table with which to make themselves comfortable, Kyle found it difficult even to snooze and observed how his friend and comrade Jack Bryson merely leaned his chair back against the wall, lifted his feet on to the table and fell fast asleep. *Impressive*, thought Kyle though he'd seen his friend do the same thing on countless occasions in deserts, on mountain tops, once on an ice-field and in bars…often in bars.

Pondering their situation, he rose, stretched and disinterestedly began a light scan of the posters adorning the walls, shaking his head at the many images and photographs celebrating the Third Reich. The Nuremberg Rallies featured as did a number of the Fuehrer. Others were of more recent vintage and captured collections of men posing with Nazi regalia in the background. In one, a group of shaven headed men wearing Nazi regalia had been photographed, arms folded, standing before a *swastika*. One of them had his right arm raised, fingers pointed stiffly in the Nazi salute.

"Sweet Jesus," said Kyle to himself as he gradually came to realise identity of the person in the photograph. He nudged the shoulder of his companion who was awake and alert instantly. "Recognise anyone?"

Removing his feet from the table, Bryson stood and moved closer to the photograph on the wall.

The angry red scar that cleaved the left eye of the Nazi sympathiser left no doubt in either man's mind. They looked at one another in real puzzlement, each asking themselves the same question. What in hell was Colonel Brand doing saluting Hitler's memory?

Kyle carefully tore the picture from the wall, folded it and put it in his back pocket.

"Maybe we should ask him about this when we see him."

* * *

Kim slowed her muscular Lexus as she and Susan entered the outskirts of Marbella.

"God, Kim, do we know what we're doing here? Surely we now have to involve the Spanish police? Liam and the two guys might be in real danger."

"It's okay, Susan. I'm on top of this."

"Kim, we're carrying guns. This can't be wise."

"I know stuff you don't, Susan. Trust me on this."

"But it's my husband we're talking about here, Kim. Don't you think it's reasonable to tell me what you know? I don't know what to think."

Kim shifted her gaze from the road ahead and looked briefly at Susan's worried face. Pondering her options, she steeled herself. "Not yet. Maybe not ever. I'll work on a need to know basis for the moment. Don't worry."

Susan continued to drive and both fell into an awkward silence, broken urgently when Susan grasped at Kim's right arm, almost pulling the Lexus inadvertently into another lane. "There's Liam...look! Over there, Kim. Walking past that garage!"

Checking her rear view mirror, Susan brought the Lexus to a halt as Susan lowered the window, shouting to attract Liam's attention. As the vehicle stopped, she opened her door and stumbled out, running towards Liam who, recognising his wife, had began hurriedly shuffling across the road with equal disregard for any traffic.

Deliriously they embraced, forcing a grunt from Liam as his pained ribs took the force of Susan's momentum. After some hurried shared concerns about the other's health, they moved swiftly, clutching one another, to the Lexus.

"Jesus, Liam. How did you get away? Where's Jack and Gus. Are you okay, Honey?"

Liam smiled. "One question at a time, Susan." He looked at Kim. "Hi, Kim. Thanks for the lift. I thought I was in for a long walk."

"We were really concerned about you three. You're dealing with some real mean *hombres*."

"Straight up!" said Liam. "They took us to what looked like a Nazi meeting hall and were going to sever my head from my body. They only let me go because Jack and Gus promised to help them in some undertaking and because they figured they had you two and the Ventura's staff as hostages." He thought further. "They don't seem to have the bargaining power they thought they had. How did you get away?"

"They underestimated Kim," said Susan, smiling. "Everyone on board's safe, the Ventura's out at sea and we have three of their men trussed up under the guard of Miguel. Perhaps once we return them to land, we can continue our honeymoon."

Liam caught Kim's glance. "Not sure about that, darling. If these men think they have Gus and Jack's attention because they're holding you two, they'd be in danger once they find out that that position's been reversed." His hand rubbed his bleary eyes as he thought through his options. "Listen, these two guys are incredible fighting machines but they wouldn't stand a chance with all of the muscle available to that gang. They would just be shot. If the police turned up, chances are they'd be held as co-conspirators. Anyway, from what they were telling the boss guy, they don't want to involve the cops."

Kim nodded somberly at Liam's appraisal, sighed resignedly and re-fastened her seatbelt. She groaned loudly.

"Buckle up folks. I guess we're going to have to get them out of there and I'm afraid I'm probably the only person who can do this without anyone being injured."

Liam's next question remained unasked as he shared a quizzical glance with his wife. Kim pulled out on to the road and continued on her way to Marbella.

* * *

Spence shot bolt upright as the phone in his office began to trill. Almost tripping over a small table and upsetting its lamp, he grasped at the phone and still fumbling, lifted it from the receiver.

"Cammy Spence."

"Mr. Spence. I have the packages you are waiting on. Is it safe to talk?"

Rubbing the sleep from his eyes, Spence concentrated, trying to remember the agreed question that would demonstrate he was who he said he was and that they could talk freely. "Thank you for calling. Have you read today's papers?"

"I have read the papers. I was most interested in the financial section."

"Which page interested you most?"

"Page five...!"

Both were satisfied that the call was between the two people expected to set up the deal. Aswad continued.

"I have the packages. You are still prepared to invest the three units that we agreed?"

Spence's frustration got the better of him.

"We've been waiting for three days. You're very late," he said angrily.

"These things are not always easy. We have agreed a price. You will, of course, want to check the merchandise but we must move immediately. My instructions must be followed to the letter."

Spence reached for a pen and wrote down the directions given him by Tarik Aswad.

"These details are acceptable. We will arrive at noon. Goodbye."

Placing the phone on the receiver, he lifted it immediately and dialed Marcus Perry who had just arrived home.

"Boss. We need you back here at the Red Lion. The Arabs just phoned. We move immediately."

* * *

In the back room, Kyle and Bryson were fully awake, attempting to make sense of their relationship with Brand.

"From here on in, Jack, we take no chances. He looks like he's in with Perry. Who knows?"

"Agreed. And these people are armed to the teeth. Now would be a good time for the Ruskie to show himself."

"Or not," countered Kyle. "If Brand's suspect, so must be the Russian."

Bryson grimaced his agreement.

"But," mused Kyle, "I checked when I was at the hospital waiting on Liam and the money Brand agreed was showing up in our accounts. Seems a bit philanthropic if he just did that in order to see us shot!" said Kyle.

"We need to think on our feet...and fast," said Bryson. "We've been stupid. We may have trusted Brand too much because of the last commission going so smoothly."

Kyle rubbed the sleep from his eyes and sat back on his chair. "You've got a point. He's prepared to give us the guts of half a mil for what, when you think of it, is pretty much a police matter. Why us? Why not the local cops or Interpol for that matter? He has all the info he needs to deal with this normally without this bollocks about needing deniability. Why does he want a consignment of thirteen cartons of drugs protected...and when you consider the amounts involved, three million pounds worth of illicit drugs isn't that much in the scheme of things. I mean it's better off the streets but it wouldn't deliver a death blow to western civilisation."

"Agreed," said Bryson. "In effect he's giving us about one sixth of the value of this stuff to get rid of the couriers, find a Russian spy and hold the stuff for him? Kind of smells a bit when you piece it together like that, eh?"

"We've been too complacent, *compadre*. But we're in it up to our ears now. What d'you think? We maintain our line with them until we figure this out? Until then we don't phone him. No contact. We work this out for ourselves. Brand can stew because he's not been straight with us."

While Bryson and Kyle were assembling their thoughts in their small room, so too was Spence in his, and just as Kim and the Brannigans sped towards the Red Lion, so too was Marcus Perry. Marbella was asleep but there was much activity amongst a few of its denizens.

* * *

Farrokh Hassan was a wanted man. Eagerly sought by all security forces and intelligence agencies in the western world and by some in the Arab world, he'd outwitted them for nine years. Mostly operating alone, he'd used a clutch of different names and nationalities to avoid capture or detection. The CIA figured he was Syrian or certainly

Middle East. British sources suggested Pakistani. Mossad had him pinned accurately as Iranian but no reliable sightings could be used as evidence of anything so they gave him a code name. Three sources had cited a tattoo on the back of his right hand. One identified it as a scorpion. Wary of his ability to sting, the intelligence community world-wide called him 'Scorpion', a *soubriquet* that pleased Hassan considerably.

Sometimes Allah had been kind to Hassan. He'd escaped apprehension by the skin of his teeth. Scorpion been shot but only injured. He'd led a charmed life but one which had been based upon equal amounts of caution and bravado. Photographs were indeterminate...perhaps the guy with the full beard, possibly the shaven headed man in dark glasses, the collared and tied accountant...his identity was a continuing mystery to uniforms in the west but his reputation was fearsome...

He'd successfully undertaken operations against western powers in several countries, even tweaking the nose of the Great Satan in his own back yard by bombing a Federal building in Boston, killing eight people and wounding several more and by assassinating a Jewish Congressman in Central Park, New York while the man was pushing his grand-daughter round the Pond. An attack on the American Embassy in Paris and the British Embassy in Rome had proved fruitless but had brought much publicity midst some structural damage. Security forces had determined that Hassan was the central figure in each but he'd still evaded capture. His ruthlessness was a byword in the security community and many would give their right arm for his head on a plate.

His motivation was unknown. Sometimes money changed hands. Most usually blood was spilled; occasionally hostages were bartered, sometimes assets destroyed but it was hard for the west to read his underlying political ethos. Was he signed up to a jihad against the west or the Jewish religion? Was he a soldier of fortune? Perhaps he was supportive of an Arab cause...an adventurer? Hassan was a Muslim; he sought the overthrow of the west. That much was discernible from his statements in hostage situations. But whatever his motives, he was a man to be reckoned with. No intelligence was available on his next target. No sources could inform on his next moves as he worked alone or as a specially detached agent for organisations whose objectives, it had to be presumed, were in alignment with his. No single cause claimed him as their own.

Scorpion was an unusual man. He tested the patience of Mossad, the CIA and MI5. American military psychologists had undertaken an analysis of his personality as far as was possible and had determined that he was a highly intelligent sociopath who merely used his war on the west to camouflage his blood lust. Had he been a normal citizen, he'd more than likely just have been a common or garden serial killer.

* * *

Farrokh Hassan was also a patient man. He'd sat alone and undiscovered in his car from the morning after the arrival of the shipment, having checked out of the hotel where he was registered as Manush Parvanda, an electronics engineer. From his vantage point he could watch the careless activities of the four Egyptians and, courtesy of bugs he'd placed within the consignment in the Dodge pick-up, could listen into many of their personal and electronic conversations when they gathered in the barn in which was housed the vehicle and the contents they *still* thought were narcotics.

Hassan too, knew of the Egyptians' arrangements for the exchange of goods for money. He had a plan, and the contents of the thirteen cartons were an important ingredient in the mayhem he proposed to unleash. He'd merely arranged for the Egyptian innocents to transport his goods from the Iranian port of Abadan to the Spanish port of Altea at no danger to himself. He now had three million pounds worth of their drugs in a warehouse in Abadan. The three million cash he intended stealing soon from the infidels was also important. Weaponry had to be purchased, forged documents paid for, alliances bought and the money due to the Egyptians would assist his scheming if he could only relieve them of it.

Little did the couriers know that the tightly sealed cartons they knew to be narcotics, that they had packed in a case in the rear of their pick-up, that they'd occasionally sat next to when smoking cigarettes, contained pure unadulterated ricin powder, the deadliest and most potent biological agent known to man.

CHAPTER FOURTEEN

The weather in Iceland hadn't improved.

"Just how far is this bloody safe house?" Brand was impatient.

"Not far now. Iceland doesn't have need of broad carriageways. Not enough people live here." Strachan concentrated on steering as the road had now narrowed to a single track and the metalled road surface had given way to crushed and rolled lava. Sufficient for an occasional journey but not suited to high speed driving. The Icelandic authorities had classified their roads A, B and smaller 'official roads'. The track leading to their cabin - as with countless other roads in the country - didn't appear on any map.

Brand looked out of his rain-lashed passengers' window and noted on either side the black scraggy rock formations on which only mosses and lichens could take hold. Steam from geysir activity rose from occasional outcrops where the earth's crust had thinned sufficiently to allow steam to escape under pressure. A strong smell of sulphur assailed Brand's nostrils and fought for air supremacy with the heavily scented aerosol that swung from the rear view mirror.

"God, this is a desolate country," he said.

Strachan explained. "Our safe house is ostensibly a holiday home. Many in Iceland have built second homes that they use for recreational purposes and let to tourists in amenity rich areas close to Reykjavík when they're not using them. They've created quite large communities with a high density of cabins, mobile homes and small wooden cabins but we have one that's out of the way. Still, ours is pretty much identical to all of the others and the fact that it's used only now and again wouldn't raise any eyebrows.

A wooden cabin appeared set below a sheer rock face as the car slowly turned a corner in the narrow black track. No trees. No vegetation. Just lava rocks and some sparse whin grass surrounded the building.

"Here we are," said Strachan. "It's been a while since I've been up but we have it checked pretty regularly. It should be fuelled and the fridge should be full of delights."

Brand looked at his podgy colleague with some disdain, keeping to himself his observation that the fridge full of delights might just be more important to Strachan than the effective completion of their mission.

"Let's get this pair inside. It'll be morning before they wake up. I'm tired and want a shower and some food. We'll truss them up and deal with them after a few hours sleep."

Ten minutes later both sleeping bodies had been carried into the cabin.

"Tie them upright on these kitchen chairs, "said Brand.

Strachan seated each of them in a sturdy, armless chair and positioned them upright, tying their arms to beams on the wall as if they were to be crucified. Satisfied he looked at his handiwork. *How ironic,* he thought, *two people of God and here we are, presenting them as if they were to emulate Jesus on the cross! Still…it'll keep them safe until they wake up.*

Brand had looked round the cabin and had returned to witness Strachan's handiwork. The head of each captive lolled on their chest.

He shrugged. "Sensible I suppose. They'll breathe easily and they're immobilised."

An Icelandic summer sun allowed only a few hours of semi-darkness but Strachan and Brand slumbered in armchairs, guns in their laps awaiting the diminishing effects of the drugs on the two in clerical garb.

Brand awoke with a start as the nun began to regain consciousness, slowly raising her head and trying to make sense of her predicament.

"Ah, Miss Petrova. You are awake. I hope you slept well."

Brand's comment awoke Strachan. The nun screwed her eyes and attempted unsuccessfully to wipe some drool from her mouth on her wimple. She spoke slowly.

"Why have you done this and why am I tied in this position. Are you a religious fanatic?"

"Your name is Svetlana Petrova. Your accent gives you away as a Russian. You are a Russian agent and are responsible for the deaths of many others... including one on British soil. You are in the company of another agent and I would like you to tell me why this is so."

"My name, sir, is Sister Seraphim. I am a nun with the Little Sisters of the Poor in Keflavik and the person seated next to me is Father Anthony. He is a pastor in the Catholic Church in Reykjavik and a good man. Why you have done this is a mystery but no harm will come of it if you untie our bonds and free us."

Strachan looked nervously at Brand, who continued.

"Sister Seraphim, then. Have it your way, but I have no doubt as to your real identity," he said with a confidence that belied his doubt. "You will tell me more about you and your faith," he asked. "But first...your accent?"

"I am from Lithuania, sir. I am twenty-seven years old and have been sent to Iceland to work with the church in Reykjavik. I am a simple woman who is dedicated to worship our Lord, and to bring peace and the love of Jesus Christ the Redeemer. I have responsibilities to others. Vulnerable people who need the care and protection of the church." Her voice rose in anger. "You are making a mistake, sir. You must understand. I am not whoever you think I am."

Brand rose from his seat, stepped forward and stooped, the closer to position his face in addressing the indignant nun.

"Miss Petrova. I have another injection which I have placed in the refrigerator. It contains sodium pentathol. You will be aware of its effects. Most refer to it as the truth serum so your story will soon be tested." He paused, looking at the pretty face framed by the religious cowl. "You are a beautiful woman, Miss Petrova. It is difficult to believe that you have forsaken men for a life of poverty and service."

"You may not believe me, sir. But what I tell you is true."

Strachan interjected. "Would you like a cup of tea, Sister?"

Brand looked at Strachan as if he was something unpleasant he'd just discovered on the sole of his shoe and sighed.

"Mr. Strachan. Why don't you boil some water and we'll have some tea then? And while you're in the kitchen, could you bring me the carving knife from the cutlery drawer, please?"

"Carving knife?" repeated Strachan, wondering what use Brand had in mind.

"If you wouldn't mind."

"Miss Petrova…"

"I tell you, it's Sister Seraphim."

"Miss Petrova. You have a reputation of being a very dangerous woman indeed so you'll understand my need to be careful in dealing with you. However, let's test your vow of poverty. Soon enough we'll test your vow of silence."

Strachan returned with a carving knife as requested and handed it warily to Brand.

"Please forgive my manners, Miss Petrova, but Strachan here seems persuaded by your denials. Me? Not so."

Taking the knife, he approached the nun who recoiled back against the wall as far as her bindings would allow.

Strachan's nervousness revealed itself. "Steady there," he admonished Brand.

Lifting the nun's white wimple, Brand took the top of her black tunic in his left hand, and placed the blunt edge of the knife against her neck. Wordlessly, he started to cut at the habit using the serrated edge, careful not to cut any flesh until a tear of some four inches had been caused to her uniform below her throat. Placing the knife on a nearby table, he spoke to Strachan who looked nonplussed.

"I have some time ago forsaken pleasures of the flesh, Mr. Strachan. But with someone as beautiful as Miss Petrova here, sometimes interrogation has its benefits. Permit me to test a theory I have."

He took an end of the torn uniform in each hand and with a couple of quick movements, wrenched the garment twice... each tear rending the habit further and revealing more of the upper body of the nun.

Inspecting his work, he turned to Strachan.

"You see, Mr. Strachan, Sister Angela here who works with the Little Sisters of the Poor is wearing an apparently expensive piece of nether-wear. This does not auger well," he said, sarcastically.

Pulling her head forward, his hand reached down the back of her tunic and pulled her bra-strap upwards so he could read the name of the manufacturer. "Ah, Mr. Strachan, it appears that this garment is made of the finest silk by a skilled craftsperson called *Guia La Bruna*. Very expensive!"

He looked at her with his head on one side, pursing his lips as if affecting a staged sorrow.

"Now, Miss Petrova. Might we start again? Or do you wish to explain to me how a nun in the service of the poor might wear a garment that must cost an amount that would feed several families for a month? It did occur to me that while you may have made the effort to disguise yourself as you have, you would have seen no need to wear less expensive underwear. Your reputation for expensive tastes appears to have been your downfall."

"I am too embarrassed to respond to your silliness. I have taken vows," she spat, now with more venom in her eyes. "I am who I say I am. This garment is unremarkable and available at any high street shop. Sitting before you like this offends me and offends God. Please cover me up. I am a nun and expect to be treated with some respect. You!" She gestured at Strachan with her chin. "Would you be good enough to cover my front. You seem more of a gentleman than your friend."

Brand nodded his consent and Strachan lifted the torn edges of her habit and tried to place them together with little success as the two parts continually separated even when lightly weighted by the wimple. He looked at Brand helplessly.

"Leave her alone," said Brand. "I'm just about to give her another injection. She'll have other things to say rather than complaining about her expensive underwear being on show." He left the room to retrieve another syringe from the refrigerator.

Sister Seraphim realised that the chords restraining her right hand were slightly looser than the ones on the left. While Brand was out of the room and Strachan was busying himself with the preparation of a cup of tea, she wriggled and pulled at the ropes until she was confident that she now had the ability to slip her hand from the tether. For the moment she would maintain the illusion that she was immobilised as the tethers on her left hand continued to hold her fast.

Brand prepared the injection in the kitchen. Strachan watched carefully.

"I haven't seen this work before. I've heard contradictory reports."

"Our psychologists refer to this as *narcosynthesis*."

He inverted the hypodermic syringe and tapped it on the side to remove any air bubbles. "The administration of intravenous hypnotic medication like this can be used to obtain vital information but I accept that some of its efficacy lies in the fact that many of those subjected to its tender mercies believe in its effect and so do not try to resist."

"So does it work, Colonel?"

"A twenty milliliters injection of a 2.5% solution will cause unconsciousness within fifteen to thirty seconds, and will last from five to ten minutes. It really only weakens resolve, impairs judgment and increases the amount a person talks but that has great value and the person who takes the drug has no recollection what they said whilst under its influence. Now I fully expect Miss Petrova to be wise to this drug but she won't be able to resist its blandishments completely. She'll tell me what I want to know…and after she recovers, she won't know what she said and what she didn't."

"But Colonel, you have much more than twenty milliliters in the syringe."

"I'll be giving your Sister Seraphim a double doze and we'll need to repeat the process several times."

Both returned to find their priest still unconscious and their nun still angry.

"This is foolishness. It is a sin against God. I absolutely forbid you to do anything other than release me and Father Anthony."

"Regrettably, I cannot comply with your request, Miss Petrova. I will administer this drug. Mr. Strachan will sit over there against the wall with a gun and a notepad and I will ask you questions. Perhaps once this is over I will have to apologise to you. We will see."

He took hold of her left arm and positioned the hypodermic. "This will take effect in a few seconds. In the meantime, you might want to say a prayer."

CHAPTER FIFTEEN

Hassan pursed his lips as he removed his earpiece and took in the import of the phone conversation between Aswad and Spence. He was already prepared but would wait until the exchange took place. Some would die. That was regrettable as the Egyptians were religious brothers but they were expendable because of the greater need to overcome the infidels globally. He told himself that their death would be justified because they themselves dealt in death by selling drugs. However, Hassan was sufficiently insightful to appreciate that the real reason they would die would be to ensure that there were no witnesses to his theft of their dollars. Any infidels involved in the transaction would die anyway. He would see to that.

* * *

Spence made his way to the small room shared by Kyle and Bryson, entering it as they stood in continued contemplation of their predicament.

"Okay, boys. We're on the move. I just took a call from the Arabs and we do the swap at noon today in a place near Moratalla in Murcia. We need a plan."

"Bit late to start planning now, Cammy," said Bryson.

"Well, if you two hadn't decked all of my men, we might have been a bit better prepared."

"Fair point. What do you want us to do?"

"Well, you'll be responsible for the transfer. We're still short on detail at the minute. I'm just waiting for the boss to come back in. Once he's figured out things, we'll let you know. In the meantime, just sit tight and relax. Things'll get exciting soon enough!"

"Is the bar open?" asked Bryson hopefully, drawing a resigned shake of the head from Kyle and a look of astonishment from Spence who looked at his watch to confirm that he wasn't wrong in calculating that it was approaching dawn.

* * *

Perry drove his Mercedes back towards the Red Lion thinking all the way of how he might use the two SAS men in relieving the Egyptians of their drugs without the need to pay over the money. *I'll need to take advice from Cammy,* he thought. *The Arabs'll know where we live or could find out soon enough. If things go wrong they'd be sure to come after us. Do we play this one square?* He shook his head. He must be getting senile. The old Marcus Perry wouldn't have let the thought enter his head.

* * *

Kim drove slowly towards the Red Lion collecting her thoughts. In the rear seat of the Lexus, Susan and Liam ministered to one another. Unexpectedly, and despite her focus upon the way she'd need to play the show-down at the Red Lion, Kim felt a pang of jealousy. Why couldn't she have someone look after her the way these two lovebirds did? Quickly she admonished herself for her selfishness. *One day, my prince will come*, she reasoned. She slowed as they arrived at the bar.

"Okay, you two need to stay here. I go in alone."

Liam began to protest but was silenced by Kim. "Look Liam. I'm local. I know these people. Please don't be concerned about me. You and Susan will just complicate things. I don't need them realising that the man who caused their recent misery has just reappeared in their bar."

"But Kim…"

"Look…a compromise. If I don't walk out of there unharmed in ten minutes…make it fifteen, you have my permission to call the police. But don't worry. I'm no hero and wouldn't be going in here if I didn't know exactly how I was going to get back out untouched by these idiots."

"You know how you'll escape?"

"I won't need to escape…I have certain guarantees because of who I know." She took a deep breath and opened the door of the Lexus…

"Here goes nothing!"

* * *

Marcus Perry turned off the ignition key having parked his Merc in the rear alleyway behind his bar and entered

176

through the back door. Turning lights on, he walked along the narrow corridor towards a conversation he heard just ahead.

Spence, Kyle and Bryson sat in the small meeting room chatting when Perry arrived.

"Okay, Cammy. Just you and me. In the back bar." He didn't acknowledge the two SAS men as he and his lieutenant left to discuss the phone call.

Bryson nursed three fingers of whisky brought to him earlier by a modestly surprised Spence.

"Gus, we need to watch our step here. This is all happening very fast. There won't be any prep. No rehearsal. All sorts of dangers in this, pal."

"Yeah. Let's wait to hear what they have to say. For all we know, they might not want us involved."

"Sounds like they've little option. Plus, they'll want us to take any risks that are going. We need to get a hold of our four by four from the hotel and one way or another we need to get our kitbags. I'd rather use our own weaponry if push comes to shove. God only knows what kind of stuff they have here."

Kyle nodded his agreement. "And let's remember…as well as uncovering the Colonel's Russian, our main objective is to capture these containers of drugs and hold them unopened until Brand takes them off our hands so we'll need to be on our toes when the action starts because we're going to have these Arab boys as well as Perry's men after us."

* * *

Kim walked towards the Red Lion and paused at a front door she hadn't crossed in years. As ever, the door was unlocked given the constant to-ing and fro-ing of people at all times of the day and night. Cautiously, she opened the door and entered a darkened bar, listening for voices. Slowly, Kim moved between tables upon which had been placed inverted chairs, clearing floor space that would be mopped clean early that morning. A thin line of light was visible beneath the door leading to the rear of the building. Kim placed her ear to the door and listened for some moments to muffled conversation before opening the door gradually and entering the corridor.

One door lay open to a room within which she heard familiar voices. Gus and Jack sat at a table, oblivious to her presence.

"Hi boys. Still drinking?"

Gus leapt to his feat. "*Kim*! What are you doing here? How did you get off the Ventura?"

"I thought you two couldn't keep out of trouble so I figured I'd better step in and help you."

"Kim, you don't understand...." said Kyle.

"Really? Last time I saw you two you were being taken off my boat with guns pointed at you."

"Yes but...."

"What the fack's going on 'ere?" A confused and angry Marcus Perry marched out of the rear bar upon hearing a woman's voice in his establishment.

Kim turned to face the enquiry. "Hi Dad. Long time no see."

Perry stopped as if frozen and Spence careered into his back. "Kimberly...what...wha'..."

He recovered a measure of his composure and his face reddened.

"You disappear for years and then show up at some ungodly hour in the back room of my pub!"

Kim's earlier instruction to herself dissipated immediately as she came face to face with her father and old enmities returned.

"I didn't disappear. I left. I left after mother died because you were responsible for her death. You and your criminal friends."

"I thought you was in Malta."

"I was. But now I'm here and I want to know what you're up to with Jack and Gus. There'd better not be any nonsense going on here because Gus and I are in love and you'd better not mess with my boyfriend!"

Kyle and Bryson, who had been watching the interaction between father and daughter with their jaws open, turned to each other and exchanged a glance that screamed, *what have we gotten ourselves into?*

Perry turned his gaze on Kyle who smiled and shrugged his shoulders, trying to buy time until he figured out how best to deal with a situation.

Perry had enjoyed a successful criminal career partly because he saw a conspiracy where none existed...and had acted on his hunches. "You!" He pointed at Kyle. "D'you think I'm stupid? D'you think I'm not up to your little games? You knew she was my daughter all along, didn'tcha?"

"We're here because your men brought us here at gunpoint. We were fast asleep when we were taken. Doesn't sound like much of a planned introduction if you ask me," said Kyle.

Perry's ire was quelled somewhat but still he nursed some harsh words for his daughter.

"You're no daughter of mine. You drift out of my life for years and then you come back into it just to try to bugger up my business interests. This boyfriend of yours owes me a bit of work and he'd better deliver on it or boyfriend or no boyfriend, he'll suffer the consequences."

"He walks out of here with me..."

"No he doesn't..."

Kyle got to his feet and spread his arms, as if separating the combatants.

"Woah, there….calm down… calm down!" He looked at Kim. "Listen, darling"…he enunciated the affectionate *soubriquet* in a staged manner…" I *will* walk out with you, but only to collect some tools that we have back on the boat in our kitbags. Jack will stay here. We do have a small piece of work with your dad. It isn't dangerous or illegal," he lied…"but it pays well and we've given our word. So once you two have said your piece, we can get on our way."

He turned to Spence who seemed as bewildered as Kyle and Bryson.

"That okay with you guys? We have some specialised equipment. I'll be back in a couple of hours and you and Jack can discuss arrangements."

Perry wasn't finished with his daughter.

"If you leave this place right now, you walk out of my life forever."

"I walk out of *your* life? You send me to boarding school for my entire childhood, then you bring me over here and never so much as give mother and I the time of day. You're never out of court, always in your pub, always in the papers, never home. I wasn't allowed to have friends. University was out of the question and if it wasn't for mother looking after my interests, I'd never had had the resources to create my sailing business."

"That bitch stole my fackin' money. Your mother. She was meant to be looking after my cash and she passed on to you. That was *my* money," he shouted.

"My mother passed her money on legally after her death. If you'd got it you'd have spent it on pursuing your career as a two-bit gangster. You're nothing but trouble and I never want to see you again. You've never been a father to me and tonight has just reminded me what a hateful man you are."

Kim turned on her heel, gesturing to Kyle. "Well, are you coming?"

"Be right there, dearest." He turned to Perry. "Sorry if this complicates things a bit. But don't worry. I'll pick up the tools Jack and I need and I'll be back straight away. I'll bring your men back from the boat. Jack will stay to explain and discuss things further."

Perry looked unconvinced. Kyle put his hand on his shoulder and spoke quietly.

"Look, we need this work. I'll be back immediately I've picked up our stuff on your daughter's boat."

"My boat, more like," said Perry reminding himself of the itch he was scratching.

Spence intervened. "It'll be okay, boss. Makes sense to me."

Perry looked long and hard at every occupant in the room before coming to his decision.

"Don't be long," he growled.

Kyle placed his arm around Kim. "Let's go, sweetheart!" They walked from the room, through the bar and into the street where Kim signaled the direction of the Lexus within which sat an increasingly agitated Liam and Susan counting down the minutes before they intended phoning the police.

***

"There's Kim now," said Liam...."and Gus is with her."

Kim swung into the driver's seat and Gus moved beside her in front. He turned to face Liam and Susan, still seated in the rear, silently awaiting an update.

"Well, sweet-pea, will you tell them the good news or will I?"

"Huh?" said Liam.

"Kim and I are lovers. We're an item. Boyfriend and girlfriend."

"Huh?" said Liam.

Kim defended her actions. "I had to say something to rescue Gus. It was the first thing that came into my mind."

"Kim, you can't treat a man like that, I thought you were serious," smiled Gus. "You've broken my heart."

Susan and Liam looked at one another. "Huh?" asked Liam.

Kim decided to clear things up.

"That man Marcus Perry who bosses those thugs who beat you up...who sent them on board and kidnapped you three... who left Susan and I to the tender mercies of his men...well, he's my father."

"Huh?" said Liam and Susan together.

"I didn't know until the old man who was guarding me let it slip. I thought I could use my relationship with my father to have Gus and Jack released but it appears that they're both up to their necks in whatever mischief my father's planning. I haven't seen my father in years because he's a very bad man. He was a very bad father and he hasn't changed." She turned to Kyle. "Gus, please have nothing to do with him. He'll only get you into trouble. Serious trouble. You don't know him like I do."

Kyle smiled at the rear seats. "You guys any clearer?"

"A bit," said Liam, then addressing his understanding to Kim, "So let me see if I've got this...you tried to rescue Jack and Gus from a situation they didn't want rescued from?...and your father is the gangster boss who duffed me up?...and you and Gus and now headlong in love?"

"Not the last bit," said Kim. "In fact, what little respect I had for him goes south if he returns to the Red Lion."

Addressing Kyle now, she exclaimed, "I'll never speak with you again."

"I thought you said your mother and father were dead," said Kyle.

"I said they were *gone*, not dead, but my father has been dead to me since my mother passed away. He as good as pulled the trigger. Even today I still use her maiden name, 'Williams' as opposed to 'Perry'."

Kyle turned back to the task in hand. "Take a left here," he directed.

Kim pulled up outside Kyle's hotel where his black Landrover was parked. Moments later the Landrover followed the Lexus out of the car park and on towards Puerto Banus where Kim used her radio to call the Ventura back into port.

* * *

Half an hour later, Kyle had checked and removed both kitbags, placed them in his vehicle and was helping old Eddie Crompton and his two colleagues off the Ventura and into the Landrover.

Kim had had time to mellow rather. She stepped from the boat, placed her hand on Kyle's arm and spoke quietly to him.

"Listen, Gus. I'm sorry you had to witness me and my father going at it. He really knows how to upset me and I perhaps said things I didn't mean but please be careful.

If this is a one-off task you're engaged in and if it's as innocent as you say, I'd love you to come back and spend some time on board. You're a lovely man and I know that Liam and Susan would enjoy your company." She swallowed hard. "However, if you prefer the company of people like my father, then it's better if I never see you again."

Kyle smiled. "Half an hour ago you were my best girl."

Kim laughed and squeezed his arm. "I'm sorry. I didn't mean…"

"Don't apologise." He took Kim's hand from his arm and held it. "Be sure I'll be back…and I'll bring that big lump Jack with me if there's still strong drink on board." He nodded at the Harbourmaster's building. "Perhaps you'll arrange for them to call you at sea if you're out and about with the Brannigans and we need to contact you?"

"Sure. Take very good care of yourself, Gus Kyle. You come back and see us."

Susan and Liam appeared on the short gangplank and echoed Kim's sentiments.

"Yeah, come back on board once you've finished your business," said Liam.

Kim qualified the offer. "Unless you're being chased by the police…."

Kyle ignored Kim's comment and smiling, spoke directly to Liam.

"Keep the girls' pistols safe in the wheelhouse. You never know if you'll need them over the next few days...now give us a hug in case I don't make it back in one piece..."

They embraced and as they did, Kyle spoke softly into Brannigan's ear.

"Might need your help to get out of this, Liam. I don't want to upset the girls unnecessarily but this is likely to go sour quite quickly and these guys will be looking for us and the Ventura so keep it out at sea...but not so far that we can't call you in to help us. Can I count on you telling Kim to bring the Ventura back here if we need help to get away from this place?"

Still embracing, Liam responded in an equally low tone.

"We won't travel far. We'll be here for you when you call. Be careful."

Kim and Susan watched the men hugging and exchanged a look. Each thought identically. *Isn't it good to see men show their feminine side now and again?*

Waving goodbye, Kyle drove the Landrover slowly off the dock and headed towards Marbella.

As the Ventura disappeared from view, old Eddie turned conspiratorially to his three fellow occupants. "I 'ad them two women naked in the bedroom on the boat.

Naked as jaybirds they was. Both of 'em stripped off.
Naked as the day they was born. Beautiful women they
was. Naked you know...naked...In the nude?"

Eddie's two colleagues smiled their disbelief and
ridiculed him as an old fool the entire journey. As they
pulled up behind the Red Lion, Eddie was still
pontificating. "I tell you...naked they was...naked." He
looked at his two cronies to test if there was belief in
their eyes.

There wasn't.

"....as a jaybird," he insisted, increasingly lamely.

Gus smiled. Whatever had happened on board, it had
certainly made old Eddie very happy.

CHAPTER SIXTEEN

Coordinated Universal Time places Iceland and Spain only an hour apart, so the morning broke roughly at the same time in these two very different locations. In the Icelandic mountains near Storidalur, another drizzle greyed the horizon of the safe house and its near view was obscured intermittently by steam from a small geyser. It still rained.

In Spain the sun rose strongly, bestowing it's warmth on parched earth.

As Perry, Spence, Kyle and Bryson discussed how best they might relieve the Egyptians of their consignment, Colonel Brand and Strachan prepared to question their two clerics, despite the priest still being unconscious.

Some minutes earlier, Brand had injected the nun with sodium pentathol and had waited briefly for it to decrease her higher cortical brain functioning. Gazing increasingly apprehensively at the still unconscious priest bound next to the nun, he'd decided that a further injection would be unwise until he'd recovered from the first. He checked his pulse and breathing and decided that all was well but that he'd let him surface in his own time.

Sister Seraphim was now, to an ill-informed observer, very drunk. She mumbled incoherently, her head rolled and her eyes couldn't focus. Brand hadn't yet engaged with her, preferring to allow her to surrender completely to the narcotic before quizzing her. Certainly, if she was Svetlana Petrova, she more than lived up to her reputation as one of life's beauties. If she was a nun, she was a loss to the many men whose heads must have turned in disbelief when a woman of the cloth walked by, her pretty face framed in a religious wimple. *I'll find out which is which soon enough now,* thought Brand.

Settling down in front of her, he checked that Strachan was armed both with his Walther PPK and a notepad. This woman was not to be underestimated. He began speaking to her to rouse her from the inner world she'd now inhabited.

"Come now...tell me your name...tell me your name, young lady." He waited while she tried unsuccessfully to formulate a response and tried again. "Is your name Svetlana?"

Again there was no coherent communication from her. *Perhaps the doze was too strong,* he reflected.

Gradually, he managed to tease some unimportant information from her and was boosted in his appraisal when she appeared to mouth the words 'St Petersburg' in her mumblings about her antecedents. *Just as per the file alleging an involvement with the FSS,* he thought. *Not Lithuania as she'd said earlier.*

Encouraged, he continued his ponderous and repetitious quizzing. Brand was no expert in the use of sodium pentathol and found himself in receipt of apparently contradictory answers as Strachan's notepad showed her responding both to Sister Seraphim as well as Svetlana Petrova; the Catholic Church as well as the FSS. Further probing elicited a positive response when Brand asked her about any association she had with England. A poorly enunciated mouthing appeared to suggest the word 'Cambridge' although Brand had been careful not to be specific in his questioning. Later she began to laugh and seemed to speak of 'Mandarin' whilst lurching from subject to subject prompting Brand to ask questions about Chinese interests to no avail. Her stream of consciousness was punctuated intermittently by imprecations and accusations, laughter and tears and it proved difficult to nail any precise information that would lead them to a convincing assessment although in the midst of her meanderings both Brand and Strachan started at her mention of a scorpion in Spain. Strachan scribbled furiously.

Standing, Brand indicated to Strachan that they might take a break. "Tea for us and water for our friend here?"

Strachan laid his notepad on the table and rose.

"I'm pretty sure she's our gal," said Brand. But give her some water and let her come round. We'll try again later."

Water and the passing of time helped the nun swim to the surface of her consciousness and she began to recover her sense of self, if only slightly. As the effects of the barbiturate wore off, she remembered the bonds were loose on her right hand. Brand and Strachan had left to converse in the kitchen. Carefully, if with some difficulty, she slipped her hand from the rope binding her right hand and replaced her arm so as to conceal her actions.

Strachan returned and adjusted the Walther in his waistband to make himself more comfortable. He sat again in his seat and lifted his notepad in preparation for a second session. Brand busied himself at the refrigerator in the kitchen assembling the hypodermic syringe.

Waiting for the Colonel, Strachan looked disinterestedly at a map of Iceland positioned on the wall to his left. That was all the time Sister Seraphim needed. She took a breath then reached quickly beneath her ankle-length tunic and withdrew a throwing knife from a sheath she always carried attached to her lower right limb. Reaching behind her, in one continuous sweeping movement, she hurled the knife in a blur at Strachan.

A movement alerted him to something untoward on his right hand side, but too late he appreciated the danger and the knife buried itself in his neck, severing his jugular vein. His carotid artery was also ruptured causing an air embolism which extinguished his life quicker than would have been the case had he just bled to death. He died silently.

Her right hand freed, Petrova leant forward and grabbed the kitchen knife placed on the table earlier by Strachan. Again in one movement she turned to her right and drew it deep across the neck of the sleeping priest, cutting his throat. Blood spilled down his chest and he slumped further forward.

Quickly, Petrova started to slice at the ropes binding her left hand. The carving knife was sharp and it made good progress as she slashed at the rope at her wrist. In her haste she drew a large and wounding cut along her left wrist and blood flowed freely. Ignoring it, she severed the binding at last and moved across to pick up Strachan's pistol from his waistband. Removing it she stood erect to find Brand facing her with his gun pointing directly at her.

"Why, Sister Seraphim, what were you taught as a Noviciate? It's almost as if you are trained in the arts of martial combat. I was right to treat you warily."

He gestured with his gun. "Place the gun back on the table. I have a pistol pointed directly at you. You have been under the influence of various drugs and are bleeding quite freely. On the other hand, I have just had a quite refreshing cup of tea and am perfectly alert. If you try to shoot me you will die before you raise the gun."

Petrova stood with her pistol pointed at the floor but made no attempt to drop it.

Brand continued. "I was very interested in what you had to say, Svetlana. You confessed to the murder in Cambridge," he lied.

Petrova shrugged.

RON CULLEY

He tested her recollection further. "You also told me all about the Mandarin".

"Did I now?"

"Yes, you did. And the Scorpion. I was most interested. But why did you kill your colleague? Might he have told me more of what I wanted to know about Mandarin once I injected him?"

"He was only involved for the money. He was a traitor to his homeland." She looked at the dead man. "His job has been done. He would only have been a liability."

"Well, you have a choice, Svetlana. There is no need for you to die here. I can take you home to Britain and you can talk to us more about Mandarin, Scorpion and Cambridge. Perhaps other matters as well. But it would be a folly to try to raise that gun. I give you perhaps a five per cent chance of making it. Perhaps my gun would jam. Perhaps the speed of youth would allow you to raise, point and shoot faster than I could pull the trigger. But you're impaired mentally and physically. Don't be silly. Put your gun on the table."

Petrova nodded her acquiescence. "Of course you are correct. I am of course disappointed that matters have ended as they have but I see I have no choice but to do as you ask."

She finished speaking. Her face contorted and utilising every muscle and sinew in her slight frame, she attempted to move with every ounce of speed her body possessed to hoist the gun to a firing position. All that moved in Brand's body was his right index finger. Petrova fell to the ground, her forehead penetrated by a single shot from Brand's gun before her right arm was able to be extended.

"*Da svidaniya*, Ms. Petrova. Goodbye!" He lowered his gun arm. "I'll see you in hell soon enough."

Brand stood in the centre of the room and slowly contemplated the carnage in complete silence. Nothing stirred. For a moment, the smell of cordite obliterated the all-present smell of Icelandic sulphur. There was no point in testing the possibility of any one of the three being alive. It was plain to see that all of their wounds were mortal.

He returned to the kitchen but this time poured himself a glass of brandy to steady himself. It had been a while since he'd gambled with his life. He'd presumed that those days were behind him. These days he was a controller of men and women...

He sipped his brandy thoughtfully. *What might she have been on about. A Mandarin? Did she mean a Chinese connection? A senior civil servant? Have we a spy in the civil service,* he mulled. *Surely she couldn't have been referring to bloody fruit? And what about 'Scorpion'? Can she be referring to the man we know by that name...or a scorpion in Spain...? Who was Brother Farrokh?*

He walked back through to the room and picked up Strachan's notepad, reading and re-reading his notes to see if they prompted anything. Finishing his brandy, his thoughts turned to the three corpses in front of him.

Returning to the kitchen, he opened the door of the pantry and took some cellotape and four cotton buds from the first aid cabinet and returned to the bodies. Carefully, he cut some tape and pressed the non-adhesive side against each of the Russians' right forefinger and, on doing this, taped each to a piece of card that he then inserted in an envelope. Reaching into his inside pocket, he took out a pen and wrote Petrova's name on one envelope and Kalinowski's on the other. Before sealing the envelopes, he inserted the swabs in each Russian mouth, gathering saliva so as to permit DNA testing upon his return back to London. A third and fourth swab took blood samples. Moving back to a room next door where he had left his briefcase, he removed a micro-camera and returned to take photographs of the three bodies.

Packing the camera and envelopes in his briefcase, he turned to the bodies again. He'd have to get rid of the two foreigners. Deniability was possible as no one knew they'd been taken...but Strachan? He wasn't married. *Lived alone,* Brand reminded himself.

Brand made a decision. He returned to the kitchen and poured himself another drink. A stiff one. Sipping half of it in one gulp, ignoring the high quality of the brandy, he walked back to the wall map Strachan had been reading just before his death. A pin with a red head marked the location of the safe house. *Not very safe for those three,* thought Brand unsentimentally as he attempted to figure out the local topography. *Hmm, we're not too far from the glacier at Eyjafjallajökull; however, you bloody pronounce that,* he mused.

He finished his brandy in a second gulp. He'd need to be wary of enthusiastic tourists who'd strayed from more usual access points but if he was careful...?

Brand stepped from the house and opened the door to a garage within which was shelve upon shelve of junk accumulated over years by earlier occupants. A few minutes searching brought him several large sacks used for earlier purposes which escaped him for the moment. A return journey brought twine.

He'd need to send in some people to clean the place up, he figured as he set about wrapping the bodies in sacking and tying them. *What a bloody mess,* he thought.

It took him an hour but eventually he had three wrapped corpses. Although he didn't work out, Brand was a naturally fit man but it took him some time and no little effort to drag the three bodies to the car. Strachan tested him most.

Taking one final look round the house he lifted both guns and locked the door securely after closing all of the curtains. It wouldn't do for some stray hiker to look in and see walls covered in blood. He'd have people up in jig-time once he disposed of the bodies.

An hour later, Brand stood over one of nature's great sights...a glacier. Moving only at a pace measurable in metres over years, nonetheless the incredible grinding and powerful surging of the ice would reduce the three bodies to mere molecules of carbon and calcium. They would never be found and if they were, they'd never be identified.

Checking to ensure once again that he wasn't being observed, he heaved and pulled at the bodies and one after the other, slid them into a convenient crevasse in the glacier. They each plummeted into the depths of the glacier and into a frozen oblivion.

Chapter Seventeen

Hassan had been following some distance behind the pick-up since they'd headed out towards the agreed rendezvous. They will be nervous, he thought so he kept his distance. It was always easier following someone when there were several parties involved so each could spell the other without attracting attention. He'd have to be careful.

He knew that the meet was scheduled for noon and that Aswad had agreed that only two persons, one a chemist, from the buyers and one from the seller's side would be present...unarmed. He also knew that the four Egyptians had plotted to arrive slightly early in order that three of them might secrete themselves closely to act as protectors of their representative. But they only had handguns. They hadn't visited the clearing they'd chosen for the exchange. For all they knew it was a popular picnic spot. It appeared that there was only one road in and the same road out...no other means of escape. Amateurs! These arrangements suited him. He'd already planned to substitute himself for the Egyptians prior to the handover. It was essential that he retained the ricin but important that he secured the three million pounds that the buyers would bring. He had to anticipate that the buyers would attempt to ensure their own safety and would also try to secure the site. He'd considered, and dismissed, the idea of removing the ricin at the meeting site having decided that it was too open to compromise. He'd have to take care of matters in advance and because of the time they'd set out, he wouldn't have too much time to eliminate the Egyptians before noon. If they didn't get a move on, they'd be late.

Hassan had consulted the map of Murcia many times in planning the retrieval of the ricin and the acquisition of the money and had determined that the roads network they were using would be too busy almost all the way to the quiet dust road they'd need to take for the last mile. He'd stop them there.

* * *

Having been up all night, Spence, Kyle and Bryson were tired. Before leaving town that morning, they'd been joined by a small man with horn-rimmed glasses. His name was Bruno Martinez de Oz who was a chemist in the employ of Perry. He was unused to excitement of the type he was beginning to anticipate but had been promised by Spence that his only task would be to test the purity of the drugs and ensure that there hadn't been any adulteration.

Spence drove Kyle's Landrover despite his fatigue. Either Kyle or Bryson would have been better equipped, having been used quite often to pulling long, two day shifts without sleep. Nevertheless, it suited them that Spence insisted on driving. They could rest or get some shut-eye.

Earlier, they'd decided that Kyle would make the swap in the company of the chemist and that Bryson, using his faithful Barrett's M82 sniper's rifle, would ride shotgun, protecting his pal from a distance. Spence was there to ensure no foul play.

"I've always wondered what three million quid would look like up close," said Kyle who was in the passenger's seat.

"Takes up a bit of space, eh? I've had to fit a million in a suitcase before but that was using £20 notes. Given all the denominations and differing currencies, we had to use six cases and you lifted then into the car so although they're pretty heavy, you'll have no problems...but of course we hope that it won't come to that. You see off the Arab and Jack here takes out anyone else who tries to interfere. We keep the money and the drugs and you and Jack are up ten grand each for a morning's work."

Martinez de Oz sat in the rear of the car looking straight ahead and becoming ever more apprehensive about the straightforward nature of his task.

The three million pounds sterling, as was agreed as an amount with the Egyptians, was comprised of various denominations of major currencies including Sterling, Dollars, Euros, even Japanese Yen and Thai Baht...it didn't matter to the Egyptians. All that mattered was that the money was in full amount, that it was in small denominations and in various currencies so as to permit easier investment.

That arrangement proved easy for Perry as currency poured in to his coffers from all corners of the globe as a consequence of the world-wide popularity of his narcotics trade. One problem it did represent was the fact that it was a product that was open to theft by better armed adversaries…or by confiscation by the police.

"Your pal good with that gun?" asked Spence.

"He's the best in the business. That rifle has taken many people out from more than a mile away."

Spence whistled approvingly. Martinez de Oz shifted uncomfortably in his seat.

"He can routinely hit a five inch square disc from that distance and if needs be, he can take out a squad of guys before they hear the shot being fired. Don't worry. If Jack's on the rifle, and not on the bottle, there isn't anyone better. I've depended on him many times in battle and he's exceptional."

"Well, let's hope those early morning whiskies haven't dulled his aim this morning. You might have cause to be grateful for his sharp-shooting today."

"Trust me. Jack's aim improves up to a point when he's had a few. Now, I'll grant you that on the odd occasion when he's had one too many, it does reduce his aim a smidgen. But the few glasses he's enjoyed over the last few hours wouldn't register on my alcohol alert."

"Then he must have some appetite."

"Aye, he does that," said Kyle.

The journey towards the mountainous area near the small town of Moratalla in Murcia continued, as did the idle banter between Kyle and Spence. Bryson slept.

After a while, Kyle, who was consulting a map, announced, "Shortly there's a small road up ahead on the left. Perhaps three hundred metres. If you pull in there, you and Jack can get off and walk to a raised copse where you should be able to see everything that comes up the road to the meeting place."

He turned in his seat. "Jack, we're here!"

Bryson awoke rubbing his eyes. "Christ, I could do with a drink."

Kyle and Spence exchanged glances.

Nice one, Jack! thought Kyle.

At the road end, Spence pulled over and he and Bryson left the car. Bryson took his rifle from the back of the Landrover and lifted a box of cartridges. He also lifted one of his hunting knives but Spence shook his head.

"Sorry, Jack. You use the rifle but the only other weapons are being carried by me. There's no honour among us thieves here. I'm afraid I only trust you guys so far. I'll have a gun pointed at your head all the way through this."

"As long as we know where we stand," said Bryson, throwing the knife back on top of his kitbag.

Spence directed his next comments at Kyle who had seated himself behind the driving wheel.

"And I want you to know that if you try to double-cross us, there won't be a log cabin in the darkest, most remote part of the Amazonian forest that you'll be safe in. We'll hunt you down wherever you run and hide. So let's play it sensible. Just you get the drugs without paying for them and we're all happy."

Bryson moved to the open window where Kyle's left arm rested.

"Okay, Gus. We'll move on up this track. Remember, you two wait here until we're in place. Give us five minutes. When we're at the copse, I'll test the microphone and earpiece. We wait until these drugs boys arrive. When you hear me coming through in your ear-piece giving you the go-ahead, you make your way up and along the dirt track to the clearing. I'll watch you all the way through the gun's telescopic sights and let you know that all's well. You're unarmed, so leave the other guy to me. I'll take care of him and you load the six suitcases into their vehicle and return here with the money and the drugs to pick me and Cammy up."

"Sounds like a plan," said Gus. "See you when it's over."

Spence and Bryson turned and walked up the track leaving Kyle awaiting their further contact.

"You okay?" asked Kyle of the small chemist in the rear seat.

"*Sí señor.*"

Kyle turned back, rested his hands on the steering wheel and sighed. *Hope he's good as a chemist because he's not going to be much help if there's a fire-fight!*

* * *

Farrokh Hassan had followed the four Egyptians from their base and knew from his earlier study of the journey he'd anticipated they'd make that they were close to their destination. As the pick-up slowed at the end of the track leading to the meeting place, Hassan readied himself.

Their pick-up moved slowly along the single track dirt road kicking up dust which, thought Hassan, must obscure their ability to see behind them. He checked his watch and noticed that they had arrived half an hour earlier than agreed. Taking a beat to appreciate the various significances of this, he eased his foot off the clutch and followed them along the track once they'd turned the first corner.

Up on a hill almost half a mile away, Bryson looked through the highly magnified telescopic sights of his Barrett. He spoke to Kyle via his radio as he adjusted the optics on his rifle.

"Okay, Gus...there's a red Dodge pick-up on the track. Stay put and I'll check that everything's *kosher* before we move.

Almost as he finished speaking he saw Hassan's Mercedes follow on behind.

"As you were, Gus. There's a second vehicle. This wasn't in the script. Let's just see what's what."

Hassan closed on the pick-up and, after trailing it for a couple of hundred metres, waited until it started down a small hill then started flashing his lights and sounding his horn.

In the pick-up there was consternation.

"Is it the police, brother?" asked Aswad.

"I can't tell. It might be the infidels or it might be just a farmer. Stop the car and we will see. Everyone must be very careful," he instructed.

Bryson witnessed the events unfolding from his eerie up on the hill.

"The pick-up's stopped, Gus. They're getting out of the vehicle."

In his car, Hassan braked and sat, waiting on a move by the Egyptians.

As the dust settled, four figures appeared; two at either side of the pick-up. Hassan saw that they were each carrying a revolver but that they were each trying to conceal it behind their back.

He brought the palms of his hands together signifying respect. "*Salaam!*" he mouthed as the four couriers walked up the hill towards his car. He smiled his mouthings again..."*Salaam.*"

The four men looked anxiously at a smiling Hassan through his windshield. They scrutinised the terrain surrounding the two vehicles. They were frightened men but they knew they had to make sense of this incident. Was this a trap or an innocent request for assistance by a local farmer or hillwalker?

As the men approached Hassan's car, they filed onto the twin ruts created by vehicle use over the years and continued to close on the still smiling driver, their curiosity wrestling for superiority over their disquiet.

Bryson's right eye tracked their every move as he maintained a rolling commentary listened to anxiously by Spence and by Kyle over the radio ear-piece connection.

Suddenly the smile disappeared from Hassan's face and he gunned the accelerator, moving the car forward with great velocity, scattering the four men like skittles. None were mortally injured but all were shocked and disorientated by being mown down. They lay in pain at each side of the track attempting to collect their sensibilities, pick up their guns and scramble to their feet.

The Steyr Tactical Machine Pistol is a 9mm blowback-operated, rotating-barrel machine pistol that can fire eight hundred rounds a minute. Hassan held one in his right hand. Before any one of the four injured men managed to stand erect, four bursts of gunfire tore through each of their bodies leaving them savaged and bloodied….and quite dead.

"Okay, Gus, our man in the car has just taken out the four guys in the pick-up. He's armed with what looks like a machine pistol. Now we need to wait and see if he's stealing the drugs or trading with us. You might want to get ready to follow him if he takes off. He's driving a green Mercedes 230 SLK Kompressor."

While Bryson was transmitting this information, Hassan pulled each of the dead men into the undergrowth next to the track and concealed them in the brush. Watched all the while through the Barrett's telescopic sights, he then returned to his Mercedes and reversed it into the same undergrowth, in the process driving over two of the men he'd just shot. Taking it back into bushes and concealing it from the dirt track, he walked towards the pick-up and, collecting his machine pistol as well as the guns left on the verge by the four deceased, sat himself in the driving seat of the Dodge.

"Just shoot him," said Spence becoming agitated.

"Not loaded yet, remember?" said Bryson. "Anyway, we wait a moment."

The red pick-up slowly continued its journey until it reached the clearing on the map earlier agreed. After a few moments, Hassan got out and put a surgical mask over his lower face and placed a pair of tight fitting industrial goggles over his eyes. Watched closely by Bryson, he pulled on a pair of rubber gloves and strolled round to the rear of the vehicle. Gingerly, he lifted the tarpaulin and checked that the consignment was as he expected it. Satisfied, he replaced the tarp, pulled down all of his protective coverings onto his neck, sucked a cigarette from a pack with his lips and lit it. Inhaling deeply, he allowed the smoke to escape from between his yellow teeth with a *hissss*.

Bryson relayed all of this to the three listeners as it happened. Kyle turned to Martinez de Oz.

"Why would someone wear protective covering on their face and hands to inspect a load of heroin?"

The chemist was now quite anxious. "Perhaps *señor*, he does not know what he has in the vehicle?"

"Unlikely. Any other explanation?"

"Then he might imagine that it is a substance that would harm him if he breathed it, touched it or allowed it to enter his body through his eyes."

"So what could it be?"

"*Señor*, I cannot tell if it is a gas, powder or liquid. It might be many things. But it appears dangerous."

"Sounds a reasonable deduction, Mr. Chemist."

Kyle thought through his options.

"Okay, Jack. He's waiting for us at the clearing?"

"Roger that, Gus."

"Okay!" Kyle launched into the Glasgow vernacular. "Me and wee Tam here will take a wander up and see him."

"I'll be watching every step. Just remember, he didn't shoot these four guys just so he could hand you over a fortune in whatever he has on that pick-up. Are you armed?"

"A revolver, just in case." So saying, he stuck one of Perry's guns in his waistband at his spine.

Bryson turned to Spence up on the hill. "Please sir, can I load my gun now?" he asked.

Spence handed him a single shell.

"What's this? The magazine'll take ten."

"One round only. If there were two, the second one might be for me."

"Listen Cammy, me and Gus are not your common or garden hoodlums. If we strike a deal, we strike a deal!" said Bryson, knowing he intended reversing that arrangement as soon as humanly possible.

"Maybe so, but I don't know you well enough to trust you with my life. One bullet! By all accounts you're good enough. That's all you'll need."

Bryson turned to see Kyle closing in on the clearing. Time was short. "Shit!" he exclaimed, "Give it here." So saying, he loaded round into the rifle and adjusted the US Optics telescopic sights until he was satisfied.

Spence threw the box of cartridges behind him at a distance from Bryson.

Through the eye-sight Bryson saw Kyle and Martinez de Oz drive up the track, the Landrover producing a lot of dust as had the pick-up.

Hassan saw the dust cloud too and moved to place his machine pistol in the rear of the pick-up next to the cartons. Bryson informed Kyle immediately. "He's tooled up. Looks like a machine pistol. Hidden it in the rear of the vehicle."

"Roger that."

A few minutes elapsed while Kyle drove the distance to the clearing. On seeing him entering, Hassan repeated the manoeuvre he deployed with the four Egyptians; placing his palms of his hands together and smiling the words, "*Salaam...salaam*," as if welcoming an old friend in peace.

Kyle drew the Landrover to a halt and waved at Hassan, acknowledging him. He and the chemist stepped out into the sunshine and walked towards the pick-up but stopped, remaining some distance from the still smiling Hassan.

"My friend. It is good to meet you after all we talked on the phone," lied Kyle.

"And it is good to meet you my friend. Did you bring the money? I want to finish things quickly. There may be people about. Let us not delay too long."

"We can't talk about the money until we test the goods. My friend here can tell us quickly that everything is in order then I will explain about the money."

Hassan shouted. "But you must have the money with you. That was our arrangement."

"First we test the goods," smiled Kyle. He nodded to Martinez de Oz and gestured towards the pick-up. The chemist walked awkwardly towards Hassan and the rear of the Dodge.

As he approached, Hassan grabbed him round the neck in an arm-lock, directing venom towards Kyle in a language Kyle assumed was Arabic. From his right hand pocket Hassan removed a small plastic bag and held it under his captive's chin.

"We have an arrangement," screamed Hassan. "Where is the money."

"Please," smiled Kyle. "Do you think I would meet with a man I have never met before and put myself in a position of having my money stolen without at least checking if the goods are everything they're claimed to be? That is all my friend the chemist here wants to do. Then we will exchange goods and leave."

Hassan exploded in rage. He pulled the goggles over his eyes and placed the mask over his nose and mouth. "I came here for money! In this hand I hold enough poison to kill you and your friend here. *Tell* him," he roared. "*Tell* him! In this bag is ricin powder. One drop will kill both of you."

Martinez de Oz blanched. "*Señor*...if this powder is what he says it is we are all dead."

"But not me, Chemist! I am protected...no?" said Hassan.

"Okay, this is not going so well," said Kyle. "Do you want to make an exchange or not? I have friends up in the hills who have guns trained on you right now, *señor*. If they think you are trying to trick us, they will just shoot you dead. *Are* you trying to trick us, *señor*?"

Hassan threw the bag to the ground, reached into his pocket for a gun he'd taken from an Egyptian's hand, and raised it.

Up on the hill, Bryson lay prone, looking down the barrel of his Barrett at what had looked with every passing moment as an incident that was bound to end in blood being spilled. Carefully he squeezed the trigger. Spence was surprised by the noise it made as the bullet spat towards its target at supersonic speed, breaking the sound barrier onwards to its target before a noise was heard by Hassan.

In the clearing, a nano-second before Hassan pulled the trigger and sent his frustrater to oblivion, Bryson's bullet smashed into the revolver leaving an astonished Hassan with a twisted and empty hand.

Cursing, he collected his machine pistol from the rear of the Dodge and dragged Martinez de Oz to the front throwing him roughly into the cabin. He fired a couple of bursts at Kyle who had moments earlier rolled to safety behind a fallen tree trunk, his own gun now drawn lest further attacks took place.

Hassan accelerated the pick-up then stopped at the edge of the clearing, braking the Dodge and opening up on Kyle with his machine pistol. Scores of bullets smashed into the tree stump leaving Kyle sheltering from the vicious hail of bullets. A further burst of machine gun fire smashed the back door of Kyle's Landrover, opening it, revealing the six cases containing cash. Yet another frenzied crescendo of bullets reduced much of Kyle's cover to matchwood and continued to force his head below the fallen tree. Hassan managed to lift three cases into the Dodge before he decided that his luck might run out at any moment.

Jumping back into the pick-up, Hassan accelerated but before leaving, in an act of malice, fired a long, continuous round into the remaining cases, shredding much of their contents. Satisfied, he laughed at his handiwork and headed back down the dirt track at speed, his escape spitting pebbles and sand behind his departing vehicle, soon obliterating it in a cloud of dust.

Up on the hill, Bryson was incandescent with Spence. "You *stupid* fucker! Your one bullet prank could have seen my pal dead. As it is, all that's happened is that your man is away with the goods, the chemist and your boss's cash. This has been one almighty fuck up and it's all down to you, my friend. If I'd had rounds, I could have taken out the tyres, shot the driver, put a hole in the middle of a silver dollar...anything. But, no...you worry that I'm going to shoot you! A man I don't give two shits about! You stupid fucker. You stupid, *stupid* fucker."

All the while, Spence was trying to appease him but Bryson was uninterruptible...and was off down the hill, walking towards Kyle screaming imprecations all the way, his Barrett slung over his shoulder.

Spence followed on cursing quietly to himself, listening to Bryson's cursing pyrotechnics and wondering how he might present this predicament to Perry without losing too much face.

Chapter Eighteen

By mid-day, Kim had awoken and joined Miguel in the wheelhouse.

"Morning, Miguel," she yawned. "Where are we?"

"Good morning, *Señorita* Kim. We are just over the horizon from Marbella. We can make shore in about half an hour if you give the command. Today the water is calm so we can stay here if you wish. The forecast is good again with fine sunny weather."

"Have our guests stirred?"

No, *señorita*. They still sleep."

"Okay, I'll make breakfast for them. I'm sure they'll be up shortly."

After making some coffee for herself, Kim bustled around the galley busying herself with the task of organising breakfast, her mind still racing from the night before. While she was washing some dishes, much to the disapproval of Graciana and Juanita, who asked her as usual what they were meant to be doing if not cleaning up, Susan and Liam appeared.

"Hi," said Liam. Is there any task on this floating palace that you don't do?"

Kim smiled. "Hey, you're up. What would you like for breakfast?"

"Coffee for two will be fine." He paused, unsure whether to continue. "You okay after last night? Susan and I have been talking. We're really sorry that we seem to have brought nothing but trouble to your door since we arrived."

Kim's face flushed. "On the contrary. I've been torturing myself all morning about me ruining your honeymoon by exposing all my old family wounds. It's completely unacceptable and I want to offer to return the entire cost of your holiday. If you decided to leave immediately, I'd understand perfectly."

Susan stepped forward and gave Kim a hug. "We won't hear of that, Kim. Don't be silly. We are so impressed by you last night and remember, it was Liam and I who first started all this by getting involved with those ruffians in Marbella. We stay. You relax. And we wait to hear if we can help Gus and Jack."

Kim held her own counsel and poured coffee for Susan and Liam. She smiled weakly. "Let's take these out onto the deck space."

After some time during which they reviewed the events of the night before, Liam decided to spend some time in the Jacuzzi, leaving the two women together.

"It must have been difficult coming across your father last night, Kim," proffered Susan.

Kim shifted uncomfortably in her seat.

"More than I'd anticipated. I suppose I knew that I'd need to confront this at some point...I mean, last night after we all went to bed I had to face up to the fact that despising my dad as I do, I *still* operated a business only a few miles from his pub. I could have chosen to work my boat from anywhere in Europe but I chose to stay close... so if I'm honest, maybe I was looking for an opportunity to bring some closure to my issues with him. This had to happen at some point but I didn't need to involve you guys."

"You were doing something to help two men we've both grown fond of over the last couple of days," countered Susan. You had no need to intervene in the way you did. For all you knew, you were putting yourself at physical risk but you decided to help them...and knowing that in doing so, you'd have to face up to your dad. That shows real character."

"Or just trying to lance the boil," said Kim.

"Do you think you'll never be reconciled?, asked Susan.

Kim shrugged. "He's an awful man, Susan. He treated my mother abominably. He beat her. He kept both of us as virtual prisoners in our home. He denied me a childhood and an education. My mother was independently wealthy and he started to use her money for what he argued were his business purposes. Mum was quite an unassertive person and never spoke back but I suppose she thought she'd had the last laugh. About five years ago she took an overdose of her medication and committed suicide but not before she'd made sure that her wealth was transferred to me. Along with her will she made a statement to make sure that the world knew what a terrible man her husband was and had it witnessed by two top psychiatrists who testified that she was in sound mind when she wrote the statement. I was awarded most of her estate and I used much of it to commission and build the Ventura." She looked around at the opulence of her motor yacht. "It means everything to me. It was my passport to sanity."

Susan placed her hand on Kim's arm. "Poor you. That can't have been easy. Yet you confronted all of that last night rather than sit here on the yacht letting anything that happened happen. You're so brave…helping these guys…and I'll tell you something else, girl…I think that Gus likes you!"

Kim harrumphed. "Nah. First off, how anyone could like someone who behaved as I did last night escapes me and second, I worry that he's just a smarter and smoother version of my father… I mean he's busy fighting his own demons and I've enough on my plate without getting involved with anyone…much less a guy like Gus. Anyway, he told me…the only people that matter to him in this world are a daughter back in Scotland and his pal Jack, who looks a bit of a character to me."

"Still think he likes you! And he's a good looking man!"

Kim reached for the now empty coffee cups and gathered them.

"Not interested, Susan. My life's too complex at present." She took the cups and headed towards the galley, smiling back at Susan. "Now you go and join your husband in the Jacuzzi and don't go worrying about my love life. You go take care of your own!"

* * *

Just as Susan and Kim were discussing his good looks, Kyle was gingerly covering the sealed bag of powder dropped by Hassan with earth and building a small cairn made of rocks over the hillock so that it came to resemble a mini-roundabout, in so doing protecting the contents for later inspection.

Satisfied, he closed the Landrover's rear door, tied it with string, and drove it down the dirt track towards the Merc, where he inspected the vehicle that Hassan had tried to hide in the undergrowth. Cigarette stubs were inspected and on the floor beneath the driver's seat, he picked up a tracking device. *Might come in handy*, he mused. Having looked the car over for any further clues as to its ownership, Kyle arrived at the road-end just as did Bryson and Spence, Bryson still howling obscenities.

"I need a drink, Gus. This fuckin' idiot could have killed you because he's a fuckin' idiot who's more idiotic than the most idiotic fucker I've ever fuckin' met!"

Spence looked on shaking his head, silently trying to convey that Bryson was being a bit harsh.

Kyle stepped out of the Landrover and walked over to Spence until he was but a pace away.

"Okay, Cammy, here's how we play it. Now, you have no cause to trust us, but you don't have any cause to doubt us either...so before I spell out how we're going to go about fixing this, I'll take your gun, please...and no funny business. Just reach round slowly and hand it to me carefully. You know you wouldn't stand a chance of doing anything else."

Spence looked nervously at the two men, one of whom towered above him and who had been slaughtering him verbally for the last five minutes.

"Don't worry Cammy. You get what's left of the money and we go look for the rest. But we work alone."

Calculating that he didn't have many options, Spence reached around slowly and took his gun from his waistband. As he brought it round he realised that neither Kyle nor Bryson had made any attempt to pull their revolvers. *Stupidity or confidence?* he pondered. *I could shoot them,* he thought but looked at Kyle standing in front of him, one hand in his trouser pocket one hand casually outstretched awaiting his gun and for peculiar reasons approaching trust that he'd later have difficulty explaining to Perry, meekly handed him his revolver.

"Thanks Cammy. Now you take the three remaining cases or what's left of them. Your boys'll have fun looking for intact notes after the bullets that riddled these cases." He nodded towards the dust track. "That guy's left his Merc just up the track on the right. The keys are in the ignition. You take it and the three cases back to your boss. Tell him we intend to finish the job. We're going to have a look for your Chemist and try to get the money back. We won't steal it although I know you and your boss will think we will because that's what you would do but we just want our ten grand fee. From what we've seen, that Dodge doesn't have any drugs in it, but something that needs careful handling...maybe ricin. Now, there's four dead guys lying up there so sooner or later the cops are going to become involved. None of us want fingered for this so let's stay calm."

He patted Spence on the arm in what he hopped was a reassuring manner. "We'll be in touch. Promise."

Spence gestured his agreement and spoke in low tones. "Be aware, boys. I'm close to the boss but there's limits. If and when you get back to us, I might just be strung up by my heels."

"Not our business, Cammy but you're a big boy. If you think Perry will have you, take the suitcases and disappear. Just make sure you let him know that we're still on the case."

Spence nodded silently, turned and began to walk up the track to the Merc. Bryson unloaded the cases containing the torn and burned remains of something approaching one and a half million pounds unprotected, for the moment, at the side of the track.

"The idiot only let me have one round, Gus. If I'd missed, you could have been shot."

"Aye, but you didn't miss. You never miss." He reached into his back pocket. "Found this. Looks like some sort of tracking device. I'm assuming it's to keep tabs on the contents of these boxes in the pick-up. Might come in handy."

"Well, our friend's long gone. Let's find a bar and compare notes on how we're going to track him down." He took his cell phone from his pocket." Our pal Colonel Brand's been leaving lots of messages telling me to get in touch. Haven't responded. You?"

"Same here. He'll think we've been shot but maybe we let him stew a bit until we can work out whether he's in cahoots with Perry and Spence."

* * *

Early afternoon saw Brand return to Reykjavik and organise trusted contractors to give the safe house a deep clean, removing any clues to what had transpired in the front room. They'd taken the weapons from him so he'd have no problems with customs clearance and one of them had driven him back to the airport where he was now comfortably ensconced in the jet preparing for take-off.

Hadn't expected that, thought Brand. I'll need to take some time to think but for sure I'll need to phone ahead and arrange to meet Barrington as soon as possible. He'll need to be debriefed, though God only knows how I explain how my carelessness in losing Strachan!

* * *

Kyle and Bryson had travelled perhaps a mile along the route taken by Hassan when Bryson called out to Kyle.

"Gus...at the side of the road!"

Kyle braked and veered into the side of the road as he saw what Bryson had noticed. Martinez de Oz was kneeling in a sand pit, his hands clutching his throat. Bryson leapt from the Landrover before Kyle had brought it to a halt and held Martinez de Oz, leaning him back on the soft sand. Before asking him what had happened, Bryson noticed that the small chemist's face was already showing evidence of a blue discolouration indicating a diminishing amount of oxygen in the blood. His breathing was heavy.

"Bruno, tell me what happened. We're going to get you to a hospital."

"*Señor*, it is too late. That man...he made me breathe the powder from a small bag. I think it ricin. If it ricin, I am dead. Hospital will only ease my pain while I die."

He grabbed Bryson's arm. "*Señor*. I have a wife and a baby boy. He only four. I don' want to die."

Bryson was joined by Kyle.

"He was forced to breathe in powder. He figures it's ricin."

"Let's get him to a hospital. We can talk to him on the way."

"He figures he's as good as dead."

"The doctors can judge that. Help me get him into the Rangerover."

Together they lifted the chemist into the rear of their vehicle and set off towards the nearest township. Kyle drove while Bryson consulted a map.

"*Caravaca de la Cruz* looks like it might be big enough to support a hospital. Perhaps only about ten minutes away."

In the rear seat, Martinez de Oz lay clutching his stomach and groaning. Bryson comforted him and asked him questions about the attack. Martinez de Oz spoke quietly and described what had happened making the point that at the point of forcing the powder upon him, the man called him an 'Infidel'.

"Better make it quick, Gus," said Bryson as Kyle floored the accelerator heading towards Caravaca de la Cruz.

Cars swerved, pedestrians waved their fists as Kyle careered along the road towards the hospital, following Bryson's shouted directions. Eventually, with Martinez de Oz fading, they screeched to a halt outside the small Hospital *Comarcal del Noroeste*.

"You carry him in, Gus. I'll alert the medics."

So saying, Bryson ran into the hospital asking anyone in garb that looked like they might be a medic if they spoke English. A young nurse responded to his obvious urgency.

"I need a doctor quickly. I have a man outside who has been poisoned. He is dying."

The nurse turned towards a desk that sat unoccupied in the corridor, lifted the phone on it and punched in numbers as she did. She spoke briskly in Spanish.

Moments later a doctor arrived and Bryson took him curtly by the arm, pulling him towards the entrance where Kyle was carrying in a now unconscious Martinez de Oz.

"Okay, Doc! This man has been poisoned perhaps twenty minutes ago. We think it is ricin poisoning. Can you save him?"

The doctor spoke rapidly in Spanish to nursing staff who took Martinez de Oz from Kyle and laid him on a trolley. An oxygen mask was affixed over his nose and mouth and needles inserted into his arms. While staff busied themselves taking readings of his vital physiological statistics in order to assess his basic body functions, Kyle eased the doctor to one side.

"We're pretty sure this is ricin doctor. What's his chances?"

Doctor Marón Mael had only five years experience following his qualification. Perhaps not unsurprisingly he'd had no direct experience of ricin poisoning but remembered the basics from his textbooks.

"*Señor*, Mortality and morbidity depend on the route and amount of exposure. Was he injected, did he touch the poison or did he inhale it?"

"We're pretty sure he inhaled it."

"Then that is indeed bad news. Exposure through inhalation causes weakness, fever, a cough, and pulmonary swelling within eighteen to twenty-four hours. Severe respiratory distress and death are likely to follow within thirty-six hours if not sooner. The period between life and death will not be comfortable."

"Can you do anything for him? He has dependants."

"*Señor*, in this hospital we try to save lives whether or not they have dependants."

"Yeah, okay, doctor. What I'm trying to get at is; is there anything you can do? Is he a dead man?"

Dr. Mael shrugged. "Where exposure is by inhalation, we'd expect to see a rapidly progressive acute lung injury, developing into laboured breathing, tachypnea, hypoxia, ventricular arrhythmia, and progressive respiratory failure."

Bryson, listening in, interjected. "Christ, doctor, what does all that mean?"

"It means, *Señor*, that he is a dead man. There is no known antidote. We will make him as comfortable as possible. As little as 500 micrograms of ricin if inhaled could be enough to kill a full grown adult. That amount would fit on the head of a pin... "

Kyle shook his head, trying to make sense of the effects of some insignificant powder that could snuff a man's life out just as effectively as one of Bryson's long range bullets.

"One final thing doctor. Can you be poisoned just by touching the stuff?

"Dermal exposure of ricin is often of little concern because the absorption amount is usually insignificant." He looked at Bryson's uncomprehending face. "That means you can touch it if you're very careful."

Kyle brought proceedings to a conclusion.

"That man's name is Bruno Martinez de Oz. He is a chemist from Marbella. He has a wife and a son. We found him at the side of the road just outside your hospital. He told us he'd inhaled ricin powder."

"But how…"

"That's all we know doctor. Thank you for helping. Now we must go."

Both men turned on their heel and left the building. Already Dr. Mael was bending over his patient trying to make him comfortable.

"We need to find the bastard who did this. Eh, Gus?"

"Yes we do, comrade. Yes we do." He paused. "And we start by having another look at that bag of powder I buried."

* * *

Some time later they drove along the dust track and noticed that the green Mercedes had been removed as had the three cases full of shredded notes, suggesting that Spence had taken them...but whether to drive back to Marbella and Perry's fury, or off into a new life, was anyone's guess. They pulled up in the clearing where the exchange had been meant to have taken place and walked over to the mound left by Kyle's protective measures.

"You sure that bag was sealed?" asked Bryson, still with an image of the blue face of Martinez de Oz in his mind.

"Yeah, clear plastic bag. Folded back on itself and tied at the top. Still, we should be extra careful."

Together they removed the rocks and revealed the sand scooped into a mound by Kyle. Cautiously, they swept it aside with their hands until the plastic bag could be seen. It was as Kyle had described. Bryson produced a small plastic drum emptied of cleaning cloths and proffered it to Kyle who, exchanging looks with him, lifted the bag between finger and thumb and placed it in the container. Bryson screwed the lid shut.

"Mission accomplished."

They both returned to the Landrover and sat in silence, staring ahead as they thought of their next step.

"Way I see it," said Kyle. "We have no option. We've got an armed nutcase running around with a shed-load of ricin in the back of his pick-up. We're told that a drop the size of a pin-head can kill someone like Martinez de Oz. You know the number plate of the vehicle. There's no way we'd be lucky enough to track this down...even if we assume that this tracking device is set to follow the ricin." He met Bryson's gaze. "We have to inform the authorities."

"Agreed," said Bryson. But we tell them just enough to track the pick-up and alert them to the nature of what they might find, no more."

Kyle nodded and they drove to a call box outside a small school on the road to Caravaca de la Cruz. Checking to ensure that they weren't being observed, Kyle stepped out, lifted the phone and dialed 112.

"Do you speak English," he asked when the phone was answered.

"Leetle," was the response.

Kyle spoke slowly. "Do you record these calls?"

"*Si Señor.*"

"Good. Now listen. You may have to play this back to someone who speaks good English. There is an emergency. A man called Bruno Martinez de Oz has just been admitted to the hospital in Caravaca de la Cruz. He is dying of ricin poisoning...RICIN." He spelled it out. "You can check. The man who caused him to inhale this substance is driving a red Dodge pick-up, number plate GI 8165 BL. He is aged in his mid-thirties, five feet, eleven inches. He is of Arabic appearance. He is unshaven. No moustache. He has short black hair, receding hairline and a slight paunch. It is thought that the rear of his vehicle may contain several boxes of ricin. He is very dangerous. That is all." He paused a second and continued his slow, modulated delivery. "Did you record that?"

"*Si Señor.*"

Kyle placed the phone on the receiver and returned to the Landrover.

"Let's go before they flood this place with cops looking for someone with a Scottish accent. Can't be too many of us around here."

CHAPTER NINETEEN

D r. Mael sat in his office awaiting his visitor. He used the time at his desk to read information he'd asked for about the potency of ricin and how it might be dealt with. It didn't make good reading. A soft knock on his door heralded the arrival of *Comisario* Romeo Natzari of the *Centro Superior de Información de la Defensa*, Spain's principal intelligence agency.

Scowling, he shook the hand of Dr Mael and accepted the seat offered by the doctor.

"Thank you for seeing me doctor." He sat on the chair offered him and made himself comfortable. "You must appreciate, we are very interested in the nature of the poison used against *Señor* Martinez de Oz."

Hardly had his first sentence been uttered than the office door opened again and another, older and more disheveled man in plain clothes entered. As he did, he flashed an ID card in the direction of Dr Mael which identified himself as Sub-commissioner César Constantino of the *Grupo Especial de Operaciones,* the Spanish policing authority that deals with counter-terrorism.

"*Señor* Constantino," said Natzari, directing his comments towards an interloper with whom he'd engaged on numerous occasions before, "You may be assured that the *Centro Superior* has competency here. We need not detain a busy man like yourself."

"*Señor* Natzari. Let us not play games. We both know that this may involve drugs or it may involve terrorism. We will work together; at least until we understand the problem we are dealing with." He sat down.

Natzari scratched the back of his neck and sighed ostentatiously.

"Very well. But please do not interrupt over much while I am asking the good doctor some questions."

Constantino grimaced his agreement.

"Dr Mael. Have you established the poison we are dealing with yet?"

"The results are not back from the lab but the symptoms are consistent with the information given me by the Englishman."

"So it was an Englishman who brought him in?"

"I think two of them. At least they both spoke English. They told me that the poison it was ricin, that the man was a chemist called Bruno Martinez de Oz, that they had found him outside the hospital, and that he had a wife and son."

"That is all?"

Dr Mael nodded. "That is all."

"Has the patient spoken?" interrupted Constantino, inducing a glare from Natzari.

"Not lucidly. He is conscious now and again but makes no sense. He is in great distress and from what I've been able to get from him…because he is a man of science, he is aware that he shortly faces a very unpleasant death."

Natzari took the lead again. "Dr Mael, you must understand that while you will wish to have your patient treated to the best of your ability, I must speak with him. If there is someone around poisoning people with ricin, many others might face the same end if we don't stop him and the information you have given me is not sufficient to capture this person. Perhaps only *Señor* Martinez de Oz can provide me with this information."

Constantino interrupted again, but this time supportively. "My colleague is correct, doctor. While this man can talk we must communicate with him or you might have many others in here with the same prognosis."

The doctor mulled over the logic of their requests and with a small hesitancy, gave his consent. "But I must be in attendance and if I say that he cannot answer any further questions, you must desist at once and leave him to us."

"Of course, doctor," said Natzari, speaking for both policemen.

Walking briskly, the two policemen followed Dr Mael along a corridor and up two flights of stairs leaving an unfit Constantino puffing as they entered the ward in which Martinez de Oz lay, gravely ill.

Approaching the bed, the doctor spoke quietly to the nurse asking after his condition. After a few exchanged sentences, he turned to the police officers. "Presently he is awake but sleepy. You may speak to him."

Natzari met with no resistance from Constantino who was still catching his breath after the walk upstairs.

"*Señor* Martinez de Oz...can you hear me?... *Señor* Martinez de Oz..."

Face contorted, mouth open in silent pain and eyes screwed shut, no response was forthcoming.

"He has been heavily sedated *Señor*. He will have difficulty making sense of what you ask him."

Natzari tried again, louder, and this time the chemist opened his eyes.

Señor. I am a police officer. I need to ask you questions. Can you tell me if you knew the man who did this?"

Martinez de Oz struggled to speak. "I did not know the man..." His lips moved wordlessly for a moment. "He called me...*Infidel*..." Again his words failed him. Further effort brought, "I have a son and a wife. I do not want to die."

The policemen shared a glance. "We know *Señor*. You are in good hands."

Again Constantino interrupted. "Did you know the men who brought you to the hospital?"

Through his pain and his terror, Martinez de Oz made a drugged but yet rational calculation. *Help the police and perhaps implicate my wife and have the money I have been paid confiscated or maintain silence and perhaps consign innocents to the same fate as I?* He thought further and decided. *May God forgive me, but I am going to hell anyway for my misdeeds...*

Constantino grew impatient at the silence as Martinez de Oz wrestled with his conscience and prompted him again.

"*Señor*. Did you know the two men who brought you here?"

His question was met with a deep sigh and the chemist closed his eyes without responding. Although he would not die until the following day, he never regained consciousness.

The two senior police officers compared notes in the foyer of the hospital.

Natzari started. "We seem to be looking for two Englishmen..."

"Not so..." corrected Constantino. "We seek two people who spoke in English and we also seek someone who has a background that permits him to refer to Martinez de Oz as an infidel. That might suggest someone with an Arab background."

"Agreed," conceded Natzari, annoyed that his mistake had been pounced on by a police officer who would doubtless take delight in his transgression later on.

As they stood deliberating on their next move, one of Natzari's officers approached with a note in a sealed envelope. Shielding it from his fellow officer, he read the details as were transmitted by Kyle by telephone. Digesting the import of the transcript, he realised that not sharing it with Constantino could be a career-ending decision. He turned the note over to his colleague with an exhalation of breath, "Sheesh", expressing his new realisation that there might be a wagon-load of this poison.

"It would appear that the English has given us the information we seek. We must move quickly. I suggest we put out as many officers as possible, monitor key roads and look for people who might fit the description. We now have precise details of the vehicle. The people we seek may be many miles away by now but we must close the area down. This, my friend, has all the hallmarks of a national emergency."

Constantino pulled his spectacles to the front of his nose and tilted his head slightly, the better to focus and digested the two paragraphs quickly.

"And we must also keep a look out for the two men who brought him in. They seem to know a lot about this. It would appear unlikely that they just found him outside the hospital as they told Dr. Mael. I will ask my staff to listen again to the recording of the phone call to see if there is background noise or other signals that can give us further clues." He replaced his spectacles in his top pocket. "This will require political decisions. If this information gets out it could start a panic."

Natzari developed his counter-argument further. "But if it doesn't we could have people die because they are not prepared. We'll have to alert our scientists and ask them what strategies we need to deploy to contain the ricin threat."

Both men nodded and headed outside to their cars where they used their radio communication to order their agreed approach. Both men also used their mobile phones to phone their most senior officer and suggest they contact politicians and decide quickly whether or not to alert an entire nation to the possibility of widespread ricin poisoning.

* * *

Brand stepped from his Lear jet and walked the few steps across the apron into a low building at London City Airport. Inside sat Sir Alistair Barrington who had been scanning a cloudless blue sky looking for the aeroplane that would bring the further detail denied him previously by telephone when Brand phoned seeking an urgent meeting.

Brand had earlier considered the prospect of flying on directly after he briefed Barrington and so had asked for the meeting to take place at the airport in order to expedite this.

Brand entered the waiting area carrying only a briefcase and looking for all the world like a middle manager on his way to a sales conference.

"Sir Alistair."

"Colonel Brand."

"I'm afraid my visit to Iceland has presented us with problems."

Barrington crossed his legs at his ankles, clasped his hands and sat back unsmiling, awaiting Brand's briefing.

"I can tell you that I met with Svetlana Petrova and Kalinowski and that they are both now dead. Regrettably, so too is my contractor in Iceland. A man called Sam Strachan. Petrova killed Kalinowski, presumably so he couldn't provide us with information, she also killed Strachan and I shot her after inviting her to lay down her weapon and return safely to London with me."

"Your gallantry does you proud," said Barrington sarcastically.

"Quite," responded Brand. "I had to use sodium pentathol and while we both understand its limitations, she did seem to reveal some information that might be useful." He remembered his samples. "Oh, incidentally, I have photographs, saliva swabs, blood samples and fingerprints for identification purposes."

So saying he took the envelopes from his pocket and handed them to Barrington.

"All three were consigned to the depths of a glacier. I wasn't observed and would expect their bodies never to be found. Strachan has no relatives and I have people tidying up his affairs in Reykjavik."

Barrington nodded his acceptance.

"Might the Russian security services know that they were meeting with you prior to their disappearance?"

"Ours was a surprise meeting. At least for them it was. No one knew we met."

"You said you obtained information from Petrova?"

"I don't know why she was in Reykjavik or why she met with Kalinowski but they were clearly engaged in conversation about someone called Farrokh, although she referred to him as Brother Farrokh...she and Kalinowski were dressed as a priest and a nun..," he said parenthetically, causing Barrington to raise confused eyebrows.

"Strachan's notes show that she was telling Kalinowski that Farrokh needed more money. Later on, under the effects of drugs, she spoke two words of possible significance, Scorpion and Mandarin. Further interrogation brought no results and at that point she killed Strachan with a throwing knife then cut Kalinowski's throat."

Barrington sat forward in his chair. "If the Scorpion she referred to is the one we know as the terrorist and if he's in alliance with the Russian dissident agents, we do appear to have a problem of some proportion," he mused. "No further clarification on the meaning of Mandarin?"

Brand shook his head.

Barrington paused in thought and considered the same possible meanings as earlier had Brand...*Chinese language or perhaps a diplomat...senior civil servant...fruit? Mandarin...? ...Mandarin?*

He shrugged. This would require more thought.

"How have you pursued the other leads we have on the rest of the Russian agents who were listed in the file?"

"I have someone looking after the activities of Loris-Melikov in Paris, one of my people is on the shoulder of Lukowskaia in Berlin and another is on the tail of Magnovska in Algiers. I've also taken an interest in the Russian agent in Marbella. The file considers him a 'sleeper' in deep cover as he's been there for some years now but the gang are presently involved with people from Egypt - a new development for them - so there's an outside chance it involves terrorist activities rather than just drugs couriering. We don't know his name as yet but I felt it would be sensible to establish his credentials and I've a couple of new men on the case; ex-SAS boys. They did an excellent job for me in the middle east."

"Has this agent come to our attention as a dissident?"

"He's listed as a possibility. We don't know why he's been placed with a gang of British criminals in Marbella, but we're informed by our sources that he's been there for years. We don't even know which member he is or whether he's a Russian or an agent from another country working on their behalf. We just know they've placed someone with the gang. I've asked my men to find what's going on and to report."

"What have they told you thus far?"

A sour look passed across Brand's face. "I've lost contact with them at the moment. They were meant to report back every day but I've not heard from them for two days now. I was going to visit them after paying a quick visit to Berlin to see how our man in Germany is getting on with Lukowskaia."

Barrington rose to his feet. "I must leave. I have a doctor's appointment. We need to make sure we're close on the heels of each of these agents. If any of them look like they're up to no good we must eliminate them immediately...and without any undue drama or publicity."

"As ever," said Brand.

* * *

Farrokh Hassan, the Scorpion, drove the pick-up carefully along a back road. At the end of the road was a derelict looking garage at the edge of a small village. Parked outside the rusting, dilapidated garage were three smallish trucks all marked in the livery of the garage. Each side of the vehicles read *Hernández De Mercancías* and signified an element of *Señor* Hernández' business; transporting farming stock and goods around the area. Slowly, Hassan drove his pick-up into the dusty forecourt of the garage noting the apparent absence of staff other than an old man in a stained white shirt and faded blue overalls who was now distracted from his ministrations on an antiquated tractor having heard the approach of Hassan's vehicle.

Smiling at him, Hassan slowly drove the pick-up past him and round the main building checking on the presence of any other people on the premises. Satisfied that the old man was alone, he manoeuvred the pick-up into the covered maintenance area and stepped from the vehicle.

Laying down his heavy metal spanner, old *Señor* Hernández wiped his hands on his overalls and walked to meet his customer.

Hassan had entered the unkempt reception area and was assessing further the likelihood of any additional staff being on the premises when the owner hailed him warmly in Spanish.

"Hola, mi amigo. Necesita ayudar?"

Raising his right arm Hassan pointed his gun directly at *Señor* Hernández and with his left mimicked the turning of an ignition key while nodding in the direction of the tracks parked on the road outside the garage.

Señor Hernández was an old man. He had lived a long
life and he sought no excitement in his autumn years.
Understanding the import of Hassan's urgent miming
almost immediately, he slowly leant below the desk
separating the two men, stopping briefly for unasked
permission as Hassan leant forward threateningly with
his gun in order to ensure that the old man was reaching
only for keys. Carefully, he selected a set of keys and
handed them to Hassan gesturing to him the truck with
which they were paired.

Hassan took the keys and moved round behind the
desk forcing Hernández back into a small room where he
kept his meagre supply of spare parts. As the old man
raised his hands further in silent submission, Hassan
remembered his training; specifically that the only
method of reliably killing a man with a handgun is to
destroy the functioning capability of the central nervous
system; specifically, the brain and cervical spinal cord.
Accordingly, the bullet that penetrated *Señor* Hernández
just below his nose caused direct and catastrophic
trauma to the tubular bundle of nervous tissue at the top
of his vertebral column resulting in its immediate
destruction and his instant death.

Closing the door of the parts' room, Hassan took the
keys and after a few false attempts, started the truck and
drove it tentatively into the gloom of the garage.
Positioning it carefully so that the two rear ends of the
vehicles closed together, he began the process of carefully
removing the boxes from their container and transferred
them from one vehicle to the other. Again he made use of
his goggles, mask and gloves until he was satisfied that

the thick plastic cartons were each secure and that there was no evidence of any leakage.

Once the boxes had been loaded, Hassan returned to the driver's seat of the pick-up and moved the vehicle to the rear of the garage where he attempted to remove all fingerprints and checked it thoroughly for items that might provide clues to his having been there before stepping aboard the truck and driving it from the garage.

Unfortunately for Hassan, although the cabin of the pick-up provided no clue as to his presence, a small device secreted within one of the cartons continued to emit the signal tuned to the receiver left by him at the clearing... as did another within the packing case he left behind. Leaving an empty cigarette pack with his Arabic notes on it was a second avoidable mistake.

* * *

Brand was over Holland en route to Berlin when the pilot woke him from a sleep and invited him forward to speak with a person who was anxiously trying to reach him. Placing his coffee and his newspaper on the seat next to him, Brand entered the cockpit and took the spare earphone set from the pilot. It was Barrington.

"Can I be overheard?"

"I suspect so."

"Then tell the pilot to divert to the nearest airfield to your people. Marbella if you can. Gibraltar or Malaga if there are problems. Phone me as soon as you've landed and communications are secure. There have been developments."

"Involving my two men?"

"It would appear so." The line went dead.

Brand spoke with the pilot who managed to get clearance to land in Marbella airport.

"We land in approximately one hour, Colonel Brand."

"Then I will return to my sleep. Try not to make the flight too bumpy."

CHAPTER TWENTY

Kyle and Bryson had pulled over just outside Bullas on the back roads of Murcia and had stopped their Landrover at a car park next to an isolated bar while they caught up on some badly needed afternoon sleep. On awakening and still fatigued, Kyle stretched, yawned and saw that the seat next to him was empty. Bryson was nowhere to be seen.

He decided to investigate the bar if only to splash some water on his face and entered to find the place empty save for Bryson and the bartender singing along with an antiquated juke box whose musical output must have been comprised of the original vinyl records chosen for its inaugural performance.

"Guantanamera... *guajira*, Guantanamera.... Guantana meeeerrrra...."

Kyle smiled at his pal singing with the barman, his arm round his new friend's shoulders, both of them now uproariously drunk. Ruefully, he noticed that Jack's free hand contained a glass containing amber liquid and that there was a half empty bottle of Scotch on the table along with several drained beer bottles.

"Haw, Gus! Pedro here's teachin' me to sing Spanish!"

The old bartender stood unsteadily and waved Kyle towards a seat at the table. He raised the bottle of Johnnie Walker Black Label in an unspoken invitation to share in its contents.

Kyle shook his head. "No, *Señor*." With his right hand he mimicked drinking from a vessel. "Coffee, *por favor?*"

"C'mon, Jack. I'm not leavin' until this bottle's dead."

"D'ye not think that a bit of sleep would have been a better idea?"

"Fuck sleep, Jack! Me an' Pedro here's enjoyin' ourselves." The refrain came round one more time and Bryson joined in again...Guantanamera... *guajira*, Guantanamera...

Twenty minutes later, Kyle had finished his coffee and Bryson had finished the bottle of whisky. They left, Bryson with his arm round Kyle to support his departure while he swore undying love for his new-found Spanish pal and waved his farewell with his free hand which now clutched a bottle of the barman's best Rioja.

Kyle helped a now very drunk Bryson into the cab and strapped him in.

Blinking sleepily, Bryson stared closely at his bottle of wine as if it were an alien object.

"Here, Gus...how am I goin' to open this?"... He pondered his situation momentarily before slowly coming to the conclusion that striking the neck of the bottle against the dashboard and smashing it would at least give him access to its contents. He was sure he could drink from the broken neck safely if only he took care. As his right arm bent back to strike the blow, Kyle grasped his wrist.

"Here, Jack. Give it here." So saying, he took a penknife from his pocket and levered a small metal screw device from its shell and used it to open the bottle.

"Fine man ye are," said Bryson as he took the bottle and drained a mouthful.

His now monotonous singing of Guantanamera descended into drunken mumblings before long and he soon fell unconscious, dropping the bottle and spilling the remainder of the bottle of wine on the floor as Kyle powered the Rangerover along the roads of the region, every so often casting his eyes at the transponder to see if the red light had turned to green, thereby indicating the nearby presence of the contents of the pick-up.

* * *

Brand's jet landed at Murcia airport and he passed through customs as easily as he had earlier arranged for his two operatives before hailing a taxi and asking to be taken to the Hotel Puente Romano in Marbella where he intended looking for Kyle and Bryson.

In the taxi he phoned Barrington and asked for the information he was denied on the jet.

"I may be putting two and two together here," mused Barrington. "But this sounds like your two men may be involved in all of this."

"All of what?" asked Brand impatiently.

"I've just had a report from a contact from Brigadier Garrick who sent me a note from the *Grupo Especial de Operaciones* who are effectively the Spanish counter-terrorism people. They want to know if I have any knowledge of two Englishmen who delivered a Spanish chemist to a hospital in Caravaca de la Cruz. I gather that the man is dying from ricin poisoning, but these two were able to tell them that he was forced to inhale the bloody stuff by someone of Arabic background driving a red Dodge pick-up, number plate GI 8165 BL. The communiqué before me tells me that the man is aged in his mid-thirties, five feet, eleven inches. He has an unshaven two day beard but no moustache. He has short black hair, receding hairline and a slight paunch. It is thought that the rear of his vehicle contains several boxes of toxic ricin. Now, might your two boys be involved in this?"

Brand looked forwards at the taxi driver who was listening to his radio and seemed quite disinterested in his hire's conversation. He decide to respond - but in as bland a way as possible.

"My first obvious observation is that my two men are Scottish but I accept that the Spanish informants probably wouldn't be able to differentiate between the accents. Secondly, the description you give suggests a professional interest in detailed observation - something I'd expect of Kyle and Bryson but thirdly, they are based in Marbella which, you tell me, is some way away from Caravaca de la Cruz?"

"Yes. It's about four hours away. About four hundred kilometers."

"Well, my boys are resourceful and energetic. It wouldn't surprise me if they were up to their eyes in this. I'm actually on my way to their hotel right now. Once I manage to check this stuff out I'll get back to you."

"See you do."

* * *

Bryson still slept as Kyle steered the Rangerover along unfamiliar roads hoping for a contact registering on the transponder he'd positioned between his legs as he drove. It's our only chance of finding this guy, he thought as he cast a sideways glance at his unconscious partner. He shook his head. I suppose I'm on my own for a while.

Driving through a small township called *El Niño*, he started as a ring-tone forced its irritating chirp above the noise of the engine. Initially, Kyle grabbed the transponder only to see that it still showed a red light indicating no contact. Momentarily confused he realised it was his mobile phone and further that for the umpteenth time, it was Colonel Brand looking to speak with him.

Resignedly, he took the phone from his pocket and answered it.

"Colonel!"

"Kyle," hissed Brand. "Where the hell are you? I've been phoning every five minutes. We agreed we'd be in contact daily."

"Yeah. Sorry 'bout that, Colonel. These phones are crap. We've hardly been able to get a signal for them plus we've had to spend some of our time at sea and there was absolutely no signal there."

"At sea?"

Kyle sighed as he realised that he'd now have to explain the 'Ventura'.

"We met with Perry's men but initially it resulted in them trying to shoot me and Bryson."

"What?" asked an astonished Brand.

"Don't worry. It's been resolved and we're now best friends…up to a point. We had to take refuge for a while on a motor cruiser called the 'Ventura' while we gathered ourselves but we're now working with Perry to retrieve the drugs consignment you spoke of."

"Have you discovered which of his men is the Russian plant?

"Not yet, Colonel."

"Right, I need to speak with you right now in order to understand what progress you're making."

"No can do, Colonel. We're on the trail of a guy who tried to steal the drugs and the money Perry had put up for the shipment."

"I need to ask you questions, Kyle."

"Yeah, well me and Bryson need to ask you some questions too, Colonel. Like why your photograph is on Bryson's wall and you looking for all the world as if you're a *Sturmführer* in the SS or something."

"Christ, Kyle. I was operational once too, you know. Why do you think I was able to tell you so much about Perry? Now don't mess me about on trivia like this. All of that can be explained."

"Well, we'll see, Colonel."

"Don't get sniffy on me Kyle. Tell me instead what you know about a chemist who was deposited in a hospital in Caravaca de la Cruz suffering from ricin inhalation."

"You know about him?"

"Kyle! It's my bloody *job* to know everything," he lied. I need to know exactly what you know and what you're doing about all of this."

Kyle relented. "Okay, Colonel. Bryson took careful note of the guy we're after. He's driving a red Dodge pick-up. Number plate, GI 8165 BL. The number plate shows the European blue badge on left with yellow stars and the capital letter E. The pick-up has aluminium sills and a damaged rear brake light. It has a green tarpaulin covering the goods in the rear and has blue scores on off side rear panel....probably scraped another car at some point. It's using *Firenza* tyres but Bryson noted that they looked worn and needed replaced so it's unlikely that the vehicle was hired from a rental company in that kind of nick.

The man we're looking for is just under six feet tall with an unshaven two day beard. No moustache. He has short black hair, a receding hairline and a slight paunch. Aged thirty-something. He was wearing a smart jacket, casual blue slacks and a black shirt open at the neck. It looks like he smokes *Bistoon* cigarettes. Not a brand I've come across. He uses a lighter and not matches, wears casual shoes unsuited for walking in rough terrain

He used goggles when he handled what we assumed were drugs but now believe is ricin poison. We've a sample of the powder but the plastic bag that contains it probably won't show up any fingerprints if he uses gloves all the time as he seems to. He also used an industrial face mask and wore pink washing up gloves when he was inspecting the merchandise... He speaks passable but poor English. Heavily accented. Looks like he's of Arabic descent and he was the guy who poisoned Bruno Martinez de Oz."

"He the chemist?"

He is...or at least, he was. Me and Bryson took him to hospital after he'd succumbed to the poison administered by our friend. The doctor reckons he won't make it."

Kyle paused after his descriptive tour de force as Brand tried to assimilate all that Kyle had told him. He was impressed.

"Well, Mr. Kyle! You've gone up in my already high estimation. Such an attention to detail!"

"Don't thank me, thank Jack Bryson. One of the key duties of an SAS sniper is observation and report and he had the man in his sights for long enough to record these characteristics. I only inspected the vehicle."

"But he didn't shoot him?"

"No. We were assessing the situation. He was covering me while I had a chat with the fellah over cocktails." Kyle's tone turned to anger. "Now, I want to know what's going on here. We see a photograph of you in a Nazi uniform then our drugs consignment appears to be a deadly poison. Seems we can't trust what you tell us. Were you aware of the consignment being ricin, not drugs when you commissioned us?"

"I certainly did *not*, Kyle and I'll be asking my own questions in that regard. But I need you to track that consignment down and I *must* find out who the Russian is." He paused, "Look Kyle, that was an excellent report. You're top drawer. Both of you."

Kyle looked at an alcohol-soaked, sleeping Bryson and grinned. *Top drawer? Christ, if he could only see him now...*

"Let's meet immediately, Kyle. We need to compare notes."

"Sorry boss, bad signal again. You're cutting out," lied Kyle. "Oh, and one more thing if you can still hear me. Bryson reckons that as our man was putting his rubber gloves on, he noticed that he had a tattoo of a scorpion on the back of his right hand."

"What?...Kyle!...Kyle!"

The line went dead.

* * *

An hour later, Kyle was still navigating his way through back roads hoping for a contact on his transponder indicating, he presumed, the presence of the consignment taken by his assailant at the clearing. Bryson still slept. Dead to the world.

This is hopeless, he thought to himself. That bastard could be anywhere.

No sooner had the thought occurred to him than the green light on his transponder started to flash. Faintly, but incontrovertibly it invited him to head east, to his left. Driving onwards for a while, he stopped the Landrover on a rise and surveyed the landscape before him. It was still sparse, dry brush and sandy soil with no evidence of human habitation. Still, a stronger signal suggested he was nearing the receiver. He shifted the gear stick into first and travelled onwards, carefully keeping an eye on the small machine he held in his left hand and following its directions as he drove.

Ten minutes further progress brought him to the village in which was located the garage boasting the signage of

Hernández De Mercancías. Stopping the Landrover at the forecourt, he checked the transponder again to satisfy himself that the green light had settled on the premises in front of him. Taking his pistol from the glove compartment, he lodged it in his waistband and with a glance at the unconscious Bryson, stepped from the vehicle and made his way cautiously towards the garage.

The afternoon sun was both hot and brilliant and Kyle screwed his eyes tight to protect them from its glare. He approached the forecourt and stepped behind one of *Señor* Hernández' trucks where he stood, observing the garage for a full three minutes before stooping and running, gun in hand, towards the relative safety of the building wall, just outside the vehicle entrance. The only sound he heard was occasional birdsong. All else was silent. Again waiting for some minutes to establish confidence in his sense that no one was moving inside the building, he advanced to a position where he could see into the darkened interior. As his eyes became accustomed to the gloom, he sank lower into a crouch as he saw the red pick-up parked at the rear of the garage.

Quietly he moved to the pick-up and looked it over for any information that might be helpful. He confirmed the number plate and looked inside the cabin. Nothing. In the rear of the vehicle, he noticed a pack of cigarettes. Inspecting them, he noted that it was the *'Bistoon'* variety he'd found earlier in the Mercedes and was about to throw the pack to the floor when he noticed some writing inked on it. Difficult to read in the gloom, he pocketed the pack and turned to the office area of the garage.

His senses were now on full alert as he moved quickly but silently to the internal door of reception. Still no sound. No suggestion of human presence. He moved into the space and surveyed the dark, untidy office before walking quietly to the door leading to the parts store. With his left hand, he turned the handle, taking care to ensure his gun was ready for immediate use. Opening the door slowly, he saw immediately the body of old *Señor* Hernández.

* * *

Outside the garage, having observed Kyle's parked Landrover, the rear of which had been peppered with what looked disconcertingly like bullet holes, police patrolman, *Guardia Civil Cabo Primera* Roberto Flores stepped from his vehicle. Flores had been the local cop for five years and knew his community well. *Why*, he thought, *does old Carlos Hernández have a vehicle like that in his garage? Perhaps he'll share a cool drink while he tells me.*

Adjusting his sunglasses and removing his police beret the better to wipe the sweat from his forehead, he walked towards the garage reception but stopped short when he saw the rear of Kyle, gun in hand standing over what looked like a body. Flores was an officer unused to drama. Mostly he was called on to referee domestic disputes in rural Murcia or to invite over-indulging farmers to remove themselves from village bars. However, his training kicked in and silently, he removed his nine millimeter Parabellum pistol from its holster and pointed it at Kyle's back.

In his most authoritative tone, Flores instructed, *"No se mueva. Ponga la pistola en la messa y levante los brazos."*

Kyle stiffened. *Shit.* He'd been so focused upon the body in front of him and its significance, he hadn't been paying attention to his environs. He hadn't a clue what instructions he'd just been given in Spanish but this was no time to assume he was being asked for a dance. His mind raced. Was he about to be shot by the man from the clearing? His eyes found the glazed panels in a cupboard in front of him containing a clutter of spare parts. In its reflection he saw with a mixture of relief and resignation that the man pointing a gun at him was a police officer. What was it Brand had said?... *'If you're in police custody, you're on your own...'* He sighed and laying his gun on a table beside him, raised his hands. *Cabo Primera* Flores repeated his grunted instruction to Kyle not to move...*"No se mueva."*

As Kyle surrendered to the notion that it looked for all the world as if he was about to be accused of murdering the old man who lay dead in front of him, he heard a familiar voice growling an instruction...

"Guantanamera, pal."

A rifle muzzle held and pointed by Bryson lifted the chin of *Cabo Primera* Flores leaving no question as to the fact of his endangerment. The police officer lowered his gun. Upon hearing Bryson's command, Kyle had been observing his intervention in the glass reflection and spinning on the now very frightened Flores he took the pistol from his hand.

With a jumble of words and gestures, Kyle tried to convey to Flores that he was in no danger and that he and Bryson had had nothing to do with the death of the body in the store-room.

Not persuaded that he had achieved either objective, he further mimed his regret as he handcuffed Flores to a wooden post and, taking his gun and radio, left, ushering Bryson out of the office door into the garage where he pointed to the pick-up.

"Great timing, Jack. I found the pick-up but there's no sign of our man or the contents of the vehicle. He must have transferred them."

Bryson's constitution incorporated an ability to shrug off substantial amounts of alcohol and although technically very drunk, to an observer, he might easily have passed for completely sober.

"Aye, but let's get out of here, Gus. Who knows if this guy's already called in his business here. We might be surrounded by cops any minute now. We'll need to get rid of this Landrover. The cops'll soon have a fix on it."

"Good shout, Jack."

As they walked back towards the Landrover, Kyle stopped and turned to face Bryson..."Guantanamera, pal?"

"Only Spanish I know except to ask him for two beers...but that might not have had the desired effect," explained his colleague as they jumped into the Landrover which sped away, Kyle at the wheel, laughing and shaking his head.

"Guantanamera, pal?"

CHAPTER TWENTY-ONE

The concierge at the Puente Romano hotel into which Brand had booked Kyle and Bryson was adamant.

"They are here *Señor*. I know this because *Señor* Bryson has made good use of the mini-bar but they are not in the hotel at present."

"Can you phone Mr. Kyle one more time?

The concierge sighed, lifted the phone and punched in Kyle's hotel room number, carefully noted by Brand.

He let it ring ten times to assure his inquisitor of the certainty of his pronouncement.

"No answer, *Señor*."

Brand smiled. "Thank you *Señor*. You've been very helpful." He turned towards the entrance of the hotel but instead of leaving, leaned into the door leading to the stairwell and climbed the three floors to Kyle's room. Tutored in burglary for the crown in earlier years, the door lock troubled him only momentarily. He entered and closed the door, his eyes taking in the scene as he did. Everything perfectly arranged. No clothes in the wardrobes. No toiletries in the bathroom and no evidence of anyone staying there. Clearly his man had moved out. He had obviously registered at the hotel and Bryson had clearly made use of his room's alcoholic refreshments but the men had obviously moved out.

What was the name of that motor cruiser Kyle'd mentioned?...The Ventura? I'd better have a look for that in the harbour, he thought.

* * *

On board the Ventura, Susan and Liam had just been served afternoon canapés with a glass of Kim's obligatory Krug Champagne.

"No word from the boys?" asked Liam.

"Nothing. With any luck, they'll be in a bar somewhere having walked away from all of this nonsense."

"Somehow, I don't think so, Kim. But if we can remain here just off the coast for the time being, I'd appreciate it. I'd like to be able to help them if they need it."

"Not a problem, Liam. I've left word with the Harbourmaster that if either Jack or Gus ask them to make contact he assists immediately."

Kim left to tend to other matters and left her guests to enjoy their relaxation.

"How are your ribs today, darling?"

"Well, I can breathe easier now and the pain isn't constant; only when I touch them." He squeezed his wife's arm."Don't worry, I'll be fine soon. I'm just glad I'm only bruised. If these guys had at me with their boots and bottles, you might be visiting me in the morgue right now."

"Liam, it's too horrible to contemplate. Thank goodness for Jack and Gus. I hope they're not too mixed up with these people."

"Well, I spoke with Gus just as he was leaving and he was keen that he would be able to call on the Ventura if needs be. He seemed sure that whatever he and Jack had in mind, it'll have these gangsters chasing them. Trust me Honey, that pair wear white Stetsons...they're the *good* guys."

"Well, sitting here in the Mediterranean sipping Champagne isn't too shabby and if it lets us help them, I'm sure we can cope with the lack of sightseeing for a few days."

Liam brought his wife's face to his and kissed her tenderly before leaning back in his reclined and cushioned chair and turning his face to the sun.

* * *

A short walk took Brand to Marbella's waterfront where the afternoon heat saw him take refuge in a shaded bar area. He ordered a beer. Taking a long slow draught to slake his drouth, he placed the glass back on the table and reached for his phone. Opening it he punched in the number that would connect him to Sir Alistair Barrington. The phone rang only once before it was answered.

"Yes?"

"It's Brand. I'm in Marbella. No sign of my men but I've spoken with Kyle and he's confirmed that he and Bryson were the men who delivered Mr. Martinez de Oz to the hospital. He's given me a lot more information on the man who is in possession of the ricin." Brand paused before sharing his next tid-bit. "He's informed me that the man has a tattoo of a scorpion on the back of his right hand."

"What!" exclaimed Barrington.

"Exactly, Sir Alistair. It would appear that we face an able and formidable adversary. The description given me by Kyle fits one of several that are currently circulating but the tattoo probably seals it. Presumably we should alert our intelligence people and tell them that the Scorpion, our most elusive terrorist target, is alive and well on Spanish soil and is in possession of enough toxin to poison an entire city."

"You'll leave that detail to me, Brand. At present, you and your two men can continue your search for him. Have you unearthed the Russian agent yet?"

"Not yet and you'll be the first to know as soon as we have." Brand sipped again at his beer. "Tell me Sir Alistair, my men were anxious to know if you were aware in advance that the product they were chasing down was ricin and not heroin?"

"Of course I was," lied Barrington. "But let me be clear. Your men are expendable. I am sure that they are able and competent operatives but let me make two points; first of all, you may have had difficulty recruiting men if they were aware that they may be dealing with a deadly poison and secondly, if I had had to protect our agents properly they would have had to meander around Spain dressed in protective garb such as may have alerted even the most stupid police officer to the fact of our interest in the matter."

"But in order to deceive them, you decided to deceive me, Sir Alistair. Am I to be considered expendable too?"

"In this game, Brand we are *all* to be considered expendable. Now you and your men get on with your task of unmasking our Russian. Do not involve others. I want to know what transpires, I want the name of that Russian agent and I want to know which side he's batting for."

Brand closed his phone and contemplated his half empty glass. *So, I'm expendable am I?*

He finished the beer in one gulp, left some Euros on the table to cover the bill and started to walk towards the marina where he assumed the Ventura would be berthed.

After half an hour of what to an innocent observer would have looked to all the world like a regular tourist rubber-necking the luxury yachts and motor cruisers tethered at their berths, Brand decided that the boat was not in harbour. He decided upon a different approach and took a hundred Euro note from a thick wad of bills. *Let's see if bribery pays dividends,* he said to himself as he approached the Harbourmaster's office.

Knocking the door, he interrupted the Harbourmaster reading sleepily about his footballing heroes.

"Sorry to disturb you sir, but I wondered if you could tell me the whereabouts of a motor cruiser called the Ventura." He felt in his pocket for the banknote.

"Ah, you must be *Señor* Kyle? I was told you would come looking for the Ventura."

"Why, yes," said Brand, keeping his hand in his pocket. "I'm Kyle. You can help me?"

"Of course, *Señor. Señorita* Kim told me to contact her as soon as you arrived. She is not far from port and will return"

"Excellent," said Brand. "I'll just wait here. Will they be long?"

"Excuse, *Señor,*" said the Harbourmaster in reply as he listened to Miguel respond to his call."

They spoke quickly in Spanish. All Brand could understand was the occasional, '*Si*'.

The exchange ended. "The Ventura is coming *Señor*. It will dock here in perhaps thirty minutes."

Brand nodded in the direction of a small collection of chairs and tables enclosed by an artificial hedgerow. A faded tarpaulin protected the few customers from the sun.

"Then I'll wait in that bar over there," he smiled.

* * *

Comisario Romeo Natzari of the *Centro Superior de Información de la Defensa*, Spain's principal intelligence agency stepped from his car and walked slowly to the murder scene inside the garage where the body of old *Señor* Hernández lay, surrounded now by police officers and forensic scientists.

Having heard on his police radio that a shooting had occurred and that the officer concerned had evinced that the culprit was a man who spoke English, Natzari made haste to the crime scene. *En route* he was made aware that the suspect had an accomplice who was a giant of a man and was even further persuaded that he was closing in on the twosome who were somehow involved in the death of Bruno Martinez de Oz.

Guardia Civil Cabo Primera Roberto Flores sat in a chair, gently rubbing his right wrist where the handcuffs had cut and bruised him as he'd struggled to reach a desk on which a phone sat. He was being interviewed by two officers as to the events he'd uncovered when he'd arrived on the scene as Constantino entered the small office.

Both men stood as Natzari announced himself.

"*Comisario.*"

Ignoring the two men, he sat on the edge of a desk next to the police officer and taking a photograph from his pocket, gave it to Flores.

"Are these the men who shot the garage owner?"

Flores studied the photograph.

"Certainly the smaller of the two men in this photograph I found over the body with a gun in his hand. I could not see the taller man clearly but from what I saw, it looks like him."

He returned the photograph to Natzari who smiled and thanked him. He spoke to the two officers who had been interviewing Flores.

"Tell the officer in command to continue here. I want to know instantly you come across anything of interest. In the meantime I have matters of greater importance to our nation to deal with."

Constantino returned to his car and sped away, kicking up dust and stones as he did so. As the cloud of sandy particles hung in the air, another car slowly made its way through the dull yellow fog and parked in front of the garage. Sub-commissioner César Constantino of the *Grupo Especial de Operaciones* stepped from his vehicle and ambled in to the premises.

* * *

Perry gazed down on a case full of burned and shredded notes and tried to control himself.

"Words fackin' fail me.... They actually... fackin'... fail me. For the first time in my fackin' life, I don't know what to fackin' say!" He turned to his clearly embarrassed and uncomfortable lieutenant. "You an' me 'ave bin together a long time, Cammy...but this!"

He closed the lid on the case.

"You need to know that if anyone else in this fackin' world brought me back what looks like the guts of thirty fackin' bob after leavin' with three fackin' million quid, he'd be fackin' dead...dead as fackin' dead could fackin' be. But it's *you*... it's Cammy Spence..." Red faced, his voice rose. "My number one fackin' man." He gestured at the three destroyed cases on the bar in front of them. "I'm in fackin' shock. Last night, my daughter, the woman closest to me in the fackin' world turns up on me doorstep wivout so much as a by your fackin' leave and the day after...the man I depend on most loses me three million fackin' smackers."

Spence stood by nervously not knowing if his boss's next move would be to shoot him dead. He'd seen Perry do it before. He'd seen men shot dead, men shot in the groin, men shot up the anus and left to die in agony, men shot in both knees and consigned to a life of pain and immobility. He knew his fate would be decided soon. Cole was stationed outside the door. He could take Perry. He was old. But Cole was armed and he was not. He could count on a hesitation by Cole because he was after all, his boss too. But....

Spence's distracted thoughts were interrupted by Perry clinking a bottle against a glass and half-filling it with whisky.

"Cammy. What the *fack* are we going to fackin' *do*? I can't fackin' shoot you…You're the fackin' brains of this operation…least ways you *used* to fackin' be." He downed the whisky in one gulp. "Cammy, you need to get that fackin' money back."

"Yeah, Marcus. I'll do that. I'll make it up to you. Thanks for…well, just thanks."

Perry recovered his usual poise. "Never mind thanks. Just make fackin' sure you fackin' get that money back…and get old Eddie and Bert in here to count what we can fackin' rescue from this lot 'ere what got shot app. Fackin' Arab. Now we're involved in fackin' terrorism and we've lost a fortune in drugs. I understand drugs but I don't know about poison. Don't even know if poison's worth any money but we need to come out of this at least level."

"Well, if you don't mind Boss, I'd like to start by speaking with your daughter Kimberly and her two guests…they might help me figure out how to get back in touch with Bryson and Kyle…"

"Don't you harm a hair on her head, Cammy."

"Course not boss…but I need a lead if we're to track down those three suitcases."

"Not a *fackin'* hair on her *fackin'* head."

Spence nodded his understanding and left, taking Cole and two others to a car which he drove to the marina to look for the Ventura. Parking close by, the men got out.

"Boss...if I'm not mistaken, that's the Ventura coming into the marina right now. I recognise it from the other night," said Cole.

"You're right, Terry. Let's go and welcome them ashore."

* * *

Claudio the Harbourmaster waved warmly at Kim as the Ventura docked. His phone rang, calling him back into his office but Kim had staff who would ensure that the motor cruiser was berthed properly. She didn't need his help.

Kim was focused upon helping Miguel drift the powerful boat gently the last few inches into dock when Brand stepped aboard uninvited and climbed the few steps to the wheelhouse where he addressed her.

"I'm afraid we've not been introduced but I must speak with you about Gus Kyle and Jack Bryson. My name is Andrew Brand."

Expecting to meet them both and now faced with a stranger with a violent red scar on his face somewhat disorientated Kim. That he wanted to talk about Gus and Jack suggested that perhaps something had happened to them. Her hand flew to her mouth.

"Oh, my God. Are they okay? Are you a policeman?"

"Is there somewhere we could talk?"

"Of course." She turned her head to Miguel. "Can you finish here?"...and led Brand to the yellow leather armchairs in the guests' lounge.

"We've not been introduced. As I said on the dock, I'm Andrew Brand." He held out his hand to shake hers.

"Kimberly Williams. I'm owner and captain of the Ventura."

It appears that we have some mutual friends...or perhaps acquaintances? Gus Kyle and Jack Bryson."

"Yes. Are they alright?"

"I believe so but they might be in danger."

* * *

Arriving at the Ventura, Spence and his three men stepped aboard, ignoring a puzzled challenge by Miguel.

"*Señor?*"

Spence, his revolver holstered underneath his shirt in the front of his waistband for the time being, smiled a dismissal, holding his hands up in what he intended to be a reassuring gesture as he continued towards the guests' lounge where Kim and Brand were seated.

"It's okay." He turned towards Cole. "Tell him to take the boat back out to sea for a while."

Cole looked to ensure he wasn't being observed and brought his gun from his pocket, waving Miguel back in to the wheelhouse. The other two watched to ensure that the boarding party hadn't drawn unwanted attention. Satisfied that no one seemed perturbed, they joined Cole and Miguel.

"Hi Kimberly," said Spence. "Sorry to interrupt."

"Cammy! What are you doing here? I'd hoped that I'd made it clear to my father that I wanted nothing to do with you or him or your bunch of no-hoper, hangers-on."

Hearing Spence's arrival, Brand turned his head to meet the unexpected interlocutor.

Both men recognised the other immediately their gaze met. Spence spoke first.

"*Herr* Brandt!...this is becoming stranger and stranger." He sat, uninvited, on the arm of the yellow sofa. "What on earth are you doing in a luxury yacht with the daughter of Marcus Perry? Last time I saw you, you were being manhandled out of the Red Lion by Interpol police."

Brand's mind was whirring but fortunately Kim unintentionally gave him thinking time by leaping to her feet and backing against a wall.

"Does *everybody* in this place work for my father? Two days ago I was happily sailing the Ventura around the Med and now I can't turn round for my father's gangsters and thugs." She looked at Brand. "Now you turn up talking about Jack and Gus and I don't know what to think."

Spence turned again to Brand. "You know Kyle and Bryson? This is just getting more curious by the minute." He paused. "I think we'd all benefit from a little chat." He moved to sit on the sofa properly and crossed his legs. "With your permission, Kimberly, we're going to take the boat out for a little tour of the bay. And while we're out, perhaps we can get to the bottom of why you have a Nazi sympathiser on board and I'll try to find out a little more about Kyle and Bryson."

Hearing a conversation taking place in the guests' lounge, Susan and Liam collected their towels and wandered through from the sun deck and into the edge of the gathering.

"Hi Liam," said Spence. "Why don't you and your lady take a seat? We're all about to have a conversation."

CHAPTER TWENTY-TWO

The motorway service station on the M1 motorway just north of London looked tawdry and drab in summer rain which had customers sprinting as best they could from their cars to the shelter of the fast food restaurants that promised respite if not edible *repas*.

Carrington's Jaguar XJ8 glided to a slow halt in the far corner of the car park. Like all of his fellow agents, he'd been taught how to avoid being followed - or at least to be aware that he *was* being trailed. He'd used every device he'd been taught and was now as confident as could be that he had arrived at his rendezvous undetected. Now all he had to worry about was whether the person he was about to meet, Commissar Second Class Oleg Kuriyenko of the Russian Secret Service had achieved a similar journey outcome. As ever, Barrington had a cover story was he to need one but as the trusted head of Britain's most secret intelligence unit, he felt confident he wouldn't need to deploy it. Meeting a Russian official whose job ostensibly was encouraging British-Russian exports but who was known to all insiders as the Russian's top intelligence official in the UK was the kind of meeting he was expected to have from time to time. Barrington was just secretive by nature and old habits died hard.

Oleg Kuriyenko was a party animal. His reputation as a fun-loving, extrovert official belied his earlier career where he'd had plenty of opportunity to demonstrate to his political masters that he could also be relied upon as a cold-bloodied killer. As his car pulled up alongside Barrington's, his beaming smile was at odds with the weather but suggested that today he was in affable mode.

He joined Barrington in his Jaguar.

"Comrade Sir Alistair," he grinned, smiling at the juxtaposition of Russian and British appellation.

Barrington didn't return his warmth. "Were you followed?"

"No. I took precautions as I'm sure you did." He paused as he adopted a more businesslike tone. "Now, Comrade, you have met with the Brigadier and have been made aware of the task our Government has set the British authorities and you have accepted the responsibility of acting on their behalf?"

"Yes. They appear quite convinced that you have some rogue operators and that you want to work with British intelligence to unearth these people and stop any terrorist activities they may have planned against our interests. The agents you've included in the dossier to the Brigadier were all known to MI6 so there's no new free information and because they *were* known, it helped them believe the narrative we've asked them to accept."

"Excellent. And you have put appropriate agents on the task?"

"Yes. I want to demonstrate that we're engaged in partnership...but not so that we come up with anything effective that would be against the interests of Mother Russia."

Kuriyenko took a small tub of mints from his jacket pocket and threw four of them into his mouth from a cupped hand. "My people have told me who you've deployed in Berlin, Paris and Algiers. We have nothing to be concerned about there. I am told that each of them are competent but will not be curious beyond their task in hand. However, we do not know anything of the two agents you have sent to Spain. Bryson and Kyle? They are unknown quantities."

"Both ex-SAS. Each a very exceptional warrior but neither have any experience in counter-espionage. I encouraged their deployment because I thought they'd put themselves about but wouldn't unearth anything we don't want out in the open. One of them's effectively a functioning alcoholic so I thought I had nothing to worry about...however," he paused for a moment, "they seem to have stumbled across the presence of the Scorpion in Spain and have associated him with possession of a quantity of ricin poison." He turned in order that he could see Kuriyenko's face clearly so as to discern an honest answer. "Is this anything to do with our work here?"

"Comrade, there are aspects of our work that are only made available on a need to know basis but this is bad news...very bad news. We must have these men stand back from any interest in ricin and in the Scorpion. They must keep to their agreed task of providing you with the name of our sleeper in Marbella. This is more important than you can imagine. All we want from this deployment is the *appearance* of Russian cooperation with the British intelligence agencies regarding our rogue agents. Nothing more. Can you bring a halt to their investigations?"

"I'll speak with their controller. What you ask will be done."

Kuriyenko nodded in satisfaction and placed his hand on the car door handle. "Good. You must understand the severity of this. No more enquiries. No more!" he emphasised.

"Agreed," said Barrington.

"As ever, your adopted nation is grateful beyond measure for the services you provide and a further sum of money has been deposited in your Swiss bank account. You will not be displeased at the amount lodged." He opened the door and moved towards his car, bidding Barrington a cheery farewell as he re-inhabited his public persona and prepared for a journey back to London.

Barrington sat motionless for a few moments as he tried to make sense of the conversation he'd just had. He was tired. The heightened levels of caution he had had to observe over many years occasionally caught up with him and this was one of those occasions. Despite entering the British Secret Service on the coat-tails of the biggest review of the agency, established to ensure that no more foreign sympathisers were ever again employed in secret work that would harm the interests of Her Majesty's Government, Barrington had found himself sympathising with much of the political philosophy of his Russian counterparts and when financial inducements came his way, it wasn't too long before he became perhaps the highest level asset the Russians possessed in any intelligence agency anywhere in the world. Protected and rewarded by them, he carried out the requirements of his paymasters to the letter, even when, as now, he couldn't quite work out the end game.

They seem only to wish to set the mood music between themselves and the west, he mulled. *They're obviously engaged in some sort of activity that will allow them to shrug their shoulders following some incident, insist their bewilderment and proclaim their active cooperation with the west in evidence. Sounds like something major's about to go off...and if they're in cahoots with the Scorpion, God only knows where this'll end up.*

Still puzzling his conundrum, he switched on the ignition and gently coaxed the car back towards London.

* * *

In a quiet valley, a deserted farmhouse, its roof missing, baked in the Murcian sunshine. Outside lay an abandoned tractor minus its wheels. On the hill opposite, Jack Bryson leaned over the bonnet of the Landrover. The crosshairs of his Barrett rifle settled on the centre of the tractor's rusting steering wheel, one kilometer away, as if it were the bull's eye on a dartboard.

"Practice makes perfect," said Bryson as he nestled the powerful rifle against his right cheek and brought his finger slowly against the trigger, settling for a moment until he was sure of his accuracy. With a loud crack that startled a flock of birds nearby, the bullet sped towards the centre of the steering wheel smashing it completely, even before any of the birds had taken wing.

"On target?"

"Bang on, Gus."

Again he put the rifle to his shoulder and this time took aim on a fence post even further away. Settling again, he adjusted and focused the crosshairs. Pulling the trigger, the round exploded dead centre in the thick wooden log tearing lumps of wood from the post.

"A fence post? asked Kyle. "Usually you pick smaller targets that test you more."

"I was aiming for the wire where it crossed a knot in the wood. Think I got it dead centre." He stood and smiled at his friend. "Haven't lost the old touch, Gus. Still got it."

"Well, we might need your artistry with that weapon sooner rather than later. It seems that our man is pretty ruthless. The way he took out those four guys and wee Bruno was impressive if only for its callousness more than its sophistication."

"We need to *find* the bastard first," said Bryson. "He could be anywhere."

Kyle remembered the empty pack of cigarettes he'd found in the rear of the red pick-up.

"Forgot about this." He proffered the pack to Bryson who accepted it and read the scrawled writing.

"Looks like something in Arabic"

Kyle retrieved the pack. "Hmmm, I certainly can't make it out. We'll keep it for the time being. It might also be an example of our man's handwriting as well as a fingerprint or two." He stood up. "Let's get moving. We may as well keep driving with the transponder on while there's a wee chance we might enter the reception area just in case he had more than one signal out there."

"So we find him, we find the drugs or the poison and we return it to Perry?"

"Probably need to do something along those lines...as well as trying to get hold of the three cases of money the guy stole." He held the rear door open while Bryson packed his Barrett rifle in his kit bag. "Also, we have to remember that the colonel seems to be anxious about Perry's Russian agent and we won't get back inside the circle to deal with that issue if we don't have something to trade." He closed the door of the Landrover. "But first we get something to eat. I'm starving...and we also need to get rid of this Landrover. The cops'll have an APB out on it by now."

* * *

Twenty miles further on towards the coast, Farrokh Hassan pulled his small truck into a lay-by and turned the ignition key to still the vehicle. He rolled down both front windows to permit a cool breeze to enter the cabin and wiped his forehead. Like most of the faithful, he sought to observe five formal prayers each day. He had already missed *Fajr* and *Dhuhr* but now he could observe *'Asr*, the afternoon obligation in order to remind himself of God and take an opportunity to seek His guidance and forgiveness. He stepped from the vehicle and shielded his eyes as he located the blazing sun in order to attempt to configure himself and place Mecca in the context of the wasteland. He observed his immediate horizon and went about his observance. There was no water available for purposes of ablutions so he knelt and repeated the words he'd used countless times, *"Allahu Akbar. Ashhadu anlaa ilaaha illallaahu wahdahu laa shareekalahu, washhadu anna Muhammadan 'abduhu wa rasooluhu."* He then recited the first verse of the *Qur'an* and after further supplication, finished by saying the words, *"Subhana Rabbiyal A'ala."*

He rose and took his phone from his pocket, returning it when he realized that he could not receive a signal in this remote part of Spain.

I must find a place where I can eat, drink and phone my brothers. Soon the Western world will know again the holy work of Farrokh Hassan.

* * *

Ten minutes into the conversation requested by Spence, some measure of confusion reigned. It had become evident to everyone that Kim, Susan and Liam Brannigan and the three members of staff were merely engaged in the organisation of a holiday in the sun. Under

Spence's suspicious glare, Brand had taken the brief moment provided by Kim's outburst to gather himself and was now back to his assured self. He'd found it necessary to insinuate himself into the role remembered by Spence and had explained that it had been true that Interpol had removed him from the Red Lion. He went on to encourage his interrogator to explore newspapers at the time which showed that he'd been handed a four year sentence for assault and robbery..."All they could prove, Cammy..." but didn't go on to say that after his role in the trial had concluded, he'd moved on to other missions and hadn't served a moment behind bars, although several major criminals based in and around Marbella were still doing time thanks to his work.

"So how come you know Bryson and Kyle?"

"Known them for years. Met them on holiday in Dublin when they were still serving officers in the SAS. We got on well. None of us is married and we agreed to meet up for a couple of weeks' sunshine here in Marbella. No big mystery. The concierge at the hotel where we agreed to meet told me they'd gone off to see people on the Ventura so I came down here."

"I can check all of this, you know."

Brand had appreciated the flaws in his alibi but hoped that the conviction with which he told his story might make it sufficiently believable to obviate the need for Spence having a word with the concierge. "Go right ahead. Be my guest. It's all true."

"So where are Kyle and Bryson just now?"

"Don't know. They haven't returned my phone calls. I was just going to give it another shot."

"Then phone them. Now!"

Brand took his mobile phone from his pocket and pulled its slight aerial to its full height. He punched in Kyle's number, now well memorised.

* * *

Kyle's phone rang as he drove slowly through the Murcian countryside. Slowing, he gazed at it and calculated whether or not it was a good idea to answer. After a few rings, he decided that little harm would come of it.

"Hi."

"Gus! Great to hear from you. Andy Brand here. I've arrived!"

"Eh?" said Kyle, confused by Brand's familiarity.

"Checked in at the hotel and the concierge told me you might be down here on the Ventura. I'm here now and bugger me if I didn't bump into an old friend...Cammy Spence...I gather you're acquainted?"

"Eh?" said Kyle.

"Yes...he's here on the Ventura along with some more of your friends, the Brannigans and Kimberly Perry...

I mean Kim…the owner of the boat." Brand smiled at Spence."Anyway, we were wondering where on earth you boys were."

Kyle decided that something was amiss.

"Colonel. Is something wrong? Are we being overheard?"

"Well, yes and no…"

"In that order?"asked Kyle.

"Quite so."

"Are you all in danger from Spence?"

"Yes. I'd have thought that likely but you simply must get out of that bar and make your way back to your friends here in Marbella. I owe you a drink."

"Take the Ventura back into harbour. We're some hours drive away. We'll meet you on board and take it from there. I assume that we're not known to them as colleagues but as friends?"

"Ever since we met on holiday in Dublin two years ago you've been promising to buy me a drink," laughed Brand.

"Okay. Got you. We'll be as quick as possible. Make sure our three friends don't get hurt."

Brand slid the aerial into its sheath and folded his phone.

"There. That's done. They're just up the coast touring. They'll be back as soon as possible and said they'll meet us in the harbour."

Spence smoothed the sides of his hair. "You must think I came up the River Clyde on a banana boat, *Herr* Brandt," said Spence.

He turned to Kim. "Forgive the Glasgow expression. It means I don't believe a bloody word he said."

He fixed Brand with a glare. "That conversation was nothing more than you providing Kyle with your alibi." He stood up. "However, if it brings our two friends back into our clutches, all well and good. But we won't be sitting on our thumbs waiting for them." He removed the pistol from his waistband and gestured at the still seated Brand. "Place your mobile phone on the table. Your wallet too. Raise your hands, face the wall and remember that this gun has a hair trigger."

Brand did so and Spence removed a small Heckler and Koch .22 pistol from Brand's pocket.

"Just in case, eh?" He stepped back from Brand and opened the wallet he'd placed on the table. It only included banknotes.

"No I.D.?"

Spence made a decision.

"Kim, take us back to the harbour." He redirected his comments to Brand. "When we get there, my men will remove Mrs. Brannigan and you as an insurance policy…"

Liam rose to his feet, his fists clenched.

"Don't worry Brannigan. She'll be well looked after but we all know how capable Kyle and Bryson are. There won't be any rough stuff if people are separated."

Liam stood his ground. "If you think…."

"I do more than think, Brannigan. I absolutely *insist*…and this gun here allows me to do so. Sit down, shut up and no one gets hurt. Inconvenience me and blood gets spilled. Yours!"

CHAPTER TWENTY-THREE

Kyle pulled off the dual carriageway, brought the Landrover slowly to a halt and removed his seat belt. He wiped the sweat from his eyes.

"Right, Jack. We need to rid ourselves of this Landrover before the cops spot us."

"Well, if we just steal an unoccupied one from a gas station we'll be identified by its cameras so we'll need to hotwire one from the side of the road. It's not the perfect answer...the cops will still be on the look-out for it but at least there won't be an army of them chasing it down."

Kyle's right foot pressed lightly on the accelerator as he nodded in agreement. They moved off almost casually in search of a substitute vehicle.

Five minutes later, as they slowly cruised the quiet roads on the outskirts of the town of Cartagena, Kyle braked sharply and reversed so he could confirm his sighting.

"Jackpot!" He reversed further, parked the Landrover at the side of the road and switched off the engine.

Bryson looked around trying to establish the cause of Kyle's exclamation. Then he saw it. Outside the front door of a large villa almost hidden from view by a shield of Almond trees, mother, father and two excited children were struggling to carry four suitcases to a waiting taxi in their driveway.

"Now, don't they look like they're about to go on holiday?"

"By the looks of the cases, at least for a week... maybe two."

Kyle and Bryson waited ten minutes after the taxi had left, observing the house. Bryson decided enough time had passed and broke the silence.

"This is *your* territory.....stealing! You're the expert."

Kyle raised his chin and grimaced his acknowledgement.

"Okay. Back in a couple of minutes. You follow me as I drive away."

So saying he left the Landrover and walked confidently to the house and knocked the front door, preparing to shrug a lot and indicate a broken-down car and the need for a phone if he was challenged. Knocking again, he satisfied himself that there was no one at home. Realising that he was only partially obscured from view, he decided that the rear door probably offered more protection and walked to the back of the house where he elbowed a small window whose glass, once removed provided easy access to the handle of the adjacent larger window. Kyle was inside in eleven seconds and had wiped the handle of fingerprints and discovered the keys to the family car hanging behind the front door within a further twenty seconds. Opening the door, he stepped out, closed the door and sat in the car, turning the ignition in the family's blue Seat almost as he sat in the driver's chair. He was back on the street signaling to Bryson to follow him within two minutes of leaving the Landrover.

Cautiously they drove to a quiet road some distance from the town where they parked both vehicles and moved their belongings from the Landrover to the Seat. As Kyle readied the Seat for departure, Tyson pulled a grenade and a large hunting knife from his kit-bag. Stooping, he swept the sturdy knife upwards in a powerful arc and punctured the fuel tank. As petroleum poured from beneath the Landrover, he stepped back and checked again to ensure that there was no one in the vicinity. He caught Kyle's approving gaze.

"Fire in the hole," he smiled before pulling the pin and rolling the grenade under the four by four. Both men stepped sensibly behind a large tree to avoid the blast and an instant later, an explosion ripped at the fuel tank and a secondary violent *crump* consumed the vehicle in fire, extinguishing all trace of its recent occupants.

"Hope the Colonel rented this vehicle under an assumed name," said Bryson.

They sat in the Seat and drove off, a cloud of black smoke behind them directing anyone interested to the rapidly burning vehicle. No one...at that point...was interested.

"Right, let's get back to the Ventura and see what's what!" replied Kyle.

* * *

Farrokh Hassan had managed to obtain a signal for his mobile phone and had made contact with a co-conspirator from whom he was to collect detonators and enough Semtex that would fill his small truck to capacity and which, when ignited, would cause an explosion large enough to cause the collapse of a small mountain.

Hassan was uncomfortable using his mobile phone. He'd heard tales that intelligence forces could now track and listen to the electronic transmission of telephone calls and so had a selection of phones he'd use then discard after every call. He used heavily coded messages and he'd travel quickly from the location from which he'd made the call in case his call was being monitored for its position as well as its message. So far, his strategy had worked. Now he awaited the man his paymasters had decided was to provide him with the explosives he needed to carry out his plan.

Sheltering from the sun beneath a tree, his truck parked only yards away on a quiet farm road, Hassan rose to his feet and stubbed out his cigarette as he heard the note of a distant diesel engine approach. On edge, he glanced at his watch to check that the timing was precise. *Yes, this must be the consignment.* He waited for more moments and a truck not dissimilar to his own in size hove into view and slowly bounced and wrestled with the undulating earth track that led to their rendezvous.

Pulling up behind the truck marked *Hernández De Mercancías,* the driver switched off his ignition and stilled the vehicle, instantly returning the farm track to the blissful silence of a hot summer's afternoon.

Hassan took his pistol from behind his back and ostentatiously placed it in the waistband of his trousers. It was to be seen that he was armed but also that he'd holstered his gun. Inside the cabin of the truck the driver did likewise.

Hassan watched carefully as the man opened the door of the truck and stepped down. *Mid-thirties,* thought Hassan. *Wiry and strong. I've to respect him. No harm has to be caused him.*

This caused Hassan some small measure of discomfort. He had remained a mystery to intelligence forces for so long because most of the people who knew who he was had been summarily put to death by him after they had served their purpose. Normally this man would have been shot after he'd delivered his goods.

The man rounded the front of his lorry, smiling.

"Hi mate...you must be *Hernández.* My name is Marius and I've got some packages for you, my son."

If Perry, Spence or any other members of his gang had been there to witness the transfer, they may have been caused terminal apoplexy as the man shaking Hassan's hand was none other than 'Happy', their slack-jawed, idiot menial.

Marius was proud of his creation. The only characteristic he shared with Happy in real life was that both were hard workers. But where Happy was a pacifist, Marius was more than capable of looking after himself...where Happy was unintelligent and inarticulate, Marius was bright and cunning...where Happy was obsequious, Marius was assertive and bold. Finally, Happy was an unemployed social inadequate....but in real life, Marius had been employed by the Russian KGB for five years before its transmogrification into the Federal Security Service.

Russia had decided some years earlier that it needed inside information on both the drugs shipments that were routed through Spain and destined for Russia as well as wanting to keep an eye on the criminal gangs, mostly British, that populated the Spanish coastline. Marius App was a perfect choice. The firstborn of Russian *émigrés* who settled in London after the Second World War, his parents had encouraged his participation in cultural affairs....mostly music and dancing. As a child he read voraciously and he was only in his late teens when he was spotted by a Russian talent scout and recruited into what was presented to the world as an educational programme that paid for his higher education in the London School of Economics. In reality it was a funding arm of the Russian Intelligence Service tasked with nurturing new indigenous talent that would promote the interests of the motherland. In the years that followed his graduation, Marius was entrusted with increasingly complex and covert duties on behalf of his employers.

Now in deep cover in Spain, he used a fictitious girlfriend to accommodate visits to Barcelona to meet his handler.

Holidays usually signified a mission of longer duration unconnected with the gang.

"Sorry 'bout this mate but I need to see the back of your right hand"

Measuring the import of the request and telling himself that it was sufficiently specific that there was little purpose in refusing it, Hassan took his hand from his pocket and proffered it, palm down exposing his scorpion tattoo.

"Do you know who I am?" asked Hassan.

"No," lied App. "But I understand that I'm paid by the same people you are. I was just told to wait for your call, make sure that you had a tattoo of a scorpion on the back of your right hand and help you move the contents of my truck into yours if you asked nicely. I don't even know what I'm carrying," he continued disingenuously.

Hassan stroked his chin thoughtfully and hesitated before replying.

"I'm asking nicely."

App smiled. "Then let's get to it. I want to shift this stuff and get back to work."

Hassan nodded and together they lifted the boxes of Semtex and some detonators into the stolen lorry until it was almost full. In tandem they pulled a new tarpaulin purchased earlier by Hassan over the body of the truck of the load in order to covering all markings and tethered it.

As they finished, Hassan considered his next move. Did he take this man at face value or consign him to oblivion in the greater interest of protecting his own identity? He looked at App who stood facing him, hands on hips and smiling. Something in his eyes told Hassan that if he wanted to eliminate this man, he'd have to do it with cunning as in a straight confrontation, he'd probably lose.

He made his decision. "Thank you Marcus. Let us go our separate ways and not speak of this again."

* * *

The gigantic Cole bid Brannigan sit on the yellow sofa by pointing a gun at him as Spence and his men removed Susan and Brand from the room. A gesture with his right hand in the direction of Kim had her sit beside Brannigan.

"Don't think for one minute that I believe that my father would let you use that on me," she hissed.

"Prob'ly right," responded Cole. "But he wouldn't give a shit if I blew away Irish here. So you behave and we all go home tonight."

"You're a big man with a big mouth and a big gun but I'd bet you'd fall like a great oak tree if it was just you and me...man to man," taunted Brannigan.

Cole laughed. "Irish! You're forgettin' that I saw you fall like a sack of potatoes the other night when you took a little punch in the face."

"Yeah, when you and nine of your pals came at me. I figure you're a bit of a cissy when you're left to look after yourself...especially if you're not handling a gun."

"Look, Irish. Don't think you can goad me into some kind of fight...that I'd win without breaking sweat by the way....so just you sit there and shut up and let me dream of the moment that I don't need to be responsible for you so I can beat you to a bloody pulp. Fackin' Irish!"

"Let it go, Liam. You can be sure I'll be reporting back to my dad that this idiot was rough with me if he so much as looks at you the wrong way." Kim stood and walked towards the doors of the lounge and looked out at a peaceful harbour scene with boat owners and crew relaxing in port or washing decks in the sunshine. *How long before Gus and Jack get here?* she pondered. *And what are Cole's orders when they do?* she asked herself.

* * *

As Kim was asking herself about Gus and Jack, the two ex-SAS men, were eating up the miles on their return to the Ventura.

"Nearly out of fuel, Gus," said Bryson. We should pull in to the next gas station."

"Okay."

It took several more speedy miles but a fuel station appeared on their right and Kyle swung the Seat Cordoba Saloon onto the slip road and pulled up at a vacant pump. Patting his pockets to ensure means of paying, he left the car and filled the tank before walking to the kiosk to pay.

A gnawing hunger reminded him that they hadn't eaten for a while and he scanned the shelves for sandwiches, noting that coffee was to be ordered from the man selling the fuel. Collecting his goods, he approached the counter and asked for two coffees, realising as he did so that the man who was serving him was dressed in chequered headgear over a shirt and denims and appeared in sartorial aspect to be of Arabic origin.

Smiling, Gus asked him, "Speak English?"

"Leetle," responded the attendant.

"Two coffees, please. To go."

"*Si.*"

A thought occurred to Kyle as the man gathered two large polystyrene cups and made ready the coffees. He reached into his pocket and produced the pack of Bistoon cigarettes left by the Scorpion."

"Can you read this?"

Hardly looking at the empty pack, the attendant shook his head prompting Kyle to produce a twenty Euro note which he folded and placed inside the pack.

"Can you read it now?"

The attendant withdrew the note and peered at the Bistoon pack, putting his spectacles on in an attempt to ensure his paymaster that he was trying to earn his money. He looked at the Arabic writing for some seconds and traced his forefinger across the writing, right to left.

"It say 'Barcelona'." He pointed to the second line of script. "It say 'Fourt of July'. 'Fourt of July'," he repeated for emphasis...and then to make sure there was no doubt that he'd earned his twenty Euros, "It say, 'Barcelona, Fourt of July'."

As Kyle thanked him and handed him further cash for the fuel and sandwiches, his eye caught the television monitor behind the attendant. With little of the digitalization that often obscures photographs taken from a video clip, a pretty clear front view was shown of both Kyle and Bryson leaving the small Hospital in *Comarcal del Noroeste* where they'd left Bruno Martinez de Oz to die

Front and centre. Looking stern. But unmistakable.

Thanking the attendant as he received his change, Kyle returned to the Seat and threw the sandwiches into Bryson's lap. He passed him both coffees with more care.

"Just been watching our faces on Spanish television, Jack. Clear as day. Don't know what the news guy was saying about us but it didn't appear to be our long awaited nomination for the Nobel Peace Prize."

"Shit! Where'd they get the shots?"

"Hospital video, I suspect. And there's no dubiety. Full colour. Looks like the cops are on to us. It's only a matter of time before that guy in the fuel station reports our whereabouts to the police so we'd better get off this highway."

Bryson took a long swig of coffee from his polystyrene cup before screwing his face up.

"Jesus Christ, this stuff is hotter than molten magma." He wedged it between the seat and the handbrake and began to open the pack of sandwiches, handing the first of them to Kyle. "We're not too far from Marbella now. Whatdya think? We take our chance and try for the exit there or get off straight away?"

"I think we go for it. It'll be another half an hour before the garage guy sees it unless he changes channels and then he's got to get a message throughout to the cops. Even if it all goes smoothly, I figure it's going to be at least an hour before they can marshal resources."

"Agreed...but don't let us get caught speeding by some bored Spanish traffic cop."

Kyle nodded. "Oh, and one other thing. The guy back there was Arabic. He interpreted the writing on the cigarette packet...it says, 'Barcelona, Fourth of July'".

"Tomorrow," said Bryson.

" Yeah, and soon the cops will know that too!"

A further fifty minutes' lively driving saw the Seat exit the highway and slow dramatically as it found itself at the rear of a ten car queue approaching a roundabout adjacent to the city's bus station. As they did so, a police car, lights flashing and siren at full pitch overtook the newly stationary cars and continued past roundabout traffic before screeching to a dusty halt atop a nearby bridge over the highway where its uniformed occupants could view the traffic flowing in both directions.

Kyle and Bryson exchanged glanced.

"Looks like we made it just in time, Gus."

"Yeah. Let's head for the bus station over there and abandon this car. The garage attendant will have been able to show them a video of us getting fuel so they'll be able to ID the car as well as me. The bus station might throw them off the scent if they find it abandoned there while we make our way to the port."

Patiently, Kyle slowly manoeuvred the Seat through the roundabout traffic and into the area reserved for car parking adjacent to the bus station. Both men scanned their environment and determined that all was well before exiting the vehicle and collecting their kitbags. Trying to act as nonchalantly as possible, they closed the car door and began to walk towards the taxi rank. Wordlessly, Kyle placed his hand on Bryson's arm, inviting him to stop. Staring fixedly at the ground as he listened to the ambient noise beyond the bustle of the crowds around them, he remained motionless for a moment before announcing, "More sirens on the way. Lots of them."

An empty adjacent cafe area protected by some small artificial pine trees provided some cover whilst also permitting the men to observe the front of the bus station. Seconds later, six mainly white coloured police cars swept into the forecourt, lights whirring and sirens blaring. Policemen poured from each car and guns drawn, hurried into the bus station whilst, from one larger black car, *Comisario* Romeo Natzari of the *Centro Superior de Información de la Defensa*, emerged and urgently sent three men towards the car park.

Kneeling, Kyle and Bryson took in the scene. As if choreographed by telepathy, they rose and crouching behind the cover of some cars which had parked temporarily in a drop-off zone, made their way towards the last police car to have entered the bus station. As with the others, the police officers had left the keys in the ignition in their urgent efforts to access the bus station quickly. Throwing their gear in the rear of the police vehicle, Bryson took the wheel and slowly reversed the car before heading it towards the exit and towards the port of Marbella only a mile away.

In order not to invite police attention too close to the port, Kyle and Bryson drove the car to a site scheduled for development near to the centre of the city and parked it behind an advertising hoarding.

"This should do for a while. The cops'll go nuts when they find one of their cars gone. It'll just add insult to injury."

"S'pose so," replied Kyle. "It's about a quarter of a mile to the harbour. Think we can get there carrying these kit bags without being noticed?"

"Doubt it."

Kyle stepped out from the shade of the hoarding and surveyed the street,

"Hold on. I'll be back in a moment."

So saying he stepped out onto the busy thoroughfare and walked over to a small shop that sold carpets, rugs and other soft furnishing materials, returning five minutes later with a large floor covering.

"Okay. Let's put our kitbags lengthwise inside this."

Catching on immediately, Bryson place both kitbags end to end on top of the now unfurled carpet and together they rolled it up, covering their belongings.

"This makes us look like home decorators or something and has the advantage of hiding our faces from everyone on one side of us."

Picking up a couple of discarded paint tins lying beneath the hoarding, Bryson placed one at the feet of Kyle and lifting the roll of carpet onto their shoulders, together they lifted the cans and with Kyle in the lead stepped out onto the carriageway on the other side.

Bryson attempted some advice on navigation. "Just keep walking downhill and we'll reach the sea in ten minutes."

They set off.

CHAPTER TWENTY-FOUR

Spence had taken his men back to the Red Lion with Brand and Susan Brannigan in tow.

"Boss'll want to see you," he said to the man they knew as Brandt.

"Fine."

Susan and Brand were escorted into the rear room previously used to hold Kyle and Bryson and a guard was placed outside. Susan moved to a window which looked out onto the opposing wall of a gloomy alley.

"Some honeymoon! How long do you think we'll have to hang around in here? It gives me the creeps."

"Let's just be patient. I'm sure everything will be resolved soon and amicably," said Brand despite his increasing misgivings.

After five minutes, the door opened admitting Marcus Perry.

"Well, Cammy. You weren't shittin' me! It really *is* that fackin' Nazi, Herr Brandt." He sat down on a chair. "Cammy here says you done time back in England after you got pinched 'ere, Mr. Hitler! Is that true, Mr. fackin' Hitler?"

"Hello Boss. Good to see you. Yeah, I got four years. I did four months in the Scrubs then got transferred to Winchester. Done two years there and they sent me home on licence. They only got me on assault and robbery. Couldn't prove nothing else."

Leaning on the window sill, Susan's heart skipped a beat. The man she'd been introduced to initially had now adopted a different persona. While her ear wasn't quite attuned to the nuances of the English accents as yet, she definitely noticed a change in Brand's demeanor and speech patterns. Her discomfort wasn't assuaged when Perry responded.

"Well now, Mr. Hitler. I lost a lot of good fackin' men that night. All still banged up. Me and Spencey here, we couldn't fackin' work it all *out*. Figured that it 'ad to be a fackin' grass what brought the cops to our door and here's you back in Marbella and you didn't fackin' think to look up your old muckers? Back in Marbella with a gun and no I.D. Up to mischief, Brandt. Eh?"

Brand shrugged his shoulders and began to fashion a response.

"Save it Mr. Nazi. We've got modern phones here now. It won't take me long to check you did your time in Winchester. And you know, Mr. fackin' Hitler...you just *know*...that if I find that you *didn't*...well, we'll be sticking the biggest gun I can find right up your fackin' arse."

Despite herself, Susan let out a cry.

"Who's the bint?"

"Name's Susan Brannigan. She's the wife of that guy Brannigan we had here. She'll do as a guarantee until we get to the bottom of all this. Kyle and Bryson won't try anything if they know we've got this pair tucked away."

Perry sat motionless as he contemplated his next move.

"'Appy!"

Footsteps outside heralded the arrival of Happy. "Yes Mr. Perry?"

"Make this young lady a cup of tea. Fack all for the Nazi until we find out what's fackin' *what* 'ere."

* * *

Reaching the water's edge, Kyle and Bryson laid the large rug on the ground and sat on a bench more used to giving temporary respite to tourists and wealthy boat owners than a couple of suspected murderers carrying an arsenal of weapons that would equip a small army. Bryson collected both cans of paint and placed them in a handy receptacle next to the bench

"Well, a frontal assault on the boat or do we take them from behind?"

Kyle thought. "Who knows what awaits us there. I figure we find a way of getting on to the Ventura without them knowing and see what gives. Seems crazy for us to walk into something that Brand has hinted might just be injurious to our health."

"That's the way I see it too."

"Give me a minute, "said Kyle. He stepped behind a nearby bush and removed his clothes other than his boxer shorts but left untouched the knife and scabbard he always had tied to the side of his right calf. Now looking more like the many holidaying tourists in the vicinity other than the sheath fastened to his leg, he clambered over a few large rocks and slipped into the sea.

Only a few moments passed before Bryson saw him return...but this time in a small row boat that, until some minutes previously, had been tied to a luxury motor yacht. Unrolling the rug, Bryson took one, then the other kit bag from the bench area and handed it to Kyle in the row boat before returning one more time and collecting Kyle's clothes and shoes.

Balancing precariously on a rock, Bryson managed to climb into the row boat and handed Kyle his gear.

"Better get dressed."

Hurriedly donning his clothes once more, Kyle pulled heavily on the oars and guided the row boat out towards the entrance to the Marina.

"Can you see the Ventura?"

"Not yet. They could have parked it anywhere in here."

"Berthed."

"Berthed then…Jesus, do you always need to correct my grammar?"

"It's your *vocabulary* this time."

"Fucksake, Gus…I need a drink."

Rowing the boat on the main waterway, Bryson spotted the Ventura.

"Over there on your left."

Kyle manoeuvred the small craft until it was located beneath the prow of the Ventura. He stilled the vessel.

He spoke quietly. "Okay. We take our pistols from the kit bag, leave the rest but tether this boat so we can bring it all on later if we need to. Agreed?"

Bryson nodded.

"First I'll take this boat round and place it amidships…"

"A fuckin' *mid*ships?"

"At the lowest point of the boat…in the middle anyway…so you can climb on board unnoticed. I hand you the rope and we tie it to the rail. You help me up and we go looking for trouble. Agreed?"

Bryson nodded again…"Afuckin*mid*ships…," he murmured again…and carefully they executed their plan until both stood, dry and armed on the walkway at the side of the Ventura. Putting his finger to his lips, Bryson took the lead and crouching, walked quietly and slowly aft where normally they'd have entered the Ventura. As he did so, he saw the great bulk of Cole seated just inside the entrance, gun in his lap and oblivious to his presence. Turning, he signaled to Kyle that they should proceed no further and stepped back to consult.

He spoke in a low voice to Bryson. "Cole. He's armed. There might be others."

Reaching behind himself, Kyle produced a silencer from his waistband and quietly screwed it onto his gun. Whispering, he said, "You take Cole. Quietly. No guns. I'll take out anyone else in the room if they move."

Another nod. A pause.

Two steps were all it took for Bryson to wheel round the door frame and present his gun one inch from Cole's nose. His left hand lifted Cole's gun from his lap.

"Make one move and say goodbye to your face".

As he spoke, Kyle had moved behind him to cover anyone else in the room. No one was there.

Bryson took charge. "I'll only ask you this once. If you lie to me, I'll just fuckin' shoot you dead. No excuses. No second chances. Is there others on board?"

Cole, now obviously terrified shook his head. "Just me!"

Kyle lowered his pistol and turned to Bryson, smiling.

"*Are* there others on board. Plural noun."

Bryson groaned.

Motioning to Cole to stand and using him as a human shield, they walked quietly through the boat, guns pointed skywards, fingers on triggers until they came to the jacuzzi where Kim was soaking in the tub, eyes closed, only her head and arms above the frothing waterline.

Kyle eyed Bryson and gestured wordlessly to him to look after Cole. He kneeled down on the deck until his face was but an inch from Kim's ear.

"Surprise!"

Kim awoke startled from her slumber and in one move grabbed the neck of Kyle's T-shirt before dragging him off-balance and head first into the jacuzzi. She rose quickly to her feet and drew her arm back to administer a blow with the edge of her right hand held rigid.

"Whoa," laughed Bryson as his friend disappeared under the foaming water…"We come in peace!"

Confused and puzzled, Kim froze as she tried to make sense of the situation.

She looked up. "Jack?"

She looked down at the back of a man trying to gain purchase on the floor of the Jacuzzi so he could rise. "Gus?"

Kyle rose from the deep and wiped the water from his eyes. "What a welcome! Where'd you learn that move?"

"I should have *finished* the move. You don't go sneaking up on people like that."

Kyle smiled. "Impressive."

Hearing the noise, Liam Brannigan emerged from his stateroom and shouted a welcome only to see Bryson stoop and wheel, his gun now pointed as an extension of his two arms into the gloomy interior.

"Friend...friend...," shouted Brannigan. "Don't shoot, Jack! It's Liam. It's me!"

"Hi Liam," said Bryson, holstering his gun in his waistband. "Come on out and see Kim beating the shit out of Gus!"

Kim still wasn't appeased. "That was a dumb move. You scared me half to death!"

"Well, it was me that got soaked."

Still smiling, Gus sat on the edge of the Jacuzzi and started to peel off his T-shirt.

"I'd better slip into something more comfortable."

"Yeah! Like a coma!"

"You tell him, Kim," laughed Bryson before turning to Cole. "Okay Big Man. We're going to sit you down for a while. Just take a seat in that chair," he said, signifying a bamboo chair helpfully constructed to assist the ligatures he intended using to immobilize his prisoner. "These knots will restrain you but the chair is light so you could still manoeuvre your way over to the edge of the boat and throw yourself off. If that's your fancy, be my guest. We won't be in any hurry to pick you up."

"I need to pee."

"Piss your pants, Quasimodo."

"Jack, that's no way to speak to anyone. You escort this man to the bathroom and I'll pour you a stiff drink."

Bryson smiled. "Dear Mr. Quasimodo, if you would care to come with me, I'll see that you're made comfortable."

He turned to Kim as he waved Cole in the direction of the toilet with his pistol.

"I'll have one of them big malt whiskies you serve up, Kim. No ice."

"*Those* big malt whiskies," shouted Kyle at his back.

* * *

Anatoly Borovsky lifted the phone on his desk. "Comrade Ivanov, this is a secure line. We can talk openly."

"That will be necessary. I want to know of progress."

"The news is mixed, comrade Ivanov. We have your man, the Scorpion, well positioned in Spain. Our agent in Marbella has recently supplied him with massive explosive capacity and he has your stock of ricin poison that will cause havoc when it is mingled with the explosive blast. Everything is on schedule for the fourth of July."

"You said *mixed* news."

"Two of our agents have gone missing in Reykjavik. We don't yet know whether this has anything to do with Operation Mandarin but one of them was on the list we gave to British Intelligence because our information was that she was involved with the dissidents within FSS."

"That has no immediate impact upon our plans unless she is presently sharing our secrets with them."

"Svetlana Petrova was one of our best agents. She will tell no one anything either voluntarily or under pressure. She has no love for the West. But she no longer appears to be in a position to rendezvous as planned with the Scorpion in Barcelona." He drew deeply on a cigarette. "I must say that the Scorpion was pleased when he was advised of this. He was never happy with our insistence on a partner...especially a woman. He still believes he's working for Iran and found it unusual that they would wet nurse him with a woman." He flicked cigarette ash into a small silver cup on his desk. "So he's happy."

"None of this troubles me overmuch."

"Perhaps the next news might. The two men British Intelligence sent to Marbella were merely intended to identify our agent out there so we could claim we were working in partnership after July fourth. Unfortunately, they have veered off-line and have discovered the presence of the Scorpion although we have no evidence that they know exactly who he is. They have also discovered that he is in possession of quantities of ricin but have no idea what it is to be used for. We have alerted one of our top people in London who has been told to ensure that they do not interfere further in the ricin investigation. Unfortunately, the Spanish police have come across a victim of ricin poisoning. He has died and they have identified the two British agents as somehow being involved. They have no reason we're aware of to imagine that they're intelligence agents...probably just think they're straightforward criminals...perhaps terrorists. They've put out their photographs on Spanish television - but without mentioning the ricin - just saying they want to interview them. I presume they don't want to start a national panic. They've also been on their trail but have not captured them."

"This is not going as smoothly as I'd wished, comrade Borovsky."

"Few operations go exactly as planned, comrade."

"Can't your agent in Marbella be tasked with removing the two British agents?"

"This is being organised. Over time we've come to expect problems emerging in the best planned of operations. Our skill, such as it is, is to be prepared to take ameliorative action."

"Then take it, comrade Borovsky. And make sure it's effective. Neutralise the two British agents and find Petrova in Iceland in case she's talking. I have invested great amounts of money in this venture and the Motherland stands to gain substantial advantage for many years if our plans come to fruition. Failure is not acceptable."

There was a click as the phone was laid down in *Novosibirsk*. In his office deep within a grand office building in the Kremlin, Borovsky frowned. These days he wasn't used to being spoken to like that. But he was concerned. Ivanov was a dangerous opponent. Politically very well connected...but so was he, he mused. But Ivanov had great wealth...great wealth. That counted...and Borovsky was a poor man. Rich, relative to the rest of the entire nation...but a pauper relative to Ivanov. *I must be very careful here,* he thought.

Chapter Twenty-Five

Comisario Natzari stood beside the newly rediscovered police car, shouting angrily at his officers whom he blamed directly for allowing his quarry to evade capture, for stealing the car and most importantly, for providing an opportunity for his boss to scream at him over the radio…thereby allowing other officers listening in to witness his humiliation.

While he stood shouting orders and demanding the apprehension of the two men in the photograph, across the road, Sub-commissioner César Constantino of the *Grupo Especial de Operaciones* stepped from his car having heard Natzari being traduced by his boss on his car radio as well as having been directed to the locus of the abandoned car. Lighting a cigarette, he looked around and seeing Natzari working himself into a rage, ambled into a nearby shop, taking the photograph of Kyle and Bryson from his pocket as he did so.

Following a visit to a third shop, Constantino wandered back over to the car where Natzari still stood fulminating over the news from one of his officers that the two men were nowhere to be seen.

He read from his notebook.

"*Comisario*, perhaps you might ask your officers to look for a large rug, some eight feet square. Coloured brown with a red fleck."

"What?" said Natzari, confused and exasperated by Constantino's relaxed manner.

Constantino gestured over his shoulder. "That shop there. The one that sells soft furnishings. The manager identified one of the two men. He said that one hour ago, he bought a rug as I've just described." He looked at Natzari's uncomprehending face. "Perhaps if we find the rug, we find the *men*?"

Stifling an urge to beat Constantino about the head if only because he was nearest to him rather than because he often out-thought him, Natzari gently simmered.

"My men didn't think to ask the shopkeepers next to the site of the abandoned vehicle whether they'd seen anything... never mind *purchased* anything? he asked rhetorically.

"Apparently not, my friend. But perhaps now they will look for the rug. Unless these men intend to hide in Marbella and want to do some home decorating while they wait, my guess is that they used the rug to conceal something. But let's be careful. For all we know it may be containers with ricin in them."

Natzari bowed to the logic of old Constantino's wisdom. He spoke through gritted teeth.

"I agree...and will so direct my men."

* * *

Cole was bound to the wicker chair having been taken to a wardroom and seated in front of a television. The door was locked. Sixty-five year old member of staff, Graciana was asked to sit outside and knit the socks she intended finishing for her two year old grandson on the basis that Cole could never escape through the porthole until and unless he lost two-thirds of his bodyweight. As well as being a patient and responsible woman, Graciana also had a cry like a *banshee*. Cole would never find a way past his guard.

Kyle and Bryson sat in the yellow leather armchairs with Kim and Liam. Bryson held a glass containing the balance of the third of three large whiskies provided by Kim.

"So what do we do now?" asked Kim.

"We get Susan back as a first step," said Liam.

Kyle shuffled uncomfortably in his seat. "Look, Liam...Kim...you're good people and Jack and I are not prepared to take further advantage of your friendship. You've been so trusting of us...and kind."

Kim uncrossed her legs and moved to the edge of her seat. She looked serious.

"What is it, Gus?"

"Jack and I have had a chat. We trust you and we'd like to be upfront with you."

"About what, Gus?"

"Jack and I are in Spain on a mission. We're financed by major players...probably an arm of Government...the *British* Government. And we're being asked to act against the gang of people notionally run by your father, Kim."

Kim's hand went to her mouth.

"We certainly didn't expect the last few days to unfold in quite the way they have but over the last wee while people have been trying to shoot us, a guy with a deadly poison threatened to kill us with it and we seem to have uncovered a plot of some kind involving a deadline tomorrow in Barcelona."

"Mind and tell them about the cops," mumbled Bryson, the whisky beginning to have an effect.

"Yes...the Spanish police found me standing over a dead body and have taken the not unreasonable view that I must have had something to do with his demise."

He looked at Kim who now looked even more shocked.

"It's okay. I didn't kill anyone. I just found the guy just before the cop found me."

"You've been busy boys." said Liam.

"Who's the man who told me he was your friend...? Mr. Brand," asked Kim.

"We're not entirely sure. He's our paymaster and until recently we had him down as a good guy. Now we're less sure. He may be on our side or he may work for your dad's gang, Kim. I'm sorry 'bout this but we have to face facts. You know yourself that your dad's been involved in one or two questionable incidents in his day."

"He's a crook...but...well, he's also my father."

"Which is why Jack and I intend to take our leave of you. We've got business to conduct and we can't cause you problems. We also have to find a way to get to Barcelona to see if we can work out what's going on. We can't trust our own boss and we can't go to the Spanish police. It's us against the world I'm afraid and coping with your interests in the matter just complicates things too much. Also...things might get a bit hairy in Barcelona and we don't want you anywhere near the firing line."

"That stuff might apply to Kim, but I'm free to make of this what I will," said Liam. "And I want my wife back safely and *pronto*!"

"Problem is, Liam...if we go after Susan and Brand, it would reduce the time we have to get to Barcelona and there's an even money chance that the bad guys win in Marbella and we end up dead or injured. Again we miss Barcelona."

"Guys, I'm not making myself clear. I'd like to think that I'm not bad at reading people and I have you two down as honourable human beings. There's no way you're going to harm either Kim or me and therefore you'd have to face up to the fact that our silence over the next two days is crucial to you. Frankly, if you don't help me get my wife back, I'd have no option but to go to the police and invite their assistance to get Susan back. Nothing, not even a potential incident in Barcelona, could persuade me to make concessions on this. You're doing things because you *want* to and because people *pay* you to. I'm going to rescue Susan because, quite simply, she's my life. She comes back safely to the Ventura or frankly, I don't *care* what I do to your feckin' plans."

Kyle held his silence, then turned to his partner. "Jack...a word. Kim, mind if we use one of your rooms?"

Kim's face crumpled as she fought back tears.

"I don't know what to think here, she said, ignoring his request for privacy." She wrestled with her thoughts as she struggled to regain some of her composure.

"Look, Gus. Tell me the truth. Are you and Jack ex members of the SAS like you said?"

Kyle nodded. "Just like we said. Dishonourably discharged because the big fellah here had one too many sherbets."

"Aye...an' what about you beatin' up the military polis? It's always me that gets the blame," slurred Bryson.

"And you've been sent to Spain to protect British interests?"

"Just like we said."

"And you need to get to Barcelona to deal with things."

"Again...as we said."

She hesitated..."I *think* I believe you, Gus...I *want* to believe you...but if you let me down, I'll never forgive you..."

"I'd never..."

Kim interrupted him and turned to Liam, now in control of her emotions and comfortable in her command.

"Liam, you're my guest on board and I'm so sorry for everything that's happened to spoil your honeymoon and put your wife in danger."

"Don't be..."

"I'm not finished. I also think that this pair haven't thought through their plans properly. How they expect you to sit still and have your wife's life threatened while they hop off to Barcelona is beyond me... So here's what I think we do. Gus? You, Jack and Liam take such steps are as necessary to free Susan. No one cares a fig for Mr. Brand unless you two think he's important to you. Once you get Susan back here, the Ventura sails for Barcelona. If the police really *are* after you then you'll be much safer off the road than on it."

Kyle and Bryson looked at each other but before they could fashion a response, Kim continued.

"Look, you two might be the best dishonourably discharged men in the British Army. You might be God knows how wonderful but you can't say that you've a better plan than one that stops Liam bringing in the police and you two getting guaranteed safe passage to Barcelona in time for your rendezvous with who knows what."

"I was just going to say..."

"Say what, Gus...that this is exactly what you intend doing? Because if you take *another* view you're the biggest fool I ever met. If you don't use my idea, who knows where the two of you will end up at."

"Don't finish your sentence in a preposition," smiled Gus.

"Jesus...Kim, he does that with me all the time. Just ignore him. Your plan makes good sense to me."

"And to me," said Gus.

Liam punched the air in delight. "Then let's get moving. I want to see Susan back here within the hour."

Bryson drained his glass and presented it to Kim inviting a refill but Liam stepped forward and took it from his hand.

"No more drink, Jack. Not until Susan's back here safe and sound. We'll need our wits about us for the next wee while. When we get back you can drown yourself in the stuff."

Bryson grimaced as he prepared his argument against the proposition.

"Liam's right Jack," said Kyle. "A coffee, a strategy and we're off."

* * *

Perry and Spence stood in front of the large television in the small, rear bar they used as an office-cum-private club. More used to showing English or European football matches for more senior gang members and their friends, on this occasion it displayed a photograph of Kyle and Bryson while a news reader spoke of the police interest in them following a murder.

"Bring fackin' Hitler in here," ordered Perry of Spence.

Brand was sticking to his jailbird cover story with Susan when Spence opened the door and bid him join Perry in the bar leaving Susan standing at the window over which an external metal grill had been placed to ensure security.

"Well, Mr. Hitler...I'm beginning to *believe* you're still going about your evil ways...them's your two fackin' pals on the telly. Seems the Spanish cops want them for a murder."

Brand had tried to prepare himself for another accusation...a beating... a threat. What he hadn't considered was seeing the faces of his two agents as large as life on Spanish TV...and Marcus Perry apparently convinced of his prison alibi.

Accused of murder?

He tried to block out Perry's background commentary and listen to what the newsreader was saying, his rusty Spanish just about holding up sufficiently to make out the veracity of his captor's assertion. *Why would they put them on TV like this?* he asked himself. *If it was a common or garden murder they would place a lot if resources behind the investigation...sure... but show photographs of two suspects on national television?*

He looked at Perry who was still mouthing away on descant but nothing was making its way through the mist of his confusion. Then it dawned on him... *Shit...they've discovered the ricin and want to track down the boys without alarming the Spanish public.* Gradually Perry's voice began to assert itself in his consciousness.

"Fackin' listen to me Mr. Hitler. You three are over here on a fackin' *job*..ain'tcha? You of all people should know that nothin' fackin' 'appens on my patch without I'm involved. You of all people should know that I get a percentage..." He stopped as a gradual realisation of Brandt's treachery became evident. His mouth twisted into a grim rictus. From the rear of his waistband he pulled his pistol. Carefully and slowly he enunciated his words.

"You... fackin'...bastard. You's over here to nick my fackin' three million *quid*." He gestured at the television. "You and them two."

He pointed the gun at Brand's face then slowly lowered it to his groin.

"Unless you explain exactly what's goin' *fackin'* on, I'm goin' to shoot you in the *fackin'* bollocks Mr. Hitler."

* * *

Standing just inside the door of the main bar of the Red Lion, Marius App *alias* Happy leaned against the doorframe mop in hand, eyes transfixed on the photographs of the two men on television...two men his handler in Moscow had just ordered him to murder.

The two guys from the fight outside, he told himself. *Shit...they were handy! This will require sufficient distance and a gun or they'll eat me alive. No time like the present.* Leaning the mop against the bar he walked through to the kitchen area and opened his locker. Glancing over his shoulder he unwrapped a small. 22 Beretta from an oiled cloth he used to clean and disguise it. App removed the Beretta...Perry would never countenance his idiot functionary carrying a weapon, even this small...and put it into his pocket. *Things might start to heat up soon,* he thought with some prescience. *Better safe than sorry. I'll need to concoct a matter of some urgency to get out of Perry's clutches. Perhaps 'Maria' will have to attempt suicide so I can go to Barcelona for a while?*

* * *

Kyle, Bryson and Brannigan seated themselves aboard Kim's four by four Lexus and began preparation for a journey to the Red Lion, the only location they could think of where Susan and Brand might be held captive.

"Remember, Liam. Jack and I do the work. You're our getaway man. Are we clear on this? I know you'll be anxious to rescue your bride but you must accept that Jack and I are better equipped to see these people off and bring Susan safely to your side."

"Clear on that, Gus. No problem."

"Then drive on."

* * *

In a small airfield just south of *Novosibirsk,* Anatoly Borovsky made ready to board his private jet *en route* for Barcelona. His entourage, often numbering in the twenties was reduced to four plus his flight crew who would remain on board while he conducted his business. The following day, at least according to his schedule, he was intent upon conducting business with many of the oil and gas fraternity who attended the political and economic jamboree that fringed the meeting of Western and OPEC representatives. But for some time he had planned an act so brutal in its impact that he anticipated a dramatic slide in relationships between OPEC and the West, a dimming of their respective economies and the establishment of a climate within which only *Russian* oil and gas...*his* oil and gas, would represent a secure investment.

Borovsky had deliberately booked his accommodation rather late in the day knowing the problems this would bring in obtaining something appropriate close to the meeting. In consequence, he and his entourage were to be housed some seventy miles outside Barcelona, in a very expensive villa in its own grounds in Figueres. Close enough to be near the action but comfortably outside the enormous blast zone he'd planned.

CHAPTER TWENTY-SIX

Susan dabbed at Brand's head wounds where Perry had pistol-whipped him instead of shooting him, Spence having earlier advised him to desist. Dragged unconscious into the room from which he had earlier been summoned, he had been permitted to receive some basic first aid from Susan who had demanded clean water and a towel.

"I think you might need medical attention for the wound on your forehead, Mr. Brand. It looks a deep cut."

She hammered on the door and after a few moments Happy answered.

"Just look at this poor man's head. He needs a dressing and a bandage. Can you get me one while I try to tend his wounds?"

"I'll get a dressing and bandage," repeated Happy, who left.

Susan returned to Brand, now semi-conscious.

"Are you okay? Do you have any other injuries?

"I'll be fine. I've had worse beatings."

"You poor man, " empathised Susan.

Brand lay back having sipped at the cup of water that Susan had earlier obtained and surrendered again to unconsciousness.

* * *

Liam cut the engine a few blocks from the Red Lion as requested by Kyle. Upon stopping, Bryson and Kyle stepped out of the vehicle and asked Liam to wait while they reconnoitered the outside of the pub. Merging with the tourists, they made their way as nonchalantly as possible to the lane on with the bar was situated. Both men used their well-trained military eyes to digest the information before them.

"No guards...occasional clientele using the bar... nothing untoward...exits free at both ends of the lane...cover available in the cafe-bar opposite..."

Kyle interrupted Bryson midst his appraisal.

"First floor window...this side of the entrance. That's Susan Brannigan."

"You're right...window sill made of wood...poorly maintained...probably rotten. Cage over the window removable by force..."

Kyle thought out loud.

"Remember how we rescued all of that sound equipment for the regimental concert in Aldershot a few years ago?"

"I was pissed but I remember the moves. Will Liam be up to the task?"

"Pretty sure he will be. We just need to hope that there's none of Perry's men in there with her."

Stepping back they retraced their steps and moments later spoke to Liam who had held his position.

"Okay Liam. We've found Susan. We need your help. Put on that high visibility jacket and take that clipboard from under the chair. You're our foreman for the next few minutes if anyone asks. Now all we want you to do is to drive this vehicle along the lane outside the Red Lion. We'll tell you where to stop. Jack and I will bring Susan…and maybe Brand… out of the window, on to the top of the Lexus, on to the bonnet, down on to the road and inside the Lexus. Once we're *all* inside you pull away…slowly and without stopping to hug your wife. You can do that later."

"Okay, got you. I can do that."

After some careful driving, Liam pulled up outside the Red Lion underneath the window as guided by Bryson.

"Right. On with the high-viz, take that clipboard and pen and look officious. Don't say anything. Just watch," said Kyle who went first and was atop the Lexus in seconds closely followed by Bryson. Peering through the window, Bryson caught Susan's eye and placed a finger over his mouth, shushing her; inviting her silence. From the scabbard on his right leg he produced his knife and handed it to Bryson who placed it carefully on the wooden sill at the upper hinge. With one mighty shove, the knife was buried two inches inside the wood. He repeated this a further three times, above, below and to the remaining side, until the hinge gave way having no support within the frame. Within another ten seconds he released the lower hinge. Susan had realised their objective and had released the window from the inside in anticipation of her rescue. Quickly, Bryson held his arm inside and offered it to Susan to climb out.

"What about Mr. Brand?"

"He can stay."

"No. He's badly hurt and needs treatment. I won't leave without him"

Bryson calculated her seriousness and decided she might well stand her ground.

"Shit!" He waved an invitation to join him at Kyle who stood on the bonnet of the vehicle ready to help Susan on to the lower lever, then redirected his comments at Susan Brannigan.

"Okay, step aside."

Kyle and Bryson stepped into the room through the open window and saw Brand lying in the corner having succumbed again to unconsciousness.

"I'll take his legs," said Kyle and together they lifted him to knee height... just in time for the door to open.

Happy stood in the doorway, a bandage in one hand and a dressing in the other just as Susan had requested some while before. Moments passed between the three sentient men as each calculated the import of the scene they were witnessing.

Happy moved first, transforming almost instantly into Marius App. Quickly he dropped the bandages and took his Beretta from his pocket. He stepped inside the door and closed it behind him.

Slowly, Kyle and Bryson placed Brand back on the floor and stood to face App.

"You two are the men the police are looking for, No?"

Kyle spoke first.

"Nah, You're mistaken. We're doing work for Mr. Perry. C'mon now, you don't need that gun. The boss asked us to take this man to hospital."

"*You're* the two guys off the telly. Cops are lookin' for you everywhere...as it happens, so am I. I'm afraid it's your bad luck that I found you before they did. Y'see I've got orders to shoot to kill."

"Whoa, calm down...shoot to kill? You've got the wrong guys. I told you...we work for Marcus Perry."

App stood back to one side to distance himself further from the two ex-SAS men.

"On your knees boys…so there's no funny stuff."

Neither man moved.

"I said on your *knees* or I'll just shoot you where you sta…" App licked his lips nervously and nodded in the direction of the key rings attached to the belt worn by each man. "Where did you get these…the key rings? Where d'you get them?"

Instantly Kyle realised they'd found their Russian agent.

"If you recognise these, then we certainly *do* work for the same people. We both work for the Federal Security Service of the Russian Federation. You are one of us. Lower your gun, comrade. Lower your gun."

Kyle stepped slightly closer to App, his palms facing the floor making calming gestures.

"I was not informed of this. I need to check with…"

"Hey, you know what they're like. These people are all incompetents. One hand doesn't know what the other hand's doing. Look, we've been sent here same as you and when you check, it'll all be explai….."

In a sudden sweeping movement Kyle brought his right leg behind him and hit App square on the side of his face. A second jump kick found his right wrist and knocked the gun from his hand. While he was still in the process of falling to the floor, Bryson moved rapidly to deliver a telling blow to his chin, knocking him unconscious.

"He's spark out, Gus. Let's get moving before someone else starts calling."

Again they lifted Brand, this time manoeuvring him to the window. Liam was down below, clipboard in hand, anxiously wondering what was taking place in the room above. Seeing his wife being ushered from the room above was his signal and he regained his driving seat in preparation for a smooth getaway. Bryson stepped out on to the roof of the Lexus and helped Susan down before returning to assist Kyle with Brand. Waiting a moment until the lane was clear, together they lifted Brand down and threw him roughly into a rear seat. Both men jumped aboard the vehicle and headed off to the port. Liam, excited and now feeling free to ask several questions at once, prompted Bryson to swivel his head and pause in his task of checking for followers and grunt, "Shut the fuck up. Drive slowly like you were asked and get us all back to the fuckin' boat."

As Susan caught his eye, Bryson realised he may have been a bit peremptory with her husband.

"Sorry, darlin'…adrenaline!"

They turned out of the lane and headed towards the Ventura.

* * *

It was dusk now as Farrokh Hassan carefully reversed his small truck into the garage unit he'd rented in Barcelona's Barceloneta District. A small, multi-racial community on the sea front of the city, Barceloneta was perfect for someone like Hassan to move around in anonymously. Only a matter of a few hundred meters from the harbour, he'd easily be able to transfer his deadly load on to the power yacht he'd also rented and would take possession of that evening.

Later tonight he would have to move the ricin and explosives on to his hired motorboat and then he would sleep in the cabin of the lorry to avoid any prospect of detection but in the meantime he was hungry. First he had to phone Armeen Borzoo, whom he understood to be his Iranian handler, oblivious to the fact that Borzoo, whilst a proud denizen of Teheran, was actually employed by the Russian FSS. Reporting that everything was almost in place, he left the call box in order to begin his prayers. He'd been careful when considering a location for his mission to select an area where a Mosque was available to believers and only a few minutes later, he found himself kneeling in prayer... *Allahu Akbar...*

* * *

Natzari's men hadn't been as thorough as he'd have wished back at the garage of *Hernández De Mercancías*. While he'd been busy instructing his men on what he'd wished accomplished, the disheveled figure of Sub-commissioner César Constantino had had his attention drawn to an old portable radio that had been left behind in the vehicle. Already checked for fingerprints and found clean, it had been left on the seat, discarded.

Constantino picked it up and turned it on. After a few seconds during which the device appeared to be making its mind up whether or not to spring into life, the radio signal locked and an Arabic voice fought for supremacy with the white noise of radio interference. *I must have that frequency checked,* thought Constantino. "Officer!"

A white coated man who was dusting a window ledge for prints turned to the sound of the voice and walked to Constantino's side.

"I was always taught that while those who would attempt to obliterate their fingerprints might clean and rub at the surface of an item, when it came to electrical equipment, they frequently forgot to check the bottom of the batteries they inserted, perhaps weeks or months earlier."

He opened the lid on the rear of the radio revealing four batteries.

"As a special favour to me, would you check for prints on the ends of these batteries and while you will want to report your findings to Comisario Natzari, would you be kind enough to phone this number and advise me of the results? If you did this immediately as I have requested, I would see no reason to inform anyone of your oversight in presuming the radio to be clean."

"Thank you Sub-commissioner. It will be done as you request."

"While you're at it, find out what radio station is currently set on the device."

"Sir," acknowledged the officer.

Now, due to Constantino's diligence and courtesy, the breathless phone call he took from the officer advised him that thumb prints found on the end of the battery belonged to a man suspected of involvement in many terrorist events...a man whose real name was unknown as yet but who was known to intelligence organisations as the Scorpion.

"Thank you officer. Now file your findings as protocol demands. I appreciate you calling me and will honour my agreement to forget about your oversight." He collapsed his mobile phone and put it in his pocket. He looked around at the fading light.

Hmmm, what do I know?...the Scorpion...ricin...the fourth of July....the murders of old Señor Hernández and Bruno Martinez de Oz, the two Englishmen and Barcelona. Not much to go on yet but I think I'll make my way up there and see what transpires. If the date of July fourth is significant, everything happens tomorrow...I'd better get a move on.

* * *

Brand had again regained a state of semi-consciousness. Ministered to by Kyle in the rear of the Lexus, he was found to be suffering from flesh wounds caused by blows rendered by Perry to the head and face, bruising and concussion.

"You'll be fine, Colonel."

"Colonel?" asked a surprised Susan.

"Long story, Susan. We've already explained ourselves to Kim and Liam. We'll fill you in on board." He turned his attentions back to Brand. "Think you can walk if we assist you? It'll draw less attention. You'll just look a bit drunk if they don't notice the congealed blood on your face and shirt. It's getting dark now anyway and you'll only be stepping from the Lexus to the Ventura."

"Let's try," said Brand levering himself into a seated position.

A few minutes later they arrived at the rapidly darkening harbour. Lights now illuminated the entire area, especially the secure entrance where Kim was waiting having just returned from the Harbourmaster's office to report that the Ventura was leaving on a trip to Barcelona. Opening the gate, she waved the Lexus onto the concrete moorings and walked behind it as Liam drove it slowly to the Ventura's berth.

Painfully, Brand allowed himself to be carried by Kyle and Bryson onto the Ventura. Miguel had been advised of the need to depart as soon as the guests had arrived and the boat sat growling at the berth in readiness.

* * *

"Fackin...fackin..."

Perry's rage was indescribable. Furiously he kicked out at the cup of water left on the floor by Susan crashing it against a wall as Spence knelt beside Marius App who was still unconscious. Gently he slapped his cheek and spoke quietly to him in an attempt to bring him round.

"Fackin'…"

"He's out cold, boss. No bullet or stab wounds that I can see. No blood."

"Fackin' 'Appy. Wake the fackah up so's we know what went on 'ere." He turned his head and shouted at one of his men who stood in the doorway. "Get a bucket of water. I need 'Appy awake right now."

Spence lifted his head and nodded in the direction of App's pistol lying under a chair.

"May have been some gunplay after all boss."

Perry stepped over and picked up App's small .22 Beretta.

"Fackin' pea shooter. This wouldn't stop a two year old fackin' baby."

Spence's ministrations began to show some success as App began to swim towards consciousness.

"C'mon now, Happy…Wake up son…C'mon now."

Perry's man returned with a metallic wine cooler full of cold water. Perry noticed his arrival and gestured his approval.

"Drown the fackah…"

Moments later App was spluttering and coughing.

"Appy. What fackin' 'appened 'ere?"

Somehow through the confusion, App managed to adopt his alter-ego and spoke as if as Happy.

"The lady asked for a bandage for the man, Mr. Perry. I got a bandage from downstairs. I came into the room. Someone hit me, Mr. Perry."

Spence was now inspecting the window frame.

"This looks professional, boss. Outside job." He looked outside onto the now darkened lane. "Ladders maybe?"

Perry held App's pistol and looked angry enough to shoot everyone in the room with the peashooter.

"Right! We *all* know who fackin' did this! It was them two fackahs who stole my three mill. Well, we'll see if they can handle us now when we're team handed…even with some of our troops still in hospital."

He turned to Spence.

"Cammy, get every single fackah we have on the books. No excuses. Get every fackah down here pronto. *Pronto*! We're going to visit my fackin' daughter down at the docks. That fackin' woman's worse than her fackin' mother. Fackin' bitch!"

Chapter twenty-Seven

Brand lay on a raised bed in a small room on board the Ventura which now sailed out at a rate of knots towards Barcelona, some four hundred and thirty sea miles away. Kim and Susan hovered over him.

Susan was solicitous. "Don't let this crowd have you up too early. You need rest. I think we can bandage your forehead wound without too much difficulty. You might have a headache for a while, though."

Brand smiled. "I promise you, I've been in tougher scrapes in the past. This scar on my right eye almost saw me lose my sight. I've a bullet hole near my neck that missed my jugular by slightly less than a country mile so I've actually been very lucky over the years given my profession."

"And what exactly *is* that profession, Mr. Brand?" asked Kim.

"*Colonel* Brand, apparently," corrected Susan.

"Military then?"

"Man and boy," lied Brand before closing his eyes and yielding to insensibility once more.

* * *

A fleet of mini-buses, cars and one motor-cycle collectively containing the remnants of Perry's gang arrived hurriedly at the entrance to the harbour posing a sharp contrast to the svelte holidaymakers enjoying the delights of the bars and cafes that surrounded some of the most expensive yachts in Europe. Everyone stayed in place awaiting Spence's instructions. When it came to operational matters, Spence and Perry long ago had agreed that Perry's emotional and occasionally reckless approach should subordinate itself to Spence's more strategic and rational manner.

"If we've got it wrong, the Ventura should be berthed five places up on the second pontoon and Terry Cole should be sitting in the rear watching out for trouble," said Spence. "If it's not there, it's likely that Bryson and Kyle have taken him out and scarpered with the boat." He turned to the two men in the front seat of the mini-bus next to him. "Jim, nip out and tell everyone to stay put until I say different...Mike, you come with me...we search this entire harbour in case they've just moved their berth. If you see the Ventura, don't board it, just come back here and we'll compare notes."

"An' get a fackin' move on as well," said a still frustrated and furious Perry.

It took a full seven minutes for Spence and his assistant to return with the news that the Ventura had slipped its moorings.

Perry's face looked like he'd swallowed some foul concoction while having had a hot nail driven through his tongue.

"Fackin' bastards...Fackin' fackin', bitch...Fackin' *useless* fackin' bitch," he shouted at everyone and no one, punctuating every word by slamming his fist on the back of the seat in front of him.

Still in a fury, he turned to Spence.

"Right, Cammy. The only way somethin's goin' to get fackin' done 'ere is if I do it m'self. You'd better come *fackin'* with me. Take your gun."

For all that Spence was his trusted...and listened to...*consiglieri*, he knew better than to contradict him in this mood, and certainly not in front of the men.

"Sure, boss."

Together they walked towards the Harbourmaster's office, Perry's face set in grim, determined aspect.

Arriving at the door of the office, Perry gave three sharp knocks on the door, barely able to contain his anger.

"'Ello?" A pause. "'Ello? You *in* there?"

After a moment, the harbourmaster opened the door to Perry and was completely surprised by his visitor aggressively pushing him back indoors and pulling a gun on him. More used to people handing in bottles of whisky as a courtesy upon leaving, he was completely disorientated by Perry's rough arrival.

"You fackin' better speak English, my son. You fackin' *better* understand what I'm saying."

"*Si Señor*. I understand your English."

"Then, you listen, son. You listen good. That boat…" He turned to Spence who had joined him in the office and closed the door behind them. "That boat…?"

"The Ventura, boss."

"Yeah, the Ventura…it ain't at home now is it? So you're going to tell me exactly where it is or I'm going to shoot you dead. Deader than dead! Do you understand me, sonny boy?"

"*Si Señor*."

"Then where the fack *is* it?"

Claudio Morales had been Harbourmaster for seventeen years in Marbella. Now and again a belligerent drunk, occasionally some pushing and shoving, once in a while some shouting but tonight he was facing a very angry man who was pointing what looked like a very dangerous gun in his very face. He didn't want to test the man's resolve while at the same time, he didn't want to act in a way that disadvantaged *Señorita* Kim of whom he had become very fond during the time she had used his port. But he was not a brave man.

Spence pulled out his gun and doubled the firepower now one inch from Morales' face.

"Barcelona, *Señor*. They are headed to Barcelona and expect to get there sometime tomorrow. "

* * *

Having completed his devotions, Farrokh Hassan took a small bag within which was ten thousand dollars cash, the fee he was to pay for hire of the powerboat for a week's languid cruising in and around the nearby ports of the Mediterranean. The owner, whilst not a member of the criminal fraternity, was flexible in his dealings with law and order and had welcomed Hassan's suggestion of a cash deal. From the boat owner's perspective, Hassan was only seeking a smaller fee than would have been necessary had taxes had to be paid on it and he would increase his profit. From Hassan's point of view, a cash transaction would not be traceable.

A taxi pulled up outside a villa on the outskirts of town. Hassan exited and paid the driver before pushing the buzzer on the gated property. He was admitted, having announced himself as Mr. Abidjan, not to the house but to the adjoining garage where the businessman shook his hand, took the satchel and casually counted the ten bundles each of one thousand dollars and presumed the accuracy within each bundle.

"Excellent, Mr. Abidjan. Now we will go to the Harbour and I will introduce you to the boat and explain some of the basics of sailing it. It is very simple. You will have no problems. "

Hassan had perfected his pleasant demeanor when it pleased him and both men chatted amicably on the ten minute journey to 'Ocean Blue', a powerful craft capable of carrying eight people in some comfort. Hassan spun a story of friends joining him the following day and his need to access the boat that night in order to provision it.

"Sure. Very sensible, my friend."

They arrived at the harbour and walked to Ocean Blue, boarding her by climbing over a guard rail made easier by a small step having been placed at the edge of the mooring by the owner.

Having showed him round, Hassan was encouraged to take the boat round the harbour very slowly so he could 'get the feel of the controls', but more so to permit the owner to establish whether or not Hassan had some basic navigational ability.

Having passed the unofficial test, Hassan returned the boat to its berth quite comfortably.

"Just like driving a car on ice," said the owner before continuing…"Now, the Ocean Blue is equipped with all safety equipment," he said with some small measure of pride. "For example, if someone falls over board we have a throw bag that will inflate upon contact with water although I'd expect that you'll have everyone wear a lifejacket while on board. This book here,"… he opened a bound folder… "This has all of the instructions and protocols you need to inform the coastguard of your intended and actual movements. All of the radio channels you'll need and so on. Importantly…" He turned to face Hassan and spoke directly to him so as to give weighted meaning to his words..."Importantly, Mr. Abidjan, this boat is fitted with a very sophisticated tracking system located on board and below the waterline. It allows me not to have need of charging exorbitant amounts of additional insurance costs because at a glance at my home computer, I can see exactly where the Ocean Blue is at any given time. It can be tracked anywhere in the world with great precision."

In other circumstances, Hassan would have resolved this matter merely by killing the man and destroying his computer, but on this occasion he was unconcerned. Ocean Blue would not travel far and the explosion it would unleash would have the owner wonder why his signal now covered a square mile of the Mediterranean.

* * *

Holding the handrail for support, Sir Alistair Barrington walked unsteadily up the steps at Embankment underground tube station, headed into a few of the stores situated in the Strand, checking faces, watching his back, journeying circuitously. Satisfied he wasn't being followed, he visited a toilet in response to the urgings of his bladder and made his way to a bar in Soho wherein sat Commissar Oleg Kuriyenko of the Russian Secret Service. When he met him only a day previously, Kuriyenko had been cheerful if businesslike. Today, his mood was grim. A meeting had been called urgently and Barrington quite expected to be informed of problems.

In this, he was not to be disappointed.

"Sir Alistair, I was quite clear, was I not, that you had to call off your people in Spain...in Marbella?"

"You were."

"I have had very disturbing reports that you have disobeyed my orders. Can you explain why Bryson and Kyle are still at large...why there now appears to be a third agent in the field...why Spanish police are now alerted to the presence of ricin? Are you aware that Spanish radio traffic at senior intelligence levels are now aware of the presence of the Scorpion on Spanish soil and that they are now aware of a potential incident in Barcelona the day after tomorrow?"

"Alas, Colonel, I was not."

Kuriyenko's voice rose to a forced whisper. "Your people were *supposed* only to focus upon unmasking our man in Marbella...a low level operative...a man of little consequence to us! They were *supposed* only to spend a few days dealing with a worthless piece of drugs trafficking. This entire episode was merely designed to permit us to demonstrate that the Great Homeland was happy to work closely with British Intelligence and that in consequence we were most unlikely to have had a hand in tomorrow's planned events."

"I appreciate all of that, comrade," replied Barrington calmly.

"Then how do you explain all of this, you *stupid* old man?"

Barrington ignored the taunt.

"My dear Commissar...we have both been involved in matters such as these for more years than we care to remember. Our respective contrivances do not always work out as planned. Initially what you asked of me was relatively simple. I arranged for two of our most inexperienced people...people who could not be associated with British Intelligence...to be deployed in Spain. While they are credible, one of them has a drink problem sufficiently severe that no one could have imagined that they would stumble across the ricin plot... or the Scorpion, for that matter."

"How am I to believe this? These people have neutralised my own agent...a trained man...and still they roam free."

"Quite. I sent their handler to Spain to manage things as we discussed but regrettably, he has disappeared and our technical people report that he has used his phone only once...and that was to make contact with Kyle. He is not responding to calls, has disappeared and we can only assume that he is dead or detained."

"I hope you understand the seriousness of this situation, Sir Alistair. We are playing for immense stakes in this matter. If your people do anything to thwart our plans tomorrow, you will be held personally responsible by me. You are aware of my reputation. I can be a good friend but I do not accept failure. You would be well advised to reflect on this. You are an old man. You should be thinking of retirement and your Swiss bank account…not of passing from this world in considerable pain."

Barrington's face did not reveal any stress at Kuriyenko's threats.

"Ah, Commissar. If only the world was as simple. You threaten me, I threaten, my handler, he threatens Kyle and Bryson and all is well." He became aware of a pressing need to micturate, knowing that when he tried to relieve himself, there would only be a few drops of urine expressed…although this would be sufficient to provide him with some comfort for another short while. He decided to end the meeting.

"Commissar Kuriyenko, I will of course do everything I can to resolve this situation. But I fear I must visit the facilities"… he looked around at the grubby interior of the bar…"such as they are." He held Kuriyenko's glare. "I shouldn't think it necessary for me to detain you further, Commissar Second Rank."

British Intelligence, in common with Mossad and the CIA are taught routinely that the Russian character is such that they never like to lose face in an argument. In dealings with them, a way should be found to allow them to exit an interpersonal exchange feeling that they have not been bettered in a dispute. In contrast, however, agents are also taught that withholding this can leave their opposite number feeling very angry, frustrated and vengeful. Sometimes, this *too*, had merit.

Sir Alistair decided on the former approach. His professionalism kicked in and he regretted his evident dismissal of his Russian superior. He continued…"Of course, Commissar, you must do *exactly* as you deem appropriate in my case if you feel I've failed you. Equally, I shall strive to accomplish all you would have me do. Now I really *must* visit the bathroom."

* * *

Anatoly Borovsky strode purposefully into his villa and threw his small briefcase on a couch. His four assistants, all male, followed him in carrying heavy bags and suitcases which they took to a number of other rooms leaving Borovsky to remove his tie and make for a drinks cabinet where he poured himself a large, neat vodka, no ice.

Raising the glass to his lips he lifted a phone and cradled it under his jaw, jabbing at the receiver a number of times almost as if to wake it from its somnolence after a period of inactivity. Satisfied, he read a number from a piece of paper and dialed it.

"Comrade Ivanov, what news?"

"Comrade Borovsky. Is this line secure?"

"It is. Now tell me…what news?"

"Our man is in place. He has all necessary equipment and tomorrow's meeting goes ahead as scheduled. We are aware that Spanish Intelligence are alert to the presence of our man on their soil…in Barcelona as a matter of fact…and that they are aware of his possession of the white powder but there has been no public provision of information on this although they have shown the photographs of two British agents on television without linking them to the poison."

"Are there now any impediments to the successful implementation of Project Mandarin tomorrow?"

"I think not, comrade. Our arrangements are now all in place. Our man is experienced as you know. Tonight he will spend in prayer. Tomorrow he will strike...and the world will recoil in fear."

Chapter Twenty-Eight

Raphael Gonzales was tired but happy. For two years and seven months he had been the project manager on a massive, new, three thousand berth Spanish cruise liner launched six months earlier. It was intended for the lucrative Miami, Mexico, Caribbean market. Now having been luxuriously fitted out, its inaugural event wouldn't even require it to leave port. The following afternoon, it would play host to a meeting of OPEC and Western Government oil and gas politicians...a big deal gathering that would market the new cruise ship - 'Sundance' - to an international audience.

As he thanked his senior team of twenty or so for their efforts in preparing the ship for the following day, Gonzalez acknowledged the work that had been undertaken by everyone and bid all in attendance get what they could of a good night's sleep.

"Tomorrow, the eyes of the world will be upon Sundance. We have some of the most powerful men in the world...sorry Julie, I've checked the attendance list and they're all men except for one or two secretaries..." Julie smiled at his teasing shaking her head theatrically at the assembled crowd in acknowledgement of her known inclination to draw Raphael's attention to any sexist slip he might make.

"From noon, our international guests arrive. We serve lunch at one o'clock and they meet in closed session from three. I gather that their time on board will not be particularly arduous and they will wish to use the time to network with each other on the top three decks. No one will remove their clothes." His second in command held his hand to his mouth in mock horror.

"By that I mean that they'll merely want to look at our magnificent spa and bathing facilities as they walk around. No one, as far as I'm aware, will wish to swim. It should be a relaxing and, I hope, rewarding afternoon for them before they commence their real negotiations in the beautiful city of Barcelona the following day after a gala dinner tomorrow night."

Raphael looked round the room and smiled affectionately at the team of workers who had assisted him deliver this beautiful monster of a ship within time and within budget.

"Although our ship, the most wonderful ship afloat, can carry three thousand guests and three thousand staff, we will only have seven hundred staff on duty tomorrow. We will have three hundred representatives of the oil and gas industries...from all corners of the world. There will be representatives of all the major religions with all of the diet and menu problems that brings and of course we'll have the ever present security teams on board. We've been negotiating with the organisers to permit one overall security detail but alas, no agreement could be reached and everybody will bring their own people. I only hope that there are no problems or we'll have everyone shooting at everyone else!" A muffled laugh rewarded Raphael for his light-heartedness.

"Security details are already on board as you know but things will really tighten up from tomorrow morning. Please...please don't forget your I.D. passes as I'll have no authority to over-ride the decision of the front of house security to refuse you boarding." He lifted his paperwork. "So that's it. Let's all go get some sleep. I'm very proud of you all."

* * *

Farrokh Hassan pulled the rope tight and fastened the tarpaulin he'd purchased to the side of the lorry. It now covered the roof and sides of the small truck, thereby veiling the signage '*Hernández De Mercancías*' on the vehicle within which he intended delivering his deadly cargo to Ocean Blue that night. Satisfied that it would remain in place for the trip of only some four hundred yards to the boat, Hassan took the folder from the driver's seat where he'd thrown it earlier and removed the keys that would give him entry to the moorings where Ocean Blue was berthed.

He would return the vehicle later to the lock-up later that night. Now he sat once more behind the wheel and slowly coaxed the lorry out if its hide-hole and drove to the dock where, unchallenged, he parked alongside his hired powerboat.

This is the most dangerous part of the operation, thought Hassan. *I must be as quick as possible.*

The steps down into the luxurious living quarters proved difficult to navigate and Hassan had many boxes of explosives and poison to carry. He could only lift one at a time and so it was an exhausted Scorpion who sat momentarily on the deck after all had been carried on board and deposited down below. Wearily he got to his feet and locked the hatch door before driving the lorry back to the lock-up. He would sleep in his vehicle within the small garage that night. Initially his plan had been to spend the rest of the evening preparing the explosive charges but he decided that sleep and relaxation...as far as was possible...was more sensible than trying to make his way back to the powerboat. Tomorrow morning he would mingle with others in the marina and be less obtrusive than would be the case if he attempted another visit tonight.

* * *

On the Ventura, Bryson sat outside in the blackness of a cool Mediterranean night as the boat powered its way to Barcelona.

"Guantanamera... *guajira*, Guantanamera.... Guantana meeeerrrra...."

He topped up his whisky glass and repeated his refrain. Kyle appeared beside him on deck.

"Last glass, Jack. No more until tomorrow's over."

"Maybe one for the road, wee man?"

"Naw. We're done here. No more drink soldier."

Bryson nodded morosely. "As you say, sir."

"We'll finish the one in your mitt and I'll see you off to bed. God only knows what we'll be up to tomorrow. We might need you in best form."

Bryson protested drunkenly. "Presently, Gus, we know precisely hee-haw about whatever's going to break tomorrow. We know there's a nut-job knockin' about with what we suppose to be a shit load of deadly poison. We know what they guy looks like. We think there's a deal goin' down in Barcelona tomorrow but we don' know what it is..."

"Pretty accurate from where I'm standing. We also know that Perry and his boys'll be on the lookout for us. He'll still think we've knocked off his three million quid and we've still got the cops looking for us and showing our ugly mugs on TV every half hour."

"Fuckin' best thing we could do, Gus would be to stay out at sea with these lovely people for a couple of months and get them to drop us on a desert island somewhere."

As Bryson delivered his solution to his friend, a glass door behind them slid open and Brand stepped out into the seated area and sat down looking pained.

"How you feelin' Colonel?" asked Bryson..."coz me an' the wee man here were just discussin' whether to make you walk the plank."

"I'll heal. But I need to speak with you boys."

"An' can we trust a word that comes out of your mouth, ma man?" slurred Bryson.

"Okay, listen up Bryson. I was once as operational as you two. I spent time working undercover with Perry's mob not because they were gangsters, but because they had links to neo-fascist movements in the U.K. and in the States. I didn't enjoy it but we put a lot of them behind bars and disrupted a lot of very ugly stuff on the far right. Now hear me good. I am who I say I am…at least to you guys. Perry thinks I'm a Nazi, Susan thinks I'm a gangster but I work for an operation that deals in awkward stuff that Her Majesty's Government want swept under the carpet. If I was a Nazi, why would I have put money in your bank accounts and asked you to unearth a Russian agent and disrupt a drugs haul? What's right-wing or fascist about that? Why would I have sent you to Palestine and got you back out again? So I could recruit you to the Hitler *Youth*?"

Kyle listed to Brand's pleadings.

"It's difficult to know who to trust at the minute."

Bryson was still truculent. "By the way…we know who your Russian agent is, old bean. We left him unconscious in the Red Lion."

"Who is he?" asked Brand, now distracted.

"Later," said Kyle. "For the moment we're up to our arse in troubles we don't understand."

"Okay, let's pool what we know," said Brand. "You thought you were taking down a drugs shipment…so did I but I was told subsequently that HMG seemed to know that there might be ricin involved. Like you two, I'm also not sure who to believe at times. They guy you identified as having a tattoo on the back of his hand is an international terrorist called the Scorpion…an Iranian. Not too many people have met him face to face and walked away. MI5, The CIA, the FSS and Mossad would all want him sitting behind a table in a room so they could have a chat with him…or dead on a slab."

"Did you know it was him we'd be meeting?"

"No. That was a surprise to everyone. But he's someone we need to take down. He's been responsible for several incidents and there's no reason to doubt that whatever he's got planned for tomorrow won't be spectacular. It won't have escaped your attention that tomorrow's date in the fourth of July."

"Yeah, we got that, Colonel," said Bryson.

"We got the info on the date and location of his planned attack…if that's what it is…"

"Sure, and you also identified him as the Scorpion and established that he's in possession of quantities ricin…"

"And half of Perry's three million quid, that he now thinks me and Gus stole from him. *He'll* be after us as well as the cops."

"Okay. He's called this caper Operation Mandarin. We've not worked out whether there's significance in the title. Nowadays, we use computer generated titles for operations so they can't be second-guessed by anyone who overhears the words...we don't know if the Scorpion's done this."

"What's the guy's name"?

"We don't know. A number of aliases. What we do know is that he's very dangerous."

"Then what can *we* do? It'll need an army to bring this boy down."

"Agreed. We make landfall in Barcelona..." he looked at his watch..." later this morning. I get a secure line and speak to people in London. We bring in appropriate support and leave it to them, then we sail off into the sun."

"We still get our money?"asked Bryson, still distrustful.

"It's already in your bank, Bryson."

Bryson turned to face Kyle. "Seems that the Colonel's solution isn't too far away from my desert island idea."

"Kim'll need fuel after this journey," said Kyle. "We've no right to intrude in the lives of these good people on board. We get to Barcelona, you..." He pointed to Brand. "You make sure that HMG compensates them for their part in all of this...generously." Brand nodded. "We get off and disappear out of their lives. You bring in the Calvary and get us home without doing time for a murder we didn't commit. We get back home, we make all the statements you want."

"That sounds about right. And if we do manage to stop the Scorpion, you'll have the ever-lasting gratitude of the intelligence communities around the world. I'll make sure that everyone knows what you did...now, you said you know who the Russian agent is?"

Kyle smiled. "Yeah. Here's a down payment on our new found trust in you. He's a guy who works for Perry as his flunky. Doesn't seem too bright but that could be an act. They call him 'Happy'. Mid-thirties, maybe. Five-ten. English accent."

"Thanks, Kyle. My people will call that mission accomplished." He sighed wearily. "Now I'm tired so I'm off to bed."

"Me too," said Bryson.

As they left, Kyle sat alone staring out into the blackness of the night, mesmerized by the wash at the rear of the Ventura. His trance was broken by Kim who kicked him playfully on his calf and handed him a glass of Champagne.

"Join me?"

"Delighted, Kim."

"I was pouring Champagne for everyone when I saw you all sitting out here."

"Yeah, just us boys talking boys' talk."

"I heard you. Seems like you can't get away from the Ventura fast enough."

Kyle eyed her, trying to understand the meaning of her comment.

"Well, we can't put you in danger. If you heard what we discussed, you'll appreciate that things might get very messy tomorrow. There's no way that I'd allow that."

"Well, Colonel Brand seems to think we can deal with this without getting involved in any violence. I just wondered if there was any urgent need for you to hurry back to Scotland. I was speaking to Susan and she and Liam would be delighted if you wanted to share the rest of their cruise with them." She hesitated…"and so would I."

The Champagne sipped by Kyle as she said this induced a coughing fit as he appreciated the weight of Kim's words.

"Stay on board? he spluttered.

"Why not. After the Colonel tells British Intelligence what's happening, you're both free to lead a violence-free existence are you not?"

"Well, other than persuading the cops that we're not murderers and convincing your father that we don't have designs on his money…you may have a point."

"At least think about it, Gus. It would be a decent reward for your efforts recently…and I'd be the happiest girl on the Med if you said yes."

She sipped the last dregs of her Champagne and took her leave of Gus, leaving him sitting on the aft deck wondering what the last exchange was all about.

"Women?"... he told himself..."complicated people... complex and complicated people!"

* * *

Kyle rose and wandered through to the main lounge area where he turned on the television. Too much adrenaline to sleep right now. Absent-mindedly, he pressed the button on the remote and moved between channels. After shaking his head at the detritus that passed for late night entertainment, he paused as he locked on to a satellite news channel. Raphael Gonzales was smiling into the camera, repeating some of the details he'd told his senior staff earlier. Oil and gas...OPEC and the west...security, heavily guarded ship...great honour for the Sundance...

"Shit! I suspect we've found the Scorpion's target. If I was a betting man, I'd figure he'd be trying to blow these people to kingdom come, if not kill them with ricin poisoning. Important target...American Independence Day...Shit! Good news must be that the ship will be hoaching with security so maybe we could just let him fall in to their hands without us showing up, he mused. *I'll let everyone sleep and tell them early tomorrow morning. They'd just fret instead of sleep. I may as well be the only one affected.*

He walked up to the wheelhouse where old Miguel was standing, one hand steering, one hand holding a cup of coffee.

Miguel raised his polystyrene cut in welcome. "*Señor* Kyle. You no sleep?"

"Too tired to sleep, Miguel. What time do we get to Barcelona?"

"*Señor*, we arrive perhaps after eleven o'clock. The Ventura she not have enough gas to go more faster. Perhaps I might have to slow down or we stop out at sea."

Kyle nodded his thanks and went below to his cabin where he took out his kit-bag and spend the dark hours oiling and checking his weaponry. *Just in case*, he thought.

CHAPTER TWENTY-NINE

Perry sat in the passenger's seat as Spence barreled down the dual-lane carriageway, driving hard towards Barcelona, a vehicular flotilla of three cars following in convoy behind him. Eighteen men in all. He'd had to call on the services of his reserve team players like oldsters Eddie and Ernie but had others who were nimble, quick and violent.

"How long 'till we get there, Cammy?"

"I'll have to slow down nearer Barcelona and the traffic we'll meet will be rush hour. Maybe tenish."

"And where the fack'll we find them?"

"Got to figure it's one of the marinas, boss. We'll just need to search for them. That's why I brought the four vehicles... 'case we need to split up.

Behind them in the mini-bus, Eddie Crompton was deep in conversation with his old pal Ernie.

"How was *I* to know she was the boss's daughter? For God's sake don't tell the old man I seen her stark naked. He'll have my guts for garters."

The cars ate up motorway miles towards Barcelona.

* * *

Comisario Romeo Natzari of the *Centro Superior de Información de la Defensa*, Spain's principal intelligence agency, Sub-commissioner César Constantino of the *Grupo Especial de Operaciones,* the Spanish policing authority that deals with counter-terrorism, and the entire Spanish Intelligence community had all come to the same conclusion as had Gus Kyle. The Scorpion's target must be the Sundance and the timing must coincide with the on-board gathering of the world's oil interests.

Constantino was closest to Barcelona as he sped, alone in his cigar-fugged police car, towards the city, overtaking all before him courtesy of a flashing light on his roof. Some distance behind him, Comisario Natzari followed on in a car full of arguing police officers having left later as a consequence of his prolonged search of the Marbella area looking for Kyle and Bryson...and because Constantino had had an early 'heads up' from one of Natzari's man.

As the Ventura, Perry's convoy, Natzari and Constantino all raced within their limits to reach the city...all oblivious to each others' mission... Faroukh Hassan sat below in his powerboat having just finished his devotions. He raised his head above the entrance to the belly of the boat and leaned his arms on the edge of the hatch, listening to the soothing sounds of the 'harbour clink' as rigging slapped gently against masts while boats bobbed serenely at their moorings. *Very peaceful,* thought Hassan.

After some more moments of quiet contemplation, Hassan locked the door so he wouldn't be disturbed, put on his gloves, goggles and face mask then went downstairs and stood for a while looking at the boxed assemblage of Semtex, ricin and detonators. This next task he knew well. He had been well trained in Libya many years before and had made very effective bombs and improvised booby-traps using photo-electric detonation, trip wires using a hacksaw blade and even once, a huge explosion triggered by a simple mouse trap. Today, however, he would make use of his favourite explosive…Semtex. He much preferred this particular plastic explosive as it was malleable but stayed plastic in temperatures ranging from -40 to +60 degrees Centigrade and was waterproof. His Russian handlers, via their man Armeen Borzoo in Teheran, had provided Hassan with the good stuff; that which had been manufactured in Czechoslovakia before 1990 at which time ethylene glycol dinitrate had been added as a tag that could help identify its source and provide a scent that could be distinguished by dogs or by specialised detection machines. Hassan's explosive material was virtually undetectable and he had enough stored below to blow a mortal hole in any ship's toughened hull.

He had to start with detonation as he intended that this explosion would be triggered by impact…the collision at speed of Ocean Blue against its target. He moved some boxes aside until he found the percussion cap which he lifted and moved carefully to the prow on the Ocean Blue and placed against the interior hull at its foremost point…the point of collision and detonation he intended. Behind it, he affixed some hexagonal booster charges, a special assembly of wax and detonating cords that would ignite the main explosive before packing several blocks of red-brick coloured Semtex tightly behind them. Now, ever more cautious, he lifted and placed the boxes of ricin in the middle of the boat before surrounding them with further packs of Semtex.

The temperature was now very high and rising within the cabin as the sun moved inexorably towards its highest point. Hassan looked at his watch. Ten-fifty. He expected the blast to occur around 1.30 so he had time yet. Reassuring himself that none of the ricin had been released during his assemblage of the bomb, he removed his goggles, face mask and gloves and wiping the sweat from his eyes, unlocked the hatch and climbed out into the cooler air.

Scanning the marina for any suspicious activity, he found none and left Ocean Blue for the mosque. He had plenty of time on his hands now. He just had to wait for the perfect moment to attack. *Nothing can stop me now*, he thought.

* * *

While Natzari was shouting at cars that blocked his path into the city, Constantino had driven to the Port Authority and had been shown upstairs to the control room.

"In here, Sub-Commissioner Constantino, we have close circuit television coverage of all routes into the port. We can access all of the marinas and most of the industrial zones and fuel storage depots that surround the port.

There are few corners in which one could hide or remain unseen for any length of time. We talk to all of the ships and craft entering and leaving the port and, as you can see, we have some of your colleagues in here today because of the security that surrounds the event on the Sundance."

"Thank you *Señor*. I am obliged." He looked round at the men and women all busily engaged in watching televisual coverage of the port, communicating with pilots and ships' captains and generally ensuring that the port was well policed and well managed. "Can I ask if you or your staff have noticed anything unusual in the past couple of days? Any uncommon faces...out of the ordinary berthings...strange comings and goings?"

"Sub-Commissioner...everything has been as usual except perhaps for the activities of your own security personnel around the Sundance."

Constantino acknowledged his assessment without comment. "Have you twenty-four hour coverage?"

"Why of course. But there's much less traffic so we only have a skeleton staff on duty."

"Do you record the CCTV coverage?"

"*Si, Señor.*"

"And for how long do you retain the coverage?"

"The Maritime Police ask us to keep it for a week but we usually keep it for two weeks. The quality of the image is very good as we have to be able to use it in court if necessary...but usually this is just for incidents in the industrial zones. Our Marinas are used by people who are very well behaved."

"Thank you again *Señor*. And may I have an opportunity to see some recent footage?"

"Most certainly Sub-Commissioner. If you care to sit at our supervisor's desk over there, I'll show you how to access all the footage we have on all of our sites."

Constantino sat at the desk and looked at a screen showing nine images of different locations.

"It would be impossible for me to look at all of these in real time. I want to see what has been taking place in the last twenty-four hours."

"Then I suggest you start by looking at the cameras which capture night scenes, Sub-Commissioner. They are all fitted with movement activators and only record when something is actually happening. Sometimes they are triggered by a bird flying across the lens or by a car on a road just inside the Industrial Zone but outside our port. But you will be able to see only when there is something to watch...not a lot of idle time when nothing is happening."

"Thank you again, *Señor*. Can you set this up for me now?"

"Of course Sub-Commissioner and I will arrange for a coffee and perhaps a *croissant*?"

"Perfection."

Constantino's eyes fell on the screen as he watched the port operating at night, trying to assess routine activity from criminal. Time was short.

* * *

Kyle waited until everyone was around the breakfast table and told them of the news item on the OPEC meeting on Sundance.

"Yes, I've heard of that ship," said Kim. "It's one of the largest cruise liners in the world, certainly one of the most sumptuous and our political leaders want to ensure that the world knows how Spain can compete with France and South Korea in building these giants of the sea."

"Well, it's probable that the Scorpion wants to ensure that it's remembered for quite a different reason," retorted Kyle.

"I agree," said Brand. "But the Spanish authorities are no mugs. There'll be a ring of steel round that ship. The Scorpion will have to look lively if he's going to damage it or harm those on board."

"Well, the Spanish authorities know about the ricin. They know about the date and they'll have worked out that the target is the Sundance. We need to get to a secure land line to advise our own people of the Scorpion's presence and they'll doubtless advise the Spaniards immediately but then we back off and let them handle it," said Kyle.

As he spoke, Miguel came into the lounge and apologised for the interruption and advised Kim that the port was now in sight but that fuel was very low so he would be travelling slowly to use less.

"Thank you Miguel. As fast as possible without leaving us stranded."

Kyle moved over to join Bryson who was pouring himself another coffee.

"You okay this morning?"

"Brand new."

"Don't know how this'll go down but just to be sure we're ready for anything, I oiled and checked all of the stuff in my kit-bag."

"Great minds, Gus. So did I. First thing this morning. My Barrett is at your disposal."

"Well, with any luck we find a phone, send the message and Brand looks after getting us away from the cops. Can't see us running into Spence and Perry any time soon."

"So, Angus Kyle. What do we do when we're loused?"

"Eh?"

"What do we do when this is over? Seems to me that you've developed a wee soft spot for the ship's captain."

"Away and don't be daft, Jack. She's asked both of us to stay aboard for the rest of the cruise but I wasn't going to say anything until I'd checked it with you."

"Jack Bryson, he say *yesssss*."

Kyle pursed his lips as if giving careful thought to the proposition.

"I can see advantages."

* * *

Hassan returned to Ocean Blue, followed the owner's written instructions and was relieved, if slightly surprised that the engine started immediately; gurgling quietly as if waiting further instructions. Again, after consulting the instructions left him, he loosened then untied the bindings that held Ocean Blue to its berth and taking the wheel, gently persuaded the craft from its mooring and out into the waterway that led to the entrance to the Marina and beyond that, the open sea.

Now having completed what he saw as the most complicated manoeuvre he had to make, Hassan's confidence grew as he continued his slow passage out of the marina, even yet still scanning the surroundings for any threat. In case he came across any such menace, he had taken the precaution of concealing a double-barreled shotgun in the wheel house and had his pistol in his pocket.

Gingerly he felt for the radio. Holding down the transmit button he spoke uncertainly.

"Hello?"

After a few seconds during which all he could hear was white noise…a reply.

"This is Harbour Control. What is the name of your craft?"

Hassan pressed transmit again."…Ocean Blue."

"What is your destination, Ocean Blue?"

"Eh…I go to Badalona…just along the coast…not far," he added in what he hoped would be a helpful tone.

"Received, Ocean Blue. Head north-west bearing 270 degrees and remain at least one kilometer from cruise ship Sundance, which is berthed at the quay at *Passeig Escollera*. Please acknowledge."

"Received, Control. Eh, out!"

He put the receiver back in its docking station and sighed with relief. He had no intention of going to Badalona or anywhere else. His final destination would be much closer to the port.

* * *

Spence stood outside a cafe built to act as a receiving station for Barcelona harbour's cable car at *Torre de Miramar* while his men smoked cigarettes behind him in the *Costa i Llobera* Gardens. Situated high on a promontory above the harbour, it permitted an unencumbered view of all traffic going into and out of the port. He had dispersed his men variously along the coastline to maintain a watching brief on those smaller ports close to the city lest Ventura elected to sail into one.

Using a pair of powerful binoculars, Spence scanned the horizon looking for the Ventura. Several times he refocused thinking he'd spotted her. Standing next to him, Perry kept up a constant stream of questions and suggestions on where to look next. A number of false alarms caused those standing behind in the gardens to move towards the mini-bus only to return to their positions and reignite the cigarettes they'd just extinguished.

Just before twelve-forty-five, the Ventura hove into view travelling very slowly. Spence focused the binoculars to confirm identification and to make doubly sure, he examined the wheelhouse and deck areas hoping to spot a face he recognised. After a few minutes he managed to pick out Kim as she walked from the lounge to the wheelhouse.

"Right everyone, that's it. The Ventura is heading for the main marina down below. In the mini-bus, people! We're going to give them a warm welcome."

* * *

Constantino's eyes had begun to glaze over as he punched the return button on the computer and brought up the next sequence of images. Scanning the screen he noticed that one of the small images showed what appeared to be a small truck unloading goods on to a boat. Interested, he enlarged it and watched a man carry goods repeatedly down into the boat's cabin. *Unusual*, he thought. *They don't seem to be provisions…all the boxes seem to be the same size. A drugs shipment?…someone else's problem.* Still he couldn't make out the man clearly due to the poor lighting.

"Evidential quality images my backside," he said quietly to himself.

Something about the truck troubled him. He checked the wheels…right size…the cabin?…proportionate to the body…then he realised what prompted his suspicion. Why would a truck with a hard shell body require a tarpaulin? He magnified the screen. Yes…certainly a tarp covering an aluminium body. He pressed the pause button, focused upon the cabin, enlarged the image and sat back with a start as the inscription written parallel to the lower edge of the driver's window came into sharp relief. Quite clearly when magnified it read… *Hernández De Mercancías…*

"Holy Mother of God…it's old *Hernández*' lorry. The one taken by the Scorpion. We have our man!"

"*Señor…*" he shouted. "*Señor…come quick.*"

Constantino jabbed his finger at the screen… "Quickly *Señor*, where exactly is this berth?"

"It's the Marina at *Joan de Borbo*, Sub-Commissioner."

"Can you show me that same space as it is right now?"

"Certainly. Let me bring it up on screen."

A few moments passed as adjustments were made.

"There, Sub-Commissioner."

Constantino looked at the row of expensive boats sitting moored at their berth. One was missing...there was a space.

"*Señor*...quickly, can you tell me the name of the boat registered to use that berth yesterday and today?"

Another flurry of punched keys and Constantino's question was answered.

"The boat is Ocean Blue. It is a powerful boat. It is owned by a *Señor* Paul Dessena who lives in Barcelona."

"Do you have an address for him?"

"Of course."

"Then print it out immediately for me. When did Ocean Blue leave its berth?"

More pressing of computer keys.

"Our records show it leaving for Badalona only ten minutes ago."

"Dear God!.. *Señor*...do you have a pilot's boat that you have available to you?"

"Of course, Sub-Commissioner. It is berthed just below us."

"Your country requires a service of you *Señor*. I cannot drive one of these boats. Will you take the boat out with me and help me find the Ocean Blue?"

"Certainly Sub-Commissioner. We can leave immediately. Let me just remind myself of its livery once more so I can recognise it afloat."

Constantino leapt from his chair as much as an ageing, overweight, heavy smoker could leap and followed the Harbourmaster down the stairs shouting the address of the boat owner, Paul Dessena into his phone and demanding his immediate arrest for questioning.

"The boat is called Ocean Blue. It is being piloted by a terrorist called the Scorpion. It left port ten minutes ago and is almost certainly headed for the Sundance. Please alert those on board and the support vessels guarding the ship immediately. This is urgent!"

It took the Harbourmaster only some thirty seconds to fire up the engines on the high-speed rigid hulled Rib and get underway. Almost as an afterthought, Constantino felt inside his jacket for his pistol and was relieved to find it strapped to his side. As the small Rib accelerated away, the burst of speed threw Constantino back in his chair.

"May God bless me and keep me," he intoned, removing his revolver from its holster; something he hadn't done in years.

CHAPTER THIRTY

All on board the Ventura moved to port to witness the grandeur of the Sundance, a kilometer and more away.

"What a size!" exclaimed Kyle. It's as big as...well it's bigger than anything I've ever seen up close."

"Oh, it's *completely* wonderful," said Kim as those watching it alongside her nodded their agreement."

"That boat must have enough booze on it to float a fuckin' battleship," said Bryson, gradually realising that his insight was to one side of the others who were captivated by its sheer beauty rather than its potential as a bar.

Kyle smiled and looked at the two naval protection vessels that sat facing outward to address any threat to the OPEC and Western oil and gas people. *No way he'd get past them,* thought Kyle as he made his way to the wheelhouse.

"Hi Miguel. Will we have enough fuel to reach port?"

"*Si Señor.* I have been careful."

Kyle smiled. "Well done Miguel."

A phone rang quietly in the wheelhouse. Distractedly, Kyle looked around to see the location of the alert and only gradually became aware that it wasn't a phone...it was the transponder that Kyle had placed in the wheelhouse in the desperate hope that when they berthed, he might wander around and get lucky finding a signal. Now he stared disbelievingly at the transponder...there was no doubt...the small green light was blinking...the tone was strong...

Kyle ran from the wheelhouse and shouted on Bryson who was at his side in seconds accompanied by Brannigan, who heard the anxiety in Kyle's voice.

"Transponder's getting a signal. All hands to the pumps. Eyes everywhere. Find the boat that's emitting the signal and we find the Scorpion."

All three piled into the wheelhouse much to the alarm of Miguel. Brannigan picked up the binoculars and scanned the horizon looking at every craft he could see.

"Liam...talk us through what you're seeing so we can *all* determine the importance of what's out there."

"Okay, Gus...There's a yacht about five hundred yards away, name's...eh...Kitty Rose. Small fishing boat... same distance, seems stationary, has nets out...can't make out its name. Powerboat heading away from Sundance about half a mile away...Ocean something...can't make it out...another yacht seems to be anchored...name's Juan something...in the distance coming towards port is a huge oil carrier...no, I tell a lie... it's carrying liquid natural gas according to what it says on the side...name's....eh...too far away...eh, name's...*Mandarin*!

* * *

In port, Spence and Perry hurried to the marina where they expected to see the Ventura make port. Spence held the binoculars to his eyes and looked for a long period out to sea in order to establish the movements of the Ventura. Eventually he was able to make sense of her movements.

"Boss, the Ventura's turning away and making a run for it. It's heading out to sea."

"Fack!" replied Perry with his customary eloquence. "Right Cammy...that boat there! Pay the fackah to follow them and catch them bastards."

Without waiting for a reply, Perry leapt aboard a large motor yacht that was beginning to manoeuvre its way from its berth. Mooring lines were being untied when Perry introduced himself to the elderly owner by saying. "There's ten grand in your pocket if you catch up with a boat out there called the Ventura. If you don't fancy the cash I'll just fackin' shoot you...'make your mind up' time, Captain."

The owner looked aghast at the boarding party beginning to assemble on the quay and looked at his wife, who was clearly terrified.

"Don't argue with him, William. He's got a gun!"

"She's right," said Spence, backing up his boss. "We'll give you a fee for your trouble…you won't come to any harm…now let's make tracks and catch up with that boat out there with the red top."

He signaled to the six men on the quayside and one by one they stepped aboard. William, now quite frightened, set to and soon had the motor yacht purring towards the harbour entrance.

* * *

On board the Ventura, Miguel had been told to put his foot down and close with Ocean Blue.

"*Señor* Kyle, we are very low on fuel…"

"As fast as possible, Miguel."

Liam came into the wheelhouse having taken Susan below into their stateroom and bid her remain out of harm's way. He had to shout to make himself heard over the noise of the engine at full throttle and the wind rush.

"Gus…I did a bit of work on Natural Gas Carriers when I worked in Congress a few years ago. These things are the most lethal things afloat. They carry quite extraordinary amounts of gas in liquid form. When these ships come into Boston Harbour, for example, they're usually accompanied by warships, fire tenders and helicopters. They shut the port down for a period because if one of them goes up, it has a thirty miles blast zone…thirty *miles*, Gus. That guy doesn't need to blow a hole in Sundance. If he has explosives aboard and hits Mandarin, he takes out the entire port of *Barcelona*...and if he has laced the explosives with ricin and it was carried on the wind, it might infect God knows *how* many miles of coastline. It would cause a major health panic. There's also a major natural gas terminal in the port of Barcelona...probably where the Mandarin's heading. If that goes up too?...This guy means business."

Kyle stared at Brannigan as the import of his information sank home.

"Can we communicate with Mandarin?" asked Bryson.

"Yes, we can do that," said Kim lifting the hand-held radio. "But it won't do much good. These things move very slowly and sometimes take maybe ten or more sea miles to turn twenty degrees off-course because of their sheer bulk. But they might have new pod propulsion systems and some armaments on board so it's worth letting them know."

So saying she began trying to contact the bridge of the Mandarin. After some failed attempts, she managed to get through and informed them of the peril they faced.

Despite a cloudless sky, conditions at sea were turbulent with a two meter swell and choppy water. Ventura handled this well but at speed, it still made for a rough ride and everyone had to hold on to an anchor point in order to remain upright.

Miguel drew everyone's attention to a small craft that was rapidly overtaking them.

"*Señor* Kyle. The Harbourmaster. He chase us."

Bryson looked out of the wheelhouse door and saw Constantino's Rib crash through the waves, heading in the same direction as the Ventura.

"Hold our course," shouted Bryson. "We don't know whether he's after us or Ocean Blue."

He turned to Kyle.

"What'll we do with Brand?" asked Bryson, still suspicious of him.

"I think he's okay."

"Would you bet our lives on it?"

Kyle thought for a moment then shook his head. "No, I wouldn't. Lock him in his room."

* * *

Constantino, pistol in hand, was intent upon somehow stopping Ocean Blue. The Harbourmaster had turned up the volume on his receiver upon hearing Kim's message to Mandarin and had repeated to Constantino a variant of Brannigan's earlier message to his shipmates on the destructive power of an exploding Natural Gas Carrier. He also drew attention to the large natural gas facility that would be within the blast zone.

He screamed at the top of his voice into the wind. "If it explodes, we are all dead, *Señor*."

Constantino looked over to the Ventura. *So who the hell is aboard that ship?* he asked himself.

His curiosity was further aroused when he noticed one of the people on board climbing on to the roof of the wheelhouse carrying a large rifle.

* * *

Hassan had by now noticed three boats to his rear heading in his direction. Initially confused, he attempted to calculate the distance between Ocean Blue and Mandarin before determining that the smaller of the boats, at least, would be alongside him before the moment of impact. He had read in his instruction manual how to lock on to a course and have the boat steer automatically so he fixed a line broadly at Mandarin amidships and took the double-barreled shotgun from the seat beside him. Checking it was loaded, he waited until the Rib came within distance.

* * *

The large motor yacht was now into its stride and was gaining slowly on the Ventura. On board, Perry was shouting expletives into the wind accusing Kyle and Bryson of trying to flee with his three million pounds. Each of his men had guns but all were pistols, less suited for longer range shooting although this disadvantage hadn't stopped Perry firing off a couple of rounds in frustration. Oblivious to the Mandarin, Constantino's Rib, or the danger he was sailing into, Perry only had vengeful eyes on his daughter's motor cruiser.

* * *

Hassan was first to fire. His first shell ripped into the side of the Rib, puncturing one of its rubberized inflatable compartments, affecting its steering and causing Constantino to ready his pistol for return of fire. A second shot hit the Harbourmaster directly who fell back, his face covered in blood, his windpipe destroyed. Light red blood poured vigourously from his throat as his hands slipped from the wheel. Immediately, the Rib began to whip viciously almost throwing Constantino overboard. He realised immediately that the Harbourmaster was dead and that he would have to take control. The windshield had been shattered by the blast and the absence of Constantino's seamanship had the Rib flounder for some minutes while Ocean Blue gained on Mandarin.

Witnessing the shooting, Bryson lay prone, trying to feel the rhythm of the boat's movement through the water. Normally a pre-requisite of any successful sniper shot was complete stillness before firing. Clearly that wasn't going to be an option here. Nevertheless, he took aim and fired at Hassan whom he could see clearly through his sights although the combined undulations on each boat made accuracy all but impossible.

He didn't even see the splash a mile away as the round passed harmlessly some twenty feet over Hassan's head.

Carefully he moulded himself into the firing position again.

Kyle had also seen the Rib holed, noticed that it was no longer proceeding directly towards Ocean Blue and that it was moving at a markedly reduced pace. Standing at the side of the Ventura to gain a better view of the race towards Mandarin, he ducked as he heard a round whistle over his head. Turning, he saw the motor yacht with men on board gaining on Ventura. Shouting to Bryson, who ignored him, so focused was he on Hassan, he drew his own pistol and crouched his way towards the stern, screaming at Kim and Liam to go below. Neither did.

Still a couple of hundred yards behind, the motor yacht was only gaining slowly and Kyle decided to take an opportunity to race quickly to his wardroom and collect more of his weaponry from his kit-bag, returning after a minute to find the gap between both boats closing markedly. Confused initially as to why this might be, he realised that the engines on the Ventura had stopped.

"Shit...no fuel left," murmured Kyle to himself.

A hail of bullets now peppered the Ventura as Perry's men let loose. The Ventura was built for elegance not defence and there were precious few places on board that permitted Kyle effective cover.

Above him he heard another round fired by Bryson...again to no avail.

Running to the end of the boat, he ducked behind a low plastic wall that housed a Jacuzzi. It offered no protection whatsoever, but hid him from view somewhat. He raised his head and recognised Perry standing on the foredeck shouting and firing at the Ventura.

"Jesus, these boys are persistent!" he murmured. *Well, let's see if they're used to handling this kind of firepower.*

First he threw one of his M84 stun grenades which exploded harmlessly in the sea but gave Perry and his men food for thought. As those on board the motor yacht took cover now having realised that there might be more of a fight than they'd anticipated, Kyle lifted his Uzi semi automatic machine pistol with its rate of fire of six hundred rounds a minute and let loose a burst which completely destroyed the prow of the boat and wounded two men.

More gunfire directed at him had him ducking again as the motor yacht, despite the new apprehension felt by all of those on board, closed then collided with the Ventura still wallowing powerlessly in the choppy waters. The speed of the motor yacht was considerable at this point and the Ventura was almost stationary. Considerable damage was done to both craft as one ploughed into the other and some of the more confident of Perry's men made ready to attempt to board the ship.

A third shot from Bryson clipped Ocean Blue but merely reminded Hassan that he was under fire. Still he closed on Mandarin.

Constantino watched the fire-fight and the collision between the two boats with incredulity. He had no idea what was going on and calculated that the only thing he could do was to chase Ocean Blue and try to get a shot off before it hit Mandarin. Frustrated, he pushed at the accelerator and increased speed but had to fight the steering to keep the Rib anywhere close to its course. Furiously he wrestled with the wheel but the Rib, while still powerful, seemed intent upon making its way towards the fire-fight between the two boats and away from Ocean Blue.

A short burst of Kyle's Uzi sent everyone on board the motor yacht diving for cover but two of the men managed to fire back and while Kyle was sheltering behind a ski-jet from their hail of bullets, they managed to clamber on board. Both ran forward along the starboard walkway giving Kyle a new problem. He could easily see off those on the motor yacht but now he not only faced attack from the rear but also faced the prospect of hostages being taken. He crouched and reversed along the port walkway.

A fourth shot from Bryson missed completely.

Hassan was now only some four hundred yards from Mandarin which now towered above him like a cliff. He was dead on target. He held tight to the wheel and repeated the words he'd used in prayer countless times before… *"Allahu Akbar. Ashhadu anlaa ilaaha illallaahu wahdahu laa shareekalahu, washhadu anna Muhammadan 'abduhu wa rasooluhu…."* His prayer was interrupted as a round from Bryson finally found a target and Ocean Blue's rudder disintegrated under the powerful force of the Barrett's bullet. The powerboat lurched to port, still progressing onwards but now heading towards the rear of Mandarin. Faroukh now had no control over the direction he was taking but was relieved to see he would still collide with his target, if now tangentially.

Miguel, Liam and Kim were still in the wheelhouse when one of Perry's men ran past, realised he'd passed a target of importance, and retraced his steps.

"No one moves." He waved his gun menacingly. "Stop this boat right now!"

"*Señor*, we *are* stopped. The Ventura it has no fuel."

"Listen mister, my name is Kimberly Perry. I'm your boss's *daughter*."

"Not any more you ain't. Think he's written you out the will, darlin'! Now *all* of you on the floor."

Perry's man didn't see the blow that sent him spinning, unconscious to the floor as Kyle entered the wheelhouse.

"Stay low… stay here. There's another man on board and more could follow. Jack's above us trying to take out the Scorpion."

He rushed from the room and headed back towards the rear of the Ventura. The second man who had boarded was found hiding next to the Ski-jet, exactly where Kyle had taken shelter moments before. He raised his pistol and his face contorted as he tried to fire at Kyle. Too slow by far. A burst from Kyle's Uzi spat eight bullets into his chest, closely grouped.

Bryson fired another shot, this time hitting the engines of Ocean Blue which started to emit clouds of smoke and reduce its speed.

Shit...that was close, thought Bryson. If *he has plastic explosives on board, a stray shot could send the lot up...but he'll still want the metal to metal collision. He still needs a direct hit on Mandarin.*

Constantino's Rib was now close to both boats and was studiously ignored by each, so intent were those on board on fighting each other. The Sub-Commissioner was not a fit man. Indeed he was a fat man but making his way to the raised prow of the Rib, he found himself almost at the same height as the lower deck of the Ventura. He climbed aboard with some difficulty and rolled on to the deck holding a rope that held the Rib tight to the Ventura. He tied the rope to a lifebelt. Moving cautiously, gun in hand, he opened a door to find Graciana and Juanita cowering in their staff quarters. With his left hand he took his police badge from his pocket and held it up for their inspection before closing the door and walking towards a door that took him inside to the lounge area.

A man unarmed, stood before him with one hand on the handle of a door. Constantino pointed his gun at him and raised his badge again

"Do not move, *Señor*. I am an officer of the law and you are under arrest."

"Hey...I'm one of the feckin' good guys," said Liam. I'm trying to get a weapon of some kind to help out upstairs."

"And you *are?*"

"Doctor Liam Brannigan. I'm a guest on board the Ventura. My wife's in this room. I want to check she's alright and get a gun to help the two boys upstairs. They're trying to stop the Scorpion from blowing the feckin' Mandarin from blowing the feckin' port of Barcelona right off the feckin' map!"

"See to your wife," said Constantino, "then we will go upstairs."

Kyle didn't see the gun butt that floored him. Even so, he spun on the floor until he found a position from which he might spring upwards in counter-attack. He stopped short when he saw the figure of Marcus Perry standing over him with a gun pointed directly at his chest.

"You Scotch fackah! You thought you'd get away with my three mill, did you? You thought you could charm my own bloody daughter into stealing even *more* of my fackin' money did you? Well you just breathed your last, my son. Just remember…you never fack with Marcus Perry!" His face contorted in a cruel smile. "Now you die, Scotchman!"

The sharp crack of a pistol shot seemed somehow small and insignificant when compared to the booming cannon noise made by Bryson's Barrett above them but they were each equally lethal when used for the purpose for which they were designed. Smoke filled the room and cordite assailed Kyle's nostrils as he began to realise that the shot must have missed. But it hadn't. He looked through the smoke to see Kim lowering a gun just as her father, Marcus Perry held her gaze for a moment before slumping to the floor, his life extinguished.

Kyle leapt to his feet and held Kim.

"Kim…I'm so sorry…so sorry."

There were tears in her eyes. "It was a choice between you and him. Not much of a choice, eh?"

He held her for a moment until more gunshots sent him running aft.

Hassan was thumping the wheel with impatience. Very slowly, Mandarin was sliding past Ocean Blue. He was close…but close enough to ignite its gas if he could just explode Ocean Blue? He wasn't sure. Looking round at the three boats now locked in a battle he didn't understand, he decided he had time to ignite the Semtex using the detonators. If he timed it properly he could just wait until Ocean Blue was as close as possible to the hull… metres away…*that should do it!*

Mandarin now towered over him like a vast wall of steel, closing on him at an angle.

It wouldn't be long now.

Bryson still fired ineffectually at Ocean Blue but now assisted by his own craft being more settled in the water and Ocean Blue losing power as well.

Still his shots went wide.

Kyle ran aft and cleared the deck of the powerboat by firing off his Uzi until all were cowering below. William, the owner and his wife had long taken refuge in the aft wardroom and as yet were unaware of the damage done to their boat although they anticipated that it would be considerable.

"Can you steer a boat?" asked Constantino.

"Sure I can," shouted Liam against the wind noise.

"Then come with me. You are strong."

Together, Brannigan and Constantino climbed back into the Rib and accelerated towards Ocean Blue. As they banked awkwardly past the prow of the Ventura, Brannigan signaled to Bryson that it was he who was steering.

"Don't feckin' shoot me, Jack! It's me...Liam!" he shouted.

With Brannigan at the wheel, the Rib sped erratically towards Ocean Blue.

Kim knelt beside her father's dead body. Wordlessly she closed his eyes just as tears filled her own.

"It didn't have to be this way Dad. I *wanted* to love you. I wanted you to love *Mum*. But deep down, you couldn't love anyone. You were a bad man, Dad and now your daughter has killed you. But you were going to kill a man who is a hundred times better than you. I couldn't let that happen...just couldn't."

Hassan hurriedly tore at the mechanisms he'd so painstakingly put in place earlier that morning.

Not much longer now and he'd set off the explosion *himself*...he started to repeat the closing words of his devotions as he completed his task. *"Subhana Rabbiyal A'ala."... Subhana Rabbiyal A'ala."*

A shadow fell over the detonator he was working with. He turned and looked up to see Constantino above him with Kyle's Heckler and Koch HK P7 rifle pointing at him.

Surprised, he held his hands aloft then brought them palms together indicating 'peace' as he had done previously before he shot the Egyptians and when he'd captured Bruno Martinez de Oz. Moving as fast as the cramped space would allow, Hassan grabbed at the gun in his pocket as Constantino fired the rifle, missing him. In his anxiety not to miss and hit any plastic explosive on board, Constantino's nano-second delay in repeating his shot permitted Hassan to aim and shoot, clipping the Sub-Commissioner in the shoulder and sending him spinning backwards.

Hearing no more movement, Hassan climbed the few stairs cautiously, gun in hand. Carefully he placed his gun hand on the railing as he raised his head above the hatch. He froze momentarily as he heard a noise behind him and cried out sharply when Liam Brannigan's shoe descended heavily on his wrist forcing him to drop the gun. A second kick, to Hassan's head was ineffective as Brannigan's soft sailing shoes carried no weight and merely glanced off. Roaring, Hassan climbed from the hatch and swung at Brannigan, connecting with his face and bursting his nose...an almost inevitable injury suffered by Brannigan in any conflict. Ignoring the pain and the blood that now streamed down over his chin, Brannigan punched Hassan solidly and saw him reel from the blow. Staggering back against a cabin wall, Hassan picked up a red fire bucket and swung it at Brannigan who retreated before its threat. He stumbled over a rope and fell backwards but as he attempted to rise, saw that Hassan stood tall before him, gun in hand and breathing heavily.

"You miserable *infidel*. You think you can stop the Scorpion? You think you can stop me succeeding in my mission? I am the *Scorpion*...I am Faroukh *Hassan*... I am known to *many* for my deeds against the west." He gestured contemptuously at Brannigan, sprawled on the deck. "I have killed many men. And when this boat explodes, I will kill many more...many *thousands* more...and you think you can stop the *Scorp*..."

Brannigan screamed as he was covered in a shower of blood and gore. Hassan's left arm blew off and the velocity of the round that hit him with such force threw him forward onto the starboard decking. Almost as Hassan's shoulder exploded, Brannigan heard the time-delayed, distant tell-tale signature of Bryson's Barratt rifle fire.

Getting to his feet, he waved in the direction of the Ventura, confident that Bryson would witness his lack of injury through his rifle sights and went forward to where Constantino lay bleeding.

"Are you okay?" asked Brannigan.

"I too, have been shot in the arm *Señor,* but it would appear that our friend had a more serious injury to his arm. In fact, it would appear that he doesn't *have* one anymore."

Brannigan left him and returned to the lifeless body of Hassan. What was left of his shoulder was still smouldering. He felt for his jugular vein in order to confirm that his wound was mortal.

It was.

Bryson climbed down from his position atop the wheelhouse and joined Kyle, Kim and Miguel.

"First things first, Jack. Let's go and make sure that Perry's men are disarmed and of no threat."

They each crouched and moved aft, guns raised...one port, one starboard...and as they approached the rear of the boat, Kyle shouted into the wind.

"Spence...Cammy...you still alive?...you okay?"

A head emerged from behind a thick circle of rope. It was Spence.

"What d'you want?"

"Jack and I have Uzi machine guns. We know how to use them. It's your shout. Either you all come out and leave

RON CULLEY

your guns where they are or we rip the boat apart and
you with it."

There was a silence for a moment as Spence spoke with
some of his men. A further pause…

"We're coming out."

* * *

Half an hour later, Sub-Commissioner Constantino
having contacted his people, watched as the Ventura
was surrounded by a flotilla of small police craft
which had sped out at his request. William and his wife
were being escorted from their boat, Ventura staff
other than Miguel were being led to safety and police
photographers were everywhere. Liam and Susan
Brannigan were sitting on the yellow leather seating
hugging one another tightly; Susan wiping blood from
Liam's face following his nose bleed. Perry's surviving
gang members were seated on a police vessel being
handcuffed. Some short distance away, the two naval
vessels scheduled to protect Sundance were now berthed
at each side of Ocean Blue and scene of crime officers
roamed its deck. A tow-rope was being affixed to the
Ventura.

Constantino, his left arm bandaged and in a sling, shook
hands with Kyle and Bryson.

"Gentlemen, you have saved many lives."

"Well, before we start, I just want you to know that
I wasn't involved in the death of the old man in the

garage," said Kyle. "We followed the Scorpion to the garage and he was dead when we got there."

"That matter will be dealt with. I know you speak the truth. We have his fingerprints from the scene of the crime and I have no doubt that our forensic team will show that the bullet in my arm and that which killed *Señor* Hernández came from the pistol he used on Ocean Blue".

As they spoke, Colonel Brand entered the room supported by a police officer who spoke in Spanish to Constantino telling him that the man whose left arm was round his neck had been locked in a room and had asked to speak with the most senior police officer available.

"That would be me, *Señor*. I am Sub-Commissioner César Constantino of the *Grupo Especial de Operaciones*. I have the honour of being one of those responsible for leading the Spanish policing authority that deals with counter-terrorism. And you are?"

"My name is Colonel Andrew Brand. My job responsibilities are not dissimilar to your own, Sub-Commissioner. I wanted to make it clear that these two men here were working under my instructions and although this matter took place in your jurisdiction, we had no intention of acting without your cooperation. We were on our way to report what we'd uncovered but I'm afraid matters got out of hand."

"I'm sure, Colonel. But what is important is that together we have stopped a terrorist atrocity that would have killed many thousands of people. Your two men have been outstanding. We were very fortunate that they were on this assignment. It was helpful too that the crew and guests of the Ventura were willing to risk their lives to save others'."

Constantino turned to Kim, sitting beside Kyle who had his arm around her.

"*Señorita,* you have the thanks of a grateful nation and I am gravely upset at the damage done to your fine craft. I have enough knowledge of insurance matters to know that you will have all sorts of problems securing the payments necessary from insurance companies for this damage as I am sure they will argue that it was caused by terrorist activity for which they are not liable…which, in all candour…it was. However, I have not become Sub-Commissioner César Constantino of the *Grupo Especial de Operaciones* without having made important contacts. You can be assured that your craft, the Ventura, will be repaired to the highest standards…and at no cost to you. When I tell those who built the Sundance how you saved their cruise liner, you can be sure they will repair the Ventura and have her back in the water soon. And allow me to offer my condolences regarding the death of your father. He was about to commit a murder and you saved a life. I am witness to this. We will want to take a statement from you and this will be difficult for you given the circumstances, but it will soon pass. Your guests and all on board will have to do the same but I will ensure that it is as simple and quick a procedure as possible."

Kim smiled weakly. "Thank you, Sub-Commissioner but presently I want only to take care of my father's funeral."

"Of course, my child."

Kyle drew her closer to him. With his left hand he tenderly swept the hair from her eyes.

Bryson stood leaning against the doorway, looking at his friend comforting Kim and drank some very expensive whisky; this time from the neck of the bottle.

CHAPTER THIRTY-ONE

Brand was led into a room in police headquarters in Barcelona that had been commandeered by Sub-Commissioner César Constantino.

"Colonel Brand, please make yourself comfortable. Coffee?"

"Thank you...perhaps some water... Your arm?"

"A flesh wound. I wear a sling only for the sympathy. And your head wound. It is healing?"

"Much better, thanks."

Constantino poured water from a cooler into a small cardboard cup using his one good hand and handed it to him.

"Yesterday we came close to a major incident being perpetrated on the good people of Barcelona. It was averted only because of your men and because of the heroism of those on board the Ventura." He paused and cleared his throat. "As you would imagine, there has been considerable media interest in these events and so far we have said nothing beyond confirming that there was an attempt to explode the Mandarin by a terrorist whose name is being withheld. As you would also appreciate there has been considerable political engagement in respect of this event and I meet with you today as you are the most senior officer involved and to tell you the outcome of discussions between our politicians in Madrid and yours in London."

"I understand, Sub-Commissioner."

"As you are aware, we took initial statements from all of those involved last night and now have a reasonably clear idea of how events unfolded. Kyle and Bryson are remarkable men but I have to tell you that our politicians are prepared to charge them with illegal importation and use of firearms, stealing a police car in Marbella Bus Station, breaking into the Red Lion premises in Marbella, malicious wounding in a street outside the Red Lion premises in Marbella, malicious damage to a window of the Red Lion premises in Marbella, stealing a vehicle from an address at *Carrer del Moll i*n the town of Cartagena to say nothing of the various and serious offences that were committed yesterday off the coast of Barcelona."

Brand looked at him with increasing incredulity. "Sub-Comm..."

"But of course we have an alternative outcome in mind," interrupted Constantino...."one which would see these ludicrous charges disappear immediately."

"What have you in mind?"

"Our politicians who take to do with such matters are, frankly, embarrassed, that our own security and intelligence forces…of course they exclude *myself* from any criticism…"

"Of course, Sub-Commissioner…"

"They are embarrassed that we were not more centrally involved in the apprehension of perhaps the world's most feared terrorist on our own soil."

"I quite understand their concerns, *Señor* Constantino."

"It pains me to put this to you Colonel…but if only the world understood that yesterday represented a *joint* action… *led* by our security forces, *supported* by a special deployment from British intelligence who were helping us close down a dangerous group of British citizens engaged in criminal activity in Marbella, it would permit us to throw a confidentiality blanket over all proceedings and everyone can go back to their day job."

"And you have had this cleared with UK Intelligence?"

"We have, Colonel. But clearly, they require you to hold to this line until they can speak with you back home." He drummed his fingers on the table. "My understanding is that your particular operation is one which is kept at some distance from traditional intelligence organisations…a sort of 'clean-up' squad which has freedom to take action normally denied MI5 or 6?"

"I'm afraid I can't say too much about that, Sub-Commissioner."

"Well, I'm sure it will be explained to you upon your return to British soil, Colonel, that your people are sufficiently pleased with the outcome of this particular operation that they wish to celebrate the success and claim joint victory over terrorism with Spain on this occasion."

"Then so be it. I'll advise Kyle and Bryson."

"Excellent, Colonel. Now, I believe you have a jet awaiting your arrival in Murcia?"

"True."

"Then please allow us to escort you back to the airport without unnecessary press and media attention. We are also arranging for *Señorita* Kimberly Williams to leave Spain for a while until interest in this dies down and while her boat is being repaired. The Spanish citizens involved will also be cared for in comfortable protective custody for a while." Constantino smiled and offered his good hand. "Perhaps we will meet again under different circumstances."

"Perhaps, Sub-Commissioner...perhaps."

* * *

Sir Alistair Barrington re-read his letter of resignation, placed it in an envelope and sealed it. Reaching into his in-tray, he lifted the pension agreement that had been prepared at his request and, pursing his lips at the generous add-ons that had been provided by a grateful Treasury, signed it also.

Miss Hetherington's trademark timid knock on his office door announced his cup of tea. She brought it to his desk, placed it before him and reminded him that he had asked to have a call placed to Andrew Brand in Oxford while he drank his tea."

"Thank you, Miss Hetherington. Will you connect us now, please? On the secure line."

Moments later, Brand was put through.

"Sir Alistair."

"Brand…I asked to speak with you today in order to advise you that I have decided to retire with immediate effect."

"Wha…well, that's a bit of a shock, Sir Alistair. I thought you'd go on forever. Was there something that spurred your decision?"

"I suppose so," he sighed. "I'm getting on now. My doctors have advised me that my prostate gland is killing me and that I may not have more than a year…two at the most…to live. Our last assignment was very successful and I've decided to get out while I still have some energy. I want to indulge myself and relax somewhat more than has been possible these past few years."

"Sir Alistair! I had no idea…Then retirement is very sensible. You'll be able to see more of your niece in Manchester. Are you leaving any loose ends?"

"One or two but then, there always would be, no matter when I decided to go. I do have one more meeting to take care of and then I'm off on a cruise round the Caribbean as I do each year."

"On your own?"

"As ever, Brand. I prefer my own company as you know." He sipped his tea. "I thought you should know that I've advised our political masters that you should replace me. MI5 would prefer their own man as would MI6 prefer one of theirs but I suspect that given your experience in your present role not to say the result you had in Spain, you may well find yourself favoured."

"I'm both surprised and honoured, Sir Alistair but I am not sure I have the diplomatic skills to be a mandarin like you."

"Well, we'll see." He lifted his cup to his lips but did not drink from it. Instead he continued…"One final matter. The FSS believe me to be one of their agents. They've cultivated my participation in their schemes since 1980. However, I assure you as a colleague and a gentleman that I have never betrayed an important secret although I have been made privy to many of theirs. Two other people knew of my role, Sir William Blakely and John Simms, one a mandarin within MI5 and one within MI6. Both now dead but the files are comprehensive. For the past five years I have been working as a double agent without anyone in UK Intelligence knowing so as to ensure that my role could not be compromised. When I return from my cruise I'll be delighted to brief you in detail. Indeed it is my intention to write a full account of these last five years while I'm away. Give me something to do when we're at sea."

"I trust your motives implicitly, Sir Alistair."

"Thank you. I appreciate that. I also have something in the order of two point eight million pounds sterling in a Swiss bank account. The access numbers are in the top right hand drawer of my desk. If you're appointed, you can decide whether to hand the money to the Treasury or retain it for some operational expenses denied you by the budget process. Certainly I must have used a few hundred thousand in that way over the years. And as my last act in my present role, I have withdrawn one million pounds which I intend using in a way that would not be permitted by the Treasury. You have my word that I will not benefit in any way from this transaction and that I will include an account of this spend within my report."

"I understand. Very helpful, Sir Alistair."

"Well, I thought I'd let you know. Anyway, I must away. I have one more meeting to attend then I'm free to do as I please. For the moment, let us keep all of this information to ourselves."

"Thank you for calling me and for your confidence in me. I wish you a long and happy retirement."

"Well, I'm afraid that neither is in prospect. Thank you anyway."

Kim took a tray of drinks to the sunny poolside whereat were gathered her three members of staff and their immediate families. They had been provided with a 'special holiday' in a small hotel reserved for their sole occupation at the invitation of the *Grupo Especial de Operaciones* who wanted further discussions with them as well as keeping them away from media interest. She handed round the drinks, smiling as she did so.

"I wanted to thank you all for everything. Not just for our recent adventure but for all your help in getting the Ventura up and running."

Graciana spoke up. "Miguel wants to say something."

Miguel looked somewhat discomfited. "*Señorita* Kim. I do not have the big words. I have enjoyed working with Ventura. You are very good person but my wife she say I am too old to do this more. I must look after my grandchildren now but I have very good remembers."

"Oh, Miguel. You have been marvellous. I couldn't have done any of this without you." She reached out and touched his arm affectionately. "You *deserve* to retire. Your grandchildren deserve to see more of you. Maria is right. But you will still visit us in the harbour?"

"*Si, Señorita.* I will still visit you in the harbour. And I will visit Graciana and Juanita and tell them all their mistakes," he grinned. Both ladies laughed back and swiped good naturedly at him.

Kim directed her smile at the two ladies. "So you both stay once Ventura is fixed?"

They both nodded and Juanita spoke for each of them. "*Si, Señorita*".

* * *

Barrington made his way to the Soho bar he'd been called to attend so urgently a few days before by Commissar Second Rank Kuriyenko. He sat alone in a corner while awaiting his arrival. A half pint of beer was all he allowed himself. Barrington had had several Russian handlers over the years, all entirely convinced of his loyalty to the Motherland. Some he liked intensely. Others, like Kuriyenko, he detested. But he was a professional. Nonetheless, if he did his job properly today his personal enmity might be satisfied just as would the interests of Her Majesty's Government.

Ten minutes late, Kuriyenko arrived, his humour just as black as previously.

"Comrade Barrington. Our disappointment in our reverse the other day is substantial. I have to inform you that my report to Moscow states that you failed to carry out my orders completely and that this led to your agents overpowering our man in Marbella, discovering and neutralising the ricin explosion and killing our agent, the mercenary, Scorpion. When they have digested my report in the Kremlin, they will not be pleased with you, comrade."

"Indeed that is a matter of regret, Commissar Second Rank Kuriyenko. I am disappointed that I have incurred your displeasure and that you have found it necessary to write to the Kremlin in those terms. However, I too have disquieting news."

He sipped his half pint of beer gingerly, hardly making a dent in its diminishing foam head.

"As you know I have served the Motherland for many years…longer, slightly than you yourself. I have been told by people rather more senior than you, Commissar Second Rank, that my services have been found to be helpful. I would hope…indeed I would be *confident*…that the Kremlin would read your report and take a balanced view of my contribution over the years. Many things I can accomplish, some I cannot and the explosion of Mandarin was onesuch. On a personal basis, I must inform you that I am dying. I have a cancer that will kill me shortly, so you'll appreciate that I'm rather more immune to threats of death, humiliation or punishment. Given my condition, I simply do not care anymore."

"But Sir Alistair, you must come with me to Moscow…we have some of the top medical…"

"No, comrade. I am assured that my illness is not amenable to any further treatment. I have made my peace with this condition. Of more immediate import is my concern for you, dear comrade. I am advised that as a consequence of your offer of assistance in regard to the rogue agents, a glowing report of your relationship with British Intelligence has been sent to FSS at the highest levels. I have read this missive but do not have a copy. Unfortunately, the wording allows the reader to imagine that you were also helpful in dealing with our resolution of the Mandarin bombing. To someone who didn't have your best interests at heart, this might permit a very jaundiced view of your work over here in London. Finally, although I have no written evidence on the matter, a meeting took place yesterday where it was clear that Dmitriy Ivanov has been negotiating with British oil interests to share in the gas field exploration in Kazakhstan in direct contradiction of orders given by the President. You must make of this what you will. I have no proof."

"But this is terrible, Sir Alistair. The Kremlin is full of very suspicious people. They will view any letter about me with great mistrust." Perhaps you could find it possible to have them clarify the missive in my favour?"

"I regret not, Commissar Second Rank. I have retired with immediate effect. This afternoon I speak with you only as a private citizen. I left at lunchtime today. My badge, ID, my passwords…all are gone or changed. I am very much yesterday's man. However, if I were in your position…"

"Yes, Sir Alistair?"

"Well, I might be tempted to exchange what I know about your biggest oil magnate for a more understanding hearing. At least it's a bargaining chip."

Kuriyenko stroked his chin thoughtfully. "It is a possibility."

"Perhaps you would be good enough to advise my friends in Moscow of my condition and of my decision to retire. My heart will always belong to the Motherland but I must stay here in London. Were I to move to Russia, all of my good work would be subject to a review by British Intelligence and much might be undone."

"I will do so, Sir Alistair. You are a true hero of the Motherland."

Following a visit to the toilet, Sir Alistair left the Soho bar still shuddering at the unhygienic men's room but smiling inwardly. In one final meeting he had managed create a fiction which enabled him to manoeuvre a large black cloud over the head of his detested Russian handler and had also provided the early shots in an internal war that might yet see the wings clipped of Russia's top oil man. A meeting the previous year with Anatoly Borovsky, Head of Russia's FSS, had left him with the feeling that he thought the oil man from *Novosibirsk* was getting rather too big for his boots.

Not a bad day's work for a retired mandarin, he decided.

* * *

The sleek lines of cruise ship Sundance carried her passengers slowly but smoothly out of the port of Miami en route to an inaugural visit to a selection of Caribbean Islands. Standing on the top deck, Champagne in hand and waving at dockhands on the wharf as befitted the very special guests of the Captain, were Liam and Susan Brannigan, Kimberly Williams, Angus Kyle and Jack Bryson.

"I'm away to get a real drink. You guys want a whisky?"

All four shook their head and Bryson sloped off to find the bar.

"D'you know," said Liam, sipping his Champagne, "the last few days have been scary. But it's been an absolute privilege getting to know you guys. Finishing off our honeymoon this way wasn't quite in our plans but we're both looking forward to spending some time relaxing with you good people without someone shooting at us."

"And I'm pleased that *you* two," she indicated Kim and Gus, "are able to spend some time together."

"Susan," admonished Liam. He turned to Gus.

"Forgive her. She's just like her mother, an inveterate match-maker and she should mind her own feckin' business."

Kim smiled. Gus shifted uncomfortably.

"Aren't you two accommodated next door to one another on this cruise?"

"Susan...!"

Listen," said Susan, the two of you and Jack are invited to spend some time on our ranch in Nevada after the Sundance docks. You'd love it there. You have the bright lights of Vegas should you wish or the peace of a horse-ranch if you'd prefer. We'd love to have you...and for as long as you'd wish. Kim, you'll have some time to kill while you're waiting on the Ventura being repaired and Gus, you look like you could do with some proper rest and relaxation as well as some sunshine."

"That's a sincere invitation," said Liam. "But you'll forgive me if I take my bride down to the cabin out of harm's way before she starts suggesting a double room at the ranch for you two! We'll see you at dinner."

They left.

Kyle clinked glasses and raised his in toast to Kim. "To my favourite ship's captain."

"Well, thank you kind sir." She sipped at her glass and screwed her face up in comic fashion. "Arrggh... this isn't Krug! I'm used only to drinking the good stuff."

"Where I come from, any alcoholic drink that sparkles is treated with suspicion. I share Jack's tastes if not quite his appetite. Whisky...Scotch whisky, that is...none of your Irish or American muck...and beer, is acceptable. Anything else is just an *aperitif*. "

"Well, you and Jack deserve all the drink you want after your heroics. You saved thousands of lives."

"Like I said earlier, I'm rubbish with money, rubbish with women, rubbish with everything. I can handle myself in a fight. My self improvement work has amounted to improving my use of the English language. I'm doing what I'm good at."

"Oh, I see you as much more than a fighting machine. You're a good man, Gus. You're good with people. You're a leader. You're…"

"Well you've got greater insight than me, Kim. My confidence in my abilities has always been pretty low."

"With women *too*, Mr. Kyle? But I see you as a handsome hunk of a man. Good sense of humour. Kind of guy *any* girl would like to take home to mum."

"You're embarrassing me," Gus smiled. "I've given up on women, remember?"

"Well, I can tell you that women haven't given up on you…at least," she finished her Champagne and allowed a steward to re-fill her glass…"this one hasn't."

"I don't know what to say, Kim. You're gorgeous, educated, skilled…just lovely. I'm just a guy who…"

"I think you're wonderful, Gus and I have an idea. I think you've been damaged by women in the past and are understandably cautious to the point of fearfulness of getting involved with any other. You think you have no skills while I see nothing but potential. Well, how 'bout this. You think you could handle the Ventura?"

"The Ventura?" Handle?"

"Yes, as in 'be in charge of'…just like me. In fact, *alongside* me. We could run it together. You told me earlier you received a decent fee for your last mission with Jack so it wouldn't be charity if you invested it. We'd be business partners... Fancy the idea?"

"Wow...Kim...I'd need to think...I mean what about Jack?"

"Well, if he's drinking he's not steering but we could find him something to do. Now that my dad's gone, my lawyers have told me that I inherit the Red Lion. Perhaps Jack could manage it? It'll certainly take a strong personality to change it from its present clientele. "

"Really," murmured Kyle under his breath...could I think...?"

"Sure you can. We don't get Ventura back until September so, until then, we cruise, maybe we go to Nevada and we get to know one another."

Kyle's face screamed uncertainty, confusion, joy and fearfulness in one complicated expression.

"Yesssss," emphasised Kim, "get to *know* one another. I'm in wardroom 978 and you're in wardroom 979. Maybe we'll bump into one another over the next two weeks? Maybe you'll call on me in my room...just you and me...talking about our business...or whatever."

"*Whatever?*"

"Sheesh, Gus. You're a basket case but I'm not giving up on you, now go see Jack and make sure he's behaving himself."

"Yeah, will do," said Gus downing the rest of his glass and taking his leave.

Looking for Jack proved more difficult than first it seemed given the gargantuan size of Sundance.

He used the time to think of his conversation with Kim as he walked the decks increasingly impressed by the myriad bars and restaurants that dotted the ship. Passing the Highland Whisky Bar, he heard the soft tones of someone singing.

"Guantanamera... *guajira*, Guantanamera.... Guantana meeeerrrra...." He looked in to see Bryson serenading a Spanish waiter.

"Haw Gus, come on aboard. I'm just teachin' wee Tam here how to sing Spanish...an' he's Spanish *himsel*'!"

Kyle took him by the arm and led him to a table. The seriousness in his eyes sobered Bryson substantially. "What's up?"

"I've been made an offer. Well, to be exact, *we've* been made an offer...by Kim."

"Saw that comin', comrade."

"Ever fancy being a cabin boy?"

"A whit?"

"A *cabin* boy...working with me and Kim on..."

"You should say 'Kim and I' there."

Kyle smiled..."Naw...the pronoun is the object of the preposition so you use 'me'...anyway, working with the two of us on the Ventura, or maybe managing the Red Lion."

"Fucksake, Gus...but don't be stupid... I'd drink the boat dry in the first week...I'd insult the guests and I'd just get in the way. So...no, I *don't* wan' to work with you an' Kim on her boat, and could you see me managin' a pub?" He drained his glass. "But *you* should take the chance. You've aye been different from me. More class by far. And you can control yer drink. See, that's where I fall down...the drink. But see you an' *Kim*? Top notch old bean. Top notch. Me, I'm a fightin' man and I'm just goin' to enjoy this cruise and wait for Colonel Brand to fin' me somethin' to do..." He held out his hand to Kyle. "But we'll always be comrades-in-arms, my brother. Always!"

* * *

At dinner that night, Kim appeared looking radiant.

"Wow, you look great dressed up?"

"Thanks...and you look handsome." She accepted the chair pulled back for her by a steward and sat down. "Where's Jack?"

"Sleeping in his room. I think the excitement of his first cruise was too much for him."

"Did you chat with him about our conversation?"

"Hmmm. And he reacted just as I'd figured he would." He nodded his thanks to a waiter who brought the whisky he'd ordered while waiting for Kim. "It's a no go, I'm afraid."

"Is that for him or for both of you?"

"I've known him since school, Kim."

"Life's about the *future*, Gus, not the past.

"I worry about Jack. Without me I worry that he'd end up dead or in a gutter."

"There comes a time when you have to let the man make his own decisions…make his own mistakes. If you've always been around to catch him when he falls, how does he know what he's capable of? Why should he give up drinking if there's always you to pick him up from the floor of a bar or sort him out after a fight?"

"Kim, I know you're right. But it would feel like the biggest act of betrayal."

"These qualities of friendship and loyalty are part of what makes me think that you and I would make great partners. I've been round the block a few times and I've set myself very high standards in men…either as colleagues…or as…friends."

Kyle repeated the word as if by saying it out loud, its meaning would become clearer…"Friends?"

"Yeah, Gus Kyle...*friends*." She grabbed his arm. "Jesus, Gus...it isn't the *woman* who's meant to make all the running but you're *impossible*. Tell me something...am I an ugly old hag?"

"Quite the oppos..."

"Am I poor company... No sense of humour?"

"Not at all..."

"So spending time with me on whatever level wouldn't be the toughest assignment you've ever been handed?"

"No it certainly wouldn't, Kim," said Kyle weakening. "In fact it would be perhaps the most wonderful assignment in the world."

"Well, that's all I'm proposing. That you and I get to know one another and during the cruise, we have a chat about where we might take things...and how fast. I'm pretty clear about how I feel about you, Gus and I hope that soon enough you'll feel similarly but I'm not stupid enough to rush my fences with a man fighting his demons as you are."

"You're lovely, Kim. I'm afraid I'm not very good at saying these things to a woman...but you're lovely."

She held up her empty glass. "I'll drink to that. It's a start."

Kyle placed his whisky glass on the table and summoning up a different kind of courage than the type he'd expended over the previous few days, leaned forward to kiss Kim.

Before their lips met, Liam and Susan joined the couple, interrupting their moment and were about to be seated when an elderly man wearing a light suit approached the table.

"I'm sorry to trouble you young people but would you mind if I joined you? I'm traveling alone you see?"

Both Kim and Gus started at his request but politeness kicked in and each outdid the other in having him sit down. Susan pulled back a chair for him to sit.

"I go on a cruise once a year said the elderly gentleman. I live alone and cruising lets me meet so many interesting people."

"It's our first cruise too, said Kyle. Very impressive. Some ship!"

"Indeed so... My name's Alistair." he shook hands with each of them.

"I'm Kim and this is my *friend*, Gus." Kim looked at Kyle and smiled broadly as she used the word 'friend' in introduction. These are our friends, Susan and Liam

"Then I have four of the people I came here to meet. I'm pleased to meet you, Dr. and Mrs. Brannigan. Where is Mr. Bryson?"

"Huh?" said Kyle.

"Mr. Bryson?"

"He's sleeping...what...?"

"We'll see one another from time to time around the ship and I'm sure we'll pass some time together and I'll enjoy that as long as we constrain our chat to the cruise itinerary." A waiter approached with the bottle of chilled *Sauvignon Blanc* that Kyle had also ordered while waiting for Kim. Five glasses were poured. "Let me explain why I'm here. I have four envelopes...one for each of you. You'll forgive me but I've treated you and Mrs. Brannigan as one person for this transaction, Dr. Brannigan." He removed four envelopes from his inside jacket pocket and sipped at his glass of wine. "Most satisfactory."

He placed his glass on the table and continued. "It's but a small gesture from, well...me, I suppose. But governments have many limitations on what they can and cannot do. I am now distant from these restrictions but close enough to Government to know exactly the service you gave recently. I imagine in the fullness of time a grateful nation might bestow on you some honour or other...they certainly should... But you probably have no idea of the calamity that would have befallen the globe never mind the people of Barcelona had you not succeeded in your mission. I'm here to tell you that and to provide you each with one of these envelopes. They each contain details of an account in a Swiss Bank, *La Banque Privee Espirito Santo*, holding a quarter of a million pounds each in your names. I do not require a receipt."

Kim and Gus looked at each other and transferred their gaze back to their elderly benefactor.

"No one's meant to know we're here," said Kim.

"So presumably you're MI5 or something?" asked Kyle.

"No. I'm actually a retired gentleman these days."

"And what did you used to be?"

"Why, in a previous life, I was a *Mandarin*, my dear boy. I was a *Mandarin*."

CHAPTER THIRTY-TWO

The End

If you enjoyed *'A Confusion of Mandarins'*, why not try *'The Kaibab Resolution'*, a 278 page thriller dealing with gun control in the USA and its links with the Irish Republican Army. There's a more substantial role for Liam Brannigan in this novel as he becomes enmeshed inadvertently in the shooting of priests at McCarran Airport in Las Vegas, Nevada where the novel is set.

You can find it here at;

http://www.ronculley.com

Ron Culley's books are read internationally, in each of the seven continents of the world...now including Antarctica following an enthusiastic e-mail he received recently. His audience is somewhat bifurcated...some preferring his pawky Glasgow humour, recalling tales of the city of his birth...others more partial to his all-action thrillers. Whatever your fancy, his web site keeps his avid readers up to date on new releases and occasional blogs as well as facilitating an exchange of comments and questions to the author.

A 437 page autobiography called *'I Belong To Glasgow'* charts the development of this magnificent Scottish city in the 50's and 60's in what is a warm and witty account of Culley's youth growing up in a Glasgow just recovering from the war years as well as his transmogrification from a young boy expelled from school via a life in public service to becoming an author. More information is provided on the same web site as above.

Another novel, *'The Waffen Speculation'*, a thriller about the Nazis in Ireland during and after the Second World War and a second book about the city of Glasgow, *'Dear Old Glasgow Town'* are both in preparation and are shortly for publication. Details can be found on the above-noted web site.

* * *

Ron Culley lives in the leafy suburbs of Glasgow, Scotland with his wife and family. The proud father of four sons and now one grandson, his *'Who's Who'* listing shows his hobbies as watching association football, irreverence, laughing out loud and convivial temulence.

Lightning Source UK Ltd.
Milton Keynes UK
UKOW050007041211

183152UK00001B/4/P